THE TRANSCENDENT

JAMI CHRISTINE

"To die will be an awfully big adventure."
J.M. Barrie, Peter Pan

DEDICATION

THIS BOOK IS DEDICATED to my sons, Harlee and Elliot, whose entrances into this world were both humbling and empowering, catapulting me on some of my biggest journeys of soul growth. I also dedicate this book to Granny, who blessed me with the honor of being present while her soul returned home, and thus inspired this story.

ACKNOWLEDGMENTS

WHERE DOES ONE begin the process of thanking everyone who had a hand in the development of a project like this? I feel the need to apologize in advance for anyone I may unintentionally leave out.

I'll start with my sons, to whom this book is dedicated. Through the journey I've been on thanks to our soul contracts with each other, I've learned to find blessing and gratitude in trauma and grief. A lot of burdens are lifted with that kind of emotional freedom! I feel it's necessary to also thank my ex-husband, Justin, for the lessons learned during our time together that helped develop this story. I hold fast to my belief that all relationships are meant to be, but not all are meant to be forever. But every relationship is meant to teach a lesson and provide opportunities for growth and greater self-awareness, and for this I am grateful, too. Thank you Mom, for taking the time to read this and provide feedback, and for helping me come up with solutions to character conflicts at the last minute. Thank you, Dad, for being my personal printer and for spiral-binding each edition as I continued to update it and pass it out to new readers. And thank you, both of you, for your endless unconditional support and encouragement, and for raising me to be the person I am today. Thank you, Ted, for being an amazing friend and fellow author, and supplying me with great feedback as well as being the ultimate grammar nazi! Thank you, Michele, for taking the time to read my story as well as give me some amazing feedback that I feel really enhanced the end result, and encouragement as well as advice for the road toward publishing (and thank you, Steve, for your advice, encouragement, and guidance as well!). Thank you, Tessa, Hannah, Kim, and Bridget for taking the time to read and provide feedback and building my confidence as a writer. Thank you, Dawn, Noah, Corrie, and Jessie for your medical knowledge to help me merge a metaphysical situation into a physical world. And thank you, Chris, for the extra push and encouragement to get this book off my computer and finally into print!

INTENTIONS

MAY THIS STORY find its way into the hands and hearts of those on their own soul-searching journey, of those in the process of their own personal awakening, and of those who seek or need any kind of support, comfort, encouragement, enlightenment, or inspiration as they navigate their way through the challenges and joys life brings to them. May you be filled with love, light, and joy.

THE
TRANSCENDENT

CHAPTER 1

THE COSMOS rushed through her as her heartbeat thundered in her ears, all of her senses amplified. Lessie Morrison was sucked against her will, abruptly and without warning, away from life as she knew it, and thrown unceremoniously into a completely different purpose.

She landed in the passenger's seat of a car, screeching through the darkness. As she was thrown back against the leather upholstery, her wide eyes caught a glimpse of a startled deer dodging the hood just before the car swerved and the headlights illuminated a telephone pole. The car jerked as it careened over the shoulder of the road and crashed through the prairie grass, the telephone pole coming at them at a frightening speed.

The driver screamed, her dark brown knuckles nearly turning white through her grip on the steering wheel.

At the very second of impact, Lessie squeezed her eyes shut and threw her arms around the terrified young driver.

Everything fell into silence. Only their breathing could be heard.

Lessie opened her eyes, taking in the familiar white haze in which they were standing, and her gaze fell on the girl, the former driver of the crashed car. She released her and stood back.

The girl squinted uncertainly through the misty light, curly black hair hanging loosely at her shoulders. "Am I... dead?" she asked in a shaky voice, finally meeting Lessie's crystal blue eyes.

"Yeah," Lessie replied, her voice casually conversational yet sympathetic. This was nothing new, and while the girl may be frightened and feeling resistance to her fate; soon, Lessie knew, all would be replaced with joy, peace, and profound understanding.

The girl blinked. "Who are you?"

"I'm called a Transcendent," she said. "I show up so you don't have to die alone." She shrugged as she added, "Moral support for crossing over, more or less." The girl responded with a blank stare, which quickly shifted to curiosity as a brilliant white light glowed before them, growing and expanding until it nearly consumed them.

The girl squinted, lifting her forearm to shield her eyes, as glowing figures with outstretched arms moved toward her from the light. They emitted a presence of familiarity, and a hint of a smile began to light the girl's features.

Their eyes met, and Lessie offered her an encouraging smile. The girl returned it, now beaming as radiantly as the spirits who joined her. "Say hi to Grandpa for me," Lessie whispered, and in a brilliant flash the girl was gone; and Lessie was engulfed by the cosmos rushing through her, catapulting her back into her own reality.

She jolted at the sound of the loud staticky *POP* as she resurfaced, and blinked several times as she focused on the kitchen table she had been temporarily removed from. She looked up to see Nana leaning back in her chair across the table, watching Lessie intently with her arms folded over her chest. A hint of a curious smile tugged at the corner of her wrinkled mouth. Lessie pressed her lips together and returned her focus to her sketchbook, where she had started a few loose strokes before she was interrupted by the Universe. She tried to pretend nothing had happened.

"Where did you go this time?" her grandmother asked in a gentle voice.

"Nowhere, just spaced out," Lessie replied, absently making a few more strokes with her charcoal pencil.

"I know that look, honey. You weren't just spaced out." She leaned forward and rested her elbows on the table, her eyes not leaving her granddaughter. "Where did you go?"

Lessie sighed again and looked up at the old woman, trying to hide the stress and frustration that she was sure was etched all over her face. Relenting, she took a breath. "It was a girl in a car accident. Dodged a deer and hit a telephone pole." Lessie returned her focus to her sketchbook.

Nana nodded, understanding laced across her solemn face. Living through a person's death right along with them was a difficult thing to get used to. She'd been through it herself countless times. Nana reached across the table and placed her hand on her granddaughter's. "Celeste, I know this is hard. I know it's frustrating. With time you'll see that it's a gift. You have awareness that many people can only dream of having in their lifetime. And insight that most don't even know is possible."

"Nana, you know I like to be called Lessie," she grumbled with a scowl, deliberately avoiding her comment. She added a few more strokes on her sketchpad, blending the deep black lines together and nodding with approval before moving on. She appreciated the normalcy of schoolwork, especially her favorite subject — art — where she felt at home behind her pencil or paintbrush. It was the escape she needed from her bizarre life.

Nana's gaze dropped to her laced fingers, and guilt settled on Lessie's chest. She knew Nana only wanted to help. She took a breath and said quietly, "I just want to be normal..."

Nana nodded, lifting her eyes to meet Lessie's. "I know what you mean, sweetie. I was a teenager once, too." Silence hung in the air between them. In a soft voice, Nana added, "It's our challenges that shape us into better, stronger people."

Lessie turned her pencil around in her small hands, no longer able to focus on the distraction of schoolwork. Her "gift" provided plenty of challenges, but she certainly didn't feel any better or stronger.

Finally, Nana stood up from the table, came around to Lessie's side and gave her shoulder a squeeze. "I'm here if you ever need to talk, you know that." Her voice was comforting, yet carried a slight undertone of defeat, and she ambled away toward the living room.

Lessie sighed as she drew her attention back to her book, then closed the cover. For once, she'd just like to forget that she was a Transcendent. She craved her former life, when she was normal, before her first calling. She stared out the window as the setting sun cast an orange and red glow across the landscape of trees and fields, slowly fading to the dark blue-black of night. The memory made its way to the forefront of her mind, as it so often did.

SHE WAS FOURTEEN years old. She stood in the kitchen with Nana and her mother, Lynne, helping with dishes and chatting about school. Nana had been living with them since shortly after her husband, Bill, died two years prior, when Lessie was twelve. Lessie's parents had grown concerned at the thought of the old woman living completely alone, as she had relied on her late husband for so much. Having Nana with them proved to be more of a blessing than any of them expected, especially Lessie.

The room suddenly faded away from her, as the *whoosh* that she had come to know all too well rushed through her, while her heartbeat sped up and the blood pounded in her ears. She felt like she should have panicked, but somehow instead she felt as though she had purpose, like some cosmic hand was reaching out and guiding her. She felt out-of-body, light as air and fluid as water, floating, but grounded all at the same time. She landed on her feet inside a roaring fire, instantly aware that she could feel no heat. Ceiling rafters collapsed around her and floor boards dropped with ashes and dripping embers to the basement below. She heard sirens outside, and searched the blaze for the presence of firefighters or rescue personnel. There was no one. Her eyes suddenly fell on a boy about her own age, lying sprawled and face-down amongst the flames, right at her feet.

It was as though the cosmic hand that had been guiding her along was still with her, extinguishing the fear that she should have felt and replacing it with an innate understanding of what her purpose was. She dropped to her knees by the boy's side, hesitating before touching him. She could see his back rise and fall slowly and painfully with each strained breath.

A splitting, creaking sound caught her attention above her head, and she looked up just as the rafters gave out. Instinct kicked in as she let out a yelp, falling forward and covering the boy with her body to protect him just as the burning rafters crashed on top of them.

Silence.

She blinked as she slowly pulled herself off the boy, watching him with wide eyes as he sat up as well and took in his surroundings with trepidation and curiosity. They were engulfed in a white haze, no longer in the fire, and watched together as a brilliant light began to grow in front of them, blinding and consuming them with an immense joy and love and peace unlike anything Lessie had ever felt before. She was captivated and awestruck by the overwhelming feeling that she was connected to a power much deeper than she ever knew existed, and she felt a strange sensation fill her with the idea that she could easily leave her world behind and gladly enter this one without hesitation. The boy's expression implied he felt the same.

Spirits began to emerge, coming for the boy with outstretched arms. He stood, his face soft with wonder as he felt the same oneness and power, and her own heart raced with the thrill of what she was witnessing.

The boy turned his head slowly to meet Lessie's eyes, and he gave her a small, contented smile that gleamed in his brown eyes. His dusty blonde hair was illuminated from the glow of the light as it only grew brighter. Lessie laughed, the sudden burst surprising her, but she was consumed with such an unexplainable joy that she couldn't help but laugh.

She gestured toward the light, as though holding open a door for him, and he gave her a slight nod, his smile growing even brighter. "Thanks," he said, "for being with me." She felt a sense of accomplishment swell in her heart.

Her breath caught as several of the beings bathed in light gracefully floated towards the boy from the glow. He smiled at her once more and gave her a wave before linking his arms with two of the spirits, and all at once he was engulfed in light, and the world around her illuminated to such piercing brilliance she felt as though she were becoming the light. Suddenly everything was sucked into gray, and she was thrown back into her previous presence in the kitchen.

Lessie blinked and took in her surroundings as a shiver ran through her. She was still holding a plate, with a towel in her hand, standing motionless, as if she had been in a daze.

"Celeste?" Lynne asked her daughter quietly.

Lessie swallowed and turned her head toward her mother, her neck muscles feeling stiff like they hadn't moved in hours. She rolled her shoulders to try to coax life back into them. Lynne and Nana were both staring at her, though with different expressions. Lynne's was a frown of concern and confusion. Nana's was a gentle, knowing smile.

Lessie shook her head, looked back at the plate in her hand and began absently moving the towel across it. "I must have spaced out..." she croaked through her dry throat. She cleared it and set the dish down, reaching for another one. Her mind felt scattered. *Was that some sort of crazy daydream?* She couldn't wrap her head around it.

They were still staring. Lessie looked back up at them both. "What?" she asked, feeling defensive.

"Where did you go?" Nana asked softly.

Lessie blinked a few times, frozen, taking in her squinting eyes and the wrinkles around their edges, and her soft smile. Nana just watched her, waiting for a response. She knew.

"What?" Lessie asked with nervous hesitation. Lynne glanced at Nana with uncertainty, then returned her gaze to Lessie.

"You spaced out, like you were... somewhere else." Nana watched her unwavering expression, searching for clues and confirmation to what she already knew. "You got called, didn't you? Where did you go?" She knew how unnerving, almost terrifying, her first time was, and maintained a sense of compassion and empathy toward her granddaughter.

Lessie looked back at her mother, whose brows were still knit with concern. Taking a deep breath, Lessie racked her brain for any memory of Nana's stories about their ability, wishing she had paid closer attention to her when she explained it before. She guessed it really never registered that it would be *her* someday.

"Well... I was in... a fire?" she began slowly, carefully, wording it like a question as she still couldn't believe it was real. She retold the story of the boy at her feet, the crashing rafters, the white haze, and the light. She sounded crazy. Shaking her head, she said, "I must've just daydreamed. It's stupid." She looked back at the dish in her hand and continued absently brushing the towel across it.

Nana's crystal blue eyes met Lessie's — their matching feature had given Nana the suspicion that Lessie would someday follow in her footsteps; and that day, her suspicion was confirmed. She placed her hand on her young granddaughter's shoulder. "You're a Transcendent, Lessie," she said quietly with a soft smile, and Lessie's heart stopped. "Just like me." Nana moved her hand to Lessie's, guiding her to place the plate on the countertop. Lessie's stomach turned nervously as she followed her lead, and she tried again to search her brain for the memory of what Nana had explained about all of it. Lynne still looked concerned, yet fascinated. Lessie felt as though she could also detect a sense of heaviness in her eyes as the realization set in that her daughter would be seeing and experiencing some things most normal fourteen-year-olds couldn't even imagine.

Lessie chewed her bottom lip as Nana took her arm and guided her to the living room, leaving Lynne to the dishes alone. Lessie perched at the edge of the couch, suddenly feeling unable to relax in her own home.

Nana studied her face, took in her presence, her demeanor, as if searching for clues as to what she might be processing in her mind, to better prepare herself for what she was about to say. She then began explaining their gift, and life as a Transcendent. Lessie's eyes grew wide at the thought of being present at the moment of countless people's deaths, at the weight of being the one to cross them over. Of course it was terrifying, yet she felt a sense of purpose that eased those fears, remembering how she felt just before the boy crossed over.

Nana leaned in closer, and added, "We're the comfort for the human mind as it faces death, and the link for souls to leave their human experience and return to where they came from." She shrugged as though this were simple, everyday conversation. "Heaven, The Other Side, whatever you want to call it."

The power behind Nana's words was staggering, and Lessie's eyes fell to her knees as her fourteen-year-old mind tried to process the magnitude of her ability.

Heaven, Other Side, Source — it was all the same to Lessie. Her family never followed organized religion, and therefore often used their own terms to reflect their personal beliefs, even though it set them apart from the majority of their small-town southern Illinois community.

"I just... I can't..." she grasped for words, overwhelmed, then slumped her shoulders, defeated. She finally looked up at Nana. "But how? How can I be in two places at once?"

Nana sighed. "I don't know all the answers, my dear. It's not like there are reference books or manuals with answers about how this works. All I have to go off of is what I've learned from the generations before me. And we continue to learn more each time."

Lessie studied her expression again. She remembered Nana saying their hereditary ability skipped a generation. "How long have you been doing this?"

"Since I was twelve," she replied. "And my grandfather helped me through, just as I'm going to help you."

Lessie shook her head in refusal. "I can't do this," she stated firmly. "I... I can't... this is too much."

"I'm afraid we don't have a choice," she responded, a slight undertone of pity in her voice. "I'm sorry. I know it's a lot to process. But for some reason, we were chosen for this job in this lifetime. We have to fulfill it." She gave her a sympathetic half-smile.

Many questions eddied in Lessie's mind. "What if this happens at school?"

"It's going to happen anywhere and everywhere," Nana replied. "You'll get used to it. Though I hate to say, people will notice that you 'space out' from time to time." She looked at her granddaughter apologetically.

Lessie frowned. She was just entering high school, already not one of the "cool kids," and now she had to add some weird "spacing out" condition to the mix? *Great*, Lessie thought. *As though being a teenager weren't hard enough.* She scowled at the floor. "You'll figure that out, too," Nana added, trying to sound reassuring.

Lessie thought back to the boy, lying in the fire, burning alive... A knot twisted in her stomach, but then released as she thought about the light, and seeing his strong, healthy presence as he began to cross over. And that light... it was incredible... She looked up at Nana. "Will I ever get to see what's in that light?" she asked.

Nana smiled at her in return, though something glimmered in her eyes that wasn't quite a smile. After a moment's hesitation, she replied, "Only when you get to cross over yourself, unfortunately. You'll have to wait until it's your time to go."

"When I die, you mean," Lessie replied, squinting.

Nana nodded with a half shrug. "Well, when your *body* dies, yes."

"Is there anyone else out there who can do this?" Lessie asked, trying to sort through her mind's constant barrage of questions.

Nana pursed her lips, squinting thoughtfully. "I have a feeling your cousin, Will, can too. He has our eyes."

Lessie studied Nana's pale crystal blue irises; how they were so uncommon from most blue eyes. Just like her own. Her thoughts traveled to her cousin — she forgot she even had a cousin. Nana's oldest son, Ron Gardener, estranged himself and his two children, William and Camryn, shortly after his wife, Jodi, passed away in a car accident. Ron and his children, who were six and three at the time, moved to Seattle and never spoke to the rest of the family again. Lessie hadn't been born yet when her aunt died, and never learned of what caused the separation.

"Why don't we talk to them?" Lessie questioned.

Nana shook her head as sadness clouded her features. "I don't know, Sweetie. I've tried."

Lessie's mind filled and overflowed with questions. And still more questions only continued to surface as the years passed and countless souls were transported to the Other Side.

SHE TAPPED HER pencil against the table next to her sketchbook. It had been three years since her first calling, and Nana did her best to help and guide Lessie. She had been through all of the emotions Lessie struggled with, and had wondered the same questions Lessie asked. She sighed, still harboring guilt. She knew she couldn't hide from her life.

Lessie stood and walked into the living room. Sinking into the soft couch cushion next to her grandmother, she leaned her head on her shoulder, and asked, "What is all this about, Nana? This life? What we do. Why us?"

The old woman sighed as she placed a comforting hand on Lessie's knee. "Those are big questions, my dear."

"But what do you *think*?"

Nana thought for a moment, then replied, "I think we're all just here to learn and grow and become better versions of ourselves. *Evolve* is probably a good word. And, like I've said before, the best way to do that is through our challenges. We happen to have been chosen for this particular purpose, I suppose."

Lessie pondered her words, frowning. "It's challenging, all right," she said in a low voice.

"And the wiser and stronger you'll be because of it," Nana said.

Lessie focused her gaze on the TV, as did Nana, both mutually exhausting the conversation. Her eyes fell on the photograph of Lessie's grandpa, Bill, smiling from the shelf on the wall alongside Nana in her younger years. Lessie mused about her and her family's complete lack of the fear of death. It was comforting to know that what awaited them in the Beyond was so amazing, so incredible, so beautiful beyond anyone's wildest imaginations, that it was almost exciting to get to leave their world behind. She wished she'd had that awareness five years ago when her grandfather died. She felt the loss and the void he left in all of their lives, yet Nana had stayed so strong through the whole process. The heart attack, the funeral preparations, the funeral and burial... Nana wasn't numbly going through the motions like most widowed spouses did. She experienced the process with full presence as though it were as real and as meaningful as the day they were married. It was beautiful, really. Lessie finally understood why Nana handled it the way she did. Because it truly *was* as special as their wedding day. She saw it for what it really was – the man she loved in this physical life got to depart and return Home. She knew he was where he belonged – where *all* of them belonged, and that someday she'd be with him again, when her time was through on this physical plane. And that... that was a beautiful thing.

Lessie sighed, lifting her head from Nana's shoulder. "Want to play Scrabble?" It was her grandmother's favorite game.

Nana's eyes brightened as a warm smile spread across her face. "That sounds fun," she said softly, and Lessie grinned, standing to retrieve the game from under the coffee table. As she set up the board and they began drawing their pieces, she thought about her family. How her parents had been so supportive, even though they couldn't fully understand what she was going through. Lessie's mother had grown up with Nana spacing out on a regular basis, and because Nana was open with her children and husband about her ability, everyone simply accepted it.

Lessie's dad, Sam Morrison, had always possessed a curiosity about what went on behind the scenes on a spiritual level, thus making Lynne a perfect match for him, given her upbringing and her mother's unique life. Their baby girl, born with crystal blue eyes like her Nana's, inspired them to give her a name with a cosmic theme.

"Would you like to go first, Celeste?" Nana asked.

Lessie wrinkled her nose. *Ugh.* "Please call me Lessie." She placed a series of tiles on the board, and relaxed into the sense of feeling somewhat normal. As the game drew on, Lessie felt a happiness settle into her heart. Despite her ability, her life, totally cramping her teenage existence; despite feeling like a weirdo, a freak; despite feeling isolated from any kind of normalcy; if she really sat and thought about it, it was all pretty cool... and it made her appreciate life on a level much deeper than she ever could have imagined.

CHAPTER 2

THE WORLD spun, and the familiar rush of blood and cosmos pounded in her ears as her heart picked up its pace. She was coming back. Another soul had crossed to the Other Side with her guidance, this time an archery hunting accident somewhere in the northern Midwest. A boy in a tree stand, unsupported by any kind of safety harness, made one wrong move that tripped the cosmic signal to transport Lessie into his world, falling alongside him as he screamed. She held her breath and squeezed her eyes shut as she reached for him and pulled him in tight, their souls vanishing together just as his body landed in a broken heap on the ground. It was a smooth transition as he let go of his earthly desires and fears and allowed her to help him rejoin with the spirits of his departed loved ones. She wondered when his body would be found, how long it would take the family to realize he was gone, and then to find him. She couldn't help but linger on those thoughts. Each time meant someone was dying alone. And usually that meant they were in tricky situations of being able to be discovered. Especially at seventeen years old.

She found herself standing at her locker, staring at the combination lock, its cool metal resting between her motionless fingers. She shook her head. She knew she had to stop thinking about the aftermath of the deaths. Her job was to assist the departure, that's it. What happened to the body had nothing to do with her. Nature and fate would all take care of it.

"Lessie...?" she heard her name like a faraway echo. "Lessie?" a little clearer and closer. She finally snapped out of it and turned to look into the awaiting dark blue eyes of her friend, Emily, who sighed with relief. "You back?"

Lessie swallowed and nodded. "Yeah, sorry." She returned her focus to her locker, twisting the lock and hugging her books to her chest. "Did the bell ring?"

"Yeah, we're tardy," Emily replied with a casual shrug, tucking back a loose strand of blonde hair that hadn't made it into her ponytail.

Lessie groaned. "You really don't have to wait for me when that happens," she said, as they began to walk quickly toward their history class. She meant what she said, though a bigger part of her was overly grateful for Emily's loyalty and friendship. She was the only person outside of Lessie's family who knew about her ability. Not only did she accept her for what it was, she was also filled with an eager curiosity about her friend's unique life.

"It's cool, you know that," Emily reassured with another shrug, meeting her eyes with sincerity. "I'd feel bad to just leave you hanging, staring off into space like that."

Lessie sighed. "People peg you as a weirdo by association because of me."

Emily shrugged again. "Whatever, fuck 'em." Lessie cracked a small smile.

They entered their history class as discreetly as possible,

taking their seats under the disapproving glare of Mr. Edwards — a tall, elderly man whose snow white hair made a stark contrast against his dark skin and black-rimmed glasses, his slacks and dress shirt always neatly pressed and his tie always neatly in place. He didn't say anything as the two tardy students entered his classroom, and instead just continued on with the lesson. Lessie's parents had explained to the school that she had a unique case of epilepsy, having absence seizures that lasted far longer than typical absence seizures do, and that the doctors have been working on trying to figure out why, but haven't had any success. Fortunately most of the staff saw Emily as a good friend who stood by her side waiting for her to check back in anytime it happened.

Lessie hurriedly flipped open her book, hoping she was guessing the right page, and tried to clue in on what she might have missed. But her focus was completely derailed... by *him*...

Time stood still as the boy in front of her turned around, as though in slow motion, his dark hair illuminated by some otherworldly light that only she could see, his emerald eyes piercing and mysterious.

"Check out again, Lester?" he jeered, using the nickname all the cool kids so lovingly bestowed upon her. All her fantasies came to a screeching halt.

Lessie glowered at him. "Ass."

"When are you ever gonna join the real world with the rest of us?" He didn't want to drop it, as usual.

Lessie tried to ignore him, praying Mr. Edwards would come to her rescue by noticing the disruption and call him out on it.

"So, like, when you're spaced out, would you know if any-one... touches you?" He gave her a disgusting smirk.

Her stomach turned as she gripped the edge of her book, keeping her glare steady and even. She didn't speak. The taut muscles in his jaw flexed as his smirk widened. *What a douchebag. Why does he have to be so hot?* A heat wave of disgust coursed through her veins.

"Mr. Griffin, would you mind paying attention?" Mr. Edwards' deep voice broke through sternly. *Finally,* she sighed, returning her focus to his smartboard, trying to forget about Mitch as he shot her one last mocking smirk and turned back around in his seat. She sank down in her chair as class continued, heat rising to her face, wishing she could just get over him. It made absolutely no sense to her why she liked this guy. Typical, overconfident, star varsity running back, always surrounded by his football posse, cheerleaders and hot popular girls swooning over him all the time. Why would she take any kind of interest in a guy like that?

Especially because most of his posse and his groupies all relentlessly picked on her just as much as he did.

She felt Emily's eyes on her from the desk to her right. Lessie glanced over at her. "You're hopeless," Emily mouthed, shaking her head, her blonde ponytail slightly swaying with the movement. Lessie's scowl deepened. Emily could read right through her and knew full well about her stupid crush. A "modern Romeo and Juliet waiting to happen," she called it. All while reminding Lessie that she really needed to get over it, because it really never was going to happen.

Maybe it was just her subconscious way of clinging to "normal." By punishing herself with an attraction to an asshole like Mitch Griffin. A really hot asshole. She huffed out a sigh. She truly was hopeless.

Lessie made it through the rest of the day without any more disruptions from the Universe. She and Emily only shared history class together, though their schedules allowed for them to walk together most of the way to several other classes. The odds of a call happening between classes when Emily was around for moral support were in her favor, but the odds of facing it alone when it happened during class were even higher.

Lessie and Emily Austin hit it off immediately from the moment they connected in third grade. Emily was fun and imaginative, and they'd create wild adventures together anytime they played. She remained curious and creative as they grew older, and her interests evolved from make-believe play to contemplating the fabric of the Universe. Together, she and Lessie entertained their curiosities about such things as ESP, astrology, reincarnation, and time travel. Naturally, when Lessie found out she had inherited her family's gift, she felt completely safe in telling her friend, and Emily had been overly excited about it and deeply fascinated ever since. Emily's acceptance made Lessie feel almost normal sometimes. Almost.

The end of the school day was always a relief for Lessie, and her spirits were already lifting as she met Emily out front. The rest of the world faded away against her will as she caught sight of Mitch riding off in his vintage red jeep, the doors and top off, taking advantage of the last of the warm weather before fall set in. One of the most popular cheerleaders, Katie Sommers, was in the front seat with him, grinning brightly. Lessie imagined herself in that seat, her arm draped around his shoulder, wearing the same grin.

"Lessie? You still with me?" she heard Emily's voice ask from the distance. She shook herself from her trance.

Blinking, she looked over at her concerned friend. "Sorry," she said, "I'm still here."

Emily arched an eyebrow at her and readjusted her backpack straps on her shoulders. "I'm going to assume that wasn't a call, and you're just hopelessly daydreaming about the worst guy possible for you." She pursed her lips then added, "Again."

Lessie's face flushed. She shook her head as they began walking toward Emily's little black Chevy Metro. It wasn't nearly as cool as Mitch's jeep, but still better than what Lessie had, which was nothing. Due to her random, involuntary spacing out, Lessie was not allowed to obtain her driver's license, which was something she forced herself to come to terms with. She often wondered, if her cousin Will was, in fact, a Transcendent, how he managed alone in Seattle. Lessie sighed, surrendering defeat to her friend's words. It was no use denying her feelings. "I don't know what's wrong with me," she began, her voice almost a whine. "I can't help how I feel, but trust me, I wish I could."

"I wish you could, too," Emily replied, her thumbs hooked in her backpack straps. "He's such a *dick*."

Lessie sighed. "And gorgeous..." she mused pathetically.

Emily rolled her eyes and scoffed. "No. It doesn't work like that. Who you are on the inside affects what you look like on the outside. He'd be cute if he weren't such a dick. But. He's a dick."

Lessie laughed in spite of it all. They approached Emily's car, and they tossed their bags into the tiny backseat. Lessie climbed into the passenger's seat, while Emily sat down behind the wheel. "So, uh," she began, changing the subject as she started the car. "Adam seemed kinda interested in taking you to Homecoming..."

Lessie stifled a groan. Homecoming. It was coming up in

mid-October, less than a month away, yet the thought of the first major social event of the year was the furthest thing from Lessie's mind. She tried to avoid such events every year. "Your cousin?" she asked hesitantly.

"Yeah," Emily responded, backing out and heading toward the road. "He's cool."

Lessie pressed her lips together. "He's a mathlete, right?"

Emily chuckled. "Yes, so a little more in your league than Mitch."

She rolled her eyes and stared straight ahead, sinking back into the seat. "No, math and art are in completely different leagues," she argued, then muttered under her breath, "So are math and crossing dead people over to the Other Side."

Emily let out a small chuckle and shook her head. "Just something to think about," she said, and she made her way to The Depot, their favorite cafe.

"How about I *not* go to Homecoming?" Lessie suggested as they pushed through the doors. The Depot was an old train station from decades long forgotten when a railroad used to run through their town. It had been converted into a coffee shop and deli that was popular amongst the after school crowd, and a place Lessie and Emily had frequented throughout high school. Upbeat acoustic music played quietly over the speakers, and the ambiance was warm and inviting both from the lighting and the smells from the attached bakery.

Several students had already arrived, ordering snacks and drinks and gathering in booths to work on assignments, listen to music, or gossip.

"You *never* go. For once I'd like my best friend to be there. It's our senior year!"

Lessie groaned. They ordered their favorite smoothies and slid into their usual booth. "You have Evan," Lessie added. "What do you need me for?"

"What about me?" A tall boy with light brown hair and blonde highlights, dark brown eyes, tan skin, and an athletic build slid into the booth next to Emily, who grinned cheerfully. He pressed a kiss to her lips. Lessie took a long draw from her smoothie, averting her eyes.

Saying she was a bit nervous when Evan Straus entered their lives their freshman year was an understatement. It was one thing that Lessie and Emily didn't have art together, which was where they both felt confident and at home; but quite another when Evan was assigned a seat at Emily's table. Lessie felt lost without Emily, but she quickly came to realize Emily wasn't feeling the same way. Lessie could never forget that night, hanging out in her room as Emily swooned on and on about Evan. His beautiful brown eyes, his light adorable dusting of freckles, his light brown hair with sprays of natural blonde highlights from the hours he spent in the pool all summer, and his perfect frame and perfect muscles, also thanks to the pool. And of course, with a bubbly personality like hers and her alluring artistic talent, it didn't take him long to fall for her just the same. Her stories of him went from gushing about his eyes and his physique, to how they have similar interests in art, and then suddenly they were joining art club together and hanging out regularly. All the while, a fear grew in the pit of Lessie's stomach that she'd been replaced, and if she didn't have Emily, then she had no one...

Lessie felt herself withdrawing from her, but Emily called

her out on it, and assured her that nobody could come between their friendship. Somehow, Emily's relationship with Evan just *worked*, and it never interfered with her friendship with Lessie, just as Emily promised.

"You two can go to homecoming together," Lessie replied.

"Duh," Evan responded, glancing curiously at Emily, who rolled her eyes.

"What she's *saying* is that she's not going. Again."

Evan's shoulders fell. "For real? You've never been!"

Emily brought her lips to her straw. "That's what I've been saying..."

"Come on, I'll just ruin your good time if I space out in the middle of it. I'll embarrass us all."

"We don't care if you space out," Evan interjected. "I mean, it's weird, but totally doesn't bother me." Emily elbowed him with a glare. He responded with an innocent shrug.

"Thanks," Lessie mumbled, taking another drink.

Emily drove Lessie home later without any further mention of Homecoming. They said their goodbyes and Lessie went inside to get started on her homework, which included completely reviewing everything she missed in history that day.

She couldn't focus. Her mind wandered to Mitch in the front seat of his jeep. She imagined riding next to him, smiling, hair blowing in the wind — one of the "cool kids," her life a complete contrast to the one she was currently living.

She stared out the window at the setting sun, and the kitchen slowly faded to the school gym, the squeak of sneakers against the polished wood floor as the football players practiced drills. Her focus was riveted on Mitch — his dark hair drenched in sweat, chiseled muscles shining, pumped from an intense practice, jersey soaked against his abs. Her heart picked up its pace. God, he was perfect.

They hid around the corner in an empty hall. Maybe Mitch secretly liked her, too. Her eyes drifted closed as his hand found the back of her head, fingers pushed in her hair. Her heart raced harder. Their lips found each other's. She'd wanted this for so long...

"Celeste—" he mumbled. She laced her fingers through his wet hair.

"Celeste?" she heard her name again, the voice softer, more inquisitive, yet far away.

She blinked.

"Celeste? Are you there?" The voice honed in, no longer far away and echoing, but present and focused and coming from Nana, standing in the kitchen at their house, studying her vacant granddaughter.

Lessie cleared her throat, shifting in her seat at the kitchen table and going back to rereading her history chapter. *Stupid daydreams,* she scolded herself. *Stupid crush on a stupid douchebag.* "Please call me Lessie," she muttered.

"Where did you go this time?" Nana asked curiously.

Lessie couldn't help but laugh. "It was that bad, huh?" She looked up to meet her grandmother's crystal eyes.

Nana simply arched a brow, a curious smile on her face.

Lessie sighed. "I was daydreaming for real this time."

"Goodness," she replied, clicking her tongue, "That must have been some daydream. May I ask what about?"

She glared down at her history book, feeling heat rush to her cheeks and neck. "No thanks..." she said, her voice level.

Nana smiled. "Some boy on your mind, if I may take a guess?"

Lessie sighed and sat back in her chair, her gaze on the trees outside the window. "I'm so confused. He's the biggest jerk in school. The one who picks on me the most for my spacey... problem." She groaned. "But he's so cute..." Her eyes went out of focus as she pictured him

Nana laughed. "We can't help our feelings sometimes," she said, shaking her head. "Just like we can't help our situations."

"Hmph. That doesn't really help me." She looked up at her grandmother helplessly. "Nana, he calls me 'Lester.'"

Nana raised her eyebrows in disgust. "Wow, he is a jerk..." Lessie smiled. Nana leaned against a chair and said, "Usually bullies act that way because they've got their own inner demons to deal with, and they don't know how else to handle it."

She sighed with a shrug. "His dad died suddenly when he was in eighth grade."

Nana nodded thoughtfully. "That can definitely affect a person's disposition and behavior..."

"Yeah, well," Lessie said, "he was a jerk before that too, so."

"Maybe you subconsciously remember him from a past life, and that's why you like him?"

Lessie pondered the idea, always eager to muse over such possibilities, just like she did with Emily. "Maybe he was actually *nice* in our past life, and we had an awesome relationship with each other."

She expected Nana to respond, but the room was silent, almost vacant. Lessie looked up, and was met with an empty expression on her grandmother's face. "Nana?" she asked, studying her and waiting. She stood motionless, staring but not staring at the wall. Lessie watched in fascination, realizing exactly what was taking place. It had been so long since she'd seen Nana get called, she almost forgot what it was like. She watched her for what felt like forever, her entire body unmoving, statuesque, except for her breath, which had slowed to a steady, deepened, sleep-like pace. Her crystal blue eyes were blank, glazed over, completely lifeless. It was such a strange sight. *Do I look like that when I check out?* she wondered. *Creepy... No wonder everyone picks on me.*

She watched Nana silently until she finally blinked, the life and personality and sparkle coming back into her eyes, and she shook her head, just as Lessie did every time she returned, trying to bring the real world back into focus.

"Welcome back," Lessie greeted, and Nana smiled softly in return, her eyes gentle and humbled. Seeing a departing soul to the Other Side was always a humbling, grounding experience.

"Mmm," she responded in a breath, recalibrating her senses.

"Where'd you go?" Lessie asked gently, tucking her mouse brown hair behind her ear, enjoying the fact that it was her turn to ask.

"He was out for a walk. I walked with him for a few steps and then he collapsed from a stroke," she replied. Lessie pictured an elderly man, ambling along. "I guess somewhere on the west coast – it was still daylight outside and there was a lovely view of the ocean." Nana shook her head. "He's lucky he was able to return Home instead of stay here. He wouldn't have been in his right mind." She sighed with pity. "That's always so sad, so hard for the family, watching their loved one continue on living without their right mind."

Lessie nodded, unable to imagine what it would be like to

have Nana there with them in body but not in mind. It almost seemed cruel. "Did you talk to him?"

Nana nodded. "Oh yes. Once we got there, he thanked me for coming to his aid, for being by his side. He had a lot of spirits greeting him, so I wished him well, and told him to say hi to Bill for me."

Lessie smiled. "You do that, too?" Nana returned her smile warmly. "I always tell my souls to say hi to Grandpa for me," Lessie finished.

Nana chuckled. "He must have quite the crowd up there thanks to us!" She took a deep breath and sighed, suddenly sounding exhausted. "I'm going to relax in the living room." After one last flash of a smile, she left the kitchen.

Callings later in life were probably more tiring than they were at her young age. It definitely took a mental toll on them. She returned her focus on her history book. Or tried to, anyway, as images of Mitch kept creeping into her head...

CHAPTER 3

EMILY AND Lessie shuffled through a rack of dresses, though Lessie's focus wasn't entirely on Homecoming dress shopping. She tried to stay present as her hands absently drifted through the satin and tulle.

"What do you think of this one?" Emily asked, holding up a long dark pink halter gown that flowed out at the bottom like a mermaid's tail. Lessie squinted against the obscene amount of sparkles, and responded with a shrug.

Emily slumped her shoulders in defeat. "Come on, Les, can you at least *pretend* to be excited?"

The corners of Lessie's mouth fell into a frown, and she let out a sigh. "I'm sorry, I feel like Adam is taking me as a last resort," she replied, referencing Emily's cousin as her "date". After much begging and pleading from Emily to go with Adam so the four of them could double date to the event, Lessie had finally conceded.

Emily laughed. "Please, Adam would be a wallflower, too, if it weren't for you," she answered. From what Lessie knew of him, Adam had plenty of friends, but rarely got involved in school social events, much like Lessie. He was overly involved in math team and academics, in Lessie's opinion. "So you make a great pair," Emily finished.

Lessie furrowed her eyebrows. "Is that supposed to make me feel better?"

Emily chuckled as she continued to scrutinize each flowing piece of fabric. "Probably not, but let's face it, we're all geeks. We gotta stick together."

"We're *art* geeks," Lessie corrected, casting a frustrated glance at her friend with her head cocked to the side. "There is a difference between our kind and his kind." She scowled. The hangers clattered together as she flipped through them a bit more roughly than before.

"What, do we have our own species now?" Emily asked with a laugh, rolling her eyes. She ran her hand across a rust colored dress, studying the rhinestone detailing.

"Might as well," Lessie murmured. She rubbed the silky dark blue fabric of a strapless gown between her thumb and fingers, but didn't bother to look at it any further. "So how come the rules don't apply to you, huh?" she asked her friend, implying her relationship with Evan. "Aren't you breaking the geek code?"

Emily shrugged. "Luck, I guess," she replied, smiling warmly at the thought of her boyfriend.

"I don't like this store," Lessie blurted as she stepped back from the rack. "I don't think this is my style."

Emily arched an eyebrow. "Homecoming dresses are pretty much all the same," she stated.

"I think I'll go in jeans."

"Oh come *on*," Emily groaned, dropping her arms and leaning her head back. Lessie lowered her head, sighing, as guilt began to settle in on her chest. Lessie wanted desperately to enjoy the event like all the "normal" kids, and she knew she needed to snap out of it and be happy for her friend. That was easier said than done.

"Let's get something to eat," Emily suggested, giving up on Lessie. She walked past her and headed toward the entrance to the store, and Lessie silently followed.

After ordering soft pretzels and drinks, they took a seat at a table. Lessie looked up to meet Emily's eyes, feeling like she really sucked at being a friend, but Emily was simply staring down at her pretzel silently, picking pieces of it and slowly bringing them to her mouth, then thoughtfully chewing. Lessie sighed sadly. Yeah, she really was an awful friend. She was about to apologize, then,

Whoosh. "Ugh, seriously?" she thought as she spun away from the mall and off to God-knows-where. *Now?* She landed in the passenger's seat of a car moving calmly down the highway. She glanced over at the driver, a boy smirking as his thumb traced back and forth over his phone as he punched out a text message. Lessie rolled her eyes and brace herself as she watched him drift off the road. He snapped to attention with wide eyes as the car bounced off the shoulder, and he yanked the wheel to the left, overcompensating. Lessie clenched her teeth as the tires caught and the car went airborne, the boy screaming and gripping the wheel as they were tossed. The sound of smashing metal crunching against the pavement filled the car as it jerked them hard against the impact. They were airborne once again. She stole a glance at the boy, who had been knocked out from the first hit. "Ah!" she shouted, caught off-guard as the car smashed into the pavement and flipped again. Her heart raced. The next hit would surely kill him. She turned and wrapped her arms around him just as the car smashed into the pavement once more.

They were instantly engulfed in silence and white haze. Lessie breathed a sigh of relief as she sat back on her heels, willing her heart to calm down.

"Did I die?" came the boy's voice, desperate and afraid.

Lessie sighed again. "Yeah."

He blinked and shook his head as his wide, fearful brown eyes met hers. "No, I don't want to die..."

She stared at him in return, unsure of how to respond. She didn't exactly have a say in the matter. She was caught off-guard by the look of desperation on his face, in his eyes. Her own face fell. "I'm sorry," she whispered.

She squinted in the light that had appeared before them, and as it grew, spirits of his deceased loved ones began to emerge with outstretched arms. She smiled as she watched, feeling the warmth, the love. "See how incredible it is? Can you feel that? Everything's going to be—" But her eyes fell back on his face, which was still contorted in despair and resistance. "Okay..." she finished, her voice falling.

"Who are you?" he asked, staring at her with searching, fearful eyes.

Lessie held his gaze steadily. "I'm a Transcendent. I help people cross over."

"I don't want to cross over," he said firmly, shaking his head.

One of the spirits took his arm, but he shrugged it off forcefully, his expression shifting to anger as he rejected the warmth and love and whirled back on Lessie. "*Please*," he begged, "You have to do something! You have to take me back!"

Her heart sank. "I – I can't..." She felt as though she were lying, and she quickly covered it with a truth. "Besides, I don't think you'll be the same if you stayed. That was a pretty bad accident. You'd have years and years of recovery ahead of you. You won't be able to do the things you love, the things you're used to. You won't be able to live the life you know..."

He shook his head frantically, "I don't care! I can recover, I can get used to a new life, I'll do whatever it takes!" He grasped at her hands then clutched at her wrists, pulling himself toward her as the spirits tried to draw him toward the light. Fear crept into her own eyes, her mouth drawn thin, as she tried in vain to stay strong and stand firm. The uncertainty in her decision tore at her. She looked to the spirits for guidance and help, but they only continued to come forward and surround them; their sole mission was to guide the boy Home. He tried to shrug out of their hold again, and as he did so, transarancy flickered through his form. *"Please!"* he begged.

"I – I'm so sorry..." was all she could manage to say, looking back at him as sorrow constricted her heart, and, instead of being guided toward the light, the spirits and the boy began fading further into transparency. He let go of her, his body finally surrendering to the inevitable, but his eyes still desperately clung to a sliver of hope that maybe she could change things. He faded further.

"S-say hi to Grandpa for me..." she choked. The last she saw were his desperate eyes as he faded to nothing.

She was back. She blinked into the sensory flood of the sights and sounds and smells of the mall and redirected her focus on Emily, who was waiting patiently.

Emily's eyebrows suddenly knit together, sensing Lessie seemed to be a bit different after this return than others. Lessie was on the verge of tears. "What happened?" Emily asked with concern, leaning forward.

Lessie shook her head. "He didn't want to die..." she said quietly. "H-he was so upset."

A sadness clouded over Emily's face as she watched Lessie with concern, unable to find words.

"I mean, this is hard enough as it is, spacing out at random, so I can go watch someone *die* and then cross them over." Her frustration began to toss and roll within her as her burning eyes lifted to meet Emily's. "Do you have any idea what it's like to be in the passenger seat of a car flipping down the highway?"

Emily shook her head, a mix of fear and wonder on her face. She remained silent.

Lessie sighed, willing herself to soften. "It's always better when we get to that light." Her eyes went far away as she reflected on its warmth and love as she so often did. "But," she continued, "He didn't want to die. He *begged* to stay. That light usually makes everyone feel better, and makes them okay with their fate. Not him. He was *fighting* it..." She dropped her hand to the table and picked at her pretzel, not really feeling hungry anymore. Her eyes followed a couple of teenagers as they walked into a store, probably looking for homecoming dresses just like Lessie and Emily were, and gossiping about crushes and mean girls and classes, unlike Lessie and Emily were. What was it like, being "normal?"

Emily sank back into her chair with a deep exhale. Her dark sapphires, filled with concern and curiosity, locked on Lessie's crystal blues. "Do you, ya know, *have* to let them cross over?"

Lessie bit into her pretzel as she contemplated the exact same question, then took a breath. "I don't... really know..." she replied with hesitation. She recalled feeling somewhere inside of her that she could save that boy, like an instinct, similar to the first time she got called and she just inherently knew what to do and how to handle the situation.

Emily's whole body pressed forward against the table, her pretzel forgotten, eyes growing wide as she took in Lessie's expression and hesitation. "Oh my God, you can *save* people?" she hissed. Her mouth hung slightly open, and her slender fingers gripped the edge of the table.

"*Shhh*," Lessie commanded, then leaned in and continued in a harsh whisper, "*No.*" Emily's face fell in slight disappointment, and Lessie added, "Or at least... I don't think so..." She thought for a moment, then continued, "The thing is, when I was there, I felt like I *could* save him. Like if I were going to do it, I'd know how and what to do and that it would work."

Emily lowered her eyebrows, then asked carefully, "So why didn't you?"

Lessie's gaze dropped to the table. "Because Nana told me we're not supposed to."

Emily sat back in her chair again, her eyes squinting incredulously. "What?"

Lessie shrugged as she tore pieces from her pretzel and dropped them to the plate. "I tried asking her about it before. And... she got kinda weird..." She looked up to meet Emily's curious eyes. "Like she got kinda upset about it, and demanded that I promise to never try to save anyone. She wasn't very clear about why, or that we were even capable of it, but," she shrugged, "I dunno, something must have happened that made her act like that, don't you think?"

"Sounds like it..." Emily responded with a small nod, looking off to the side as her voice trailed. She shook her head, her eyes suddenly flashing. "I dunno, Les, if you felt like you were capable of saving him, and he wanted to live, you should be allowed to at least try..."

Lessie narrowed her eyes, looking levelly into Emily's. "Are you saying that the next time someone wants to live, I should try to keep them here?"

Emily smiled. "Shouldn't that be their choice anyway?"

Lessie thought for a moment, looking down at her forgotten pretzel. "I suppose it should be..." she replied quietly.

CHAPTER 4

LESSIE KICKED her shoes off in the foyer, and her mother turned and smiled in greeting as Lessie sauntered into the kitchen.

"Hey Les, have any luck?" she asked before turning back to the cutting board.

"Nah, I wasn't really feeling it today," Lessie replied. "We're going to try again another time." She glanced around. "Is Nana home?"

Her mom hesitated, her eyes clouded with concern. She answered in a quiet voice, "She's in the living room. She fell asleep on the couch." She paused, then added, "Again."

Lessie's heart constricted as her eyebrows creased. "Is she okay?"

Lynne shrugged. "She won't say. She's mentioned a few times that she doesn't feel well, but she won't do anything about it." She shook her head. "I don't know what to do with her..."

Lessie's gaze drifted to her feet as a lump formed in her throat. Nana had always been spunky, rambunctious, and full of life. She struggled with the idea of her feeling ill or tired. "I'll go see if she's awake," Lessie said quietly, and Lynne nodded as she watched her daughter leave the kitchen.

True to Lynne's words, Nana was sleeping on the couch,

wrapped in an afghan. Lessie turned to return to the kitchen, not wanting to disturb her, but stopped when she saw Nana's eyelids flutter.

"Hi, Celeste," Nana greeted, her voice quiet and groggy.

"Hey, Nana," she replied, offering her a soft smile. She approached the couch and knelt down on the floor next to her head. "Are you feeling alright?"

Nana groaned and attempted to stifle a wince as she pulled herself up to a seated position. "Just tired is all," she reassured her, but Lessie sensed there was more behind her words. "How was your shopping trip?"

Lessie frowned and shook her head. "I don't think I'm into this whole Homecoming thing," she responded, her voice gloomy.

Nana's face fell. "Why not? You've got a date, right? That boy you showed me a picture of? He's pretty cute..."

Lessie smiled in spite of herself. "Kind of... But he's such a *nerd*." She paused, then added, "I know I have no room to talk, but he's just not my type. Plus he's going with me because basically nobody else will."

Nana chuckled, her voice cracking. "So what, exactly, is your type?"

Lessie snorted. "I guess I don't really have a type, do I." She said it more as a statement than a question, her voice filled with dismay. She then shrugged and added, "Maybe my type is someone who spaces out at random but handles getting picked on about it better than I do."

Nana sighed sympathetically and reached up to give Lessie's shoulder a squeeze. "I know it's not easy. Trust me, I've lived through it, too. But, everything happens for a reason." Lessie gave her an appreciative smile, though her words didn't truly resonate. Nana returned her smile, just before she yawned. "I think I'm going to rest a bit more, Sweetie." She carefully lowered herself back on the couch.

Lessie studied her pale face while chewing her lower lip. "Are you sure you're okay, Nana?"

The old woman's papery eyelids began to drift shut, but she responded softly, "I'm just fine, don't you worry. Just tired is all." And within seconds, she was asleep.

The weight of the unknown suddenly pressed heavily on Lessie's heart. She stood up as her gaze lingered on her grandmother, and returned to the kitchen. Her mother was sliding a pan of chicken breasts into the oven. "Mom, something's definitely not right with Nana..."

Lynne turned to face her after closing the oven door and setting the timer. "I know..." was all she said, trying to mask the unease in her voice. Her eyes seemed to carry the same weight Lessie felt in her chest.

Lessie's father entered the room, placing his briefcase on the counter and giving Lynne a kiss. He glanced back and forth between the two, having overheard their conversation. "Maybe we should encourage her to see a doctor."

Lynne shook her head. "I tried talking to her about that, but she doesn't think it's necessary."

Sam's mouth twisted to the side in a half-frown. "Well, hopefully it's just a bug," he said, his eyes still harboring concern.

Lessie felt a twisting in the pit of her stomach that whatever was going on with Nana wasn't "just a bug." And by the look on her parents' faces, she sensed that they felt the same way.

A text message buzzed on Lessie's phone in her back pocket,

and she retrieved it, silently grateful for the distraction. She read the text from Emily.

>>*Ever heard of astral travel?*

She arched an eyebrow, released a small smile, and shook her head as she stared at the lit screen in the palm of her hand.

"Emily's at it again," Lessie commented after noticing her parents' inquisitive gazes.

"I'm tellin' ya, that girl has a secret closet full of flow charts and line graphs and candid snapshots of you," Sam joked.

"Oh, Sam," Lynne scolded, though humor laced her voice.

"What?" Sam said defensively. "I've never seen anyone with an interest that far-reaching." He leaned against the counter and grabbed a handful of M&Ms out of the candy dish. "What was the last one? Astronomy?"

"Astrology," Lessie corrected.

"What's that got to do with what you do?"

Lessie laughed again. "It doesn't. She's just interested in everything." She shrugged. "And just knowing what I can do has her interested in what else could be possible." She looked at them both. "I mean you can't help but wonder if there's anyone else out there that has some sort of mysterious ability, kinda like mine, can you?"

"Of course," Lynne finally answered, meeting her eyes. She pressed her lips to the side and added, with a hint of hesitation in her voice, "Like Will..."

Lessie blinked in the silence that followed her mother's words. The prospect of her cousin, Will, being a Transcendent had been mentioned before, but the estrangement in the family prevented them from ever knowing for sure. A shadow of sorrow cast across her heart at the idea of Will having to face his strange life completely alone, without the mentorship of Nana. The shadow grew darker at the thought of Nana possibly not being there to guide her, either.

Lynne grew distant as she continued to work on dinner preparations, until finally, Sam stepped to her side and wrapped his arm around her waist. "Your brother may come around someday," he offered gently. Lessie knew her mother battled resentment toward her brother abandoning the family, especially when his anger stemmed from a personal issue with their mother. Why did he choose to take it out on the whole family?

She smiled appreciatively. "I'm not so sure, but thanks." She squared her shoulders as she took a breath. "It's his life, and his choice, not mine. Best we can do is live the best life we can, and not get upset about the way others choose to live theirs."

"That is very true," Sam said with a smile. "Your wisdom is one of the things I love most about you."

Lynne smiled in return and pressed a kiss to his lips. "Kinda can't help but look at things the way I do after growing up with a mother like mine."

Lessie averted her eyes back to her phone and turned slowly on her heel. "Ooookay, then, I'll just be in my room," she said, trying to hide the disgust in her voice.

>>*Mom and Dad are making out in the kitchen again,* Lessie typed as she made her way toward the stairs to her room. >>*So, please, I beg of you, fill me in on astral travel.*

>>*OMG, it's crazy, I just came across it!* Lessie rolled her eyes after reading her friend's response. *Yeah right,* she thought, knowing full well Emily was pouring over Google looking for more explanations to make sense of Lessie's ability. >>*Okay, so*

like there are yoga traditions that believe there are different levels of human existence, called Sheaths of Existence...

>>*Go on...?* she typed after a long pause of waiting for her friend to continue.

Her phone began ringing in her hand, and Emily's name displayed across the screen as Lessie stood in the middle of her bedroom floor. She answered it immediately.

"Too much to type," Emily said with an excited laugh. She didn't let Lessie respond, and dived right into a verbal explanation from where she left off. "Okay, so Sheaths of Existence, and they range from the physical body, like our bones and organs and stuff, all the way up to our spiritual body, like our soul. And so the astral body is like our aura or energy or whatever you want to call it."

Lessie nodded as though she could see her. "Yeah, we've talked about auras before," she said. Despite growing up in a small-town Southern Illinois community that seemed to have a culture all of its own that didn't have room for beliefs in such things as Sheaths of Existence, she certainly believed in all of it. Really, how could she not?

"Right, but this takes it a step further," she replied. "So the astral body is the energy of the physical body. It's you, but like *another* you. Like a double."

Lessie's eyebrows knit together. "Go on..." she encouraged, taking a seat on the edge of her bed, the springs in the mattress lightly groaning.

"So the astral body is thought to be a link between our brain and our mind." Her voice was excited, almost giddy. "So then there's astral *projection*," she continued emphatically, "which is taking the astral body and *separating* it from your physical body." Lessie felt an excitement bubbling inside her. Emily certainly landed on some information that hit close to home... She pressed on, "Like shifting your consciousness into your astral body and out of your physical body!"

"And astral travel?" Lessie asked eagerly, leaning forward, clutching her phone to her ear.

"Is moving around in your astral body. Traveling, anywhere and everywhere, whether in this physical world or to a completely different plane."

Lessie leaned forward further, resting her elbows on her knees, her head in her hand as it swam with the new information. Was this what happened to her every time she was called? "Holy shit, Em, you may have hit the mother lode here..." she breathed.

"I know, *right?*" she exclaimed, practically coming through the phone. "I mean, this is, like, *exactly* what's happening to you, only for you it's involuntary!"

"So, what, do you think I can control it somehow?" Lessie asked, her heart beating faster at all the possibilities that were racing through her head.

"I don't know, maybe!" she answered with excitement. "And I'm thinking, from the way this sounds, *anyone* could do it." She paused, then continued, "With some practice, anyway. You probably have to be really good at meditation..." Before losing her train of thought, she shifted the subject back to Lessie. "But think about it! This makes so much *sense!* You space out like you do, and your physical body is still right where you left it, but your *energy* body is somewhere else! Like you're in two places at one time!"

Lessie's mind raced. "It *is* exactly like me... I wonder if Nana has ever heard of this?"

"You would think she would have said something to you if she did," Emily replied.

Lessie nodded, a giddiness growing within her. "I can't wait to ask her... This is so crazy!"

"Lessie! Supper's ready!" Lynne's voice carried from downstairs.

"Hey, I gotta go," she said to Emily. "This is awesome, though, let me know what else you find."

"Oh, I will!" she replied. They said their goodbyes and hung up, and Lessie raced downstairs.

Lessie's thoughts shifted to Nana as she began helping serve the chicken. "Is Nana coming to eat?" she asked, glancing in the direction of the living room.

Lynne's face fell slightly. "I'm pretty sure she's still asleep." She looked to Sam. "Should we wake her?"

He gave her a look of sympathy and said, "She should probably eat something, but if she's not feeling well she needs the rest, too."

"I'll go see if she wants to get up," Lessie said, and walked quietly into the living room. She found Nana where she left her, fast asleep on the couch under her afghan. Lessie knelt down on the floor next to her and placed her hand on her shoulder. "Nana?" she said softly, giving her shoulder a squeeze.

Her eyelids fluttered open. "Oh hi, Honey." Her voice was still groggy.

"Supper's ready. You should probably come eat something."

She lifted her hand to rub her palm against her eye. "I'll try to eat a little. I'm not all that hungry, though." She pressed herself up on the couch and shifted her legs, landing her feet on the floor. Lessie took her arm and helped her up to stand, which took more effort than she felt it should have. But once Nana was up, she seemed to move just fine into the kitchen.

"She lives!" Sam greeted her, trying to keep the mood cheerful, though they were all equally concerned.

"I've just been extra tired lately; don't you worry about me," Nana stated as she took a seat at the table.

Sam brought up Lessie's conversation with Emily once they had all begun eating, curious as to what she discovered this time. Lessie brightened as she began eagerly explaining what she'd learned. Her family hung on her every word, especially Nana.

"So you're saying we involuntarily create a, what did you call it? An astral projection?" she asked, clarifying, as she absently picked at her chicken with her fork.

Lessie nodded again. "That's definitely what it sounds like." She took a bite and chewed while pondering what she wanted to say next. "I wonder if we could voluntarily project and travel...?"

"Just be careful if you do try it," Nana replied with a hint of warning in her voice.

They spent the rest of dinner casually conversing about Lynne's and Sam's days at work and Lessie's upcoming Homecoming dance that she wasn't looking forward to. When dinner was finished, Lessie returned to her room and texted Emily again.

Her thumbs flew across the touch screen keyboard. >>*Did you find anything out about how to do the astral travel thing?*

It didn't take long for Emily to reply. >>*Funny you should ask!* And she immediately followed her response with a link to a video of a guided meditation. Lessie chuckled. Of course Emily would have a video. She began to wonder if she would be any good at it. She'd never actually meditated before, and when she was called, it didn't take any thought from her; it just happened.

Her phone buzzed again, and she read the message on the screen. >>*So where are you gonna go if you try it?*

Lessie considered the possibilities. Where *would* she go? >>*I dunno...* she replied.

>>*You should visit somebody,* Emily suggested. >>*Maybe try to find someone who can do what you do?*

Lessie's thoughts were immediately transported to her cousin, Will, and her eyes involuntarily drifted to her laptop on her desk. She had sent him and his sister, Camryn, friend requests on social media, which they had accepted, but their relationship never extended beyond that. All she learned from his profile was that he was a software engineer primarily working from home. She'd never spoken with either of them, and still had no concrete proof that he was like her.

>>*I think I know where I'll try going first...* Lessie typed.

LESSIE COULDN'T SHAKE the hesitation she felt toward exploring Emily's discovery. Though she spent the next day watching videos of meditations and researching the concept of astral travel, guided by the links Emily shared with her, she still felt a nagging sense of uncertainty toward attempting to visit Will. What if it actually *worked?* She didn't know him, and didn't know if his father's resentment carried over to him. But, the more she thought about it, the more her desire to have a connection with someone who could relate to her unusual life outweighed her fears of the family rift. If, of course, he was a Transcendent at all.

Lessie stayed up late finishing last-minute homework before

once more reviewing the video Emily had sent her. It was nearly midnight by the time she finally felt ready to try it. There was still the possibility it wouldn't work, and she wouldn't have to worry about anything. But if it *did* work... She tried not to think any more about the multiple possible outcomes. She bit her lip, knowing school would be a challenge the next day if she didn't try to get some sleep, but her eagerness had her feeling alert and energized.

She lay back in her bed, willing herself to relax, and closed her eyes. She tried focusing on each muscle group in her body, from her face and scalp down to her toes. She began taking her mind down as though descending a staircase, just as she remembered in the video, slowing her breathing as she went lower and lower into her subconscious. She visualized darkness when she reached the bottom. She then imagined opening her eyes in her physical body, and focused on the feeling of lying on the mattress, limp and motionless. So far, the exercise seemed to be easier than she anticipated. With a slow breath, she imagined her body as an energy field, rising up out of her and floating above her, in the same position she was in as she lay on the bed. She studied herself, taking in the way she looked from the back – her tousled, mouse-brown hair, her small shoulders, the curve of her spine as it made way into her narrow hips, her small calves and sharp heels. She spent time really taking it all in, and once she felt comfortable there, she took another breath and visualized a shift, a floating sensation up off her mattress and into the body floating above her.

She opened her eyes. Floating above the bed, she looked at the ceiling from her new perspective, then lowered herself to stand on the floor to take in the rest of the room. She stared at her meditating form for a moment, right where she left it on the bed, and a strange sensation washed over her. She looked down at her astral self, holding out her arms and hands, then back at her physical body once more. "Weird," she said out loud, testing her voice. Still the same... She walked over to her desk and tried to pick up a pen, but her hand went through it instead. Not the same. She otherwise felt exactly as she did during a call to a departing soul.

She looked around once more, pressing her lips together. Her hesitation returned as she thought about her cousin in Seattle, a tightness of nerves taking hold of her heart. Maybe she wasn't ready. What about visiting Emily? Would she know she was there? Her nerves relaxed at the prospect of visiting her friend first, and decided to put her original idea on hold.

Lessie closed her astral eyes and pictured herself hovering above her house. When she opened them again, everything was just as she pictured it: stars dusting the sky above her, her roof below her, and a bird's eye view of the fields around her. She flew higher and grinned at the sensation. She could feel the air around her faintly, cool and comfortable against her skin, but not as strongly as she would feel it if she were physically there.

She closed her eyes again, imagined hovering over Emily's house, and opened them. So far, so good. Smiling curiously, she lowered herself down and pictured being in Emily's room, closing her eyes once more, and as soon as she opened them she found herself standing on her friend's floor. Beige carpet, purple and mango colored paisley comforter tangled around her on her bed, cream colored walls covered with paintings and drawings she had done in art class, as well as posters of their favorite bands and framed photographs featuring Lessie and

Evan. She had a bookshelf against the wall stuffed to the brim with a mix of teen fiction novels and metaphysical reference books. Anything and everything she took interest in wound up in print form on her shelves, and Lessie knew it'd be a matter of time before a book about astral travel showed up amongst them.

Emily was face-down on her bed, her arms sprawled out with one arm dangling off the edge, and the side of her face was squashed into the pillow, her mouth hanging open as she breathed loudly, borderline snoring. Lessie chuckled at the dramatic appearance. "Hey, Em," Lessie tried speaking, her voice sounding just like her regular, physical voice. "Can you hear me?"

Nothing. She didn't even stir. Lessie pursed her lips to the side, furrowing her eyebrows. She approached the edge of the bed and tried pushing Emily's shoulder, but her hand didn't seem to make contact, just like when she tried to pick up her pen. "Emily!" she tried again, a little louder. Still nothing. She sighed, feeling slightly defeated, then thought again about visiting Will. Maybe it *would* work if she visited somebody with the same ability? If he even *had* the same ability. She suddenly had the pressing desire to find out. It seemed to be working somewhat naturally for her, especially for it being her first attempt. She took another look at her unconscious friend, and drew in a steadying breath. "Well, wish me luck..." Still, Emily didn't budge. Lessie braced herself, closed her eyes, and imagined transporting herself to Seattle.

CHAPTER 5

HE DRIFTED through a dream. It was the same one that troubled his sleep since he was thirteen years old. His first calling — only in the dream, he wasn't the one called. He was the one called to.

He was in the woods, alone, running. He'd been running for so long, but the woods were endless. He couldn't seem to find a clearing — just constant trees for miles. He wasn't sure if he was running from something, or to something. But every time it was the same. Running.

He stumbled over a root, but as soon as he recovered, his foot landed on soft earth, pressing through leaves, and suddenly the awareness consumed him as strongly as his sudden gripping fear that there was no earth underneath his foot — he was falling.

He screamed, flailing, grasping, but the leaves and brush caved in around him as darkness swallowed him. He landed hard on a soft mud floor, but it wasn't soft enough to prevent his body from breaking. He cried out again. Where was the boy, coming to save him? He was alone. No light to greet him and take him Home. Only darkness.

The ground overhead opened up, and sunlight dappled in momentarily as he squinted toward the heavens. The temporary reprieve was suddenly broken with darkness again as the menacing silhouette of a massive log broke through and fell into the pit, its rotting center cracking as it pushed through the leaves and brush, coming straight for him. He stared, terrified, as though its journey to the bottom were happening in slow motion, and he shook himself from his trance just in time to back away, but not quick enough to escape. The log crashed across his legs, and he released a primal howl as he felt his body become severed in two. He was supposed to die! The boy was supposed to be with him; but he never came, never offered any comfort in his presence. Never brought him to the light.

He couldn't move. Pain rocketed through his body, and his head spun. He tried to grasp at what energy he had left to pull free from the log, but it was no use. He gasped for breath as fear consumed him once more, pushing at his body from all angles, inside of him and out, until it began transforming into panic. His heart raced. He wanted to scream, but his voice was gone. He squeezed his eyes shut and fought against the weight of the log once more. He couldn't feel his legs at all. He pushed against the rough bark, grunting and struggling as his breath came in rapid bursts, sweat beading at his brow.

"Will!" came a female voice, echoing from the distance.

"Help!" he cried, his voice strained. Hope began to surface. She could bring him to the light!

"Will, wake up!" Her voice was louder, clearer. His eyes darted around the dark pit. Nobody was there. He strained against the log once more.

"Will!" He felt two small hands grasp his arm.

And suddenly, finally, he died. Sweet surrender, beautiful freedom, he embraced his journey with open arms as the weight was gone and the darkness shifted into light.

He opened his eyes. He blinked, furrowing his brows. He was in his room, not the white haze. He turned his head to find a semi-transparent girl standing alongside his bed, looking concerned, or perhaps even worried. Her hands were on his arm, and she quickly withdrew. He blinked again and moved, but he felt as though his body were air. The blankets around him didn't move, the mattress didn't sink or shift under his weight.

"What the—"

"Don't freak out, I can explain," the girl said, bringing her hands forward.

He sat up, but his body stayed on the bed. He gaped at the sight. The rest of his surroundings were completely undisturbed and normal — the stack of books on his nightstand, notebooks on the floor, the organized chaos of his desk, blinking lights and whirring fans of computers, dual monitors covered in sticky notes, and the edge of a keyboard visible beneath another stack of notes of codes and equations. He turned his focus back to the girl and squinted. "What is this? Who are you?" She looked familiar.

"Lessie Morrison, your cousin," she explained in a gentle voice.

His gaze traveled to the floor. That's why she looked familiar. He had seen her picture on social media. He jerked his head back up to meet her eyes again. Her crystal blue eyes — just like his. Was she... Could she...?

"You're a Transcendent, aren't you?" she asked, her voice almost a whisper. "That's why this is working. That's why you..." She gestured toward him, a physical body sleeping peacefully, and an astral projection, sitting next to it.

Transcendent. He had never applied a name to what he did,

though he vaguely remembered his father using that term. He was terrified when it first happened — at home one Saturday afternoon, absorbed in a video game, when he was called to the boy running through the woods. He fell with him, felt his fear, his panic, heard him scream when they landed in the pit. The log fell from overhead, and he lunged to push the boy out of the way; but as soon as he touched him, they were gone.

When he returned to the living room, "Game Over" flashing on the TV screen, he felt disoriented and confused. His father was staring at him with a nervous, pained expression.

"You okay there, Son?" he asked hesitantly.

"Dad... What just...?" He was afraid to explain what he just saw. Was he crazy? Would his dad think he was crazy? His father seemed to battle mixed emotions, then finally surrendered to asking Will to explain what just happened. Will found the courage to tell him where he had just been, and what he saw. His father then explained the family trait with a strained voice — that his mother could do it, too, and that he'd grown up around her "spacing out" at random, to cross souls over to the Other Side. Will tried to ask him why she wasn't part of their lives, but Ron had nothing more to say. It was the closest he'd ever been to being "supportive" of his son. His emotions and bitterness only got the better of him after that. Will journeyed on through his life deciphering the mysteries of his "ability" completely alone.

"Yeah," he croaked, finally answering Lessie's question. He held her gaze, but revealed no emotion.

"I am too!" she exclaimed, her face brightening, but she quickly withdrew upon seeing no reaction from him. He pondered the concept. There was someone else just like him...

His gaze fell to his knees. He was twenty-five years old now. He'd done this alone for so long, what good would it do to have someone to talk to about it now?

"What are you doing here?" he finally spoke.

Her face fell. She suddenly looked nervous and out of place. "Um," she stammered. "I..." She bit her bottom lip and shrugged. "Astral traveled here?"

"And you decided to visit me?" He squinted uncertainly.

She blinked. "Wait... You know what this is?"

He shrugged. "My life is kinda fucked up. Tried researching to try to make sense of it. I've come across it before. 'Bout the only thing I found that made sense."

She sat down next to him on the edge of the bed. "Have you tried it?"

His brows creased. "Why would I want to? I do it involuntarily, why would I want to add to my problems?"

She shrugged. "Just to test our abilities, I guess." She sighed dejectedly, and they sat in strained silence.

Will sat with tight lips and clenched jaw, his eyes faraway, almost lost. There was so much to process all of a sudden. He broke the silence. "How did you know how to get here, anyway?"

Lessie recalled her adventure, hunching slightly, as though under pressure of interrogation. "I felt like I was imagining it all, actually. I had no idea what I was doing, because I don't know where you live exactly. So I just, I don't know, maybe it was intuition? I allowed the landscape to 'light up'," she held her fingers up in quotes, "to guide my path, and I followed it, then a section of the city lit up, and your apartment complex lit up, and then your apartment lit up, and here I am. I guess I still feel like I'm making this all up, or dreaming it."

Will silently processed her words. If he hadn't already researched the concept himself, he would have thought he was dreaming, too. Hell, maybe he was.

Lessie cleared her throat after another period of heavy silence. "I was kinda hoping you'd be happy to see me..."

His eyes lifted to hers, his expression unchanged. Expressing emotions wasn't his thing. Trusting people even less so.

She shifted awkwardly. She seemed to be processing whether or not it was a good idea to have visited him. After a moment of thought, she pursed her lips and took a breath. "Look, as far as I'm concerned, there isn't a problem between you and I." She bit her lip after he didn't respond right away, then added, "I hope you feel the same..."

His chest rose with an inhale, as memories of his Dad's bitterness flooded his mind. More memories followed, the months of doctor appointments when his dad got the idea that perhaps drugs could turn off his ability, so he could live a "normal" life rather than constantly remind his father of what he could only imagine were dark memories. The relief he felt when his dad finally gave up, but the abandonment he felt when his father closed himself off emotionally for good. Pain pressed against his heart and tightened his throat. Lessie had nothing to do with that part of his life. Finally, he nodded. "We don't have a problem."

A small smile tugged at the corners of her lips, just before sadness clouded her features as she took in the pain in his own expression. She lowered her eyes. "Will... I'm so sorry you had to deal with this alone." She shook her head. "I don't know how you did it all these years." She seemed to withdraw, sorting through a multitude of thoughts, as though she had no idea where to start or what to say next. "Will, Nana is sick," she finally spoke. "And... I'm not sure she'll pull out of it..." Lessie swallowed hard as pain lanced across her face.

His heart sank. "Is that why you're here? Nana won't be with you much longer, and you're afraid of facing your life alone?" He tried to withhold his anger, but she must have sensed it, as she recoiled slightly.

"No, that's not..." she whispered, her voice trailing. "I'm sorry... I can't expect you to... care."

His chest constricted. He was always too quick to fight, to defend himself and his situation. But he couldn't help it. He had been so *alone* for the past twelve years, feeling rejected, shamed, and shut out. Why should he suddenly accept his cousin into his life?

He lifted his gaze, and his heart sank further at her sadness — her lowered head and fallen shoulders. It wasn't her fault they'd never met. He sighed. "I care," he finally said quietly, though unsure if he was telling the truth. "She is my grandma, too."

They held each other's gaze for a moment longer, until finally, she nodded. "I'm sorry," she repeated. "I'm sorry you didn't have her in your life."

He shrugged. "It is what it is. I figured things out."

"It didn't need to be that way. She really did want to be there for you, too." Her eyes clouded with sorrow.

"She didn't even know I was... one of you guys."

"She assumed." She lifted her head, and shrugged. "You have our eyes." She took a breath before continuing. "Besides, you're her grandson. Regardless of your ability, she wished she could have been part of you and Cam's lives." She exhaled, and her eyes fell to the floor once more. "She never wanted Ron's issues to hurt her relationship with you guys."

He nodded. "I could have reached out."

"Why didn't you?"

He shrugged, but didn't answer.

She lifted her hand to squeeze his knee. "Will. We need each other. You don't need to be alone anymore."

He pressed his lips together, lowering his head as his shoulders rose slightly. "I'm used to being alone."

"Come on," she urged, her hand still on his knee. She stared at him pleadingly, and he lifted his eyes to meet hers.

"Why should I suddenly let you into my life?" His voice was almost a whisper.

"Because we're family."

They held each other's gaze silently. Family. Family meant nothing to him. The only family he knew was his father and sister. Sure, his sister had tried time and again to break down his walls, to express some sort of love and acceptance, but he'd rejected it every time. It wasn't that he didn't love her in return — it was that he was gun-shy, from having felt rejected by his father for so many years. He was hesitant even to allow friendship into his life.

But something about Lessie's presence struck a chord deep within him. A shadow of something that had fallen dormant all those years, a yearning to break down the walls and welcome love, for once. But how could he trust her? She was part of the family his father harbored such anger toward — the family he'd shut out after his mom died. Surely his father had good reason for his separation from their lives?

He stared at her hand on his knee, then brought his gaze back up to her eyes. "I don't trust people very easily," he admitted in a quiet voice, and her face fell. "But." He took a breath. "I can try."

A hopeful smile reached her eyes, and he placed his hand on hers. He smiled in return.

CHAPTER 6

DID YOU have a dream or anything about me last night?" Lessie pressed as she met Emily at her locker before first period. She woke that morning with an eagerness to fill her friend in on her experience the night before.

"No..." Emily replied, her brows lowered over her questioning eyes as she gathered her books and shut her locker door. "Why?"

Lessie groaned, but she held onto the hope that everything that happened the night before wasn't just her imagination. "I tried the astral travel thing."

Emily's eyebrows shot up. "Yeah? What was it like?"

Lessie leaned against the lockers next to Emily's, dropping her head back and looking at the tiled ceiling as she hugged her books to her chest. "It was amazing, actually." She turned her head to look at her friend, then added, "It felt so *real*, like I was flying, and out-of-body, but it was sort of different from when I'm called... But then sort of the same..." She shook her head. "It's hard to explain."

"Sounds really cool..." Emily said with a fascinated smile.

"I tried visiting you first," Lessie continued, and Emily raised her eyebrows again. "But you didn't even budge when I tried to talk to you. You were face down all sprawled out on your bed."

Emily chuckled. "Yeah, that's pretty much how I sleep..." she admitted as they began their walk to class.

"I visited Will next."

Emily's eyes widened. "You did?" She shook her head, suddenly eager for information. "And?"

"Well, he was asleep when I got there, but he seemed like he was having a bad dream. I tried saying his name, but he said, 'Help,' or something, so I touched his arm, and that's when he woke up. But, like, a copy of him sat up — his body stayed asleep."

"Whoa!" Emily exclaimed, grinning. "Just like what I read about!"

"Yeah," Lessie replied, shaking her head. "It was crazy. We talked..." She sighed sadly. "But it felt like he didn't want to talk to me, or didn't trust me. I think dealing with this life alone, plus whatever his dad told him, must have really done a number on him."

"You should reach out to him again," Emily suggested. "But, like, an email or something."

Lessie nodded, remembering the walls Will seemed to have around him. "I might let some time pass. I'm not sure what to think of any of it."

They continued walking side by side toward their first period classes, navigating their way through the bustling hallways, each of them pondering their own thoughts about Lessie's experience. The sudden appearance of Adam broke them from their thoughts as he walked toward them in the opposite direction. His thumbs were hooked in the straps of his backpack around his shoulders, and he was so tall, Lessie almost had to crane her neck to look up at him. He was wearing a plain white polo tucked into jeans, as though his nerdiness needed any more help being accentuated. He had the same deep blue eyes as Emily's, only his were hidden behind dark rimmed glasses. His light brown hair was neatly combed, and, if Lessie was honest, he had a very nice physique that she wouldn't have minded checking out a little more if it weren't already so awkward for her that he was her pity homecoming date.

"Adam!" Emily greeted him with a grin.

"Hey!" he responded with equal enthusiasm, pausing in the hallway.

"You going to the game next Friday?" Emily asked.

Adam shrugged, pushing his fingers through his thick light brown hair, then adjusting his glasses. "I usually don't; but hey, if that's all part of this Homecoming thing, then I guess I can give it a shot." He gave Lessie a wink and a smile. Lessie grimaced and shuffled her feet on the floor, avoiding eye contact.

"It *is* part of the whole Homecoming thing," Emily replied as she elbowed Lessie in the ribs. Lessie scowled, but Emily ignored her and continued, "So we'll see you there! I can drive. I'll text you a time!"

Adam grinned. "Sounds good to me." He bumped his knuckles against Lessie's shoulder, which was too much physical contact for her liking. She swallowed and glanced his way, forcing a smile. "Catch ya later!" he finished cheerfully, and he pushed by them, heading to his next class.

Emily grinned at Lessie, then rolled her eyes when she realized Lessie wasn't reciprocating her joy. "Come on, Les, lighten up. He's cool."

"He's a total nerd," Lessie responded with a groan, shaking her head. They began walking again as a tone echoed through the hallways for the next class period.

"He's a cool nerd," Emily corrected. "He's fun, you'll see. Why can't you just give him a chance?"

Lessie barely heard the last of Emily's words, distracted by the group of students they were passing by. Katie Sommers was draped over Mitch's shoulder as he leaned casually against a locker, his arms folded over his chest. Before Lessie could lose herself in imagining her own arm wrapped around those shoulders, she quickly averted her eyes, but not quickly enough to miss him sneering at them as they passed. Her heart sank. "Hey there, Lester." The rest of the group chuckled and snickered.

They kept moving as Lessie felt her face burn. Emily groaned, her eyes narrowed. "Ah yes, that's right, because you're still hung up on that *dick*," she muttered under her breath, her brows lowered over her angry eyes.

"I am not," Lessie retorted unconvincingly, absently tucking a strand of hair behind her ear. After a pause she added, "What does he see in Katie, anyway?"

Emily rolled her eyes dramatically and stopped in front of her classroom door. "You're pathetic. See you in history class."

Lessie sighed. "Whatever." And continued in the direction of her own classroom.

As soon as class was over, Lessie snatched her phone out of her pocket, secretly hoping to see a notification of a message from Will, but instead found a text from her mother.

>>*Took Nana to the hospital. She was in a lot of pain this morning and finally gave in. Having some tests run, will keep you posted.*

Lessie's heart plummeted, and she suddenly felt clammy. She thought back to her conversation with Will the night before. It was the first time she had openly admitted that she wasn't sure if Nana would pull through.

By the time she made it to third period, her nerves were completely frayed. She had gotten another text from her mother that Nana was being transferred to a larger hospital in St. Louis, which was the nearest city to their small town. >>*Call you at lunchtime, try not to worry. Love you.* It was the last message Lessie had received from her. She felt sick.

"You okay?" Emily asked as she took her seat in class next to Lessie, eyeing her hesitantly.

Lessie shook her head, willing away a wave of nausea that threatened to take over as her stomach churned violently. She was certainly not okay. And as if things couldn't get worse, Mitch turned around in his seat in front of her, the same sneering grin on his face he always wore in her presence. "Hey Lester, ready for Homecoming? I hear you're taking the star mathlete with ya." He wiggled his eyebrows. She held her breath, but he persisted. "Works perfectly for him, I'm sure. Any way he's gonna get any experience with a female is if she's unconscious."

Something inside of her snapped. She narrowed her eyes, pressed her lips together, and stood up with her books gathered in one arm. With her free hand, she swung hard and slapped him across the face with a loud *crack*.

She left the classroom stunned in silence behind her.

Her footsteps echoed against the tile and the lockers as she quickly made her way through the halls. As soon as she was out of the building and in the school courtyard, she flopped herself down on a bench under a tree, her books toppling off her lap as she sat breathing heavily. She dropped her head in her hands as tears began stinging in her eyes. Her phone buzzed next to her on the bench, and she hesitantly picked it up.

>>*That. Was. AMAZING. :-O*

Emily. Lessie couldn't help but crack a small smile, despite the torrent of emotion surging through her. But amidst her anguish and frustration and brewing grief, feeling her hand connect with Mitch's face was the most satisfying feeling she'd had in a very long time.

It didn't last long before her thoughts traveled back to Nana. Her heart sank as she pictured her friend and mentor in a hospital. She couldn't be sick — she had *years* left in her... Lessie glanced down at her phone, then tapped her mother's name in her contacts. Her heart picked up speed again as she brought the phone to her ear.

"Lessie, aren't you supposed to be in class?" Lynne asked as soon as she picked up.

"I'm skipping," Lessie responded curtly.

"Celeste," Lynne scolded.

"Can't really focus anyway. What's going on with Nana?"

Lynne sighed. "They detected cancer..." Lessie simply breathed against her hammering heart, unable to accept her mother's words. But she continued in a strained voice, "It's stage four..." Lessie's knees began involuntarily tapping together as she leaned forward on the bench, her stomach twisting into knots. "She has a pretty big mass on her pancreas," Lynne added. "They're seeing if there are any options for her. But, stage four on the pancreas is never a good thing."

Lessie pressed her head into her hand as she leaned her elbow on her knee. Her mind was spinning rampantly in all directions. "So..." she finally spoke, her voice almost a whisper, "Is she gonna make it?"

Lynne paused as she took an uneasy breath. "Probably... not... Celeste."

Silence hung in the air again as Lessie's world began to crumble. Tears threatened to spill over as she swallowed hard, feeling dazed and lost. "H-how much longer do they think she has?"

"Probably not long, with a diagnosis like that. Could be months, could be weeks."

Lessie choked, the tears finally falling. "What the hell, Mom."

"I know, I know..." Lynne said consolingly, holding strong, "I can't believe it, either."

Lessie let the tears fall for a moment as Lynne quietly waited. Finally, Lessie spoke again. "How is she? Emotionally, I mean."

"Fine," Lynne replied. "Of course, she's perfectly fine."

Lessie nodded. Naturally, Nana would accept that her time was drawing near. Lessie, however, could not.

Lynne took a breath, then added, "She's okay with this, Les. You know that. She's been looking forward to being with Dad again all these years. And you both know what awaits on the Other Side. She's ready to move on."

Lessie choked on a sob as her raw emotions barely remained intact. "I know that," she said through a watery voice. She wiped her eyes with the back of her hand. "But *I* don't feel ready."

Lynne sighed. "It's out of our control. Remember what she always says — everything happens for a reason. Let's take this a step at a time, okay? Go back to class. You shouldn't be skipping."

"I slapped Mitch before I left," Lessie admitted randomly.

"Oh my God, Celeste." She didn't exactly sound disapproving, which elicited a small smile on Lessie's strained face. "We need to find you a healthier outlet to channel your emotions."

"I thought that was pretty healthy," Lessie remarked, eyeing the palm of her hand as she sat back on the bench.

"I'm not going to reply to that." She paused, then continued,

"But Lord knows he deserved it. Look, everything is going to turn out just fine, just the way it's all meant to be, so try not to worry about it. Go back to class, and I'll keep you posted if there's any news."

Lessie nodded. "Okay," was all she could say.

Worry and sadness and anxiety tugged at her heart after they hung up, while at the same time she enjoyed a giddy satisfaction in her retaliation on Mitch. She was grateful for her bold move, as it turned out to provide the only positive emotion in her sea of negativity.

"Oh my God, Les, that was *awesome!*" Emily exclaimed as she caught up with Lessie at her locker before fourth period.

Lessie couldn't help but respond with a small smile as she twisted her lock between her fingers. "I really needed that..." she admitted, and she swung open her door to switch out her books.

"Where did that even come from?"

She shook her head as she closed her locker door, and they began walking the short distance to Emily's locker. "I'm just kinda stressed about Nana being sick..." Lessie said, her voice mellow. "And I wasn't in the mood to deal with his crap." She hugged her books to her chest as she explained what had recently transpired with her grandmother.

"Oh Les... I'm so sorry..." Emily breathed, sympathy clouding her features.

They stood in silence for a moment, not knowing what else to say, both in disbelief that Lessie's spunky, lively, fun-loving grandmother may not be with them for much longer.

As if the day couldn't get any worse, just before lunch, Lessie was suddenly shoved unexpectedly face-first into the lockers. An "Oof!" escaped her lungs as the metal doors clattered against her weight, and a hand gripped her shoulder and spun her around, revealing that Lessie had been ambushed by Mitch's girlfriend, Katie. The tall, thin blonde shoved her back into the lockers once more with the heel of her manicured hand. Lessie glared at her, trying to hide the fear that was rising in her chest. Three other cheerleaders showed up behind Katie, forming a wall around them, glares and sneers coming at her from all angles. "What the *hell*, Lester?" snapped Katie. Lessie swallowed and remained silent, trying to keep her gaze firmly on her assailant. Katie grabbed Lessie by the hair, yanking her head back behind her as Katie brought herself closer to Lessie's face. Her neck ached from the angle and her head hurt from the wad of hair Katie had clutched in her fist. "You think you can just slap my boyfriend in the face?" Lessie swallowed again, feeling certain the fear was apparent in her eyes as she could feel Katie's hot breath on her face. Her perfect blonde hair in its perfect curls, perfect blue eyes, perfect makeup, perfect body... It was all in Lessie's face, and was unfortunately turning out to be very intimidating. "How about I slap *you* in the face, *huh?*" She raised her hand to strike, and Lessie flinched.

Before Katie had a chance to swing, her own blonde head was yanked backward and her whole body followed, a look of complete shock etched across her wide-eyed face. It took Lessie a moment to process the scene that was unfolding before her as she released some of the tension she held in preparation for Katie's blow.

Adam towered over Katie with her hair in his fist, and he casually met Lessie's eyes and said, "I'm a bit old-fashioned, I don't like to hit girls. You wanna do the honors?" He offered her a smile and gestured his free hand toward Katie as though it were an act of chivalry, and it took Lessie a moment to get her bearings straight. The rest of the posse stood back, uncertain as to how to handle the situation, as Katie grimaced, clawing at Adam's fist at the back of her head. Lessie supposed this didn't happen to them often.

Lessie met his eyes in disbelief as she rubbed the back of her head where Katie had ahold of her moments ago. Finally, she shook her head. "I'm good," she replied, "I don't need to stoop to that level." Then she added with a nervous smile, "Thanks, though."

He shrugged, then turned his head to face Katie's nervous face, her hair still in his clutches and her head craned back. He met her eyes and said quietly, "You need to keep a better watch on that boyfriend of yours, what with all the sexual references he keeps passing at my friend, here." He leaned in closer and muttered, "We may not be on your level of popularity, but if I were you, I wouldn't fuck with us." He let go of her hair with a shove. "Have a nice day," he said with a courteous nod, and headed into the cafeteria. Lessie gulped back her shock. Casting one last glance at the disheveled cheerleader, she followed behind Adam, her mouth gaping in disbelief.

She caught up with him in the lunch line. "Well, that was pretty badass..." she managed to say once she found her voice. It rendered a chuckle from him, the corner of his mouth crooked upward in a half-smile. It was kind of handsome... Lessie cleared her throat again. "Thanks for that."

He shrugged. "It's nothin'," he replied. He pushed his glasses up the bridge of his nose. "I usually like to keep the peace, but when I see shit like that, I can't help but step in." He grabbed two trays and handed one to Lessie. "Nice one with Mitch earlier, by the way." He smiled with a glint in his dark sapphire eyes behind his thick glasses. He did have pretty eyes...

Lessie groaned. "How did you hear about that?" she asked, already knowing the answer.

"It's all over school," he replied. "You can't go hitting the star football player and expect to get away with it. Emily filled me in on the details, like the bullshit Mitch has been saying to you. He's a pig. Totally deserved to get slapped." He then smiled, as they inched forward in line, and added, "Which, I gotta say, *that* was badass!"

Her cheeks burned scarlet. Was she seriously having this conversation with Adam? She was realizing he wasn't exactly what she expected. "Thanks," she mumbled.

After a pause, he spoke again, changing the subject. "So, uh, am I supposed to wear something that matches your dress?"

"Uh... Um..." she stammered, caught off guard.

"Homecoming?" he added, arching a brow and smiling slightly.

She pulled herself together and shrugged. "I guess, but I haven't really picked one out yet..."

He gave her a sideways glance. "You know it's two weeks away, right?"

She furrowed her eyebrows. "Yes, mother, I know."

Adam chuckled as he began loading up his tray. "I'm not tryin' to control your life, sorry."

Lessie shook her head. "It's fine. I just have a lot going on right now, that's all."

"Want me to come help you pick something out?" he said innocently.

Lessie grew rigid at the idea. "No!"

He shrugged. "Just offering." They neared the end of the line in silence, but before it was their turn to pay, he said, "Look, I'm not trying to be your boyfriend or anything. And I'm sorry you've got a lot going on." She averted her eyes, her brows creased. He finished, his voice sincere, "But just try to have fun with this, okay? It's our last Homecoming dance, let's just roll with it."

She fell silent, shocked at how forward he was, and the confidence he exuded. Before they parted ways, Lessie forced herself to speak again. "Hey, thanks again for helping me out." She offered him a half-smile as she met his eyes.

He shrugged. "Anytime." He returned her smile before heading to his table. He had a really nice smile...

CHAPTER 7

LESSIE ENTERED an empty house after school, which twisted her sinking stomach even tighter. She tossed her backpack on the table and pulled out a chair, slumping into it and leaning her elbows on the cool wooden surface, her chin resting in her hands. She stared out the window, ignoring her backpack and the homework inside it. It wasn't like she'd be able to focus on it anyway.

She felt as she should have been handling this better. Death... It's what she did. It was a normal thing for her. She knew she should feel happy for Nana, just like Nana was happy for her husband when it was his turn. But she just couldn't. She still needed her.

Her mind wandered to slapping Mitch, but even that didn't bring her the satisfaction it brought earlier, as now the whole school was talking about her behind her back. She shuddered as she recalled the assault from Katie.

And then there was Adam...

I should try to find a nice Homecoming dress... she thought absently. *I'd like to look good at his side...* She blinked, sitting up straighter. *Wait, what?*

She jumped as her phone buzzed with an alert, jolting her

away from her thoughts. She picked it up, squinting and igniting with a fluttering sense of hope.

New Message from Will Gardener.

"Will?" Her heart was suddenly hammering, her brain firing rapidly, all other thoughts completely gone and forgotten. She hesitated opening it, knowing that if it were anything negative, she didn't think her heart could handle it.

She decided to take her chances. Her finger shook as she opened the message.

Lessie, hey, about last night. I just wanted to say, thanks for coming by. That had to have taken guts, and I didn't give you enough credit for that. I'm not used to people caring, and I'm not used to having someone to talk to about this. But, I'm willing to try. Figured I'd start by sending this message.

Will

She stared at it with wide eyes. *Oh my God...* The breath she'd been holding burst from her lungs as tears began to sting at her eyes. Her thumbs began rapidly flying across the touchscreen keyboard in response.

>>*Will, thank you. I was actually starting to wonder if last night was all just a dream...*

She quickly tapped "send" and waited, her breath hitched in her tightened throat.

The ellipse popped up, signalling that he was typing a response, and her heart leapt into her windpipe, hammering away with abandon.

>>*No, it was very real. Maybe let's meet up a more normal way next time though. Like a video chat or something.*

She grinned. The feeling of her cheeks stretching into a

display of any kind of joy had almost become foreign to her after her emotional day, but she welcomed the feeling. >>*I'd like that. If you're game.*

>>*Yeah, I'm game.*

She beamed as she gave him her contact information, and felt a new wave of nervous jitters wash through her as she waited for him to call. Before she was completely consumed by nerves, her video chat app began ringing. She tapped to open it, her finger shaking all over again.

The window opened up, displaying a small thumbnail of herself in the corner as Will's face filled up the main screen. It was really him... thick sandy brown hair, crystal blue eyes that looked just like Nana's and her own, and sharp features that reminded her of her mother. He looked just like he did the night before when she met him on her astral journey.

She stared in disbelief for a moment before letting out a breath. "Wow..."

"Hey," he greeted, giving her a hesitant smile. She was glad to see him smile, especially after his uncertain mood the night before.

"This is so crazy..." Lessie stood from her chair in the kitchen and headed up to her room, her phone grasped in her hand as she stared in awe at the real Will Gardener. As soon as she got to her room, she closed the door behind her and fell onto her bed face down, propping herself up on her elbows.

"So," he said, breaking the silence. "Sorry again about last night."

Lessie shrugged. "I understand. I'd probably be the same way. But I don't want you to be alone anymore."

He gave her a small nod. "Yeah." He glanced down,

seeming to search for words, then returned his focus to the screen. "What's the latest on Nana?"

She sighed as her face fell slightly, and filled him in on what she learned from her mother that day. "Mom and Dad are still up at the hospital," she finished. "I haven't heard anything lately."

"I'm sorry, Les," he said softly, his eyes filled with genuine sympathy.

"Well, like I said, I can't expect you to care, or feel sorry for me. But, thanks."

Will shrugged. "I could have done something about my relationship with Nana. She's tried reaching out to me. But I guess I let Dad's feelings about the family control mine." He sighed heavily, shaking his head. "I should have come back home to live with you guys. I don't know why I put up with the life I lived."

"How could you help it, Will?" Lessie cut in, feeling a pang of sympathy for him. "Losing your mom is a pretty big deal... Your dad and sister are important people. You couldn't just leave them."

He nodded slowly, thoughtfully. "You seem wise for your age."

She laughed. "Thanks. Occupational hazard."

"True that," he replied with a nod and a knowing smile.

She sat up and turned her attention to the sound of the click and creak of the door opening downstairs. She turned back to her phone after hearing her mom call her name, and said to Will, "Mom and Dad are home. I should go."

Will nodded. "No problem. I'm sure I'll see you soon, in one form or another." He gave her a small smile that reached his eyes. "Thanks for finding me."

She grinned as a warmth filled her heart. "Thanks for writing, and talking." They said their goodbyes, and Lessie quickly left her room to join her family downstairs, still savoring the joy of getting to connect with her estranged cousin, and the hope of actually breaking down his walls.

She stopped short mid-descent on the staircase, and her heart sank as she took in the sight of a suddenly frail looking Nana hanging on the arms of Lessie's parents as they assisted her into her room.

"H-hey guys," Lessie said softly.

"Hi Lessie," Lynne replied gently, offering her a comforting smile as her daughter stared at her grandmother.

"Nana..." Lessie spoke, her voice growing hoarse. How had she declined so rapidly? Nana looked up at her and met her with a sympathetic smile.

"Hi Sweetie," she replied in a tired voice. "I'm going to get some rest, I'm on a lot of pain killers. I'll see you in the morning, okay?"

All Lessie could do was nod, and she helplessly watched them disappear into Nana's room.

ONCE RETURNING HOME after school the next afternoon, Lessie hesitantly approached Nana's silent, darkened room. She poked her head in through the door, waiting for her eyes to adjust to take in the old woman's sleeping form. Her chest slowly rose and fell under the sheets with her steady breath.

"Nana?" Lessie whispered softly, not wanting to wake her, yet at the same time desperately craving conversation with her.

She saw her stir slightly, then release a soft groan. "Les?" she said, her voice cracking from her lengthy sleep.

Lessie's heart pounded faster as she hesitantly entered the room. "How are you?"

"Mmm," she hummed softly. "Okay, I guess. So tired. But come in, I feel like it's been forever since I've seen you."

Lessie immediately felt her eyes filling with tears. "Yeah. Me, too." She approached the other side of the bed and crawled in next to her grandmother, lying on her side to face her. She looked so much older all of a sudden. "This happened so fast..." she whispered, trying to restrain her tears.

"I know... kind of surprises me, too..." Nana said, offering her a sympathetic smile. "But it's okay, you know that, right?"

Lessie swallowed against the lump in her throat. She started to say yes, just to agree with her, but she knew it wasn't true. Instead she choked out, "No..." and she could no longer hold back the tears as they spilled over. She blinked furiously against them.

"Oh, Honey," Nana whispered, reaching to pull her granddaughter into an embrace. "I won't be gone, you know that."

"But I won't get to talk to you, or see you, or ask you questions, or tell you about my life, or hear about yours..." Lessie sobbed against her, finally surrendering to her anguish and letting it all spill out. She sucked in a ragged breath. "I feel so stupid. Death is part of... *everything*. I *know* that. And part of me wants to be excited for you... but..." She struggled to finish, both unable to find the words and having trouble speaking.

"But you also know you won't have me around anymore."

Lessie nodded, letting the tears spill all over again. "I feel so selfish," she managed to say.

Nana squeezed her again. "It's not selfish. It's perfectly normal." She kissed the top of her head. "And, remember, it's our challenges that teach us our best lessons, and help us grow as people. You'll find a way to see the beauty, Sweetie, and you'll be stronger for it. Just be open to receiving the messages along the way."

"Messages?" Lessie replied softly, her tears finally slowing.

Nana shrugged, then pulled back to meet her eyes. "The Universe has mysterious ways of speaking to us. There are signs everywhere, all the time. You just need to watch for them. And be open to them." She shrugged again, then smiled. "Or just ask. Ask and you shall receive. All you have to do is ask the Universe, or ask God, or ask Spirit, or whatever you happen to call that higher power, and you'll get your answers one way or another. You just have to be open to receiving them."

Lessie nodded thoughtfully. "I don't know if I need a sign so much as I just need help accepting this..."

Nana smiled and hugged her again. "Well, then ask for that, too."

CHAPTER 8

EVERYTHING MOVED so fast. Never in all her life did Lessie imagine that her grandmother, her Nana, would be taken from her so abruptly. Mere months ago she seemed so vibrant and full of life; but that moment as Lessie stood in the doorway, taking in her weak, sleeping form in the dark room as night peacefully made its way into the world, she was a shadow of what she used to be. It had been two days since Nana had told Lessie to ask the Universe for a sign, or for help with comfort and acceptance, but she had yet to find it. She tried to choke back the tears that stung in her eyes as a lump grew in her throat. She still struggled. Nothing had happened to make it easier. She wanted to handle it with the same grace that Nana had handled her husband's death — knowing it was the next step in their soul's evolution.

She hung her head, folding her arms across her stomach as she leaned harder against the doorframe.

She knew her mother was struggling with the thought of Nana leaving them, too; though she did well to hide it. Not only that, but Lynne also struggled with brewing resentment that she had to handle the passing of her mother without the help of a perfectly capable brother. Regardless, Lynne put on her brave face for her daughter, and instead turned to Sam for comfort in private. Lessie was all too aware of this, and while she appreciated her mother's act of strength, she was left feeling that much more alone.

"Why does this have to happen..." she whispered from the doorway, hugging her arms tighter against her chest. She sighed softly, the weight in her heart feeling more obvious upon her exhale, and just before she could turn to leave the room, the familiar *whoosh* of cosmos consumed her and swallowed her in.

She landed on her feet on a carpeted floor in a dark room, slivers of light stretched across the floor and walls from the street lamps outside. Her heart made a sudden leap in shock when she realized a glowing young girl sat on a bed in the middle of the room, staring pensively at an identical lifeless body lying next to her.

She looked serene, her ankles crossed as they hung off the edge of the bed from underneath a simple white nightgown, her hands folded neatly in her lap, her face soft as she studied her motionless form. Her soft blonde hair was pulled back into a loose ponytail at the back of her neck, and her body was thin and frail. She slowly turned her head to meet Lessie's curious and shocked gaze, seeming completely unfazed by the stranger in her room.

"Hello," the girl greeted.

"Um... Hi," Lessie responded uncertainly, squinting at the girl.

"Here to take me over?" she asked casually.

"You know why I'm here?" Lessie questioned, shocked.

The girl shrugged. "Apparently I'm dead, or, at least my body is, and a bright light hasn't appeared yet, so I figured you have something to do with the process."

Lessie suddenly found herself flooded with questions. "What happened?" she asked hesitantly.

"I had leukemia for a really long time," the girl replied as though simply giving a weather report. "It almost took me last year, but I made a recovery. I dunno, was just desperate to live. So I did."

Lessie nodded slowly, already captivated by the girl's story and what could possibly make her feel so at peace with dying at such a young age, especially after having fought so hard to live once already. She asked, "And now?"

The girl shrugged. "I spent the year doing a lot of soul searching. I learned more about myself, and God... I started getting bad again in the last month or so, and I realized I'm okay with whatever happens this time. Didn't think it would happen tonight, though, but that's okay." She sounded like she meant it, her lips curling up into a soft smile.

Lessie furrowed her eyebrows in confusion. This was definitely all very new to her. "It's okay?" she repeated inquisitively.

The girl offered her a smile again. "Yeah. I'm ready to go. I know there's more on the Other Side. This life..." She waved her hands around her, her palms up, "It's all just a dream, right? Like, temporary? The real stuff is where I'm going." Lessie blinked, trying to make sense of her words. "Anyway," the girl continued with a smile. "I guess we better be off then." She scooted to the edge of the bed as though she were about to stand, but Lessie didn't move. Her mind was still reeling as she tried to process the situation. The girl stopped, remaining seated, noting Lessie's hesitation, her head tilting to the side as she studied her curiously. "Unless... You don't want to?"

Lessie shook herself from her reverie. "S-sorry, this is just...

different for me. Normally I show up just before the person dies, so I can be with them when it happens."

The girl gave her a curious smile, then said, "Don't you work for God? Like, you should have all the answers. This shouldn't be anything new to you."

Finally, Lessie relaxed into her strange environment as she cracked a smile and released a small chuckle. "Heh, no, I'm just some girl from Southern Illinois who has a *really* bizarre gift." She shrugged her hands out to the side then dropped them back to her hips. "I'm called a Transcendent. I don't even know what it's like over there. It's a tease every time. I mean, I can *feel* how amazing it must be, but I never get to cross over into it. Pretty cool that you get to see it, huh? I just get to watch."

The girl's eyes had widened at Lessie's explanation. "Seriously?" She looked off to the side, pondering. "That's crazy..." She then met Lessie's searching blue eyes once more. "I always wondered if... mysteries... like that existed. There's so much more to this world, to this Universe, than any of us can even begin to dream!" Lessie grinned at her words as she continued, "It's amazing, isn't it?"

Still grinning, Lessie nodded. "Yeah, it is." She then grew solemn as several questions rose to her mind. "Aren't you worried about your family? They're going to find you here, having died in your sleep. They'll be devastated..." She felt a pang of sadness in her heart at the thought of her parents having to lose a child. No parent should ever have to go through that.

But again, the girl simply shrugged. "Of course they will be. We're all taught to believe there's a natural order to things. Parents get old, they become grandparents, those children grow, the grandparents die as the next parents get old and become grandparents, and so on and so forth. But, if a parent dies while the child is young, or worse, a child dies before a parent... well, we're not able to handle that, because it's not in the order we know and understand." Lessie nodded, listening intently to her words. "It's like we forgot, or have never been taught in the first place, that there's a reason for everything, even if it doesn't make sense. Every bad thing that happens to us is a chance to grow, to learn who we really are and what we're made of. If we can view it that way, we can really rise up into some amazing people." She smiled. "I think my parents will pull through this eventually, and be that much stronger because of it. And we'll all be together again on the Other Side."

Lessie slowly released a breath, staring in awe at the girl. Her skin prickled with the deep sense of truth the girl spoke, and she was even more moved by how what she said resonated so clearly with what Nana had said all her life. Tears stung in her eyes as she suddenly realized that the Universe had brought her to this girl, connecting her to the truth she needed to hear to finally accept Nana's fate.

The girl turned her head back to her lifeless body. "This cancer has been hard, and I hated life and hated God through quite a bit of it, but when I almost died from it last year, I guess I sort of had an awakening." She looked back up at Lessie, smiling. "I lived for a reason, and I needed to figure out that reason and fulfill it."

"And do you feel like you did?" Lessie asked eagerly, her voice choked with emotion.

The girl's smile brightened. "I suppose so, or I wouldn't be here, would I?" She thumbed in the direction of her abandoned body. "I'd still be there, breathing, sleeping."

"So what was it, then? The reason you lived, that is."

"Well…" the girl began, a thoughtful look traveling across her face as she glanced off to the side. "I learned a lot of these things through journaling. That helped me put my thoughts together and made me realize how connected we are, and how this time here in our human lives is only temporary, and we're here to grow as spiritual beings and then take that knowledge with us back to the Other Side."

Goosebumps traveled over Lessie's skin again. She squinted, half-smiling. "You got all that out of journaling?"

The girl laughed. "Okay, so I read a bunch of stuff online, too. Then I wrote about it. But it felt right. Like I just *knew*, ya know?"

Lessie smiled. Nana had spoken of those same concepts so many times before, but hearing it from this girl carried new meaning for her. Losing Nana, her mentor, was her challenge. But pressing through life without her, and learning and growing from that challenge, would only make her stronger. Her life suddenly shined with a new sense of purpose.

The girl smiled, sensing the glow that Lessie exuded as she reflected on the power of the girl's words. "It feels right to me," she continued. "It's the reason I can sit here and not be afraid, and instead be excited about what lies ahead for me." The girl held Lessie's gaze, thought for a moment, then continued her story. "My mom is a minister. She and I had long, deep conversations about all this. About the meaning of life, and our purpose, and why things happen that seem so bad and so terrible, and we both agreed that these terrible things are meant to teach us the most powerful lessons, so we can grow into the best people. And help others do the same when bad things happen to them. She began sharing some of our thoughts in her sermons, and suddenly more and more people began to come to her for comfort and wisdom. She credited it all to me, but I know it was all in her heart, too." She smiled warmly at the thought of her mother and the great work she was doing in their community, all because her daughter battled leukemia and they chose to learn and grow from it, rather than mourn it.

Lessie felt a tear slip down her cheek, and wiped it away quickly. The girl chuckled. "It's okay! Don't cry! My parents will be heartbroken when they find me, I'm sure, but they're strong, they'll pull through it, and they'll do amazing things because of what they learned with me. Because I was given a second chance at life."

Lessie chuckled pathetically as more tears gathered in her eyes. "I'm not crying 'cause I'm sad," she said softly, smiling. "I'm just so... blown away by all this..." She shook her head. "My grandma is dying, and I was struggling with that..." She met the girls' eyes with another laugh. "Ironic, right? Here I ferry people to the other side all the time, but I can't handle my own grandmother's death." She shook her head and continued gesturing toward her, "And here I wind up with *you*, and you hand me everything I needed to hear to get through it." She sighed, looking deeply into the girl's bright eyes. "You've served much more of a purpose than you know. You're an amazing soul." Another tear slipped down her cheek. "Thank you."

The girl grinned and stood, reaching out to embrace Lessie. Before Lessie could warn her, the connection the girl made with her secured the link, and the room disappeared. Lessie returned the embrace, and once they finally parted, they found themselves standing in the white haze. The girl stood back, her hands remaining clasped gently around Lessie's wrists. She absolutely beamed, her whole being growing brighter. "Thank you for the ride, friend."

Lessie grinned at her. "Hey, it's what I do," she replied casually with a chuckle, and the smiling girl turned to face the light as it began to grow. Spirits emerged from the light with arms outstretched to greet the girl and take her Home.

Lessie watched as the girl's eyes grew wider and brighter, her mouth hanging open slightly. "Whoa..." she breathed. She turned to look at Lessie, her expression so full of excitement that she seemed as though she were about to burst. "This is so freaking *cool!*" she exclaimed, unable to contain herself.

Lessie couldn't help but let loose a hearty laugh, thoroughly enjoying the girl's enthusiasm, her awe and wonder feeling utterly contagious. Her heart felt so full at that moment, seeing the girl's vibrant joy, and experiencing the moment for what it truly was — a beautiful, incredible passage from one life into the next.

The girl linked arms with the spirits, and her being glowed even brighter. She looked over her shoulder at Lessie and flashed her a wide, excited smile, then raised a hand to give her a departing wave. "Thanks again, see you on the Other Side!"

Lessie raised her own hand to wave in return, still smiling brightly. "Thank *you*," she responded. "Say hi to Grandpa for me!"

With one last grin, the girl turned her head and stepped into the light, and all of Lessie's surroundings burst into a blinding, brilliant luminescence as she squinted against it. She was suddenly transported back, the familiar whooshing sound crashing around her, and with a staticky *pop* she was instantly on her feet right where she was before she was called, getting ready to leave Nana's doorway. She blinked a few times as her eyes adjusted to her surroundings, the room almost feeling dull and lifeless compared to where she'd just been. She wiped at a tear that had escaped down her cheek as emotions surged inside of her. She turned to face her grandmother again, who was still lying in bed, asleep, and smiled.

"How cool..." she whispered. "You'll get to do that soon..."

She then turned and headed back up to her room

CHAPTER 9

LESSIE AND Emily, once again, found themselves poring over racks of Homecoming dresses. It was the Friday afternoon of the last weekend they had to shop before the dance, and Emily, who had already found her dress, was trying to help Lessie decide on one before she ran out of time.

Lessie emerged from the fitting room and smoothed the satiny fabric at her waist, as Emily's eyes widened and jaw dropped. "Damn, girl..." she breathed.

Lessie looked up to meet her eyes, chuckling and grinning sheepishly. "You like?"

Emily nodded quickly, eyes still wide in awe. Not only did the dress fit her perfectly, hugging her in all the right ways, the gradient teal complementing her eyes perfectly, and the intricate beadwork sparkling at the bottom; but she emitted a certain glow from a newfound cheeriness and confidence, of which Emily was dying to know the source. "Oh yeah," Emily replied, "I like..."

Lessie laughed as she turned around, eyeing herself in the mirrors. She pushed her fingers into her frizzy hair, suddenly frowning. "I'm sure it would look even better if this weren't such a mess," she grumbled.

Emily grinned, arching a brow. "You suddenly care about your hair?" Lessie shifted sheepishly. "Well," Emily continued, "Lucky for you I have hair appointments scheduled for us that day."

Lessie automatically returned her grin. "What would I ever do without you?" she laughed.

Emily shrugged. "You'd be a sad little introvert with no life," she replied. "Now come on, pay for this thing and let's go eat so you can tell me who you are and what you did with Lessie!"

Lessie bought the dress, and the two proceeded to the food court where Emily practically ran to a table, eager for Lessie to fill her in on what suddenly changed. She listened with wide eyes as Lessie told her of the profound experience she had the night before with the girl with leukemia. Her heart filled all over again, just as it had when she heard the girl's words of deep wisdom. The girl had gained that wisdom from the challenges she had faced and grown from; and it only built on Lessie's new awareness that she, too, had wonderful growth ahead of her.

Emily hung on Lessie's every word, then fell back into her seat with an awestruck exhale, shaking her head. "Synchronicity," she said, her eyes thoughtful and faraway. "Things line up just the way they need to when you need them to."

Lessie nodded. "Mom and Nana always said things happen for a reason." She smiled, meeting Emily's eyes. "They weren't kidding."

LESSIE INHALED DEEPLY as she pulled her denim jacket tighter around her shoulders against the cool fall air, taking in the dark blue sky, the brightly illuminated football field, and the bleachers filled with cheering fans. She normally felt claustrophobic in such environments, but she managed to relax and go with the flow, enjoying her friends' company and finally allowing herself to feel like a normal teenager as they moved through the crowd at the Homecoming football game.

She felt a rush of warmth and a tingling sensation travel up her spine as Adam casually put his hand on the back of her shoulder and smiled down at her from his towering height. "Want to sit down?" he asked, breaking her from her momentary trance.

"Um... Y-yeah, sure," she stammered nervously, suddenly feeling awkward. Her eyes darted to Emily, who was pressed up against Evan's side, before moving to focus on Adam and shooting him a wary smile.

She took a deep breath and gazed out over the football field. The grass glowed a vivid green under the spotlights, brightly contrasted against the dark night sky. They climbed the bleachers and took a seat as the band burst into celebration for a first down, and students dressed in dark green cheered and clapped along.

"I'm excited about tomorrow," he said casually as they found a seat. "Do you dance?"

Lessie went rigid. "N-no, not really..." Her stammer elicited another chuckle from Adam.

"It's not really my thing either. I don't go to many of these. But I'm up for it if you are!" He flashed her a toothy grin, his deep blue eyes bright and alive behind his dark rimmed glasses.

"I-I'm not sure about that..." Lessie replied awkwardly, leaning her elbows on her knees after tucking back a loose strand of hair. "I like to avoid crowded places."

"Because of your thing?" Adam questioned, causing Lessie

to stiffen all over again. "Epilepsy, right? Ya know, I never heard of absence seizures until I met you. What's that like, anyway?" Lessie's heart leapt into her throat at his forward question. "Like when you zone out. Do you know what's going on when that's happening, or remember anything?"

"Heh," she chuckled nervously, then met his inquisitive eyes. He was genuinely curious, but not in a judgemental way, and she felt herself begin to relax. "Sorry, that's confidential," she replied playfully.

He squinted, holding a small grin. "You're part of some alien conspiracy, aren't you?" he questioned, and mischief crossed her features.

"Dammit," she muttered, feigning frustration. "Now that you know, you can't be allowed to live."

"Hell, just when things were starting to get good," he responded, still grinning. Together, they refocused their attention on the game, as a newfound giddiness bubbled inside her.

THE DAY OF HOMECOMING flew by in a blur. Lessie's nervous jitters had begun to creep in during her hair appointment with Emily. Her hand shook as she applied her mascara later. And she could barely pull her dress on straight as she fumbled in her bedroom in front of her full-length mirror. Emily just laughed at her.

Lessie's nerves only escalated as she caught sight of Adam's car approaching her house, and she felt certain she'd pass out from her sudden inability to breathe when her date stepped out from the driver's seat. She met Adam's eyes behind his dark-rimmed glasses, which seemed to be an even deeper, more captivating shade of ocean blue brought out by the teal shirt he wore, adorned with a black tie. He was absolutely handsome, and she was not prepared for it.

She humored her mother, who snapped picture after picture of the four of them. Lessie nearly choked when Adam slipped his hand around her waist for the pictures her mother wanted of just the two of them.

Lessie's heart lifted as she watched her grandmother hobble onto the front porch, supported by Sam's arm, to watch the four prepare for their evening together.

Lessie hugged her fiercely before they gathered in Adam's car. "You look beautiful," Nana whispered, her eyes filled with light. "And your date is quite the handsome fellow, too." She flashed Lessie a wink, and heat rose to Lessie's cheeks. "Have a good time, okay? Don't worry about anything else."

Lessie gave a stiff nod, but smiled nonetheless. "I'll try, Nana."

Their dinner reservations were at a popular steakhouse, and, finally, nearly halfway through dinner, Lessie felt herself relax. They talked casually, joked, laughed, and so far the Universe was leaving Lessie alone. She was beginning to feel hopeful that she'd survive the night, after all.

Her nerves were back full-force as they entered the school. She smoothed her dress along her waist and down her narrow hips, and Emily laughed as she nudged her. "Seriously, Les, you're a mess. Try to relax. You look amazing!"

Lessie eyed Emily, trying to focus on her friend rather than her surroundings. "So do you," she replied with a nervous smile, and she meant it. Emily's blonde hair was half up, half down in graceful curls that brushed across her bare shoulders, her strapless dress a perfect shade of deep magenta that both contrasted and complemented her dark sapphire eyes. It hugged against her small waist before flaring out at the bottom, and was embellished with tiny glittering rhinestones that flowed in a gentle stream from her bust line, curving down her waist, around her hip, and spilling out around the bottom hem. Lessie's smile relaxed as her shoulders loosened. She was at Homecoming, with three wonderful friends. She suddenly felt determined to enjoy herself. "Let's do this."

Emily grinned, linked her arm into Evan's as Lessie did the same with Adam, and together, they entered the gymnasium.

The expansive room was transformed into an Under the Sea theme complete with kelp streamers and glowing pearlescent balloons. Loud music blared and thumped from the band on the stage, as colored lights flashed through the darkened gym. Before Lessie choked on her own restricted breath amidst the sea of dancing students, Adam reached his hand around her back and pulled her in close. "You ready?" he asked, smiling down at her.

She looked up to meet his dark azure gaze, and smiled hesitantly in return. "Ready as I'll ever be," she responded bravely.

The four soon found themselves on the dancefloor, moving to the music and grinning broadly. As Emily wrapped herself in Evan's arms, Adam leaned in closer to Lessie.

"See? No problem!" he shouted, grinning.

Lessie rolled her eyes. "You don't understand! The alien conspiracy I'm involved in could take over at any minute!"

Adam laughed loudly. "Well, hopefully they decide to let you come back! I'm having fun!"

Lessie shook her head, grinning, and allowed herself to let go of her fears and enjoy the night.

The driving beat of the music wound down to a slow,

melodic rhythm, and couples began pairing up on the dance floor. Emily and Evan were already ahead of everyone, falling into step, arms wrapped tightly around each other as Emily rested her head on Evan's shoulder with her face pressed into his neck. Lessie turned in the direction of the tables to make her escape, but stopped, caught by Adam's eyes and inviting smile. He shrugged, and offered a hand to her, which Lessie stared at with hesitation, her body going rigid as the butterflies erupted into life in her stomach. "Shall we?" he asked casually, and Lessie swallowed against the lump in her throat.

She reached her hand up to join his, praying he didn't see how badly she was shaking. He smiled warmly as their eyes met once more. He drew her in close to him, leaving at least an inch of space between their bodies, which was good since she was fairly certain her hammering heart would knock him over if she got any closer. Taking the lead, Adam began moving them together in rhythm to the music.

"Having fun so far?" he asked as she stared out across the dance floor, trying not to allow her body to become paralyzed with fear and whatever other emotions she had stirred up inside of her.

She shrugged, trying to act casual. "Sure," she replied. "You?"

He grinned and tightened his hold on her back. "Yes, I am. Thanks for going with me."

A smiled escaped. After spending so much time hating the idea of going with him, feeling as though they were set up out of pity, she found herself oddly appreciating the situation. "Thanks for taking me," she replied sincerely, and she smiled as their eyes met again.

And at that moment, she was sucked from the dance floor.

Oh no! No, no, no! she screamed in her head as she was taken far away from the dance, leaving behind a vacant, motionless body.

"Lessie?" Adam asked, cocking his head to the side, suddenly feeling as though he were dancing with an off-balance statue. He looked into her empty eyes with concern.

It wasn't long before Emily caught sight of the couple. "Oh shit," she muttered under her breath, abandoning Evan and rushing over to Adam and Lessie.

"What's going on, is she doing that thing?" Evan asked as he joined them. Emily wrapped her arm around her immobile friend and looked pleadingly at her boyfriend. Students all around them were already starting to stare and whisper.

"Yeah, help me guide her over to a table," she ordered.

"Let me help," Adam offered, but Lessie wasn't budging, and if they tried to push her forward, she'd surely fall. Much to Emily's dismay, they were beginning to attract more attention.

"What's wrong with her?"

"What is she doing?"

"That is super creepy..."

The whispers were flooding in from all around, and suddenly Emily felt a gripping pang of sympathy for her friend. Maybe going to a busy school event wasn't such a good idea after all.

"Fuck off, leave her alone!" Emily shouted at the gathering crowd, and finally Adam scooped the statuesque girl into his arms and carried her to a table as far from the crowded dance floor as they could get. He managed to get her to slump down into a chair, her vacant eyes drifting out across the room.

Adam tried to talk Lessie back to reality, snapping his fingers in front of her face and growing more worried by the second.

He looked desperately at Emily. "How long does this usually last? Can we get her to snap out of it?"

Emily shook her head, folding her arms across her chest nervously. Evan wrapped a comforting arm around her back, chewing his lower lip. "No, you have to wait for her to come back," Emily answered, hoping Adam took the term "come back" as more of a metaphor. "Sometimes it only lasts a minute or two, sometimes it lasts longer." She glanced over at the crowded dance floor. Some of the students had returned to dancing, while others still eyed them curiously. Her heart sank as she spotted Mitch and his gang of football players and cheerleaders staring directly at them, whispering amongst themselves and sneering. "I hope for her sake it's over soon..." she added.

"Back the hell off!" Adam suddenly shouted, abruptly standing up and waving his arms out at the gathering crowd, causing Emily and Evan to jump back. "She can't fucking help it!" He moved forward as part of the crowd began dissipating, some wearing guilty expressions, others clearly unfazed. "You're all a bunch of assholes!" He glowered at the last of them, zeroing in particularly on Mitch's smirking girlfriend, before finally returning to the table. He stopped dead in his tracks when he made eye contact with a very distraught Lessie.

He blinked, then rushed forward and knelt down next to her, clasping her hands in his. "Jesus Lessie, are you okay?"

Lessie swallowed and licked her lips, her eyes darting over the crowd that was now back to dancing and acting as though nothing happened. She was still getting her bearings about her after crossing a soul over to the Other Side, and her heart constricted in her chest as so many confusing emotions washed over her. Her fears coming into reality. The unwanted attention she attracted. The horrible timing. Everyone staring and whispering. Adam having to witness it. Adam sticking up for her...

Her eyes shot back to meet Adam's, whose face was still wrought with concern. "Of course I'm okay," she snapped back, then immediately regretted her tone. He did just defend her. Before she could apologize, her eyes were drawn back out to the crowd, where she caught sight of Mitch, Katie, and several of their friends whispering and snickering amongst themselves while staring in her direction. Her face burned as her eyes narrowed angrily. She stood up and snatched her phone, already processing what she'd have to tell her mother when she called for her to come pick her up. Her stomach twisted.

"Les?" Adam hesitantly asked as he stood, and she shot him one last look.

"Thanks for sticking up for me," she croaked against threatening tears, then cast a pained glance at Emily and Evan before making a beeline out of the gymnasium.

Adam met Emily's eyes, both feeling defeated, before he drew back his shoulders and held his head higher. "She's not leaving," he stated, and he took off after her.

He found her at the front entrance to the building, already on the phone with her mother as tears spilled down her cheeks.

"It happened again, Mom... In front of everyone," he heard her sob into the phone as he approached her. He gently placed his hand over hers and met her eyes as he drew the phone away from her ear.

Not breaking eye contact, he brought the phone to his own ear. "Mrs. Morrison? It's Adam. Everything's going to be okay. I'm going to talk to Lessie, don't come get her yet. We'll call you if we need you." Lynne hesitantly thanked him on the other end of the line and wished him luck, and they both hung up, Adam's eyes still locked on Lessie's.

"I can't stay here," Lessie stated adamantly, her voice watery.

"Yes, you can," Adam replied evenly. "And you're going to."

"No, Adam, did you see the way they were looking at me?" Lessie's eyes filled with tears once again. "I'm a freak! They were all whispering and staring and—" She choked on a sob before she could continue.

"So what?" he shouted back, and she recoiled slightly. "Who gives a shit what they think?" His eyes were narrowed as they bored into hers, and she narrowed her own to mirror his.

"You don't understand..." she muttered, breaking eye contact and looking down at the floor. The image of Mitch whispering and staring at her, sneering, replayed in her mind. Her heart ached, but perhaps more for the fact that she still harbored feelings for him.

"Yes, I do," Adam replied, his tone softening slightly. "No, I don't have what you have, but I'm not one of the cool kids, and I'm sure people are doing their fair share of whispering about me, too."

"Whatever," Lessie retorted, not believing him. "You've got it all together." She waved a hand in front of him, palm outstretched, and continued, "You're smart, you're confident, you're good-looking." She didn't intend for it to sound like she was openly admiring him, and instantly grew nervous that she sent the wrong signal. Her words seemed to hit him like a brick as he drew back, blinking and suddenly looking fidgety. She held strong, unmoving, aware she couldn't take back her words.

He straightened and pulled himself together. "Well...

Thanks..." he responded awkwardly, and drew his attention back to the situation at hand. He gestured towards her and said, "And so are you."

She arched a brow at him, folding her arms over her chest. "I'm what?" she asked. She certainly did not feel smart or confident, and after her embarrassing scene and flood of tears, she didn't feel very attractive, either.

"Smart. And g-good looking." Heat rose to his cheeks at his involuntary stutter, and Lessie pretended not to notice, holding her ground. He wiped his palms against his pants as he pressed on, "And you can work on your confidence!"

She eyed him under lowered brows with pursed lips, arms still folded over her chest. She didn't respond.

He threw his arms out to his sides. "Why do you care what other people say about you?" he exclaimed, his voice a startling echo. He quickly lowered his tone. "What does it matter what those people say or think about you?"

"It's embarrassing!" she retorted, eyes flashing.

He waved his hand in reference to the crowded gym, where the music had resumed its lively pulse. "Are you here for them?"

Lessie held his gaze, hesitating. "N-no..."

"No. You're here with us. With your best friend, who loves you, her boyfriend, who accepts you," he placed his hand on his chest, "And me, who doesn't give a shit about some condition or weird quirk you have, because I think you're cool and I'd like to enjoy my evening with you."

She stared at him as the whole world screeched to a halt. Suddenly there was nothing else around her but Adam, and a flood of tears welled up inside of her, threatening to spill over again, but this time for an entirely different reason. He thought she was cool? "I—" she started, but Adam interrupted her, grasping her shoulders gently but firmly.

"So you're going to be a good friend and be here for Emily, because I know you love her just as much as she loves you, and if that's true then she should be all that matters. Now pull yourself together and get back out there and have a good time with us."

Damn... She stared at him in shock. Nobody had ever talked to her like that. They held each other's eyes for what felt like forever, and she thought she saw something flicker in his expression before he let go of her shoulders and stood up straighter, blinking. "You good?" he asked, and she noticed his breathing had become quicker.

Her own breathing was a bit labored as well, she realized. She nodded slowly, still staring at him with wide eyes. "Yeah," she exhaled in response. "I think so."

The music had shifted into a slow song again, and Adam slowly offered her his hand, giving her a cautious smile. "Want to try that again?"

She glanced down at his hand, then back up to meet his waiting eyes. Nervously, she reached forward. "Not really," she replied with a quiet, shaky voice, "But, you're pretty persuasive, so..." Her voice trailed off as she placed her hand in his, and he grinned brightly, causing the butterflies to erupt all over again. She couldn't help but smile back as heat rose to her cheeks.

"Awesome," he replied, and led her back out to the dance floor.

CHAPTER 10

LESSIE FELT considerably more upbeat as time passed, despite Nana's continued steady decline. The occasional pang of grief would strike, but she only needed to tap into the strength and wisdom of the girl she was called to several weeks ago to build her back up again. Nana was at peace with the direction life took, and trusted that everything was happening according to a Divine Plan; and therefore, Lessie could only feel the same way.

Having developed a friendship with Adam only added to her strength. Emily nagged her on a daily basis as to what their official relationship status was, but Lessie never had an answer for her, and instead responded with a blush and a grin. Lessie was finally starting to feel at ease with life, having mostly let go of her frustrating crush on the unsuitable jock thanks to the new distraction of Adam, and appreciating the unconditional friendship that surrounded her.

As the end of October inched closer, Nana declined further; and the week before Halloween, Lynne and Sam agreed it was time to call in hospice. The nurses tending to the frail old woman only accentuated the reality that the end was near. It seemed as though all she did anymore was sleep, and any responses they were able to elicit from her in conversation were slight moans and throaty gurgles. Lessie felt a twinge of sadness at the realization that she wouldn't get to have a vocal conversation with her grandmother anymore.

She sighed as she lay in bed staring at the dark ceiling, and her thoughts traveled to Will. She hadn't talked to him in awhile, and after glancing at the clock to see that he'd probably still be up, she decided to video chat with him. She clicked her bedside lamp on as her phone sang until he picked up, and his smiling face filled the screen. She was glad to see him smiling more since the first time they met.

"Hey," he greeted. "I've actually been thinking about you these last couple days."

She smiled, grateful that he was still warming up to her and slowly breaking down his walls. "Yeah, sorry I haven't been in touch, been kinda busy with school and Nana and everything."

"How is she?" he asked, eyeing her with concern.

Lessie sighed sadly. "Hospice is in. It's just a matter of time."

Will shook his head. "That's crazy how fast she went down..."

Lessie nodded. "I know." She thought she detected a hint of sorrow in his eyes, and wondered if he was bothered by the awareness that he'd never get to see his grandmother.

"How's your mom?" Will asked, breaking her thoughts.

"She doesn't let on to me much about how she feels. She just acts strong all the time."

"I just wondered if she's pissed about my dad not being around to help while their mom is dying."

Lessie sighed and thought before answering. "One of the cool things about Mom is how forgiving she is. She doesn't like to get worked up about other people's decisions in how they live their lives, and she does the best to live hers. But, I know she does get frustrated about him not being around."

Will nodded. Not wanting to dwell on regrets, Lessie proceeded to tell him about her experience with the girl who died of leukemia, and his eyebrows raised the whole time as he silently took in her story. "Have you ever experienced anything like that?" she asked after she'd finished.

"No," Will replied as he let out a breath, shaking his head again. "That's wild..."

Lessie nodded. "It was definitely Divine intervention. Makes you wonder what else is going on out there in the Universe, doesn't it?"

Will responded with a slow nod. "I wonder a lot of things."

Lessie leaned into her hand. "Like what?" she asked, hoping to coax more conversation from him.

He shrugged, hesitating on sharing his feelings, then finally surrendered. "I guess I wonder if our death is predetermined, you know? All the times I'm called, it's seconds before the person's death. But so many times, like in a car accident, I feel like there's enough time that the person could correct the car and avoid the pole. Instead, it seems like death is inevitable, almost like it was planned."

Lessie chewed the inside of her cheek. She couldn't deny having wondered the same things herself. "It does seem that way. But there's really no way for us to know how it actually works. Is there?"

He shook his head. "I don't know. I try not to think too much about it. It's not like I'll ever get answers." His face grew solemn, and Lessie's heart sank.

"Yes you will," she said, wishing she could reach out and touch him. "We have each other now. I can tell you all the things I learned from Nana. And we can discuss our questions with each other, maybe come up with our own answers."

He sighed, then nodded as he pressed his lips into the ghost of an appreciative smile. "I'm still getting used to the idea of having someone to talk to."

Lessie smiled. "I'll keep working on ya." He finally gave her a genuine grin. She squinted her eyes as another thought came to mind. "Will... When I visited you, you seemed to be having a bad dream..." Her voice trailed off, unsure if she was crossing any boundaries.

Will shrugged. "Just a dream I've been having since I was thirteen," he replied.

"What about?" she pressed.

He hesitated, then finally answered. "Of my first call, only I'm the kid I got called to. Running, then falling into a hole. And waiting for someone to come cross me over, but I never die." His expression remained stoic.

Lessie stared at her cousin through the screen, then finally let out a breath. "Well... You don't have to run anymore." She tried to offer him an encouraging smile.

He nodded in return. "I didn't miss the irony that in my dream, I finally died, but it turned out to be you waking me from it. I actually haven't had that dream since." He returned her smile, and her heart filled with warmth at the sincerity in his voice. She suddenly felt that, by his simple statement, they'd mended the years of separation, as though they'd never been apart.

"Thanks, Will," she whispered with a glowing smile.

After saying their goodbyes, Lessie set her phone on her nightstand as she reminisced of their first meeting, and her first time with astral travel. Her eyes suddenly flew open wide as a realization occurred to her — she could possibly still be able to speak with Nana, after all. Grinning, she settled back against her pillow, eager to use her newfound knowledge to have the connection with Nana that she could no longer have physically. She slowed her breathing and quieted her mind, letting her eyes drift shut and allowing her body to sink into the mattress. She went through the steps — picturing herself floating above her physical body, transferring her awareness into that presence, then slowly moving about the room until she got her bearings about her.

Once settled in her astral form, she closed her eyes and transferred herself from her room to the first floor. She grew nervous as she entered Nana's dark room, and listened to her slow, rhythmic, albeit rattled breathing, before breaking the silence. "Nana?" she spoke, her nerves jumping even more. She placed her hand on Nana's arm, just as she had with Will.

And to her excitement, the contact created the link, and the old woman's spirit sat up from her sleeping form. She looked around curiously, before finally landing her gaze on Lessie. She arched her eyebrow. "What is this?" she asked, her expression turning immediately to that of surprise at the sound of her own healthy voice.

"An astral projection," Lessie explained, smiling. Her heart was soaring. "I don't know why I hadn't thought of it sooner," she continued. "I was so afraid I wouldn't get to talk to you anymore before you... crossed over... But I can!"

"This is fascinating..." Nana marveled, looking around

curiously again, then back down at her withering, sleeping form. She frowned. "Ugh, I look terrible."

Lessie couldn't help but chuckle. "Well, death isn't exactly glamorous," she replied. "How are you feeling?"

Nana returned her attention to her granddaughter and smiled. "Great right now," she answered. She then shrugged, and added, "Could be better, otherwise. The morphine works, though. It's strange, I feel like I'm in the midst of a calling most of the time. I feel out of body sometimes, and other times I'm very aware of my physical body and how I have no control over it anymore. It's a bit unnerving, but then I'm so drugged that I don't really care."

The corner of Lessie's mouth curled up into a sympathetic half-smile, fascinated by her grandmother's experience, and she sat down next to her on the bed. "Are you excited?" Lessie asked, her voice almost a whisper.

Nana met her curious gaze, a warm twinkle in her crystal eyes, and she smiled softly, knowingly. With a small nod, she replied, "Of course I am. I've thought about this moment ever since my first calling, the first time I saw the light."

Lessie smiled, understanding. "You're finally going to get to see what's over there..." she mused, putting herself in her grandmother's shoes, imagining what it must feel like to know that next stage of the journey was so close. She rested her head on her grandmother's shoulder and sighed, thinking about how far she'd come, about what excitement lay before Nana. "I'm so grateful I got the chance to talk to that girl. She really changed things for me."

Nana smiled appreciatively and patted her granddaughter's knee. Lessie had told Nana of her experience shortly after it happened. "I've never experienced anything like that," Nana said softly. "You learned something all on your own, something I've never encountered before. You really will be just fine without me."

Lessie sat up to face her grandmother and smiled, and pulled her into a strong embrace. Tears brimmed in her eyes, and she squeezed her grandmother tighter as they spilled over.

As Nana leaned back, she held Lessie's gaze for a moment, turning serious. "Celeste, will you do something for me?"

Lessie nodded without hesitation as she wiped her fingers across her cheek. "Of course," she replied instantly. "Anything."

"Will you get in touch with your cousin Will? I don't know if the bond can be mended with Ron, but his problems aren't yours to bear. I could never shake the feeling that he's a Transcendent like us, and it always ate at me that I couldn't guide him like I've done for you." She sighed as she lowered her head, then she lifted her gaze to Lessie once more. "Knowing that you can help him from here on out would make me very happy."

Lessie's heart skipped a beat, and a smile stretched across her face when Nana finished. "One step ahead of you, Nana," Lessie replied, her voice soft, and Nana's brows raised. "I visited Will the first night I tried astral travel, and we got to talk, just like you and I are right now." Nana's eyes grew wide, and Lessie continued, "He *is* a Transcendent, Nana." She told her of the conversations they'd had since the first night Lessie had visited, and how he'd slowly been letting his guard down and opening up to a friendship with Lessie.

Nana's eyes shined with tears of joy, and she quickly pulled her granddaughter in for another hug. Lessie's heart constricted, gripped by Nana's emotions. "Oh, honey," she whispered into her granddaughter's neck. "I can't tell you how happy this makes me."

Nana's words flooded Lessie's heart, and she was unable to withhold the tears that spilled over once more. She sniffed back a sob as they held each other for a few moments longer. Finally, they released and Lessie leaned back, meeting Nana's shining eyes again. "Nana?" she asked hesitantly. Nana nodded for her to continue. "What happened? Why did Uncle Ron cut everyone out?"

Nana's face fell as she averted her eyes to her knees. She took a breath, then said slowly, "I suppose you deserve to know the truth."

Time suddenly stood still as Lessie realized she'd finally get answers about the family rift — answers to questions Lessie and her parents had long ago given up on asking. She leaned in closer, ready to hang on every word. Nana sighed, looking up to the ceiling as though there were support to be found there. "I was the one to cross Jodi over," she stated quietly. A deafening silence followed.

Lessie didn't immediately reply, as her brain took a moment to process, then suddenly erupted with questions. Nana met her eyes searchingly.

"Wait... What?" Lessie squinted in confusion. "I thought you had to be the person's same age in order to get called to them?"

"I honestly don't know how it happened. Maybe the rules don't apply if you know the person? Or maybe you have to be relation of some sort? I don't have answers to this one. I've toiled over it for years."

"Wow..." Lessie breathed, her voice trailing off. She shook her head. "But what reason does that give Uncle Ron to cut you off?"

Nana sighed, pausing for a moment as she carefully chose her words. "I mentioned that I was there; I was hoping to bring him comfort, but instead... He thought I could save her. Bring her back. And he was furious that I didn't."

Silence fell again as Lessie tried to wrap her mind around all that Nana was telling her. She squinted as questions surfaced. "*Can* you save people? Bring them back?"

Nana hesitated. "My grandfather said it's forbidden to try. And it's dangerous to try." She shook her head, then changed the subject back to Jodi, as though not wanting to continue discussing the possibility of saving people. "I don't know why I got called to her. It was the first time I got called to someone who wasn't my age, and the first time I got called to someone I knew. My grandfather never gave me any insight on that happening; so if it had ever happened to him, then he never told me. But what he has said before is that there are no mistakes. Every calling is part of a Divine Plan, some more than others. Just like your girl with leukemia. We are brought together for far more reasons than just to assist them in their passing, or to be with them so they don't have to do it alone. While, of course, the people we cross impact our lives greatly, sometimes it happens to be us — the ones assisting the crossing — that impact others' lives. And we may never know the reason, but my grandfather insisted that no matter what, there is *always* a reason, and we are *all* connected in ways we may never know."

Lessie nodded thoughtfully, feeling an overwhelming stir at the magnitude of her grandmother's words. "I agree with him," she finally replied, her voice quiet. She furrowed her brow as a thought crossed her mind. "Nana, how did your grandpa die?"

Nana shook her head. "It was his time." Lessie wasn't sure

she believed her. "There was a reason I got called to Jodi," Nana continued. "Maybe this rift in the family was all part of the plan. I don't know why or what, and it seems as though I won't ever get to know while I'm here physically. But," she shrugged, then finally smiled softly. "I'll get to know all the answers soon enough."

Lessie's gaze trailed to the floor as she turned the new information over in her mind. She suddenly felt eager to tell Will, to pick his brain and perhaps, eventually, find a way to mend the bond between Ron and Lynne, to stop her uncle from allowing his grief and his grudge to further poison him. Lessie's brows knit as she looked up to meet her grandmother's eyes. "Nana, have you kept this a secret all these years?"

Nana's gaze fell to her knees. "I told Bill. But otherwise, nobody knows."

Lessie frowned as her heart constricted. "Why?"

Nana inhaled, then let out a slow exhale and she shook her head. "I don't know. Maybe I was afraid." She met Lessie's eyes, revealing a sadness in her own. "I'm a human with flaws too, you know."

Lessie pondered the pedestal she had viewed her Grandmother on, and even her own parents as well. *I guess we're all humans just figuring life out and making mistakes along the way,* she thought. "Well, I'm glad you told me," she said quietly as she met her grandmother's eyes once more.

"I'm glad I did, too." They held each other's gaze for a moment longer before Nana brought her hand back to Lessie's knee. "You should get back to sleep, Sweetie," she suggested.

Lessie nodded slowly, pressing her lips to the side. "Yeah.

I feel like I want to spend as much time as I possibly can with you, though," she added, her heart heavy.

Nana brought her hand back up to wrap around Lessie's slumped shoulders. "We'll get a bit more time," she replied. "Especially since you discovered this, I won't leave without saying goodbye." She smiled and pressed her lips against Lessie's head.

Lessie swallowed a lump in her throat and offered her grandmother a sad smile. "Good," she whispered.

CHAPTER 11

NOVEMBER ROLLED in cool and crisp, tree branches exposed from fallen leaves, announcing the onset of winter. And just as each leaf fell, Nana declined further. Hospice was in regularly, keeping her comfortable as she lay in bed, constantly sleeping, occasionally opening her glazed eyes slightly before letting them flutter closed again.

Lessie spent as much time as she could lying in bed next to Nana, talking to her about school, Adam, and the possibility that she might have a crush on him; and even better yet that she's finally starting to let go of the crush on Mitch. She knew Nana could hear her, and was happy to talk casually with her even though she couldn't verbally respond.

Her final day was drawing near. Lynne, Sam, and Lessie could all feel it, sense it. Lynne had attempted several times to locate her brother in Washington so she could contact him, but each time she had no success.

It crossed Lessie's mind to inform them of what she learned from Nana about Ron's reason for abandoning the family, but every time she thought about it she decided against it, not wanting to burden her parents with heavy information to add to their already full plates having to deal with Nana's condition.

As Lessie drifted off to sleep, she felt herself awakened by a feeling very similar to being called, yet she was still in her room. She sat up slowly from her physical body, which was sleeping soundly in bed, and looked around her room curiously, wondering for a moment what was going on, before realizing that Nana's astral form was standing next to her, smiling, with her hand on Lessie's shoulder.

"Nana," Lessie whispered, her eyes growing wide. "Are you... Did you...?" She struggled to form the words as they caught in her throat.

"No, honey," Nana broke in, still smiling. "I'm still alive. Just trying out this astral travel thing you told me about." She stretched her arms out and studied them, then looked around the room. "I wish I'd known about this earlier in life!" she said with a laugh. "I could have had a lot of fun with it!"

Lessie grinned. "It's pretty cool. This is the first time I've been visited by someone, though. Kinda weird..."

Nana's smile softened. She took a seat next to Lessie on her bed. "Do you visit Will often?"

Lessie shook her head slowly. "No, not often, but we have been in contact. I plan to visit him after you... you know..." She lowered her gaze to her knees, suddenly feeling strange as she struggled with a mixture of grief and joy.

Nana placed a hand on Lessie's shoulder. "I want you to be there when I go," she said quietly, and Lessie lifted her head to meet her grandmother's crystal eyes again, her own eyes shining with curiosity and sadness. "I know you'll be there anyway. You and your mom and dad. But I want you to be there as *you*.

Don't try to do this astral projection thing so you can see me cross over. I want you to experience it from a normal human perspective."

Lessie cracked a small grin. "It crossed my mind a time or two that I'd try to see it happen from this standpoint."

Nana smiled knowingly. "I figured it did. But there's something special about death when you can't really see what's going on spiritually. I experienced that when Bill died. There's something profound about being present in the moment, and *feeling* what's happening rather than seeing it. I want you to experience that, too."

Lessie could feel tears burning at the backs of her eyes as the reality of her grandmother's words sunk in. That this was truly the end. She suddenly choked on a sob. She leaned against her grandmother, and Nana wrapped a comforting arm around Lessie's shoulders. "It's a curious thing, being this close to the veil," she said quietly, her voice distant and thoughtful. Lessie didn't respond, but Nana felt her listening and silently urging her to continue, so she did. "I know we're there on a fairly regular basis, crossing souls over, but it's different when you're having your own personal experience." She thought for a moment, then continued. "I've only ever been this close once before, and that was in the final week of my pregnancy with your mother. With Ron, everything was too new for me to really understand what I was experiencing, or to really grasp it; but with your mom, I had already been there and knew what to expect physically, so all that was left was to tune into the experience spiritually. I felt this connection with her soul. I don't quite know how to explain it, but it felt as though she was still connected to the Other Side, and would be until she drew her first breath. And since I was carrying her, it gave me that connection to the Other Side, unlike I had ever experienced it before, even though I was so frequently there crossing souls over." She sighed, then looked down at Lessie. "Honey?"

Lessie lifted her head to meet her grandmother's eyes. "Yeah?"

"I kept a journal while I was pregnant with your mom. I remember writing about that experience the week before she was born. I want you to read it. Perhaps it will give you an idea of what this is like. Either way, it'll give you a little more understanding of what I'm experiencing, and why I want you to experience it from a normal human perspective."

Lessie contemplated the enormity of Nana's request, and suddenly felt a driving urge to find her journal. "Where is it?" she asked, sitting upright and holding her gaze.

Nana smiled softly. "It's in my cedar chest in my room. I keep all my treasures from my life in there. I dated all of them, and all the entries as well. Just find the one from the year your mom was born, and find the entry from a week or ten days before her birthday. I remember it like it was yesterday, so I'm pretty certain that's where you'll find it." She gave her a squeeze. "I'll probably be on my way tomorrow," she added with a whisper.

They held each other's gaze for a moment as tears welled up in Lessie's eyes once more. "Nana..." she whispered, then fell into her arms. "I'm going to miss you..."

Nana drew her in closer, stroking her back. "I know, Sweetie. But I'll still be around."

"Can I find you like this, do you think?"

Nana shrugged. "I'm not sure if it works that way once I'm on the Other Side. But don't worry, I'll find a way to reach you. You'll know."

Lessie sucked in a ragged breath and rested against her, savoring that final moment in silence.

As soon as Nana returned to her physical form, Lessie's eyes popped open, locked on the ceiling with a new sense of determination. She immediately sprung up, not wanting to waste a single second in finding that journal. She snatched her phone and turned on its flashlight, then left her room and descended the stairs as quickly and quietly as she could. Pushing the door open slowly, she crept into her grandmother's dark room and shined her phone's light on the cedar chest at the foot of the bed. She winced as the heavy lid creaked, pausing a moment to make sure all was still silent except for her grandmother's slow and steady breathing, then quickly lifted it all the way, shining her light on the contents. Nana's wedding dress was packed away neatly, along with several candles from different occasions, photo albums and a framed picture of her with Bill when they were young. Finally, Lessie's eyes fell on a stack of books bound in leather or fabric, and she lifted them to study their spines, where dates were scrawled on the edges. She found the year her mother was born and retrieved the book. She held it to her chest and stood slowly, carefully lowering the lid of the chest. She gave a startled jump when she heard Nana moan softly from the bed, then calmed herself immediately, smiling. The sound could have easily been mistaken as a sound of pain, but it was the only sound Nana could physically make anymore as she continued to deteriorate. Lessie knew she was communicating with her. "Thanks, Nana," she whispered into the dark. "I love you."

She rushed upstairs, throwing herself into bed and

immediately flipped through the pages to the date Nana had told her. It was exactly ten days before her mother was born.

I am nearing the end of this part of the journey. I can feel it. I can feel a shift, like a wind change. I feel like I'm transitioning into another world.

I missed this part with Ron. I was too caught up in being tired and fat and heavy and achy, wanting it all to be over with. I never saw this other world I can see now. I was there — I think all pregnant women go there, just before their baby crosses over. Only so many don't see it. Most miss it.

I'm in it. But I want to hang onto it. It's full of so much mystery... And in my life where there isn't a whole lot of mystery, this is a rare gift. I want just a little longer to explore it. It's like I can touch the veil... I am the closest I'll ever be to glimpsing the Other Side and actually getting to feel it, aside from crossing into it completely. I am a vessel, a ferry from the other side of the veil, and so I'm granted the opportunity to glimpse it, like so very many other women, like I was three years ago, too. But unlike so many other women, I'm aware of it this time. I'm reaching out my hand, just barely touching this realm I've been so curious about for so long...

This is why I am pregnant. In all my years of being so close to the Other Side, I never experienced it like this before, on this level. I am filled with gratitude that in this lifetime, I get to truly be aware of and connected to the Divine Truth that we are spiritual beings having a human experience. And that I get to know that on a deeper level now. I thought I knew it before. I certainly did on a deeper level than any "normal" human, but this... this is so much more.

In all my years of ferrying souls to the Other Side, I now get to ferry one from the other side. What a unique and beautiful experience that is for someone like me...

I am going to savor this moment for as long as I can. My connection to the life I've grown inside of me, and the connection that life has given me to the Universe in which we are all connected...

LESSIE PLACED THE journal on her lap, staring up at the wall as her head swam with thoughts about what she had just read. It was so deep... She naturally couldn't relate, having never been pregnant herself, but her grandmother's words helped her see it from an angle she had never looked at before. And it deepened her understanding of what Nana was experiencing now. She lowered herself back onto her pillow and closed her eyes. She hoped she could connect to the experience of Nana's crossing and *feel* it the way she described it to her. She suddenly felt a sense of excitement grow in her at the opportunity that lay ahead of her.

She drifted into a peaceful sleep.

LESSIE STAYED HOME from school the next day, all three of them silently aware that Nana's time was fast approaching. The hospice nurse agreed, confirming what they already knew.

Lessie's parents were quiet and reserved, moving about the house on autopilot, checking in on Nana occasionally, observing her slowing breaths, her mottled skin, her sallow face. Lessie overheard her mother express her frustration to Sam that she had no way of contacting Ron to inform him of their mother's condition, but nothing more was said about the issue. Lessie sat at Nana's bedside the entire day, flipping through her journals, feeling a connection with her grandmother she had never experienced before. The old woman had written of her struggles, her challenges, her difficulty accepting the burdens in her life, and later on her realizations for why she was dealt those burdens. Lessie smiled as she read through Nana's discoveries, now able to see the source of Nana's insight that for every burden there was an equal or greater blessing. Not once, however, was there mention of what happened with Jodi, and later with Ron. It was like she wanted to erase that part of her life from her memory. Regardless of the missing details that pulled at Lessie's curiosity, she appreciated at least getting to read what Nana *did* share in her journals. Lessie felt an insurmountable gratitude for the lessons her grandmother taught her. She reached out and placed her hand on her grandmother's, taking in the stark contrast of life and death in their skin.

They were at the veil. Nana was there, and Lessie was in the presence of it. She closed her eyes and slowed her breathing, allowing herself to feel the energy of the room, of her grandmother, honing her senses in on the experience.

She sensed an energetic shift, subtle as the breeze, and her awareness was involuntarily drawn to Ron, Will, and Camryn. Lessie smiled, suddenly filled with a sensation, or perhaps a recognition, that Nana was traveling, seeing her son and grandchildren before she departed, reassuring herself that, despite not being part of each other's lives, they were all okay and doing just fine. Lessie felt a sense of satisfaction inside of her that didn't feel quite like it belonged to her, and suddenly she realized that she must be experiencing Nana's emotions.

She felt the shift again, and brought her awareness back to herself, opening her eyes and taking in her grandmother's limp, semi-lifeless form. She tuned into her grandmother's presence in the room. She could feel it, a familiar feeling of simply knowing someone was in the room with her. That feeling was coming and going, as though sometimes Nana was in the room with Lessie, and then moments later Lessie was in the room alone. It was a curious feeling that she just simply sat with it, letting it be.

"Lessie?" Lynne's soft voice broke her daughter's thoughts.

Lessie looked up to meet her mother's concerned eyes as she stood in the doorway. "Yeah, Mom?"

"You okay?"

Lessie nodded, and her eyes traveled back to Nana. "Yeah," she replied. "Just thinking. And feeling."

Lynne stepped forward into the room and slowly made her way to sit in the chair next to Lessie. "Feeling what?" she asked.

Lessie shrugged, unsure of how to explain. "Just... I don't know... It's like she's in and out. Here and not here. I think she's traveling."

"Hmm," was all Lynne said. They sat in silence for a moment.

The hospice nurse came in to check on Nana, going through her routine, then watched her thoughtfully. She finally brought her focus to Lynne and Lessie, who were eyeing her expectantly. "It won't be long now," she said gently. "I'll let Sam know, and let you be alone with her. Let me know if you need anything." She quietly left the room.

Lessie and her mother sat in silence for what felt like seconds and days at the same time before Sam entered the room. He sat down next to Lynne and took her hand, resting their entwined fingers on his lap. "You okay?" he asked softly.

Lynne nodded as tears welled in her eyes. "Fine," she stated simply. She then brought her focus over to Lessie. "How are you?" she asked, her expression both concerned and searching.

Lessie met her mother's eyes for a moment, then brought her attention back to Nana. "I'm okay," she replied sincerely.

Lynne nodded in reply. She took a breath, then said, "I'm proud of you, for coming to terms with this as well as you have. I know it's not easy to know she won't be here to guide you along, but you're going to be just fine. Dad and I are here for you, even though we don't understand what your life is like, with the experiences you have, doing what you do... But we can try."

Lessie formed a soft smile. "It's okay, Mom. I've learned a lot in the past few weeks. I know I'll be fine." She took a breath, then admitted, "I wanted to tell you... I talked to Will."

Lynne's eyes widened. "You did? When? How?"

Lessie shook her head, shrugging. "There's a lot to fill you in on. He's a Transcendent, too." She smiled affectionately as she met her mother's wide eyes. "It all happened in perfect timing," Lessie continued. "Neither of us have to be alone anymore with all this. And it makes it easier since Nana won't be here to help me along. I still have someone. And, maybe, we can figure out how to draw the family back together again." She felt a sense of eagerness to share what she knew about the rift, but held back.

Lynne smiled sadly. "I don't know if that's possible. But it's a nice thought."

Lessie returned her mother's smile before they all refocused their attention on Nana, as her breaths slowed even further.

The veil.

Lessie's awareness shifted to its certain, though unseen, presence. The light, too. It was strange, knowing how it felt, knowing it was there, but not being able to see it, or feel it quite on the level she'd felt it so many times before when she'd crossed over so many souls. She could still feel her grandmother's presence moving in and out of the room. Her periods of absence were growing longer than her periods of presence.

Together they waited. Nana exhaled, long and shallow, and they held their own breaths expectantly for what felt like an eternity, never hearing her draw an inhale.

"Mom...?" Lynne whispered, and all three of them jumped when the old woman drew in a ragged breath.

"Jesus, Mom, way to scare the hell out of us," Sam commented, holding his chest.

Lessie couldn't help but grin as Lynne shook her head, her eyes wide and shining. Again, they waited. Again, Lessie felt her presence moving in and out. It was there. She knew it was all there; the light, the veil, that soft glowing haze of the room fading out and the Other Side fading in, the souls and spirits from the Other Side coming to join her, to take her.

She could feel it all happening, acutely aware of the energy and spiritual activity around them, while feeling a strange mixture of frustration and fascination at not being able to *see* it like she had so many times before. This was her grandmother's departure, and instead of being with her at the edge of the Other Side like she had for so many strangers countless times over the past three years, she was instead sitting in her room, physically present, experiencing it just the same as her mother and father were.

She felt Nana's presence wane once more, fading, and then vanishing. Though nobody could see them, Lessie intuitively knew that the spirits were present, coming forth from the light to take Nana into her next life and the next stage of her great adventure.

She let out another shallow exhale.

Silence fell in the room.

Nothing could be heard but the sound of slow, quiet breathing coming from the three people who remained.

"She's gone..." Lynne finally whispered.

Lessie reached out to grasp her mother's hand, and together they sat silently for what, again, felt like both seconds and an eternity at the same time.

Time stood still, frozen as though it weren't something measurable at all, but before that awareness could set in, the seconds resumed ticking by. Sam and Lynne both stood up slowly. Lynne leaned forward, placing a kiss on Nana's forehead. "I love you, Mom," she whispered, her voice catching in the back of her throat.

Sam reached forward, giving the woman's arm a squeeze. "Bye, Mom," he said softly.

Lessie finally stood, leaning forward and kissing her on the forehead as well. "Good job, Nana," she whispered, smiling, and giving her hand a squeeze. "Say hi to Grandpa for me."

Together, they quietly left the empty room.

CHAPTER 12

THE SOFT brush of fingers across his forearm awakened Will's senses, and he opened his eyes to the semi-transparent form of his cousin standing at his bedside. Her eyes held a new sense of awareness, as though she'd just returned from an enlightening voyage.

His astral form sat up as his physical body remained asleep on the bed, and Lessie released his arm as she sat down next to him. He pressed his lips together with a sadness in his eyes that told Lessie he knew exactly why she had come. He remained silent.

"It was amazing, Will..." she whispered, shaking her head in wonder, and he released a smile. The connection he felt with her was still a foreign concept to him, yet his comfort in her presence felt so natural in just the few short times they'd seen each other.

"What was it like?" He dropped his legs over the edge of the bed as he moved to sit next to her.

Her eyes traveled to the ceiling as she searched for words. "I wasn't sure what to expect. It was nothing like what we do. I only got to *feel* her cross over, not *see* it. But... it was amazing..." She retold her experience, and he listened intently. Her eyes dropped to her knees as her voice softened. "I'm so grateful I got to be there with her..."

Will remained in pensive silence, his mind consumed as he imagined death from a perspective other than his own. Suddenly, Lessie broke his thoughts. "Nana was there to cross your mom over."

His heart skipped. Eyes widening, he slowly turned his head to meet Lessie's nervous expression as she drew in her bottom lip. "Wait... *what?*" he burst. He shook his head. *"How?"*

Lessie dropped her gaze. "I don't know. Nana didn't, either. She'd never been called to someone she knew, or someone who wasn't her age, before. It broke all the rules. If there even *are* any rules."

"Dad must have known this..." Will breathed, staring at the floor

Lessie nodded. "That's why he cut everyone out. Nana tried to tell him she was there, hoping maybe it would comfort him, but instead... well." Her face fell.

"Why would he get mad about that, though?" Will questioned.

"He thought Nana should have saved her."

"How?" Will exclaimed, his eyes shifting back up to meet hers. "How could he expect that of her?"

"I don't know," Lessie whispered, holding his gaze, then frowned. "I can't believe she kept it a secret for all these years. I wish I knew why she didn't want to tell us."

Will shook his head, eyes wide as his mind spun with questions. He thought of his father, his grudge, and how petty it now seemed. Anger suddenly burned in the pit of his stomach as he realized how different his life could have been had his father only listened to Nana. "How could he just assume we can save people?" he said in a low voice through clenched teeth.

Lessie shook her head. "I don't know. But Nana always said never to try..."

Will furrowed his brows. "Why?"

Lessie shook her head again, frowning at the floor.

Will frowned, too. "Seems like she was hiding something."

Lessie simply nodded, but didn't respond.

A small pang of grief washed through him. He'd never known the woman; and yet he could have, if he'd just responded when she'd reached out. He grimaced against the frustration that he'd let his father's feelings govern his own. That he'd missed out on a relationship with his grandmother, who could have been a mentor to him, just like she was to Lessie. He could have asked her his questions, pondered the mysteries with her, rather than muddling through them alone.

He lifted his eyes to meet Lessie's, taking in the ethereal glow that surrounded her. She was here now, part of his life. Perhaps things could change.

"I want to come to the funeral," he heard himself say, and her eyes widened.

"What?" She shook her head, then added, "Will, that's... you'd..." she struggled for words, then finally said, "I can't expect you to do that for a person you don't even know..."

He interrupted her. "I want to." He shifted in his seat to face her. "Dad feels the way he does, and I can't change that, but I can change me. I want to be part of the family."

He held her gaze as her eyes filled with tears, and she leaned forward and drew him into a hug. "That would be awesome, Will," she whispered.

THE NEXT MORNING Will prepared himself to completely step out of his comfort zone and call his sister, which caught her off-guard. He never called her, having closed himself off from getting close to anyone, especially family, after living his life in the shadow of his father's resentment. With his new connection with Lessie, he tried to build himself up to allowing more connections and relationships in his life. He figured he'd start with his sister.

"Will, is everything okay?" Cam asked, her voice nervous.

"Nana died," he stated, cutting to the chase. "They're having a memorial service for her, and I'm going out there. I wanted to see if you wanted to come before I bought my plane ticket."

Silence hung between them before finally Cam spoke. "Okay, hang on, you just threw a lot at me. First of all, how do you know this?"

"Our cousin, Lessie, told me." Cam struggled to make sense of his words as he explained how they met and the relationship that has since transpired. He fell into conversation naturally as he pressed on, channeling strength from his new friendship with Lessie. Finally, when he was finished, Cam, though stunned with the new information, agreed to go with him.

SILENCE HUNG BETWEEN the siblings on the plane as they absently stared out the window at the orange glow of the sunset reflecting on the aircrafts and vehicles as they taxied to the runway. They tuned out the drone of the safety protocols presented by the flight attendants, their minds on their destination that awaited them. Finally, after the plane leveled out above the darkening clouds, Cam broke their silence. "I've always felt like Dad's grudge was a bit... Extreme..." She turned to face her brother, tucking a strand of brown hair behind her ear. "I've tried so many times to get him to explain what happened, but he'd never tell me."

"Well, now we kind of know," Will replied. "She could do what me and Lessie do. When he told me about it after it first happened to me, he was so... Distant. He never wanted to talk about it again." Will shook his head. "I always felt like something was wrong with me."

"Nothing's wrong with you," Cam replied. She sighed, her brown eyes dropping to her knees. "I'm glad we're going out there. It's not fair that we missed out on so much. What you do — that's *amazing*, Will. Our family probably knows *so much* about it, and we missed out."

"It's not amazing," Will cut in with a low voice.

"It is, though. Dad's shit just made you feel bad about it. But you have a special gift." She met his eyes. "Sorry that sounds cliche. But I believe you do."

He let out a breath. "Thanks."

Will spent the rest of the flight opening up about how he came to meet Lessie, what he'd learned from her already, and how her presence made him feel a sense of comfort and normalcy he'd never experienced before. Camryn hung on his every word with wide eyes, captivated and awestruck at what incredible mysteries her family history contained. Will eased into the conversation, feeling a sense of warmth in not only having someone to talk to about his unique life, but in being accepted. St. Louis glittered like a reflection of the stars above it as they made their descent; and they both glowed, uplifted, as they left the airport terminal. After picking up the rental car, Cam drove them to the airport hotel, both their minds consumed with thoughts of what the next day might bring. They woke early the next morning with a nervous excitement to meet their long-lost family.

WILL AND CAM stood on the front step of the Morrison residence carrying boxes of breakfast foods from a local restaurant, shifting awkwardly as they waited.

"Will," Lessie breathed, grinning, as the front door swung open.

"Hey," he greeted, feeling an eruption of nerves within his stomach as he took in the sight of her. "You're real and in the flesh," he added, finally releasing a smile.

Lessie laughed and, as Sam smiled and took the boxes from Will and his sister, Lessie drew Will into a tight embrace. His nerves began to ease as he returned the hug, trying to relax into the foreign sense of peace and belonging he felt in Lessie's presence.

His gaze lifted to meet his aunt's misty eyes, and without words, she drew him and his sister into a fierce embrace. Lynne squeezed them tight, and finally took a step back as she brought her hands to their faces, exchanging grins filled with emotion.

"I can't believe it," Lynne breathed as a tear spilled over. Cam's eyes misted as well, as Lynn continued. "It's been so long... I'm just... So happy, I can't even find words." She choked on a laugh as she drew them in once more.

"It's so good to finally see you again, Aunt Lynne," Will said as he returned her embrace. He lifted his eyes to Sam and Lessie. "All of you."

A SIMPLE MEMORIAL was held at Lessie's family's house. Nana chose to have her body donated, and otherwise didn't want the traditional arrangements of a visitation and funeral. It started off steadily as cars began filling the driveway. Nana had been involved in many organizations in the community and had stayed actively involved in decades-old friendships. It was heartwarming to see the love and support pour in, and all the lives Nana had touched. Stories and memories of Nana and Grandpa's lives filled the day, and Lessie felt caught up in the whirlwind of it all.

Adam didn't leave Lessie's side the remainder of the day after he, Emily, and Evan arrived. She felt a sense of warmth and comfort in his presence, though he seemed awkward around her, shifting uncomfortably and laughing nervously. Lessie escaped to use the bathroom upstairs later in the afternoon, then took her time as she adjusted her plain black dress and gray sweater in her full-length mirror, and affectionately touched her grandmother's birthstone pendant that hung from her neck on a thin gold chain. As she ran her fingers through her wavy, mouse-brown hair, she jumped at the sudden appearance of Emily in her bedroom.

"Sorry!" Emily apologized. "How ya doing?"

Lessie offered her a smile as she relaxed. "Fine. This day is going by in a blur, though."

Emily nodded. "I feel like I haven't gotten to talk to you at all. Adam has been up your ass all day!"

"Oh," Lessie replied, as a blush crept up her neck. "I don't really feel like he's up my ass... He's just trying to be there for me. He seems kinda uncomfortable, though. You think this type of memorial is weird for him?"

Their eyes met for a moment, Lessie's innocently curious, and Emily's amused as a smile curled the corner of her lips. "I'm pretty sure that's not why he's acting uncomfortable..." Emily replied.

Lessie's brows furrowed as she considered Emily's words. "Well... what's his deal, then?"

Emily chuckled. "He's crushing hard on you but can't do anything about it because, well, your grandma just died."

The blush finally made it to Lessie's cheeks as she averted her eyes. Given the circumstances, she hadn't had a lot of time to focus on her feelings about Adam, though she knew feelings were definitely present as they spent more time with each other at school.

The magnitude of everything surrounding Nana's passing, as well as her excitement of having her cousins in town, definitely consumed all her attention. She looked up to meet Emily's smiling face, and chuckled nervously. "What happened to all his crazy confidence?"

Emily shrugged. "I guess he gets nervous around pretty girls..." She flashed her friend a wry smile.

Lessie let out another nervous chuckle. "Have you two been talking?"

Emily's smile widened as she casually shrugged. "Not any more than we ever have. But when we do, he won't shut up about you. It doesn't take a genius to figure out how he's feeling. Especially seeing how he's acting around you today..." She playfully wiggled her eyebrows.

Lessie rolled her eyes in response. "Well, great, now that's all I'm going to be thinking about, and I'm probably going to look just as awkward. Thanks."

Emily laughed. "Do something about it! Just be his girl-friend already!"

Lessie considered her for a moment, then let out a breath. "It's kind of my grandma's funeral, Em. Now isn't exactly the time or place..."

Emily shrugged again. "I'm sure Nana wouldn't have seen anything wrong with it."

Lessie smiled. She was right; Nana never wanted funerals to be sad events. She would have appreciated Lessie pursuing a possible relationship and creating joy during a time in which most people mourned. "You're right," she answered simply, flashing Emily a grateful smile.

Emily returned her smile, and together, they left Lessie's room.

Just as Lessie feared, she fell into an equal state of awkward shyness around Adam, suddenly acutely aware of his presence and his own uneasy disposition. At the same time, she couldn't help but feel a sense of gratitude toward her friend for bringing her attention to the situation.

She realized, with sudden clarity, that she was ready to move forward into something with Adam. She smiled at the thought, and sighed at the realization that she was more interested in this sweet, cute, confident, and not to mention better-suited guy rather than another certain someone, who hadn't so much as made an appearance in any of her daydreams in quite some time. Finally.

Emily and Evan helped the family clean up after the last of the guests left, while Lessie and Adam left the house, arms laden with two bags of trash to bring to the bin at the end of the driveway. It was a silent night, and stars danced cheerfully in the clear sky. They tossed their bags into the bin and Lessie pulled her sweater tighter as a chilly breeze blew past them, rustling the last remaining brittle leaves in the trees. "Thanks," she said with a smile, glancing his way, as she slowly began walking back toward the house.

"Oh, sure," Adam replied.

"It's beautiful out tonight," Lessie commented, appreciating the mild chill for the November night, as she took a seat on the wooden bench swing that hung under her favorite tree.

Adam looked around uncomfortably. "Yeah," he agreed, then said, "Did you want to get back inside?"

Lessie shook her head. "Nah, I need a bit of a break. Some fresh air." She smiled at him and patted the seat next to her.

"Oh. R-right," he replied as he sat, looking terribly uncomfortable.

Lessie couldn't help but laugh. "Okay, who are you and what have you done with Mr. Confident?"

He glanced at her quickly and feigned confusion. "What? What do you mean?"

"You're acting all weird!" she exclaimed, still grinning, then nudged him in the arm. "Lighten up!"

He squinted at her. "You're... oddly happy... considering your grandma just died..."

She shrugged. "It helps a lot to know she was at peace with it," she replied. "We had some good conversations before she died. It gave me the closure I needed." She looked up to meet his eyes. "I'm gonna miss her, but I'm happy for her."

Adam nodded thoughtfully. "That's good," he replied, and gave her a crooked smile.

She chuckled again. "*You*, however, have been acting weird."

He swallowed hard, his adam's apple shifting visibly in his throat. Dense silence hung between them.

"What are we?" she finally asked, her heart picking up speed as she cut to the chase after realizing he wasn't going to speak.

He stiffened as he sat up straighter, his eyes widening slightly. "W-what?" he asked, his voice cracking.

"We've obviously gotten closer. Gone out a few times, had fun each time..." Lessie shrugged, then met his nervous eyes again. "Where is this going?"

He swallowed again. "I..." he started, then said, "Where do you want it to go?"

She could feel butterflies taking wing in her stomach again as the question was turned back on her. "Uh... Well..." She took a steadying breath, then took in his face: those gorgeous dark blue eyes hidden behind his glasses, his thick light brown hair; and he did look handsome in his dark blue collared shirt, buttoned almost to the top. She could see the dip between his collarbones just above the top button of his shirt, and was mildly surprised to find that, of all things, somewhat alluring. She swallowed, then said, "Do you like me?" as she dragged her eyes back up to meet his.

He blinked, reeling at her question, and an internal battle seemed to ensue. Finally, he took a breath, and, locking his eyes on hers, he replied with a soft voice, "Yeah, I like you." His cheeks instantly went red.

Relief washed into her. The butterflies and her furiously beating heart only grew stronger, but her confidence did, as well. Her eyes traveled to his lips... they looked soft and inviting as he waited nervously for her response. He was visibly shaking.

His eyes followed hers, catching where they undoubtedly

traveled, and he shifted nervously. He gripped the edge of the bench, his palms growing sweaty, and licked his lips.

She smiled softly, then began leaning forward. *Do it do it do it do it,* she kept urging herself, trying to ignore her thundering heart. She closed the distance quickly, pressing her lips softly against his as her eyes fluttered shut.

His breath caught, and after a few seconds of wide-eyed paralysis, he relaxed into the situation, fears eased. He closed his eyes and gave his full attention to the moment.

She relaxed, too, once she felt his tense body let go and enjoy the experience. It suddenly wasn't so terrifying anymore, but thrilling, exhilarating. *I'm getting my first kiss!* shot through her mind, and she tilted her head to get a better angle. He followed her lead, deepening the kiss, and hesitantly brought his hand up to her shoulder, then around to her back. She lifted her own hand to cup his cheek, and she moved it back to push her fingers into his hair. *Oh wow, he has really soft hair,* she thought absently as her hand found the back of his head and pulled him closer to her. He shifted on the bench to make his angle more comfortable, and her heart flipped as her mind continued to spin excitedly. She felt him sigh against her, and a smile stretched across her lips as she kept them pressed against his. Slowly, they separated, staring dumbstruck into each other's eyes.

"I like you, too," Lessie finally said in a soft voice.

Adam huffed out a laugh as he brought his hand to the back of his neck. "Heh, I kinda figured that." They stared at each other for a moment longer, before finally Adam said, "Can we do that more often?"

A laugh burst from Lessie's throat, her eyes sparkling as she nodded happily, "Yes, we should definitely do that more often."

As though it were an invitation, he grinned before leaning forward and pressing his lips against hers once more, this time drawing her into an embrace, all nerves set aside. *There's my Mr. Confident,* she thought happily.

They lost track of time, lost in each other, before finally they separated, holding hands and swinging lazily on the bench as they stared at the stars, Lessie's head resting peacefully on Adam's shoulder. "We should probably get back inside before anyone starts to wonder..." Lessie commented with a sigh.

"Yeah, I was thinking that, too," Adam agreed, though he didn't sound enthusiastic about the idea. He turned his head to meet her eyes. "So, does this mean you're my girlfriend?"

Lessie grinned. "Are you asking me to be?" she asked playfully.

Adam chuckled, smiling. "Lessie Morrison, will you be my girlfriend?"

She leaned forward and pressed a quick kiss to his lips, then leaned back an inch to meet his eyes. "Yes, Adam Austin, I would love to."

CHAPTER 13

LESSIE SAT on the ground, tucked snugly against Adam's knees as he sat on a straw bale with Evan and Emily in Lessie's backyard. They gathered around the fire pit, basking in the warmth of the roaring flames in the cool mid-November night.

"So, my family has a big Thanksgiving gathering every year..." Adam said. Her heart sank as her mind traveled to the embarrassment of possibly spacing out in front of Adam's family. She swallowed hard, but didn't respond. "We always get together the Saturday after Thanksgiving," he added.

"Ooh!" Emily exclaimed. "You should come! I'm bringing Evan with me!" The two exchanged a grin.

Lessie rolled her eyes. Her heart sank further. The friendship surrounding her carried with it a warmth she was insurmountably grateful for, but she continued to find herself reluctant to face social settings. She took a breath, and said, "You know I would love to, but—"

As if right on cue, before she could finish her sentence, she was swept from her existence with the all-too-familiar *whoosh* of cosmos.

This happens, she thought with a frustrated sigh. She braced herself, expecting to land in the front seat of a car as they careened towards certain death. Instead, she found herself in the middle of the woods. Snow was falling through the thick trees in the dark silence, and not even a breeze was blowing to rustle what few leaves were left on the barren branches. The only light came from the moon filtering through the brambled canopy. Lessie felt a brief sense of gratitude that her ability took away her sense of pain — she was aware that it was freezing cold, but it had no effect on her.

She looked down and drew in her breath. At her feet, in the accumulating snow, was a girl, curled up tightly with her arms hugging her knees. She wasn't nearly dressed warmly enough for the conditions, and frost had developed on her hair and lashes, her skin looking ashen and her lips blue. Lessie dropped to her knees, her mind racing with questions. She absently thought to look for signs of life before realizing, of course, she wouldn't find any. What are you doing out here?" she whispered with heartbroken pity. "Come on, let's go." She brought her hands to the girl's frozen form and the world disappeared around them, replaced by the familiar white haze.

The girl blinked as she sat up. Her skin was pale, but much more alive. She brushed her tangled blonde hair from her face as she looked around. "Am I dead?" She brought her eyes to Lessie's, which were still filled with sorrow as she knelt next to her.

"Yeah," she replied with a small nod. "Why were you out there?"

"Running away from home," she answered sadly, lowering her head. "I didn't mean to die, though."

Lessie's face fell. "Why were you running away?"

The girl considered Lessie for a moment. "Got sick of getting beat up and starving," she replied quietly. She seemed to be processing the recent turn of events in her life, until finally her eyes came back in focus and she let out a surrendering exhale. "I've never stood up for myself, never tried to take care of myself. Running away was the first thing I ever did to try to make my life better." She chuckled, shrugging, seeming to relax into her fate. "Didn't get me very far, apparently."

The light had begun to grow, cutting through the haze and enveloping them in warmth and joy, and the girl smiled as the spirits emerged. Lessie smiled as well, watching the girl take in the profound beauty of it all. "I'd say you got a lot further than you give yourself credit for," she said.

The girl turned back to Lessie. "Yes, it looks like you're probably right," she replied as she stood to join the spirits. "Thanks."

Lessie nodded. "Say hi to Nana and Grandpa for me." The girl grinned, and turned, suddenly consumed by the golden light in a brilliant flash, and vanished into its depths along with the spirits. At that same moment, Lessie was swept back into herself, the familiar sounds of whooshing and static accompanying her all the way, finishing with a *POP* that only she could hear as her senses returned.

Firepit, roaring flame, sitting in the grass, leaned up against a strawbale between Adam's knees, Emily and Evan watching her curiously. Dark night, starry sky, cold late autumn breeze, bundled in her hoodie and shielded from the air's bite.

Friends. Family. Love.

Not everyone gets to experience that in their lifetime on Earth. Lessie sighed, settling in against Adam's knees as she recalled the girl's words. Abuse and neglect were her normal. Those were foreign concepts to Lessie. She had the love of her parents, her cousins, her friends, and her boyfriend. Her boyfriend who wanted to share the love of his own family with her, innocently trying to invite her to his Thanksgiving gathering. And she was about to decline because of her fear that she'd have to endure the small embarrassment of possibly spacing out in front of everyone? Which may not even happen at all? She frowned at her knees, feeling a sudden sense of shame for letting her inability to accept her uniqueness get in the way of appreciating the love that surrounded her.

"But what?" Adam's voice broke her thoughts.

Lessie looked around as she felt the three pairs of eyes on her. "What?"

"You were saying you would love to, but... Then you were gone." He said it as though it were completely normal. It didn't go unnoticed as she felt a warmth grow in her heart at his easy acceptance of her abnormality.

"Oh," Lessie breathed. She turned to look up at his waiting face, the glow of the fire illuminating his features in burnished gold and bronze and amber, his eyes reflecting the flame as they fell on hers. She smiled, then pulled herself off the ground to sit next to him on the bale, her hip pressed against his. "I was going to say, but *that* happens," she waved her hand in her face to reference her spacing out, "But..." she continued, "I'd love to." She offered him a genuine smile, raising a shoulder slightly as she waited for his response.

He grinned. "Really?"

She nodded. "If you think your family will like me, anyway."

"They'll love you!" Emily broke in excitedly. She grinned from her position on her straw bale, pressed up against Evan with his arm draped around her.

"And so long as they won't think I'm weird or crazy if...

that... happens." Lessie's shoulders drew up by her ears as she awaited Adam's reply.

Adam chuckled. "There's a lot more to you than epilepsy. Don't let a condition define you or make you think less of yourself. Plenty of people have health conditions, and anyone who judges them for it is an asshole." He lifted his arm to wrap around her shoulders, pulling her against him. She leaned her head on his shoulder, cushioned by his thick hoodie, breathing in his masculine scent as well as his support and friendship. She felt a small pang of guilt every time "epilepsy" was used in regards to her secret life, but if it meant feeling the acceptance of true friends, she let it slide.

THE WEDNESDAY BEFORE Thanksgiving, school dismissed before lunch, and the four gathered in the parking lot, eager to start their long weekend.

"I didn't think this day would *ever* end," Emily complained as she readjusted the strap of her backpack on her shoulder and straightened out her denim jacket. "You guys want to get lunch at The Depot before we head home?"

"Sounds good to me," Evan replied with a smile. Before Adam or Lessie could voice a response, the roar of an engine interrupted any attempt at saying something audible, as an old red jeep blew past them.

Lessie narrowed her eyes, observing the driver: Mitch Griffin, with his cocky grin and plastic girlfriend half in the passenger's seat, and half draped all over him with a similar expression. Fortunately, it was too cold out for him to have the top and doors off, but it didn't stop his smug appearance as he thundered out of the school parking lot. Lessie pulled her jacket tighter and laced her fingers into Adam's as she watched her former crush draw attention to himself. She felt a sense of gratitude that she could safely say she had *finally* moved on.

"What a douche," Evan said with a scowl and a shake of his head, and Emily snorted in amusement.

"No kidding," Adam agreed, also scowling as his eyes followed Mitch's jeep as it tore out onto the street. "He thinks he's such a badass."

"Guess he's having his party," Emily commented as they continued walking toward their cars. Lessie rolled her eyes at the thought of the party Mitch had been throwing on the Saturday after Thanksgiving annually since their freshman year. They always waited to hear about somebody getting busted, but somehow they all managed to evade any consequences. It was an open party, a free-for-all for anyone who wanted to come, and each year it only seemed to get bigger. Mitch hosted his parties at his grandparents' farmhouse, which had been vacant since his grandfather died and his grandmother moved to assisted living. Lessie recalled a time, not long ago, that she secretly wished to be part of the "in" crowd; cool enough to attend those parties and perhaps even be noticed by Mitch in a positive way. She squeezed Adam's hand tighter. Those days were far behind her.

"Wanna go?" Evan asked with mock eagerness, grinning and elbowing Emily as she unlocked her car.

She flashed him a look of disgust as she tossed her backpack inside. "Ugh. How does he even get away with those stupid parties, anyway?" She stole a glance at Lessie before climbing into her car, and Lessie smiled and shook her head as she wrapped her arm around Adam's waist. She felt a sense of freedom, which Emily must have picked up on, as she flashed her friend a relieved smile of approval.

Adam gave Lessie a squeeze around the shoulders as he nodded toward Emily and Evan. "We'll catch ya at The Depot."

THANKSGIVING WEEKEND arrived with the threat of snow, but instead it remained a crisp, dry cold without a drop of precipitation in sight as Lessie stuffed herself on the smorgasbord of food with Adam and his family inside the cozy warmth of his grandparents' house. He had a fairly large family, and it was Lessie's first time meeting all of them, including his parents, Matthew and Anne, and Adam's younger brother, Noah. They were sweet people, though Noah seemed to possess a bit of rebellion in him. She felt welcome the instant they all met. Adam's extended family was the same way — both his grandparents, Cleo and Richard, were elderly and kind, with wispy gray hair and deep smiling wrinkles at the corners of their eyes. She had met them long ago at a few of Emily's special events, and it warmed her heart to see them again, and them likewise. Lessie hoped she wasn't expected to remember everyone's names right away as Adam introduced her to his aunts, uncles, cousins, and new baby second cousin.

Everyone had contributed at least two dishes, and Lessie sampled everything on the buffet, feeling pleasantly miserable as she leaned back in her chair between Adam and Emily.

"Having fun so far?" Adam asked Lessie, smiling.

"I ate so much I feel disgusting right now," she replied with a grin, "but yes, I'm having a really good time."

The night drew on with board games, football on TV, coffee and dessert, and discussing plans for Christmas, which felt like it would be there before they knew it. Lessie chatted casually with Adam's other cousins, and some with his brother, Noah, though the young teen spent most of his time battling with Emily's brother, Ben, on the Xbox.

Lessie felt a sense of contentment in the environment, surrounded by so much joy and love throughout the family. She didn't want the night to end, but reluctantly said goodnight to Adam's grandparents and the rest of his family at nearly midnight as she and her three friends piled into Adam's car, feeling sleepy and lethargic with full stomachs and even fuller hearts. She had made it through the evening unscathed by an unexpected calling, but she realized that even if it had happened, she probably wouldn't have cared.

Adam dropped Emily and Evan off first, then drove down the country road to Lessie's house. "I'm glad you came," he said with a smile as he put the car in park in Lessie's driveway.

Lessie grinned. "I am, too," she replied. "Thanks for inviting me." She leaned in to press a kiss to his lips. They were two weeks into their new title as girlfriend and boyfriend, and Lessie still enjoyed the thrill of butterflies every time their lips met. She hoped it would never get old.

LESSIE DRIFTED SLOWLY into a sound sleep as soon as she was in bed, dreaming of Adam's smile, his dark blue eyes, kissing him while wrapped in his warm embrace. A smile spread across her lips as her eyes drifted shut. It had been weeks since her mind was consumed with thoughts of a different boy upon falling asleep, and as she settled deeper into her blankets, her smile widened at the realization, appreciating the sense of freedom it brought with it. She had a boyfriend. A *nice* boyfriend who was actually compatible with her, and she loved the direction it was headed. Her eyes began to flutter shut as she welcomed sleep.

Whoosh...

She groaned as she was broken from her relaxed surrender. Into an impending car crash, no less. She forced her senses to wake up as the vehicle, which seemed somewhat old, hit a ditch hard and was thrown upward and into a field, gaining speed as they suddenly dropped down a hill toward a telephone pole.

"Shit!" the driver gasped frantically as he fumbled with the steering wheel. Probably drunk, she assumed, turning to face him and preparing to reach for him once they crashed, but her heart stopped dead in her chest.

CHAPTER 14

❝ NO...❞ LESSIE gasped, her heart sinking about as fast as the vehicle was speeding down the hill.

The driver screamed, throwing his hands up to shield himself, and Lessie clenched her teeth and squeezed her eyes shut as she threw her arms around him. The shattering of glass and crunching of metal was faintly heard as the world faded into white haze.

"Oh God..." she breathed, tasting bile in her throat as her stomach violently turned. She dropped back onto her heels, opening her eyes, taking in the sight of the driver, who was now sitting next to her. She shook her head. "Nononono no... Mitch..." She felt panicked, desperate, as she pushed her fingers into her hair at her temples. This couldn't be happening. Feelings, painful feelings, were brought to the surface, like a scab ripped off a forgotten wound that hadn't quite healed yet.

"Lester?" he asked, narrowing his eyes.

She choked on a half-laugh, half-sob, as she dropped her hands to her lap. Of course, he had to be an ass even when he was dead. "Yeah," she breathed out a defeated sigh. "It's me."

"What's going on?"

She swallowed a lump in her throat and took in a ragged breath. "This is where I go when I space out."

"Am I dead?" he asked after a short pause.

She couldn't hold back the sob that broke forth. "Yes," she cried. "I'm sorry..." Helplessness clouded her eyes as she tried to catch her breath. He'd be gone when she woke up the next day. The whole school would be affected... The thought was suffocating.

He squinted against the light as it began to appear, then whipped his head back to face her. "I don't want to die." His voice was a firm whisper.

Lessie's breath hitched as she met his fearful green eyes, tears staining her cheeks. "What?"

"I can't die," he stated more loudly, clearly, his eyes locked on hers and his gaze piercing.

Lessie swallowed hard, holding his desperate eyes with hers. "Mitch... That was a pretty bad crash..." She shook her head, and cast him a look of pity. "I can't imagine you'll ever be the same..."

He clenched his teeth in determination. "I'm not supposed to die," he stated adamantly, beginning to sound panicked. His eyes were pleading. "Take me back."

Her stomach turned again, her heart still hammering furiously in her chest. *Nana said not to...* The thought was fleeting. Regardless of what she'd been told, somehow, somewhere in her heart, she felt certain she had to do something.

The spirits emerged, and their white glowing figures gently took his arms. He stood, shrugging out of their hold. Lessie stood as well. "Lessie," he choked, begging her with his eyes, fear emanating from him. This was all wrong... The spirits reached for him again and began to lead him back. "*Lessie!*" he screamed louder, lurching forward with clenched fists, trying to fight, to no avail. As he broke loose of one of the spirit's hands, his body faded with a hazy flicker.

"Mitch..." she whispered, watching helplessly as his struggling outline began to fade even more. Every fiber of her being leapt to run after him. He was supposed to live. He wasn't finished yet. One last look at his desperate, pleading face, his eyes crying out to her for help; before he faded completely, she set her jaw. She squeezed her eyes shut, and exhaled, projecting her energy toward him, driving purely on instinct.

Breeze, and silence. Or perhaps, an ethereal music. She couldn't quite tell, but she felt her soul smile, her heart expanding. She was everything and nothing, expansive and concise, all at once, feeling as though she were united with a great and powerful energy, and everything felt right, everything felt complete.

It was the most beautiful, powerful, incredible feeling she'd ever experienced. Any fear, any worry, any burden she ever carried within her vanished like a distant, faded memory, as she merged with something much more powerful than herself. She felt laughter, her being soaring with new freedom. It was as though she had always belonged in that light, as though she were always supposed to *be* that light. Parting with her physical form to unite with this much more glorious, joyful sense of purpose seemed brilliant, and she smiled with the thought. As her being surged with light and happiness and completion, her body called out to her like a beacon in the distance. A thread of connection tugged her back enough to remind her of her purpose, and she redirected her energy to envelop Mitch's spirit like a warm embrace. They joined as she pulled him gently back, and he clung desperately to whatever he could make sense of, closing his eyes tightly as he was jolted back with her, suddenly engulfed in darkness.

Lessie breathed heavily, her eyes still shut tight. She felt like the world was spinning too fast, her entire presence like pins and needles as she came down from an immense high. She was somewhat disappointed to leave.

"Damn, this is a good one," she heard a female voice say, and her eyes popped open to find herself sitting in the passenger's seat of Mitch's jeep in the dark, empty night. Her heart jolted and her stomach turned violently, jarring her from the beauty and magnificence of the world she had just come from, as her eyes fell on his crushed body.

It was horrible. The steering wheel was smashed sickeningly deep into his chest, and his head hung limply over the top of it, his blank eyes open and vacant. The dashboard had his left leg shattered beyond recognition. His right leg was significantly damaged as well, as it was trapped between the caved dashboard and the seat. She wanted to throw up. The sight before her burned into her mind, etched into her soul, and she didn't think she'd ever recover.

Lessie tore her eyes from the gruesome sight to the glowing figure of a girl standing next to him, the driver's side door open. She wanted to ask who she was, where she came from, but she couldn't find her voice.

The girl looked up to meet her eyes. "Hey!" she greeted a little too cheerfully. "Never seen you before!" She flashed Lessie a bright smile, then returned to focusing on Mitch's lifeless body. Lessie's eyebrows knit in confusion as her senses slowly began to regain function. She was still unable to speak. The girl breathed through tight lips, her exhale making a slight whistle.

"Three broken ribs and a punctured lung. He's lucky it was only three!" She gave a small chuckle and brought one hand to his back and the other underneath to his chest, her ghost-like palm moving through the steering wheel he was still draped over. A bright green glow began to radiate from her hands. "It always surprises me how many people drive vehicles that don't have airbags," she continued to ramble as she worked.

Finally, Lessie felt her body coming out of her temporary paralysis. "What are you doing?" she croaked, then cleared her throat, looking expectantly at the girl.

"Saving his life!" she chirped, glancing up at Lessie with a quick smile before returning to her work. She then chuckled again. "Well, technically *you* saved his life. Can't very much live without a soul! I'm just saving his body."

Lessie stared wide-eyed at the girl until the green glow dissipated and vanished. "That took care of that!" She began moving her hands to scan the rest of his body, falling still when her hand came to the back of his neck, just below his skull. She blew out a whistle. "Yikes. Hangman's fracture. Instant death!" Lessie's stomach turned at her words. The glow began to emanate again from her hand, lighting up his neck. As she worked, Lessie watched with widening eyes as Mitch's eyelids drifted shut and peace graced his features. The girl smiled. "Spinal cord should be good as new, but he'll most definitely have a bad case of whiplash! And he'll need a brace while his C2 heals. Not that you care," she added with a shrug. She then traveled down to his leg. "Ooh, femoral artery," she said with a grimace, and held her hands just below his knee. The green glow returned, and once it vanished again, she stood back with a look of accomplishment.

"But... what about the rest of his leg...?" Lessie stared at the mangled mess trapped under the smashed dashboard.

The girl gave Lessie an inquisitive look. "What do you mean? I just fixed it."

"*Look* at it!" Lessie commanded, frustration rising in her.

The girl returned her attention to his leg and shook her head with a smirk. "I know, *right?* He won't be keeping that! A lot of the vessels were severed. I cauterized the artery, but that limb will be dead before he ever gets to the hospital."

Lessie gaped at her. "W-what?"

"It sucks, right?" she exclaimed, looking less-than-sympathetic. She prodded his shoulder with her index finger. "He looks athletic. This will probably put a damper on that!" She squinted at Lessie's shocked expression. "What's the matter with you?"

Lessie continued to stare, open-mouthed. Blinking, she finally gathered her bearings and spoke. "Uhh... I know him."

The girl thought for a moment. "Hmm. That doesn't happen often. But cool." She shrugged, then began moving her hands over his chest as though searching for something. "What does he play? Hockey?"

"Football..." Lessie replied, her voice trailing.

The girl nodded. "I was close!" Lessie just stared. She was not close. Her hand stopped over his chest. "He still has a lot of internal hemorrhaging." The green glow appeared under her hands once more as she sat and hummed to herself, as though simply waiting for a hot pocket in a microwave. "Ooh!" the girl suddenly exclaimed, her eyes brightening. "Maybe he'll get one of those cool prosthetic legs that runners get to use! You know? The kind that looks like a giant shoe horn?"

Lessie's face couldn't look any more horrified. "What is

wrong with you...?" she breathed. The girl just laughed, and Lessie gasped in frustration. "You fixed his lung! Fix his leg!"

The girl shook her head. "Sorry, I can only heal fatal wounds. Severed arteries, punctured organs and whatnot." She shrugged casually. "Can't really do anything about broken bones." She raised one of her hands and held it over what was left of his leg and closed her eyes to concentrate, while the other remained busy at his chest. Nothing happened. She opened her eyes to meet Lessie's. "See?"

Lessie continued to stare at her, aghast.

The girl chuckled. "Chill." She shook her head as she tucked a strand of her straight brown hair behind her ear. She brought her hand back to join the other, and the green glow returned under it. "You need to loosen up. Life's too short to take it so seriously. Especially with a life like ours!"

"He almost *died*!" she protested, suddenly breathing heavily.

"Even better — he *did* die, and we brought him back!" She grinned proudly as though they just won at the science fair. "He's apparently meant to live, or what you just did wouldn't have worked, and I wouldn't have gotten called here to do what I do."

"Called?" Lessie repeated curiously, then recalled what the girl just said. "Life like ours?"

The girl nodded. "Yeah, I'm just a regular girl like you. You're not the only one doing what you do, you know."

Lessie's eyes narrowed. Sure, she assumed there were others out there with "gifts" like hers, but how would she ever find them? She never bothered giving it much thought.

"My name's Stephanie," the girl introduced. "And your friend here will be fine. Life will be different though! But, hey, that's what life's about! Ya can't live without suffering at some point.

It's how we learn our lessons, grow as people, ya know?" The green glow dissipated once more and she raised her hand and patted Mitch's shoulder. Lessie watched in amazement as his back rose and fell with a shallow breath, as though he were merely sleeping on the steering wheel. Stephanie smiled. "This is just part of his journey. And he's got quite the journey ahead of him, too! If he can get through it, I'm sure he'll find that life will be pretty incredible on the other end of all this. It's gonna take some work though."

Lessie nodded, staring at Stephanie's bright expression and processing her words. "*If* he can get through it?"

Stephanie replied with a sideways nod. "That's what free will is all about. It may have been his fate to have this accident, but it's his choice whether he makes an emotional recovery or not. That's the hardest part of these kinds of traumas." She grinned as she closed her eyes and got a sense of his vitals. Opening her eyes and still smiling, she stated, "He's good to go, my work here is done. Nice meeting you...?"

"Lessie," she replied.

"Cool. Lessie. I'll probably see you again sometime, I usually get linked to the same Transcendent. But hey," she pointed her finger at Lessie and continued, "I've been told that saving people like you did can have some pretty nasty side effects. Just warning you."

"Side effects?" Lessie asked nervously.

Stephanie laughed, causing Lessie to scowl. "Yeah, I don't recommend making a habit of this." She winked at her. "But, gotta do whatcha gotta do! See ya!" And with that, she vanished.

Lessie was left reeling, but before she had a chance to process any more of what just happened, she was ripped from her existence and thrown back into her physical body in her bedroom, her last fleeting awareness being Mitch drawing in another shallow breath.

Her head suddenly felt three hundred pounds heavier, as though her brain were trying to force its way out of her skull. Her stomach lurched as her body began to writhe, and she choked as her stomach lurched again, her throat feeling thick and her mouth beginning to water. She barely rolled herself over to swing her feet off the bed before she heaved the contents of her stomach onto the floor. An animalistic cry escaped from her chest as her whole body screamed with pain, her head feeling as though it were splitting in two. Before she could muster another sound, she heaved again, dropping to her knees.

"Celeste!" she faintly heard her mother cry as she burst into the room. Everything faded to black.

CHAPTER 15

L ESSIE DANGLED her legs over the edge of a cliff at the Grand Canyon as she sat on the red gravel ground amongst the junipers and sagebrush. She sensed the breeze in the dry, yet warm southwestern air as though it were really brushing across her skin, and a sense of adventure was ignited in her as she realized the whole world was at her fingertips.

She had surfaced in and out of consciousness after returning from saving Mitch the day before. She had just enough time, and energy, to talk her parents out of calling 911, explaining there was nothing a hospital could do for her, before she blacked out again. The pain was too much to bear as she gradually came to, leaving her feeling as though she had no choice but to stay out-of-body. She had visited Will first, waking his astral form in the early morning hours to tell him of her discovery.

He eyed her uncertainly as she pulled his semi-transparent form into a seated position, and immediately said, "I saved someone, Will." He responded with wide eyes and fallen jaw.

She recalled the experience, trying to find words to explain it. How it wasn't just anyone, it was one of her classmates. The feeling that he wasn't supposed to die yet; and how he didn't want to, either. How she was reluctant, at first.

"I knew he'd never be the same," she said in a low voice. "The accident was *so* bad..." She couldn't suppress the images of his lifeless, broken body as they crawled back into the forefront of her mind, her stomach turning and heart hammering. She felt hot tears burning her eyes as she grimaced against the memory. The image consumed her senses. "I'm so glad we never see the aftermath of death, Will, and we go straight to the veil. It was *so* horrible..." Tears shined in her eyes as she brought her palms up to her head, pressing her lips tightly, clinging desperately to staying in control.

"Hey," he said as he brought a comforting hand to her back. "Breathe, Les, it's all over, and he's fine. Everything's okay..."

She took deep, steadying breaths. "Sorry..." she whispered, squeezing back the tears and swallowing hard. Her hands fell limply to her lap. She forced the images out of her mind and continued to tell him of her experience. He kept his arm around her back. "It was all instinct," she continued, "like I knew what I was doing, even though I had no clue what I was doing." She paused as she lifted her gaze to the ceiling. In a whisper, she said, "I saw the Other Side, Will..." She brought her eyes back to his. She couldn't form any more words.

His expression shifted to eager interest. "What was it like?" he asked in an equally soft voice.

She let out a chuckle that sounded more like a gasp, shaking her head in wonder. "It was so incredible... I kind of didn't want to leave." She dropped her gaze to her hands in her lap. "I almost forgot to come back... But, somehow I remembered what I was doing, and got hold of his spirit and drew him back. And then there was this girl there when I opened my eyes, and we were back in the jeep." She told him of Stephanie, how she healed Mitch's injuries and brought his body back to life. Will continued to stare with wide eyes.

"Damn..." he breathed, his expression far away. "You hear about miracles happening... Just like this kind of thing..." He met her eyes with curiosity. "Do you think all miracles happen because of people like her? Like us?"

"Will, I think there are far more mysteries to this Universe than we can even begin to imagine..."

They held each other's gaze for a moment in silence, marveling at the possibilities that they couldn't even begin to know of, until finally Will asked, "So, what happened when you got back?"

Lessie told him of Stephanie's warning, and the excruciating pain she endured when she returned. And that, even though she knows he's okay, she couldn't stop seeing Mitch's lifeless form. Will exhaled heavily, shaking his head, unable to speak as he eyed her with concern.

"Are you going to be okay?" he asked softly.

Lessie took a breath. "I don't know. I'm trying to keep my mind off of all of it."

"I'm here for you, okay?" he said quietly, with an undertone of hesitation. "Nobody's going to understand what you're going through."

Her heart warmed at his gesture, and a small smile came to her lips as she met his eyes. "Thank you," she whispered.

Will's gaze dropped to his knees as he brought his hands together in his lap. They sat in silence, until finally, Will spoke softly, "Do you think Dad knows we can save people?"

Lessie's brows furrowed. "Why would he?"

"Why else would he be *so mad* at Nana, to the point where he cuts her off from his life, because she didn't save Mom?"

Lessie's eyes widened as she stared at her cousin for a moment, considering his words. She then shook her head as she looked down at her knees, still thinking. "But, why would *he* know that, when Nana wouldn't even tell *me* that?" She looked up at Will again, eyes squinted in consideration as the gears turned in her brain. "Nana has always been adamant about *not* saving anyone, but she never mentioned if we *could.*"

"Why else would she be adamant about something like that?" Will asked, his voice low.

Lessie shook her head. "I don't know..."

A BALD EAGLE soared overhead, bringing a serene calmness that softened her shoulders as she watched it glide on the breeze. She had stayed with Will until the sun rose and it was time for him to physically wake, and she left with a sense of completion, as though she had gained a brother.

The pain in her body was still more than she could bear, so as quickly as she had returned into herself, she left again, pondering the concept of traveling around the world. She was elated to find her theory worked, and she continued to marvel at the possibilities as she watched the eagle. The night before, as she fell screaming to the floor and her parents rushed frantically to her aid, she choked out that she'd saved someone, and talked her parents out of dialing 911. Early the next morning, she managed to elaborate on the reason for her sudden illness after she realized there was no way she'd be able to function at school. She never explained that it was *Mitch.* Her parents stared with wide eyes as she told the rest of her story in a weak voice, and, after ensuring she'd be okay, they stepped outside her room.

She could barely make out her mother whisper to Sam, "There was a *reason* Mom told her not to try to save people..."

"I know, but it's done," Sam replied in a low voice. "Maybe she knows not to do it again now."

Lessie had spent the day traveling as she recovered. She felt significantly better as the day wore on, but the splitting pain in her head and weakness in her muscles forced her to continue to rest.

Her thoughts wandered back to Mitch, and she carefully directed them away from the accident and instead to his recovery. Earlier that day, she had managed to check in on social media as she lay limply in bed, squinting at her phone's screen and trying to ignore her headache in order to see if she could learn the latest news. Her entire newsfeed was overflowing with prayer requests, updates, and posts from concerned friends about him and his accident. Her heart sank when she read that he was still sedated, but her skin prickled with an eerie sensation upon reading that he had three broken ribs and a broken neck, and had undergone surgery for a below-the-knee amputation of his left leg. She forced the horrifying images of those very injuries from her mind. Her skin prickled once more upon reading repeatedly as she scrolled:

It's a miracle he lived.

God must have a plan for him!

Mitch's survival is a true miracle, praying for a smooth recovery on this difficult road ahead!

Stephanie. The miracle was merely Stephanie. Lessie was there. She watched as Stephanie discovered his injuries, healed what would have otherwise killed him, agreed there would be no way he could keep his leg...

She shook her head at the memory. Her mind traveled to Emily's texts that lit up her phone throughout the day.

>>*OMG Les you're missing a crazy day... The whole school is freaking out about Mitch!*

>>*Holy crap someone just said they had to amputate his leg... How fucked up is that??*

>>*The whole football team is losing their shit!*

>>*Are you still alive? Why aren't you answering my texts? What's wrong with you?*

>>*I'm at lunch. Adam is worried about you. A couple of church groups just organized prayer vigils for Mitch, you should see this... It's pretty powerful to watch...*

THE EAGLE LANDED on a branch farther down in the canyon, tethering Lessie's thoughts back to the vast desert landscape. She couldn't imagine the state the student body would be in had Mitch not survived. Had Lessie been unable to save him. If someone like Stephanie didn't exist...

Were there other people out there like her? Like Stephanie? People doing things she'd never even heard of yet? Or possibly never would?

BY THE END of the day, Lessie's headache had somewhat dissipated, though she still felt weak and drained. Emily arrived at her house after school, and nervously poked her head into Lessie's bedroom.

"You've *never* been this sick," Emily remarked from the doorway, afraid to enter the room. Her eyes traveled across Lessie's limp, prone form, her hand dangling loosely off the edge of the bed, her pale face smashed into the pillow. "Should I be wearing a hazmat suit?"

Lessie managed a chuckle. "I promise you, I'm not sick with anything you can catch." She rolled to her side and attempted to press herself up to face her friend. "And if you *can* catch this, we have way bigger issues to deal with."

Emily eyed her curiously as she stepped inside the room, closing the door behind her. She placed Lessie's books and homework on her desk before slowly taking a seat in the chair facing her ill friend. "Go on...?" Emily pressed.

Lessie took a breath and cut to the chase. "I saved Mitch's life."

Emily sat, blinking. "Come again?"

"I got called. To Mitch's accident. Saturday night." Lessie spoke slowly and plainly, watching as Emily put it all together, her eyes growing wide and her jaw going slack. Lessie nodded, assuring Emily she was telling the truth, and dropped her head back onto the pillow. "I saw... Everything..." She took a breath, her stomach turning and her whole being protesting against her elaborating, desperate to avoid having to relive it again. "His leg..." she forced, bringing her eyes back to Emily's, concentrating on her face so as to avoid seeing the image she was describing. She continued explaining what happened, what she had seen, and what she had done. She finished with telling Emily about Stephanie. "That miracle everyone is talking about? The miracle that he lived? It was her."

Emily shook her head slowly, her gaze falling to the floor as she wrapped her mind around Lessie's words. "So what about Mitch?" Emily asked, as she lifted her eyes back to Lessie's. "Do you think he remembers any of this?"

Lessie turned her head, still resting on the pillow, to eye her friend as she chewed her lower lip. "I have no idea."

CHAPTER 16

HAZY MEMORY... Voices calling to him, strapping him, bracing him, lifting him...

Blinding pain.

Darkness.

The chopping blades of a helicopter propeller. Voices, machines...

Darkness. Peaceful, calming darkness.

Panicked crying. *Gen?* He tried to reach out to his sister but couldn't move.

Darkness again.

VOICES. SO MANY voices. Why were there so many people? Mitch squeezed his closed eyes tighter, then relaxed them again, keeping them shut. *Stop talking...* he thought. Rude. Couldn't they see he was trying to sleep? He felt miserable. He could faintly hear the sounds of whirring and beeping. He tried to process things against the fog in his brain. *I'm not in my room...* he realized, tuning out all the chatter and focusing on the beeping sound. *That sounds like...*

He hurt. Like he got hit by a truck. His whole chest ached, and it was painful to draw in air. He couldn't turn his head, then quickly realized it was braced in a collar. And his legs felt really weird, especially his left... He swallowed hard, his throat raw and scratchy. He moved his thick, sticky tongue against his teeth and grimaced. *I need water...* he thought absently. He stirred, feeling a tugging at the back of his hand. *Stuck... something's stuck on me...* his mind fumbled as it processed. The voices kept talking. *Quiet...* he commanded, keeping his eyes shut. His forehead wrinkled in frustration. *Where the hell am I...?*

He slowly opened his eyes, his vision blurry at first. After blinking a few times, he took in his surroundings as best he could with his braced neck. He was in some sort of bed that had him lying in a slight incline. His eyes traveled, recognizing it was a hospital room. Monitors beeping, tubes coming out of him... He didn't have a shirt on, but something was wrapped loosely around his chest. And, to his surprise, the room was completely empty. *Where'd everybody go?* he wondered, his eyes darting around. He could have sworn there were at least five or six people in there with him.

His heart stopped as his eyes fell on the lower half of his body. "What the fuck..." he gasped, his voice a hoarse croak. His right leg was bound in a thick cast, but his left leg... His stomach dropped. It ended just below the knee, a stump wrapped heavily in thick white gauze. *Where the hell is my leg?* His brain began working on overdrive, frantically flailing as if he were about to fall off a cliff. He wanted to move but couldn't, the beeping on the monitors picked up speed, and suddenly the door swung open. A young female nurse entered the room, her long chocolate ponytail swinging behind her as she burst through the door, and her large amber eyes wide with concern.

"Mr. Griffin!" she gasped. "You're awake!" She gave him a gentle smile. "My name is Dawn. Try to calm down, now, Honey."

Mitch attempted to move, but grimaced against the pain. "What's going on?" he rasped.

"You had one heck of an accident. It's a miracle you're alive, really," Dawn spoke. "You were in a car accident late Saturday night, you must have ran off the road and hit a telephone pole. You had a bad concussion when they found you. You were in and out for a bit, but once you stabilized you were in surgery for..."

"My leg...?" he choked, his eyes wild and panicked as he stared at her, desperate.

Her face fell. "Sorry, Sweetie... It was crushed beyond repair. There was nothing they could do, no way to even begin to fix it..." She sighed sadly. "The whole limb was dead before you got to the hospital. I'm so sorry." She paused, then continued. "We kept you sedated until this morning." Her face brightened. "I'm so glad to see you're awake! We figured it'd be a matter of time before the last of the anesthesia wore off. Doctor Park was your surgeon, he'll be in later today to explain everything more for you."

He tried to shake his head, struggling to sit up, but failing, only causing a searing pain in his chest and neck and an aching throb in his head. "Oh, no, Sweetie, don't move," the nurse advised, outstretching her hand. "Those ribs still have quite a bit of healing to do, and your neck... well..." Her voice trailed off. "I really don't know how you survived that..." she whispered, almost to herself.

"I... I need my leg..." he rasped.

She cast him a sympathetic, yet hopeful, gaze. "We have a team of incredible therapists lined up. You'll be walking again in no time."

He stared at her, hope beginning to flicker inside of him.

"And... I can play football again?" His voice was finally coming back, though it was still gravelly and hoarse.

Her face fell again. "With time. Anything is possible. But strenuous activity like that will have to be put on hold. We'll focus on walking first, then work your way up to running." She gave him another hopeful smile. "But, I have faith you'll be good as new, like nothing ever happened!"

His mind went to his football scholarship, the promise of college and his future, all caving in like charred logs consumed by flame. It was over. Before despair could completely devour him, the chatter of voices returned. Nothing he could make out at first, but annoying nonetheless. He slowly brought his hands up, ignoring the uncomfortable tug of the IV, and pressed their heels to his temples and squeezed his eyes shut. "Can you tell whoever it is that's talking like that to be quiet?" he groaned. "Why are the walls so thin?"

The nurse eyed him curiously. "I... I don't hear anything..."

He opened his eyes to meet her confused gaze, his own expression matching hers. "You don't hear that?" he asked.

She shook her head, looking slightly concerned.

Tell her I'm glad she took the locket.

He blinked. That was definitely a distinct voice. Dawn looked unfazed. "You didn't hear that?" he asked, studying her.

She shook her head again. "No... Sorry..."

The locket, tell her I'm glad she took it.

He furrowed his eyebrows. "What damn locket?" he muttered, squeezing his eyes shut.

"Pardon?" Dawn asked, her interest piqued.

He opened his eyes to meet hers. "Some lady keeps saying to tell you she's glad you took the locket." His eyebrows lowered even more. Dawn looked stunned as her hand absently reached up to her chest, touching where the pendant of a necklace might hang. She reached beneath the collar of her orange scrubs and withdrew a silver heart on a chain.

Yes, that's it. She felt guilty that she took it, didn't even give her sisters a choice, even though she knew she wanted it the most.

He felt driven beyond his control to relay the messages as they continued rolling in, feeling strangely out-of-body as he did so. "She said not to feel bad that your sisters didn't get it, she knew you always had a love for it, so she wanted you to have it anyway."

The nurse's eyes grew wide with shock. "Mom...?" she whispered.

Mitch blinked, then squinted. What the hell was happening here? "I need a drink of water," he mumbled, feeling confused and disjointed.

Tears had welled in the nurse's eyes, and she furiously blinked them back as she nodded, still clutching the small heart-shaped locket. Without another word, she left the room.

Thank you.

His eyes searched the room. Nobody was there. "Sure, whatever," he mumbled, still feeling a fog rolling through him. Before he could process anything further, the nurse returned with a plastic lidded cup with a straw, and, after increasing the incline of his bed so he could sit up, brought the straw to his lips from her stance at his side.

"How did you do that?" she finally whispered, breaking the silence.

"What?" he asked after taking several long draws of the cool, refreshing liquid. He could feel his body responding already.

"My mom... How did you know?"

He looked up to meet her stunned, watery eyes. He wasn't sure how to answer her. "I... I just heard it... and felt like something made me tell you..." He gave her a shrug. "I don't know."

She nodded. "Well... thank you." She gave him a half-smile, a tear slipping down her cheek. "I needed that." She squeezed his shoulder, set the cup on the table next to his bed and rolled it within his reach. "Your mom and sister are on their way up from the cafeteria. They'll be glad to see you're awake." She gave him a soft, grateful smile, then quietly left the room.

He lay blinking in his bed, unsure of what just happened, then sank his head back into the pillow, closing his eyes. The voices picked up their chatter again. *Shut up...* he thought, as the fog swirled in.

CHAPTER 17

LESSIE BREATHED in the woodsy, citrusy scent of
Adam as she pressed her face into his flannel-clad
chest, enjoying the feeling of his arms wrapped tightly
around her, encompassing her in more warmth than her
wool coat could provide. She smiled as she breathed. It
was the last day of school before winter break. A gentle
dusting of snow had begun falling, and the light accumulation as well as the continuing flurry made the world feel
quiet and magical, enhancing the moment Lessie shared
in Adam's arms outside the school building.

With Mitch out of school for the duration of December, and
talk of him steadily dying down as his conditions improved,
Lessie was able to gradually return to the way things were before
his accident, slowly tucking away her fears and apprehensions
over the situation into the back of her mind as she enjoyed her
days with her friends and boyfriend. The nightmares became
less frequent, as did the intrusive visions of his accident. Will
was her rock as he talked her through what he was certain
was PTSD, helping calm her mind and redirect her thoughts;
meanwhile allowing Will the opportunity to break down more
of his own walls. Life got easier as time went on, edging closer
to Christmas break.

The town was filled with holiday spirit, its tree-lined streets twinkling with strings of lights, garlands adorned with red bows were strung on the lampposts and hung from the awnings of the historic buildings, and storefront windows displayed scenes of winter wonderlands. Along with the cheerful, cozy Christmas atmosphere in her hometown, Lessie also had the distraction of finals to study for as the first semester drew to a close, and Christmas festivities during their two-week break from school to look forward to. Everything was going to be okay.

Adam pressed his lips to the top of Lessie's head, bringing a warm smile to her face as she closed her eyes. "What am I gonna do with myself, not getting to see you every day?" he sighed into her hair.

Lessie chuckled. "We'll talk every day, video chat or text or whatever, and you can come over anytime." She leaned back from him, her arms still hanging around his waist as she met his eyes.

"Get a room!" Emily's playfully jeering voice carried as she hopped down the school's steps.

The two reluctantly separated, though Lessie laced a gloved hand into Adam's bare fingers. "Like you're any better!" Adam retorted, nodding toward Evan who was trailing behind her.

"So what's the plan?" Emily asked cheerfully, blowing off her cousin's remark as she drew her scarf tightly around her chin. Snowflakes were already frosting her loose blonde hair.

"I'm hosting New Year's again, so you guys better be coming to that!" Evan exclaimed, looking at the three expectantly.

"Of course!" Lessie said, grinning, stifling any residual fears of her "gift" kicking in and embarrassing her in the middle of it. Thanks to her boyfriend's help, she'd grown a new sense of confidence and had survived enough events that she felt comfortable attending more. Adam gave her hand a squeeze, smiling at her.

"Let's get through Christmas first," Emily interrupted. She grinned at Lessie. "You coming to our family Christmas?"

Lessie returned the grin. "Absolutely!" she replied. Two for two. She was getting the hang of accepting invitations to social gatherings.

Emily beamed, stepping between her cousin and best friend and draping her arms around each of them. "I freaking *love* that you two are together. It's like we're *all* family!"

"Speaking of family," Adam spoke, smiling. "Mom said I could invite you along to church Christmas morning. Want to come?"

Lessie's smile faltered slightly as she immediately made eye contact with Emily, who ever-so-slightly raised her eyebrows. Lessie had never been to church — it had never been Lessie's family's "thing," and she hadn't ever put much thought into it.

Lessie cleared her throat and met Adam's eyes with a smile. "Yeah, actually I think I would." Emily subtly arched her brow as she released her arms from Lessie and Adam, returning to Evan's side, and Lessie replied with a small shrug. She was genuinely curious to experience a church service, and Christmas sounded like the perfect opportunity to see what it was all about

LESSIE WOKE EARLY Christmas morning, earlier than she ever really cared to, to get ready for a much-anticipated church service with Adam and his family. She had grown increasingly curious about attending, but had no idea what to expect. She knew the Christmas story, but she was most eager to find out what drew everyone to the weekly services, and what went on there.

She slid into black leggings and pulled a long-sleeved gray tunic over her head that hung almost to her knees, then topped the look off with a dark blue scarf. After brushing her hair and teeth and applying a bit of mascara, she quietly made her way down the stairs, knowing her parents were fast asleep. They were supportive when Lessie informed them of her Christmas morning plans, albeit curious as to what she would think of her experience.

Adam arrived several minutes later, awkwardly standing at the front door as Lessie pulled her black boots on and shrugged into her thick winter coat. She slid her gloved hand into Adam's arm, and pulled him into a tight hug.

He bent to capture her in a deep kiss. "Mmmm," Lessie hummed into him before pulling away, smiling contentedly. "Merry Christmas." She could come to be perfectly fine with this church thing...

"Merry Christmas," Adam replied, casting her a similar smile. He pulled the passenger's door open for her. "You look beautiful," he complimented as she climbed into the car.

"You look rather fine yourself," Lessie replied, grinning. He did look handsome, wearing a dark blue button-up dress shirt and black slacks, and a heavy denim coat overtop.

"So you've really never been to church?" Adam questioned as they pulled out of the driveway.

Lessie shook her head. "Nope." She smiled as she turned her gaze to him. "But I'm excited to see what it's like."

"Your family knows about the Bible, right?" He turned the wheel as they pulled out onto the highway. There may have been lines of concern etched in his features.

Lessie nodded with a partial shrug. "Sure, or at least Dad

does. He was raised sort of religious, but quit going to church when he met Mom."

Adam's brows knit at this information, but didn't question. "Do you know the Christmas story?"

Lessie nodded again. "Sure, baby Jesus born in a manger, and all that."

Adam smirked as he shook his head. "I'm glad you're coming with us," he said, smiling briefly in her direction as he drove through town.

Lessie returned the smile. "I'm excited to see what this is all about."

It was certainly more beautiful than she expected. She gazed in awe as they entered the church, first greeted by soft Christmas hymns playing from the organ in the loft. The elaborate decorations captivated her: the massive Christmas trees on either side of the altar, adorned with shining metallic red and gold ornaments and glittering white lights; the holly wreaths sparkling with their own lights; the multitude of candles glowing throughout the church; and the life-size nativity scene to the side of the altar. Swags of pine surrounding thick candles sat in the window sills, and small wreaths hung from the sides of each pew, pulling the coziness of the Christmas scene throughout the entire church.

"This is beautiful," Lessie whispered as they joined Adam's family in a pew toward the front. They slid in next to Adam's parents and brother, who had already joined his grandparents along with his aunts, uncles, and cousins. Lessie waved cheerfully at Emily, who sat with her parents and brother at the other end of the pew.

The service was long, yet fascinating. The story of Jesus's

birth was told, after a long production of bringing the baby statue to the nativity set and placing it in the manger, and the pastor drew out a long sermon about Jesus's presence in their lives and the wonder of God coming to them in the form of a human baby, making himself man so that he could one day save everyone from their sins. Those parts confused Lessie, though she did her best to follow along and make sense of the pastor's words.

He read passages from the Bible, and she was fascinated by the truth she was able to pull from it in her own understanding, but even more so fascinated at everyone else's interpretations. God made himself "man" in the form of Jesus... but that happened every day, didn't it? Every child born was a manifestation of God in human form...

It seemed as though the people gathered there clung to their faith. The pastor spoke of the state of affairs of the country and the world. He spoke of the tragedies and terrible things that happened, but their faith that one day Jesus would return and save them all was what kept them strong.

Lessie's eyes began to leave the pastor to take in the congregation. She watched as they nodded, grimaced, or smiled in response to the pastor's words as he spoke. Some hung on his every word, while others were beginning to nod off. But they all seemed to believe his words without question, and all carried a unanimous belief that one day their Jesus would return.

Lessie's mind wandered as she contemplated the thought that one day this man would come back and put an end to all suffering. She reflected on wisdom Nana had shared with her before: that suffering was necessary, in order to learn lessons and grow. She thought back to the day she met the girl with leukemia and crossed her over, how at peace she was, accepting that life was meant to be challenging. She thought of Mitch, and how she hoped he could grow from the challenges he faced. And herself; what a better person she'd become because of the difficulties in her life. Putting an end to all suffering would simply mean they'd just be in Heaven, where suffering didn't exist. Then what would the point of being human be?

AFTER THE SERVICE, Adam's parents, Matthew and Anne, thanked Lessie for joining them as they made their way back to the parking lot. A light snow had begun to fall, and a thin white blanket covered the ground. "We're glad you could come," Anne spoke, her voice sincere and her smile matching as she pulled her scarf tighter around her neck.

"We hope you enjoyed it," Matthew added.

Lessie closed her coat and pulled her gloves on as they walked toward Adam's car. "I did," she replied, smiling at them politely. There was sincerity in her voice, as she felt enlightened from the conclusions she drew while contemplating the sermon. Adam gave her a warm smile.

"I'll text you later," Emily said with a smile as she joined with her parents, and Lessie nodded.

After wishing each other a Merry Christmas and saying their goodbyes, Adam and Lessie climbed back into his car and began the drive back to Lessie's house.

"So you really did enjoy it?" Adam questioned, stealing a glance at Lessie as he drove carefully across the freshly fallen snow.

"Yeah," she replied, feeling her guard coming down and preparing to be honest with him. "It was fascinating."

Adam nodded thoughtfully. "So, why doesn't your family go to church?"

She shrugged, relaxing into her seat. "We kind of have our own beliefs. My whole family does." He squinted in response, but remained silent, so she continued. "We feel comfortable with it, and just never really felt the need for organized religion."

"What do you mean, your own beliefs?"

She pursed her lips in thought, suddenly realizing this was the first time she was placed in such a situation. Lessie had only ever discussed religion with Emily, but Emily knew her story and her background. Not only that, but Emily's family didn't regularly participate in organized religion, either, and only attended on major holidays. Lessie never had to explain her lifestyle to anyone before, and explaining it while avoiding the fact that she crossed into the spirit world on a regular basis was no easy feat. "It's kind of hard to explain," she finally responded with furrowed brows. She glanced in his direction. "Why do you go to church?"

He blinked, then finally replied, "For the connection with God, I suppose."

Lessie nodded, trying to put herself in Adam's place. He'd never felt that connection to the Other Side like she had so many times. Never felt that warmth and love, that peace and oneness with Spirit. He had nothing to base his beliefs on except what he'd been raised to believe, which mostly came from the Bible. And how trustworthy was that? she wondered. Having been written by men and retranslated as it was passed down over the centuries... She suddenly found herself eager to understand more. "So, what is 'God' to you?"

Confusion shifted over his face. "W-well..." he began, as

though he weren't sure what kind of answer she was expecting. "I guess, He's everything, everywhere. He made us, made the world we live in. He protects us, guides us..." He squinted once again, tilting his head as he gazed out over the road. He glanced at her briefly. "What is God to *you?*"

Lessie smiled. "Well, first of all, I don't call it a 'He.' I call it The Universe," she answered. "Source, Higher Power, whatever. Usually I fall back on Universe, though, because, like you said, God is everywhere and everything. We are all connected with that God-energy, and we can tap into it anytime we want. I don't look at 'praying' as asking God for help, as though God is something separate, like a parent. I think we *all* are God. *I'm* God, *you're* God.

"If we want something, or need help, we just need to tap into that God energy." She held her hand to her chest. "It's in all of us, and we're all connected to it. To the Universe."

He simply stared out the window, brows still furrowed, and she wondered if her words were making any sense to him. She decided to press on. "That's basically why we don't go to church. Not that we find anything wrong with it. But Mom and Dad say there's a lot of focus on not sinning, and believing in Jesus, and stuff like that. And God being a separate thing."

Finally Adam found his voice, and let out a small chuckle. "Heh, there's so much more to it than that." Lessie smiled again and waited for him to continue. He turned the car onto her lane. "Jesus *died* to save us from our sins."

"What does that mean, though?"

Adam's eyebrows knit. "It means that we sin, we make mistakes or bad choices; but if we believe in Jesus, we'll return to Heaven."

Lessie nodded thoughtfully, considering his words. "So, where do you think one would go if they *didn't* believe in Jesus?"

"Hell, I guess."

She frowned. "Do you really believe such a place exists?" He didn't answer. "What about the people who don't believe in Jesus, but they've been perfectly good people all their lives?" Still, no response. She turned her body slightly to face him. "What if *this* is Hell? It's the opposite of Heaven, right? Maybe our souls have to cross into this plane *first*, to suffer, but then try to grow from it, right? Then we go back to Heaven when this life is over, and we come back again to suffer more and learn new lessons, and then return to Heaven again, and so on, until we finally reach enlightenment."

Adam stared at her blankly, his mouth slightly agape, before dragging his eyes back on her lane. "Where do you get this?" he finally asked.

Lessie laughed, leaning back. Her smile met her eyes. "I just like to think about that stuff. I also get it from my parents, and Nana. And a lot of it," she placed her hand over her heart, "I just feel." She paused as she held his eyes. "Isn't that how you feel about what you believe in?"

Adam remained silent as he slowed to park in her driveway, his expression still lost and blank. "I..." he started. "Yeah...I guess?" He fidgeted in his seat before adding, "It's just how I was raised."

"Have you ever questioned it?" she asked, her tone genuinely curious and her eyes matching.

He considered her for a moment, squinting. "Why would I question it?"

"Why wouldn't you? Isn't that how we learn more? By

asking questions?" He continued staring at her silently as they sat in her driveway. She didn't move to exit the car, as she found she was enjoying their conversation. She found an element of exploration in getting to talk with a participant of organized religion, and she was curious to open new doors and ask new questions.

He sat silently for a moment, until finally, he said, "I guess I never thought to ask questions... You shouldn't question God..."

Lessie frowned slightly. "Well, it's not really a matter of questioning *God*... it's more just questioning why you believe the things you were raised to believe."

He lifted his head to meet her eyes, and changed the subject. "Did you feel anything? Get something out of it?"

Lessie shrugged. "I dunno. I found it interesting that they have this hope of Jesus coming back someday. I think everyone should believe in something that brings them hope and gives them comfort, so if that's what works, then that's really great."

"You don't believe that?"

Lessie shrugged again. "I just think God is in all of us. *Part* of us. The 'Second Coming" will probably be the day everyone realizes that. We don't really need Jesus to grant us access to God or anything like that. We've already got access. I kind of wonder if Jesus was here just to remind us that we're *all* God, but somewhere that message got lost in translation."

This time, Adam shrugged. "Well, the Bible makes it pretty clear..."

"The Bible was translated a lot over a *long* time, though," Lessie replied. "Not to mention, written by humans."

"Of course humans wrote it. But God worked *through* them. They interpreted his message, and wrote it down."

"Hmm…" Lessie replied thoughtfully. "So, what if I'm inspired by God, and I believe God is speaking through me, so I write it all down. All these things I've said just now, what if that's God speaking through me, just like the old writers of the Bible? You think anyone would believe me? Would my words be added to the Bible?" Adam chuckled at the thought. "I'm serious!" Lessie shot back, though she smiled as well. "What if I'm being inspired by God *right now*, and you're just laughing at me?"

Adam shrugged as he picked at a piece of loose vinyl on the steering wheel with his thumbnail. "I don't know. I guess nowadays it would be hard to get people to believe you…"

Lessie laughed. "Funny how that works."

Adam seemed to be lost in thought as they sat in the driveway. She reached to give his knee a squeeze and smiled at him, breaking him from his contemplation. "Thanks again for taking me along. I did enjoy it."

Adam gave her a smile that seemed forced at first, though it quickly warmed with sincerity. "Thanks for coming," he replied, then leaned in to pull her into an embrace, followed by another deep kiss, which lingered long enough to leave any discomfort from their conversation in forgotten shadow.

CHAPTER 18

A FRIGID early February wind blew, making the warm indoors a stark contrast to the bitter outdoors as Mitch hobbled his way into the school building with his sister, Genevieve, close at his side. The high school sophomore had been feeling particularly protective of her older brother, especially as his first day back at school since his accident drew nearer.

He stood rigid in the large open school foyer, gripping his crutches, his heart suddenly hammering wildly in his chest. He had been kept up-to-date on his studies by a private tutor, though his classes were the least of his worries. He was more concerned by the fact that all eyes would be on him as he limped through the hallways on his crutches, still getting used to his prosthetic leg. It was attention he really didn't care to have.

And then there were the voices. They continued their other-worldly chatter since the day he woke up from his anesthesia after the amputation. Some worked their way to the forefront, their voices carrying stronger and clearer than the others if they had a particular message to share with someone Mitch was anywhere near. For the most part, he was able to ignore them and continue on with his life. But, ignoring the stronger, more direct voices caused him to fall just short of going insane. He found refusing to relay their messages was similar to being held underwater, unable to surface until he surrendered.

The idea of having to deal with that at school was terrifying.

His mother, Ruth, and Genevieve took his strange new ability in stride. Not long after his first incident with the nurse and her late mother, Ruth's grandfather came to Mitch as he lay in the hospital bed and urged him to speak for him to his granddaughter.

Ruth stared at her son, wide-eyed and dumbstruck, as he rode the current of his great-grandfather's voice. He was a man Ruth always respected and looked up to, sometimes even more so than her own father. "He said to stop beating yourself up," Mitch spoke, his voice soft yet strong. "Micah's death was not in vain, and there was nothing you could have done to prevent it from happening the way it did."

Ruth shook her head, still dumbfounded, tears welling in her eyes. She'd never spoken to her kids about her inner demons surrounding her husband's death; yet, there it was, brought out in the open from her son's mouth. Genevieve stared with wide eyes and gaping mouth, her gaze shifting between her mother and brother. She was an open-minded individual, and she had quickly come to support her brother in whatever this strange new ability was. It strengthened their bond as siblings while, unfortunately, their mother remained distant and reserved, much as she had since Micah died four years prior.

Mitch was silently grateful for his sister's unwavering support as she stood next to him in the hallway, pulling her long, dark hair into a ponytail and casting him a gaze that said, *You ready?*

Was he ready? He noticed a few people were already

staring at him as he gathered his bearings, taking in the familiar surroundings with new eyes. He felt he couldn't move.

"Mitch?" a male voice broke him from his trance. He slowly turned his head to focus on the source of the voice, Carter Gregson, his friend and the varsity wide receiver. The tall, dishwater blonde, husky boy stood staring at Mitch before finally snapping out of it and coming forward, smiling. He clapped him on the shoulder as soon as he reached him, and greeted, "Good to have you back, man!"

Mitch cleared his throat. "Y-yeah," he replied, giving a quick nod. "Good to finally be back, I guess." Genevieve watched the exchange silently, clutching her books to her chest, feeling ready to fight if anyone tried to give her brother a hard time.

"How you feeling?" Carter asked, his brown eyes traveling down to Mitch's seemingly normal lower extremities.

Mitch shifted uncomfortably and readjusted his crutches. "Fine," he replied, even though his non-existent left foot itched and his neck ached. He felt his sister's eyes on him. He turned to face her. "You can probably go, Gen," he spoke, giving her a weak smile.

She cast him a wary gaze. "You sure?"

"He'll be fine! I'll walk with ya," Carter broke in, grinning and nudging Mitch with his elbow.

Genevieve chewed her lip. "Okay. Text me if you need anything." Her eyes then became stern. "I don't care if it's not allowed in class, I'll have my phone on me and if any of the teachers have a problem with it, I'll shove it up their—"

"I'll be fine, Gen, really," Mitch interrupted.

His sister sighed, still looking unconvinced, but reluctantly agreed. "Fine." She left her brother with his friend and former teammate.

Former, Mitch thought, tasting the bitterness of the word. The pain of the reality of no longer being able to play football stabbed him suddenly and unexpectedly. He felt the clap of Carter's hand on his shoulder again, nearly knocking him off balance. "The whole team is excited to have you back, man," he stated, smiling, and they began walking slowly down the hall.

"Oh, that's cool," Mitch replied halfheartedly.

Carter sighed. "I guess it's good timing since football is over. No matter what, you'll always be part of the team, got it?"

The knife in Mitch's heart twisted painfully. Timing? The timing didn't change the fact that the whole situation *sucked*. Sure, football season may be over, but he was riding on a scholarship to a great university based on his skill in the sport. His dreams for his future were crumbling around him as he was left standing on one leg and staring at a vast unknown. He had to completely reroute his future, and without football, he felt he had nothing. He refrained from answering Carter, suppressing his despair.

They rounded the corner into a hallway, and found several of the football team and cheerleaders gathered around his locker. "Oh em gee! Mitch!" his girlfriend, Katie, squealed as she bounded up to him, her blonde curls swinging at her shoulders. She pulled him into a tight embrace, which he attempted to return despite the difficulty of his crutches.

"Hey, Baby," he greeted, forcing a smile. She hadn't visited him nearly as often as he hoped she would. She had stopped by the hospital a week after his surgery, but seemed as though she felt awkward and out of place. She came with him to his family

Christmas gathering, and spent New Year's Eve with him as well, despite the fact that she seemed more absorbed in her phone, texting her friends, who were at a party she was disappointed to be missing. She had only visited him once more since then.

She caressed his face as she stood close to him, her blue eyes pitying and sorrowful. "Sweetie, I'm so glad you're back."

Mitch sighed, his forced smile faltering slightly. "Me, too," he lied. He suddenly realized he was annoyed with her. Betrayed, almost. Perhaps he was a bit hurt, as well, but he wasn't about to let that show.

"Dude, what's it like?" Blake Hathaway questioned eagerly, nodding toward Mitch's lower half. He was the only one who lacked the tact that held everyone else back from asking the same question they were all wondering. Mitch shifted uncomfortably once more, suddenly feeling like a circus sideshow.

"Um, it's not fun," he replied honestly.

"Are you still going to get to play?" Blake pressed, and Carter punched him in the arm.

"What's it look like, you idiot?" the large-framed boy chided.

"People with missing limbs can still play sports! I've seen it!" Blake retaliated, punching him back.

"It probably won't be for a while, will it, Babe?" Katie asked sadly, cutting in before a fight broke out.

Mitch slowly shook his head in response, trying to keep his face set and strong, then let out a deep exhale. "No," he said in a gruff voice.

"Dude, what about your scholarship?" Blake asked dumbly, and Carter punched him again. "Ow!" Blake rubbed his arm as he shot Carter an offended glare.

"You can't ask questions like that, you ass!" one of the

other cheerleaders, Grace Beckham exclaimed, narrowing her eyes at Blake.

"I should start heading to class," Mitch broke in with a low voice, deliberately avoiding the subject of his future. "It's gonna take me awhile to get there, anyway."

"I'll walk with you, Baby," Katie cooed as she grasped his elbow.

"Me, too," Carter added as he joined Mitch at his other side. "But I ain't callin' ya 'Baby,'" he kidded, and elbowed him in the arm.

Mitch was glad to leave the group, the memories of what his life used to be and the reality of his future became too painful as it stared him in the face. He hobbled on his crutches, wishing he had pushed himself harder in therapy as he learned to navigate life with his prosthetic leg, even though he pushed himself hard enough already.

Katie... His thoughts were suddenly interrupted by a female voice. *Not again,* he thought as he squeezed his eyes shut, hoping he could just ignore it this time. He kept moving so as not to raise any questions from his friend and girlfriend. *Not now...* he thought. *Please...*

Katie... the voice persisted.

"Ugh," Mitch groaned as he stopped and rubbed the palm of his hand vigorously against his forehead.

"Babe, are you okay?" Katie coddled as she stopped with him and touched the back of his arm, casting him a look of concern. Carter stopped and eyed him closely as well.

Mitch shook his head. "Fine, just... Headache. Been getting them a lot." He grasped his crutches once more and continued to move forward.

"You've been through a lot, man. Take it easy," Carter spoke as he followed behind Mitch.

Katie, you must mend what you've broken with your sister...

"Please leave me alone," Mitch muttered under his breath as he stopped again and held his forehead. The familiar, suffocating feeling of being held underwater began flooding in, and he physically gasped for a breath.

"What did you say, Baby?" Katie questioned, her voice still pitched with concern.

I'm okay, I can breathe, I'm okay, I can breathe he repeated in his head like a mantra, but it was no use.

Katie, please talk to your sister, the elderly female voice urged, drowning out all other sounds in the hallway, and Mitch felt a sense of desperation wash through him, causing him to feel as though his lungs were collapsing.

"You need to talk to your sister!" he finally burst, stopping and jerking to face Katie, who stopped in her tracks, gaping at him as though he had hit her. He sucked in a deep breath and exhaled heavily as they stared at each other in silence.

Silence. Mitch closed his eyes and took a steadying breath. Maybe the woman was gone... He turned and kept walking, trying to pretend as though nothing had happened.

Katie wasn't about to let it go that easily. "What was that about?" she pressed, keeping her voice even, though Mitch could sense that she was fighting to stay calm. He always knew there was a competition between the two girls, more so instigated by Katie than by Korie. A rift had formed between the two shortly after Korie's freshman year when she failed to make it on the cheerleading squad. Korie was now a sophomore and had since joined the volleyball team, befriending Mitch's sister and becoming her own kind of star. He never knew why the rift formed, but never bothered to ask, either.

"Nothing," Mitch responded gruffly as he continued walking, and he distantly heard Katie come back at him with more questions, but her voice was drowned out by the woman's urgent words.

You must tell Korie the truth, apologize to your sister!

And suddenly, without warning, the woman's voice seemed to come at him not in the form of words, but as memories, as his mind was all of a sudden infused with knowledge. Cheerleading tryouts.

Katie's searing jealousy of her sister, who was prettier and funnier and more talented than she was. No doubt Korie would be the star cheerleader if she made it on the team. Korie desperately wanted to cheer. Katie rigged the tryouts results. Korie didn't make the team. She was devastated. Katie pretended to be sympathetic, but Korie sensed Katie had something to do with it. She confided in her grandmother, whose voice and memories and knowledge cascaded violently and furiously into Mitch's mind as he stopped and held the heels of his hands to his eyebrows, his crutches pinned tightly under his arms as he held tight to his balance.

And, just as suddenly as it started, the voice and the memories stopped, and Mitch was once again left in silence. He breathed heavily, processing, seeing his girlfriend in a different light. He turned his head slowly, squinting at Katie, who was waiting for him to reply to whatever she had said, her arms folded over her chest and her lips pursed.

"How could you do that to Korie?" Mitch breathed, his eyes narrowed, forgetting that he was the only one who heard the voice, and that neither Katie nor Carter had any idea what just happened to him, or the knowledge he now possessed.

"What are you talking about?" Katie demanded in a low voice, her expression suddenly turning angry and defensive. Carter watched the exchange with confusion.

"You rigged cheerleading tryouts?" Mitch asked, and Carter's eyes widened in surprise as Katie's face burned red.

"What are you talking about? Where is this even coming from?" Katie's voice rose as her anger built, her stance rigid and her fists clenched at her sides.

Mitch shook his head and his face fell, suddenly filled with mixed feelings. Disappointment churned inside of him, yet he was also very aware of how crazy he must sound, throwing this at her out of nowhere. Carter continued to stare at them in shock and confusion.

There was no turning back now. Mitch set his jaw and met Katie's eyes. "Your grandma is disappointed in you, and would really like to see you make amends with Korie. Just admit what you did was wrong, and apologize for it. That's all."

"What do you know about my grandma?" Katie demanded in a hiss through clenched teeth, squinting through blazing eyes.

"I just... Heard her." Mitch suddenly felt sick, and wanted to crawl in a hole, especially as he realized they had attracted the curious gazes of onlooking students in the hallway. He gripped his crutches and began walking, leaving the two behind; Carter staring dumbfounded as his gaze darted between his two friends, and Katie seething with anger and violation, clenching and unclenching her fists at her sides.

"You *what?*" she balked, and he paused, glancing at her over his shoulder. She threw her hands up, taking a step back. "You know what? Never mind. Whatever you just did?" she tapped her skull, squinting angrily at him. "Not cool, Mitch. So not cool." And she stormed past him down the hall, parting the sea of students on her way.

Mitch swallowed hard as he watched her go. His first day back was not off to a great start. "Dude," Carter said quietly, jolting Mitch back and away from his fleeing girlfriend. "What... What was that?"

Mitch shook his head as he grasped his crutches and began walking again. People were still staring at him, causing his skin to prickle. He shot angry glares at the onlookers and barked, "What are you lookin' at?" causing them to quickly redirect their focus and return to their lockers or chatting amongst themselves.

"Mitch?" Carter asked carefully as he towed closely behind.

"Look," Mitch spoke, a little more harshly than he meant to, as he stopped abruptly, nearly causing his friend to crash into him. Carter backed up a step with wide eyes. Mitch sighed, averting his eyes to the wall. "I don't know what's going on with me. Just forget it, okay?" He finally turned his head back to meet Carter's questioning brown eyes.

He nodded, though his burly shoulders hadn't dropped their tension. "Okay," he said quietly. "Whatever, man..."

And without another word, they continued their walk to their respective classrooms.

MITCH BREATHED A sigh of relief at the end of the day when he finally made it to his locker. He survived, and while he constantly heard the background chatter of voices, none of them tried to come to the forefront and demand his attention. He concealed himself with his locker door, practically crawling inside to hide from the world, as he loaded his books into his bag, which was a challenging feat with his crutches and wavering sense of balance. Once packed, he closed his locker door, and practically jumped out of his skin as his dark green letter jacket came flying into his face.

"What the—"

"We're *done*, Mitch Griffin," the furious blonde barked through an angry snarl. All Mitch could do was stare, limply clutching his jacket, as she fumed at him. "What you did to me earlier, that was *totally* fucked up! That stuff was *personal*. You have no business getting in my head, and I don't want to be around you if you're gonna be doing... fucking... *voodoo* shit like that!"

Mitch finally found his voice. "I wasn't in your head..." he started, but she cut back in, pointing a finger at him.

"My grandma is *dead*, so however you knew that..." She threw her hands up, shaking her head. "Whatever, I don't even know. But she never liked me anyway. Korie was her favorite. So all that shit you said was lies. And... And you were in my head! That's *fucked up,* Mitch! Stay out! And don't get near me anymore!"

And at that, she spun and stormed out of sight, leaving him in her dust staring numbly down the hall.

"That was harsh, man..."

Mitch jolted again at Carter's unexpected presence. He turned to face his friend. Or, at least he hoped they were still friends. "What, you feeling brave enough to be near me? What if I do voodoo shit to you, too?" He scowled as he stuffed his letter jacket back in his locker, then worked his backpack onto his shoulders, first one arm while the other clutched a crutch, then switching to the other.

"Hey, man, I don't understand what's going on or whatever, but I'm still your bro." Carter shrugged, though he looked somewhat nervous. "I'm here for ya. And... I dunno, man, I dunno if you were in her head or whatever, but you kinda made it sound like her dead grandma was talkin' to ya or somethin'..."

Mitch continued to scowl, avoiding eye contact. He wanted desperately to run and hide. Unfortunately, it'd be awhile before he'd ever be able to do much running.

"So, like, I guess accidents can mess ya up and stuff," Carter continued, sounding more hesitant as he stumbled through his words. "But, like, if you're hearing voices or whatever, I dunno if that's what's going on or not, but if you are, they make medication for that. Maybe you could ask your doctor about it, or something?"

Mitch continued to avoid his eyes, though his words struck a chord with him. There *was* medication out there... would it work to suppress these voices? He almost relaxed at the idea of freedom...

"He doesn't need medication," came Genevieve's stern voice from behind Carter. Both boys turned to face the tall brunette, standing firmly with her arms folded over her chest and her sharp features set in determination.

"It was just a suggestion," Carter explained, but Genevieve waved him off.

"Whatever," she barked. "Just be a good friend. He's been through a lot, okay? Now beat it."

She pursed her lips and glared threateningly at him, until

finally he backed down, glanced at Mitch, shot him a quick, "Later, Dude," and left.

"Let's get out of here," Mitch mumbled, eager to get to his sister's car and, better yet, home. Genevieve nodded, and together they silently left the building without further interruption.

As soon as Mitch and Genevieve were safely within her car, she turned abruptly to face her brother and said, "You have got to find a way to control those voices, or at least try to ignore them." She eyed him sternly.

Mitch shook his head, frowning. "I can't," he replied. "It doesn't work like that. They keep getting louder and louder until I feel like I have no choice but to answer them. I don't know how to explain it."

Genevieve sighed. "People are talking, Mitch. You attracted a lot of attention in the hallway with Katie. I think people are wondering if you're crazy..." She cast Mitch a sympathetic gaze. "Craig Fitzgerald asked me if you're right in the head..."

He sat silently, feeling a sense of hopelessness wash over him. Just when he thought his life couldn't get any worse, it continued to crash and burn. "What did you tell him?" he muttered.

Genevieve shrugged. "I told him you've been through a lot and you're still dealing with it. And to fuck off or I'd rearrange his nuts."

Mitch snorted. It was probably the first time he'd shown any sort of amusement since his accident. Ever since their father died, Genevieve had developed a fierceness he'd never known someone in such a small frame could possess. She had a sense of control and dominance about her that was as striking as the blow of her volleyball spike, and could be just as damaging if on the receiving end of it. He admired her strength in the face of tragedy. His mother had become a recluse after her husband's death, distant and uninvolved, and Mitch... He sighed, looking out the window and reflecting. He'd turned into a complete asshole, belittling and degrading those who weren't in his "social class" to gain what he thought to be power and respect.

How did Genevieve, who was only eleven years old at the time their father died, turn out to be the only one in their family who pulled through with any kind of strength?

He thought of Katie sabotaging her sister's success, and, despite the pain of rejection, he realized he was better off without her. He brought his eyes up to meet his sister's. "Thanks, Gen." His words were genuine and heartfelt, a rare thing coming from him.

She smiled, appreciating the uncommon sincerity. "That's what family's for," she replied softly.

Mitch hung his head as he sank back into his seat, his heart suddenly feeling heavy. "How are you the only one of us that came out ahead after Dad died?" he spoke in an almost whisper, looking down at his knees.

Genevieve sighed sadly as she turned her key in the ignition. The car rumbled to life, and she shifted to back out of her parking spot. "I cry a lot," she replied simply, making her way slowly out of the lot. She shot him a glance. "You should try it sometime. It's not good to keep all that bottled inside."

Mitch huffed. "I don't need to cry," he grumbled. "All that's gonna do is make me feel like a pussy."

Genevieve rolled her eyes. "First of all, if you want to use genitals as insults, it's 'testicle', not 'pussy', because nuts are way the hell weaker if you think about putting them through what a pussy can handle. And second, what are you saying about me?"

He turned his head to meet her eyes as she briefly glanced at him, before returning her focus to the flow of traffic exiting the parking lot. She was anything but weak. He admired her strength and ferocity and take-no-shit attitude. He had the attitude, too, alright. Except his attitude just made him a complete dick, and he knew it. "No," he responded. "You're not."

"Not what?" she shot back.

He allowed a smirk to break his darkened features. "A testicle."

She threw him a quick nod. "Damn straight." She turned the steering wheel sharply as she drove out into the street and began their trek home. "So. Crying. You should try it."

Mitch stared out the window as they drew farther away from the school, his smirk vanishing. "No," he responded curtly, and closed the subject.

CHAPTER 19

❝ DID YOU hear what happened to Mitch yesterday?"

Emily eagerly asked Lessie as she approached her at her locker the next morning.

Lessie pursed her lips as she gathered her books for first period Spanish. She had heard the rumors traveling, but hadn't caught any details. "Not really, but I know Katie dumped him," she replied, closing her locker door and giving the lock a spin. She turned her head to meet her friend's wide blue eyes. "Why...?"

"I finally got the details this morning. He apparently called Katie out on something there's no way anyone could know about," Emily answered excitedly, bouncing on her heels.

"So?" Lessie asked, tilting her head to the side. She began making her way to her next class with Emily walking closely at her side.

"*So,*" she continued, her voice growing more animated, and she hopped in front of Lessie, stopping her in her tracks and facing her straight-on. "I've read in numerous places that people who have near-death experiences often come back with some sort of enhanced psychic ability." She lifted her hand excitedly and touched a finger to her head. "Like the NDE triggers something in their brains and then they can see auras or they're clairvoyant, or, possibly in Mitch's case, clairaudient."

Lessie squinted at her incredulously, her heart suddenly picking up its tempo. "So, are you saying...?"

Emily looked fit to burst as she grinned and nodded her head vigorously. She struggled to keep her voice down. "I think Mitch might be a medium!"

Lessie swallowed hard against her tightening stomach, then, after a short stunned pause, pushed past her friend. Her heart pounded harder as goosebumps prickled her arms and spine. "I don't know if I can handle that right now..."

Emily's face fell as she watched Lessie walk a few steps, then jumped to catch up to her. "What do you mean, 'handle that right now'?"

"I mean, I feel like it took me long enough to get over what happened in the first place. Now you're telling me I gave him psychic powers?" Lessie pressed her lips together as she made eye contact with her friend, whose face was much less animated after Lessie's reaction.

"Well..." Emily replied, her voice trailing off. "I wasn't really thinking of it like that..."

"Of course not," Lessie grumbled, suddenly feeling agitated.

Emily's features fell in momentary hurt before she drew herself together. "Sorry, you know I think all this is really... fascinating..." she said in a hushed tone.

Lessie sighed audibly. "I know. But this isn't some sort of science project or sci-fi movie." She stopped and turned to face her friend outside her classroom door. "This is real life. *My* life. And now I feel like I fucked up someone else's." She glared into her friend's pained eyes, hating how much her anger had risen, but unable to suppress it. She let her shoulders fall, exhaling heavily as her face softened. "Sorry." She shook her head, then added, "See you in art." Without waiting for a response, Lessie turned and entered the Spanish classroom.

As she sank into her seat, her thoughts remained on Mitch. She couldn't help but feel responsible for his situation, his misery, despite his desperation to live...

"Hey, man, I have a solution," Carter announced with a grin as he approached Mitch at his locker. Mitch had welcomed the weekend with eagerness after his first three days back. But Monday had come too quickly, and with it came his nerves all over again. Surviving the remainder of the school year was becoming a very daunting concept.

Mitch arched a brow and frowned. "A solution to what?"

"You need a date for the Valentine's dance this Friday night!" Carter grinned wider.

Mitch shook his head as he shut his locker door with a clang. "I wasn't planning on going to that," he responded sullenly. He slung his backpack over his right shoulder and gripped his crutch under his left. More and more his confidence and stability grew on just one crutch, and with that came a sense of freedom.

Carter's face fell slightly. "Come on, man, you can't let this control your life! You still need to get out and have fun!"

"Limping around while all my friends are dancing doesn't sound like fun," he muttered under his breath.

Carter shook his head, ignoring him. "Look, Presley Stevens, that cute redhead cheerleader? She's had a crush on you for a while. I told her I'd pull some strings and maybe you could go together!" He grinned proudly.

Mitch glowered at him, clenching his teeth. "You what?"

Again, Carter's face fell. "What? She's cute, kinda shy, but you two will totally have a great time!"

Mitch shook his head vigorously as he stared at his friend, his eyes flashing. "What the hell, man? You could have asked me first before telling her you'd 'pull some strings.' Now I feel like I *have* to go! And seriously, I wasn't planning on it!" He pushed past his friend and began his trek to class.

"S-sorry, man, I was just tryin' to help," Carter stammered as he began trailing behind Mitch.

Mitch ignored him as he pressed on and, as fate would have it, he passed a group of junior girls gossipping amongst themselves, one of whom was Presley Stevens.

She caught Mitch's eye and tucked a strand of her coppery hair behind her ear, her freckled face beginning to redden. He sighed internally and thought, *What the hell,* and stopped at the group of girls. A silence fell over them as they all turned to stare at him, but he held Presley's gaze.

"Presley, right?" he spoke with an undertone of authority.

"Y-yeah," she replied sheepishly, her face growing a darker shade of red as she tucked her hair again.

He shrugged nonchalantly as he said, "Wanna go to the dance with me this Friday?"

Her eyes nearly popped out of her head as the girls around her struggled to suppress their squeals. "O-oh my God, *yeah! Yes,* I-I'll go with you!" she stammered, nodding, her face so red her freckles nearly disappeared.

"Cool," Mitch replied, flashing her a casual smile. He retrieved his phone from his jeans pocket, exchanged numbers with her, smiled casually once more, and continued making his way toward his class. He could hear the eruption of squeals amongst the girls from all the way down the hall, and he couldn't help but smile to himself. *Oh yeah, I still got it,* he thought smugly, his confidence boosted. It was just what he needed. Maybe he shouldn't have been so hard on Carter... He stole a quick glance at his friend, who also wore a smug grin, and he shook his head. *Nah.*

LESSIE STARED ABSENTLY at the empty chair across the table, her dinner untouched and forgotten on her plate.

"What's eatin' ya, kiddo?" Sam asked carefully, eyeing her from his seat.

Lessie sighed as she glanced down at her steak. "Just miss Nana, I guess. Wish I could ask her what to do, or how to take any of this."

"What happened?" Lynne questioned, her face falling in concern.

Lessie pressed her lips together as her thoughts replayed her day. She prodded a piece of broccoli to the edge of her plate. "Mitch came back to school yesterday."

Lynne and Sam exchanged a glance. "How is he?" Lynne asked cautiously.

Lessie shook her head. "I just wonder if I did the right thing."

Nodding thoughtfully, Lynne replied, "I guess, if it weren't meant to happen, it wouldn't have worked. Have you talked to him at all?"

Lessie scoffed. "Yeah right. I don't think he remembers anything, and he's always been so *mean* to me. I don't think that'll change."

"His dad died not long ago, right?" Lynne questioned.

Lessie nodded.

"And I suppose he can't play football anymore..."

Lessie sighed, sinking into her chair. She felt partly responsible for his mess.

Lynne studied her daughter's expression, then said, "Sometimes, the death of a dream can be even more difficult than the death of a loved one." Lessie squinted as she lifted her head to meet her mother's eyes. Lynne took a breath, then continued. "It's a lonely grief. You go through the same stages of loss, but people understand your pain when you've lost a loved one. You have support, and comfort. When a dream dies, it's as though part of *yourself* died, because that dream was part of you. Yet, people don't understand why you can't just move on, or look on the bright side." She shook her head sadly. "It's not that simple."

Lessie, still squinting, said in a quiet voice, "Why are you telling me this?"

Lynne held her eyes. "Because he's probably not going to be any nicer to you, if bullying is his outlet for grief." Her eyes filled with sadness. "Just remember the battle he's probably fighting, and try to be patient."

Lessie frowned at her forgotten dinner. Perhaps she really did make a big mistake...

CHAPTER 20

FRIDAY AFTERNOON arrived with an early dismissal, and as soon as Mitch and Genevieve were home, he began rifling through his closet for his formal shirts, slacks, and dress shoes. He immediately slid his prosthetic foot into the left shoe, sighing with relief that it seemed to fit without any trouble. He willed himself to relax and enjoy the evening. He had even agreed to pick Presley up himself, arranging to drive his mom's SUV. He had been released to drive the week before he returned to school, but preferred to avoid it when he could, as being behind the wheel surfaced too many triggers for his unstable emotions. But, he'd be damned if he let that get in his way that evening.

"How do I look?" his sister asked as soon as he left his room. She twirled in her red dress that perfectly accentuated the few curves her narrow body had to offer. She tugged a large dark gray flannel shawl around her shoulders, its fringes hanging around the hem of her dress and trailing down to her classy black boots. Her dark hair was pinned back loosely, half up and half down, and her mascara enhanced the sparkle in her dark brown eyes.

Mitch pursed his lips. "If I see Henry groping on you, I'll beat his ass."

She responded with a grin. "You look pretty handsome yourself."

"Thanks," he answered, brushing off the compliment as he turned to his mother.

The heavyset woman was curled up on the couch under a quilt, her focus consumed by the TV series she had been watching constantly since she got home from work. Her dark hair fell limply at her shoulders, the many silver strands glinting in the lamplight.

''Where are your keys, Mom?" Mitch asked, his voice carrying over the TV.

"On my nightstand," she replied absently. Her eyes never left the screen.

Mitch sighed, shaking his head, and gripped his crutch as he made his way to her room.

He searched out the switch on her lamp in the darkened room, then scanned the cluttered mess on her nightstand until finally he spotted her keys. He stopped, his arm suspended in the air, as his eyes fell to the corner of the room.

There, on the floor leaning against the wall, was an old steering wheel. Its grips were worn but the Jeep emblem in the center was clear and polished. Just like he had left it.

He felt his stomach lurch as the room spun out of control. He squeezed his eyes shut tight as he was swept into the undercurrent of anger and hurt and regret and hatred, which all bubbled up inside of him like the bile that had made its way to his throat. In a fit of rage, he snatched the car keys off the small table and stormed out of her room.

He stopped in front of his mother, blocking her view of the TV, and glared at her. "What the fuck," he growled.

A look of surprise and concern traveled across Ruth's formerly vacant face as she met his angry eyes. "What's wrong?" she asked quietly, her voice hesitant.

"Why did you keep that thing?" he shouted, his body beginning to shake from anger.

"Mitch, I don't know what—"

"The steering wheel, goddammit!" His nostrils flared as he swung his arm out violently to point in the direction of her room. His voice continued to rise. "Why would you keep it? Why would you want to keep something that would constantly remind me of the day that fucking *ruined* my *life*?"

Ruth hadn't flinched, hadn't shown any sign of being affected by his outburst. Genevieve held her breath at the far edge of the room, her eyes wide and shining. Mitch's whole body shook and his chest heaved against his strong inhales and exhales, as he glared daggers at his mother.

She finally sighed, looking down at the floor. "That was your dad's jeep, too, you know," she replied in a voice so low they could barely hear her. Genevieve bit her lip as Mitch's face softened, though his shoulders and back remained rigid. "His hands were on that wheel, too." She looked up to meet Mitch's green eyes, which were beginning to carry a glimmer of regret. Her own eyes were laced with sorrow. "We had our first date in that jeep, drove away after our wedding in that jeep." She looked down at the floor again. "I drove him to the hospital in that jeep," she finished in a whisper.

Mitch swallowed hard. All he could do was stare at her. His

heart suddenly felt like a lead weight. Genevieve drew her lips together as she continued watching the exchange at the edge of the room. Mitch let out a shaky exhale, his sudden regret gripping him as fiercely as his hatred toward the object that offered their mother one of the only connections she had to their father. Ruth's life had ended when the doctor approached her, guilt and grief etched across his face, to tell her that her husband faced some complications during the surgery and didn't make it. Her life ended with the loss of her partner, similarly to how Mitch's ended at the loss of his leg.

It had been four years, nearly five, that Micah had been gone, and Ruth had gradually withered away as she was sucked into the abyss of depression. She lost her will to live, and had lost touch with her own children as well, when they needed her the most. Mitch suddenly felt a wave of disappointment ebb through him. He opened his mouth to release his anger, to yell and fight and make sure she understood how she had failed all of them. But he stopped himself as something in her dim eyes broke him. She lost part of her world. Of that pain, he was no stranger. Would he allow himself to just wither away, too?

He swallowed hard again, clutching his mother's car key in his fist. He had a date to pick up, and a dance to get to. A life to live. "Sorry," he muttered. She didn't react, her eyes simply drifted back to the TV screen as soon as he stepped out of her way.

"You kids have fun tonight," she said half-heartedly, her eyes not leaving her show.

Mitch met his sister's wet eyes as he made his way to join her at the front door, and together, they left the house with heavy hearts.

Henry had arrived, pulling up to the curb, and Genevieve

pulled herself together, smiling and waving before she turned and met her brother's eyes once more. She pulled him into a tight embrace. "Have fun, okay?" she whispered at his neck.

Mitch gave her a squeeze around the waist. "Be careful," he replied, and after one last encouraging smile, they parted ways.

LESSIE WAS WRAPPED in Adam's arms as soon as they entered the dance floor. The gym was decked in red streamers, glittering hearts, and pink confetti, which enhanced the air of cheesy teenage love. "Have I told you how beautiful you look?" Adam whispered as he wrapped his hands around Lessie's waist, smiling down at her.

He always managed to release the butterflies in her stomach, and once again they took wing as she felt heat rise to her face. "Only, like, seven times so far," she kidded, grinning in return. She had found the light blue dress several weeks before on a shopping date with Emily and had fallen in love with it immediately. It brought out the crystal blue of her eyes, which shined as she gazed at her boyfriend with admiration.

Emily and Evan joined them to dance as an upbeat hip-hop song filled the gymnasium, but Lessie was immediately distracted as she caught sight of Mitch entering the gym on his crutch with a redheaded cheerleader on his right arm. For once since he'd been back at school, he looked somewhat relaxed, or maybe even happy. She couldn't help but smile as she moved to the music, redirecting her focus back on Adam, who was laughing at something Emily said and following the rhythm with them.

Once the song was over, the four made their way to the snack table, which was laden with finger foods and Valentine candies. Lessie picked a few white chocolate dipped pretzels, but before one made its way into her mouth, Emily was nudging her in the ribs. Lessie looked up to question her friend, and followed Emily's nod towards the other side of the gym.

Lessie froze upon seeing Mitch looking rather uncomfortable, struggling almost, as he spoke with a wide-eyed teacher. His date shifted awkwardly next to him as he spoke, and several others stopped what they were doing to listen in. Lessie and Emily continued to watch the scene unfold: Mitch speaking, Mrs. Perkins shaking her head as her wide eyes began to shine, students stopping to eavesdrop, until finally Mitch stopped, looking around nervously, and Mrs. Perkins took his hand and said something that looked like "Thank you." Mitch gave a quick nod, then left as swiftly as his crutch would allow him to. His date followed quickly behind.

"Mitch! Wait!" Presley shouted as she ran to catch up with him. Before they knew it, Mitch was at the snack table, which was near the exit, and Lessie and Emily continued to silently observe, as did the rest of the students nearby.

He stopped and turned to face her. "I'm sorry," he spoke.

"Mitch, it's fine!" Presley replied. "I don't think you're crazy!"

He shook his head as his eyes flashed. "Everyone thinks I'm crazy." He snapped his head towards an onlooking student. "You! I bet you think I'm crazy!" he barked angrily, and the student quickly shuffled, averting his eyes and rushing back out to the dance floor.

"Mitch..." Presley warned, reaching to take his arm, but he jerked away.

"What are you looking at?" he shouted at another student, who backed away slowly, still eyeing Mitch with uncertainty.

Presley grasped Mitch's arm. "Come on, we should go," she

commanded, and tugged him toward the exit. He finally obliged, and they were gone.

The remaining students were stunned into silence, and the music suddenly felt distant. "Whoa..." Emily breathed.

''What do you think's wrong with him?" Evan questioned.

Emily shook her head. "I don't think anything is wrong with him," she replied.

"He thinks he's talking to dead people," Adam cut in, squinting his eyes and folding his arms over his chest. "So yeah, *something* is wrong."

"You don't believe that's what he's actually doing?" Lessie questioned, glancing toward her boyfriend.

He shrugged, meeting her eyes. "No. He's hearing voices or something. Things like that can happen after a bad accident. It messes with your head."

Lessie narrowed her eyes. "Do you believe it's possible at all?"

Adam pursed his lips. "Nah," he answered. "It's just a glitch in the brain or something. I don't believe any of that hocus pocus stuff."

Lessie's face fell as her heart sank. "Oh."

CHAPTER 21

LESSIE SLAMMED her locker door shut after fourth period P.E. Monday afternoon, where she had to watch Mitch sit the class out once again. Their schedule had changed for second semester, and, as if by some sick twist of fate, she no longer had History with Mitch, but instead P.E. As if staring at the back of his head first semester while she had a raging crush on him wasn't bad enough, she now had to watch him sit in the sidelines during the one thing he loved most and used to be *good* at — sports and physical activity — as he tried to obey his doctor's orders while he healed. It was like the Universe was rubbing it in her face that she'd ruined his life.

She was ready to meet up with Emily, Evan, and Adam for lunch and try to get her mind off of Mitch. Emily arrived just as Lessie was giving her combination lock a spin, looking as though she had something to say, but struggling to hold it in.

"What?" Lessie questioned, cocking her head to the side as she eyed Emily curiously.

She sighed. "I just keep hearing all these rumors about Mitch. It's crazy!" She cast Lessie a sympathetic gaze. "I know you don't want to talk about it, though."

"Not really." She initiated the walk to the cafeteria, and Emily slowly turned to join her.

"So, have you been called lately?" she asked, attempting to change the subject. "Ya know, since we're on the topic of strange abilities."

Lessie grimaced slightly, then shook her head. "Not at school. I did a couple nights ago, car accident, which is pretty usual, but during the school day I've been more or less left alone."

And suddenly, Lessie stopped in her tracks, her jaw going slack and her eyes shifting out of focus.

Emily couldn't help but laugh, rolling her eyes. "Nice timing, Les." Lessie stood stone-still in the hallway as Emily waited for her, leaning against the lockers with her arms folded over her chest and watching as the rest of the students in the hall made their way to the cafeteria, shooting curious glances in Lessie's direction, and then quickly scuttling away with averted eyes after being shot a threatening look from Emily.

And then there came the steady click of rubber-footed metal against tile approaching the two girls. Emily stood straighter, silently begging Lessie to come back, but she was still vacant, and Mitch only drew nearer. Emily braced herself to fight, unsure of what to expect, knowing that if Mitch was anything like his old self, it wasn't going to be pretty. She set her jaw and waited.

Squeak, click, squeak, click. Suddenly, Mitch paused, staring at Lessie momentarily, as though processing a thought, then shifted his gaze to meet Emily's guarded eyes, squinting. She blinked nervously. *Did* he remember something?

She was about to bark at him, tell him to leave, when suddenly, Lessie came back.

She blinked a few times, cleared her throat as she regained

composure, and went rigid as she met Mitch's eyes. He squinted under furrowed brows, but before he could say anything, *if* he was going to say anything, Emily finally found her voice. "What are you lookin' at?" Her tone was dangerous. Mitch's uncertainty quickly shifted to anger as his shoulders stiffened in defense. "Well?" she barked again. "You know full well what it's like to feel like a freak! Fuck off!" Her face was set in an angry snarl.

Mitch finally clutched his crutch tighter and took a few steps before eventually breaking eye contact, shaking his head and scowling, and wordlessly made his way to lunch.

Lessie exhaled heavily, not realizing she was even holding her breath. "What was that...?" she whispered.

Emily shook her head. "I don't know..."

MITCH DRUMMED HIS pen against his notebook in his fifth period anatomy class, his mind consumed with thoughts of Lessie. Something about the way she had looked, spaced out. He'd never really noticed it before. It was almost as though she were ... *gone...*

And not only that, but immediately upon laying eyes on her in her "spaced out" state, something triggered in his head. A bright light, a desperation, a feeling of being torn in two separate directions; yet he couldn't make sense of any of it.

Seeing her like that made him feel as though he were waking up from a very intense, very vivid dream. One he couldn't shake, knowing it had some sort of meaning and significance in his life, yet he was unable to determine *what.*

The feeling followed him like a dark shadow the remainder of the week and, gradually, dreams began making their way into his slumber, jolting him awake in a cold sweat on numerous occasions in the middle of the night. A gripping fear, a sense of losing control, and darkness, immediately followed by light. A silence that was strangely comforting, but then a new sense of determination broke the silence, driving him to fight. But for what, he didn't know.

His dreams were broken, almost as if pieces of the story were missing, but every night was the same — the fear, the darkness, the silence, and then suddenly, an impossibly bright light, and warmth and love and joy, all of which he felt a vehement objection to. Something that should have been so welcoming was found to be the complete opposite as he fought to stay away from it, *begged* to not go. He felt powerless, terrified, and desperately incomplete. He wanted to scream.

Sometimes he did, jarring his sister awake, who would burst into his room panting, eyes wide with fear.

"Mitch?" she would gasp, chest heaving, looking completely disheveled.

"Just a nightmare," Mitch would choke in response, sweat beaded on his brow. And then, after collecting themselves and willing their nerves to calm, they would each return to bed.

Every night the same dream. Yet he had no idea what it meant. Nevertheless, he had the sinking suspicion it had to do with his accident.

Nearly a week and a half after catching sight of Lessie spaced out in the hallway, guarded by her friend, he encountered it again.

The same thing, only this time it was before third period, as the halls grew empty while the students thinned out in their respective directions. She stood motionless at her locker, staring blankly ahead, shoulders slumped and jaw slack. Completely alone. The same vision was triggered, or was it a memory? The bright light, the despair... She had something to do with it, and he was suddenly overcome with an insatiable need to find out what it meant. His heart hammered. Turbulent emotions roiled within him — fear, confusion, but mostly, anger, which had only been building since he returned to school. Constant memories of his old life, his *good* life, stared him in the face, taunting him and viciously reminding him that he would never get that part of him back. He gripped his single crutch tightly, grateful that his strength had continued to improve as his movement was becoming more fluid, and took a few steps toward her.

And waited.

CHAPTER 22

❝ WHERE DO you go?" Mitch demanded in a low voice, his eyes narrowed.

Lessie jolted with a gasp upon meeting Mitch's eyes as soon as she returned to her physical body. She swallowed hard as her skin prickled. Her eyes darted around the empty hallway before landing on Mitch once more. He was inches away from her, breathing through his flared nostrils, his face set with urgency. He leaned on his crutch, though Lessie could see his confidence had returned as his strength improved.

She realized it would be pointless to argue. It was the moment she'd been dreading, yet was eager to face and get it over with. Their paths had crossed and, whether they liked it or not, were intertwined. "I already told you," she answered in a quiet voice, her eyes locked on his.

He faltered. Her words triggered that same feeling inside of him — the bright light, a sense of desperation, a need... But he couldn't quite place anything else, or sort through his mixed emotions. He clenched his jaw, but remained silent.

Lessie stood strong, taking a steadying breath. "You don't remember, do you?"

He faltered again, then reset his face, his muscles rippling at his jaws. A foreign sense of nausea turned in his stomach.

"You died," she whispered, keeping her face and voice even. "But you... Didn't want to..."

No. He didn't want to hear the rest of it; he didn't want to believe any of it was true. "Fuck you..." he hissed from the back of his throat through clenched teeth.

Lessie licked her lips, her eyes still locked on his. She remembered her conversation with her mother — to be patient with him as he dealt with his grief. She thought of his strange new ability, his life, which had been turned upside-down, and his struggle to make sense of it all. And he had to do it alone. She drew in her lips. He was different, "gifted," just like her. And she suddenly felt overcome with the realization that she *wanted* him to know her secret. That she wanted him to remember. "I cross people over, Mitch. That's where I go." She held his gaze. "You died when you wrecked your jeep, and I got called to cross you over, but you—"

Anger came to a slow boil as he took in her words. "Bullshit!" he spat, his eyes flashing, and she recoiled slightly. "You expect me to believe that?"

Silence echoed in the empty hall, until finally, Lessie's own eyes narrowed. "I know you do."

His eyes flashed again as her words stabbed his turning stomach. His anger gripped him, clawing at him for release. Nothing made sense anymore, nothing was as he thought it was; but he knew she was right. He believed her. And that brought his anger to a full rolling boil. "I *should have* died," he responded in a low growl, unwilling to be overheard yet wanting to shout at her, scream at her, spill out all of his anger and despair and hatred for his life right there in front of her, tear her down until there was nothing left because this was *her fault*. He was shaking, teeth clenched, face turning red, but still his voice remained low. Frighteningly low. "This is no life." He gestured with his free arm to his crutch, and to the lower part of his leg, where his prosthesis was holding him up, tucked securely under his jeans. "I'm worse than dead. I'm alive, with *nothing* to live for."

He glared at her, his anger almost palpable as she backed into the lockers, her eyes wide as her heart broke. She wanted to cry, to run; but she was afraid to move, and almost felt as though she couldn't even if she tried. So she stared at him, with shining eyes, his fierce gaze locked on hers.

He squeezed his eyes shut momentarily as another vision surfaced in his mind. Lessie's face, which hadn't been there before, not even in his dreams, watching him desperately as he felt himself moving toward the light. She moved toward him with determination and outstretched arms, and the memory faded. His eyes popped open, his glare venomous, flashing with a hatred so palpable that it nearly slammed against her as she pressed hard against the lockers, her breath catching in her constricted chest. Her heart began to race. They were still alone in the hall, and she desperately hoped for someone to turn the corner and save her.

"This is all your fault," he spat through a snarl, leaning in so close she could feel his hot breath on her face as the back of her head bumped against the metal door. His words seared through her heart, and if she weren't so afraid of him at that moment, they would have broken her.

"Get away from her!"

Lessie exhaled in relief at the familiar voice, turning her head to see Adam approaching with a piercing, threatening glare. Mitch backed up slightly, standing straighter.

Once Adam was within arm's length of Mitch, he grasped his shoulder and gave him a quick shove back, causing Mitch to stumble slightly with wide eyes. Adam glared daggers at Mitch, using Mitch's handicap and his own height to his advantage as he towered menacingly over him. "Haven't you made her life hard enough?" Adam demanded, and Mitch's shocked expression quickly turned back to anger.

Oh, I believe it's the other way around... He ground his teeth in his clenched jaws as he fought the urge to say his thoughts out loud. "Go to hell," he muttered instead.

Adam leaned in closer to Mitch, pressing an angry finger into his chest. "I see you giving her a hard time again and I'll personally make sure *this*," he gave Mitch's crutch a tap with his foot that was just hard enough for it to slip slightly, briefly causing Lessie and Mitch both to wonder if he was actually going to knock it out from under him, "is the least of your problems," he finished, his glare remaining locked on Mitch's wide eyes.

Mitch leaned in toward Adam, trying to make himself taller, though Adam still had a good five inches over him. He narrowed his eyes, still clenching his jaws. Lessie cut him off as he opened his mouth to speak.

"Stop it!" she burst, stepping forward from the lockers. "Both of you just *stop it!*"

Their eyes remained locked as they backed down slightly. Mitch opened his mouth again to speak, but Adam cut him off, bringing his finger back up to him again. "Don't try me, Gimpy," he threatened, causing Mitch's jaw to fall open, though his eyes still burned with the same anger. Adam dropped his hand as he stood straighter, backing off from Mitch, but not removing his eyes from him.

"Adam!" Lessie gasped, her mouth agape.

Adam took her arm as though he didn't hear her. "C'mon," he said in a low voice, and after shooting a quick glance at Mitch, who stood angry and stunned, she walked down the hall with Adam, clutching her books in her arms.

"Thank you," she said quietly. "But you didn't have to call him that."

"Oh please!" Adam retorted in exasperation. "After all the times he's called you *Lester?*"

"I'm just saying, his life turned upside-down, you can't blame him for acting the way he is. Insulting someone based on a disability isn't exactly... nice..." She chewed her lower lip.

Adam groaned. "I can't believe you're sticking up for that dickweed."

She glanced at him quickly, then averted her eyes. "Sorry," she muttered. "Thank you for sticking up for me." After a quiet pause, she said, "Why aren't you in class?"

"It's English," he replied, eyeing her with confusion, as though she should have known the answer to that question. "We always walk together, remember? You never showed up. I was about to go without you then thought... you know... your thing happened. So I went to look for you."

She felt a pang in her heart at his kind gesture. It was moments like those that swelled her heart and rekindled her love for him.

"What were you doing with him, anyway?" he asked before she could thank him.

She sighed. "My 'thing' happened." She shook her head. "He was there when I came back."

"Why? What did he say to you?"

They stopped outside the classroom door as Adam eyed her with concern. "Just being his usual asshole self," she replied, then gave him a smile that didn't reach her eyes. "Thanks again," she added, then turned to duck into class, hoping not to draw too much attention to herself, leaving him alone in the hallway, confused and uncertain, before he finally entered the classroom as well.

HER RUN-IN WITH Mitch weighed heavily on Lessie's mind the rest of the day, so much so that she couldn't shake the burning need to make some sort of peace with him, as impossible as that might be. She moved against the flow of students making their way through the hallway at the end of the school day, her nerves tearing at her stomach, and fear gripping her heart. She approached Mitch with trepidation, questioning her every step, before pausing just feet away from where he stood at his locker, gathering his books. Lessie swallowed hard and gathered her courage.

"Mitch," she stated, standing at a careful distance. She could see him visibly tense at the sound of her voice, and watched as the muscles in his jaw flexed as he gritted his teeth. She took another steadying breath. "I-I'm sorry," she stated carefully. "About earlier."

Not moving, and still standing stiffly at his locker, Mitch squeezed his eyes shut. "I don't want to talk to you," he muttered, trying to maintain control of his emotions.

A heavy silence hung between them as Lessie tried to breathe against the pain in her heart. "You really don't remember anything?" she questioned softly, her voice strained.

"I have enough to deal with because of what happened,"

Mitch replied through gritted teeth. "Why would I want to remember it?"

"I didn't mean that," Lessie replied. "I meant... The Other Side... The light... You don't remember?"

Mitch took a deep breath and didn't bother to suppress the annoyance etched across his face. He opened his mouth to speak, to spew off more angry words at the girl who ruined his life, and Lessie tensed, sensing it coming, again sparking the question in her as to whether she made a huge mistake. Who was she to play God? Maybe he really was meant to die, and it was all a test that she failed miserably...

Before the words could leave his mouth, Mitch suddenly went rigid, clutching his crutch with a white-knuckled grip, bringing the heel of his right hand to press firmly against the middle of his forehead. He grimaced for a moment before finally regaining composure and relaxing slightly. Taking a deep breath with softly closed eyes and an air of annoyed obligation, he spoke, "Nana?" as if confirming someone's name.

Lessie's senses were jolted as she stared at him with wide eyes. "W-what?" Her heart began to race.

Mitch sighed heavily. "She says you did the right thing," he stated gruffly, then grasped his crutch and pushed past her, hobbling as quickly as he could move down the hallway.

Lessie stood in stunned silence, reeling, before finally turning slowly, seeing his form disappearing around a corner. She pulled herself together and leapt to catch up with him.

"What was that?" she demanded as she approached him. He ignored her as he continued his brisk hobble. "Mitch!" she shouted, leaning in closer as she walked alongside him. "Answer me!"

He halted, turning to glare at her. Through clenched teeth,

and eyes locked on hers, he growled, "I *said* I don't want to *talk* to you."

Her own eyes narrowed as he broke eye contact and continued limping away on his crutch. She refused to back down, keeping up with him as he hobbled down the hall. "No, you're talking to me, damnit. What just happened?" She grasped his shoulder firmly.

He whirled on her this time, jerking his shoulder to throw off her hand, then leaned forward, causing her to recoil slightly as his nose came within inches of her face. His eyes blazed with fury. "What just *happened* is part of my new *fucked up life!*" he burst angrily. His nostrils flared as his glare cut her to her core. She swallowed hard against the pain. He waved his free hand at her. "*Everything* about my life is *fucked up*, Lester! All thanks to *you!*" He jabbed a finger into her shoulder, and she winced as she took a step back, eyes wide. "So back off, and get *out* of my *life!*"

They held each other's gaze for a moment longer, his eyes still blazing with hostility and hers still wide with shock, until finally he huffed through his nose and turned once more to leave. This time, she did not follow him.

"Les...?" she heard a hesitant voice behind her. Slowly, she turned to face her friend. Emily's face was contorted with concern and unease. "What was that?"

Lessie shook her head as she turned once more to watch Mitch disappear down the hall toward the exit, his crutch making a rhythmic *squeak, click, squeak, click.* Her heart panged with a jolt each time his crutch met the tile, until he finally hobbled out the door and vanished.

Without warning, almost surprising her, her chin began to

quiver as tears stung at her eyes. Shaking her head, she let the tears fall as her heart broke.

MITCH PAUSED ONCE he reached the open air outside the school building. He tensed, expecting Lessie to show up behind him, but she never came. He was alone. He hobbled on his crutch toward the parking lot in the direction of his sister's car.

"Mitch!" Genevieve called out from behind him. She ran to catch up. "You okay?" She eyed him with concern as she walked alongside him.

"No," he replied curtly.

"What happened?"

He shook his head. It barely made any sense to him that Lessie would have anything to do with his survival. Attempting to explain it to anyone else would be next to impossible. He threw the car door open, tossed his backpack into the back, and fell into the passenger's seat.

"Tell me what happened," Genevieve urged as she sat down behind the wheel, still studying him with concern.

"Let's just go home," he muttered.

"Does this have something to do with the voices?" she asked.

"I *said* let's go *home*." He scowled, facing forward.

"Because nothing's wrong with you, Mitch. I think you have a gift that could change people's lives, and—"

"*Take me home!*" he roared, finally shifting to face her with a menacing snarl.

She drew back slightly at his outburst, then pressed her lips together tightly, turning to the steering wheel. She silently put the key in the ignition. As they pulled out of the parking lot, she said in a soft voice, "I'm sorry. I just... Maybe there's a reason for all this."

"I don't want to talk about it," he muttered. She nodded, and they rode in silence back to their house.

CHAPTER 23

THE SEGMENT on public speaking. It was the part of the school year Lessie dreaded most, and her feelings only escalated as she fidgeted, waiting her turn to present her speech in her English 4 class. It was short, to the point, and something she hoped she could breeze through quickly without any cosmic interruptions.

She had already spoken to Mrs. Andrews beforehand. "If something happens... like, my thing happens... Just, ya know, move me out of the way so I don't have to stand in front of the class like an idiot."

The tall, thin brunette had smiled warmly from behind her purple glasses. "I'm sure you'll be fine, Miss Morrison."

Lessie listened to Adam present his speech. Not only was he brilliant in math, but he was incredibly talented with words; not to mention a stickler for proper grammar. The class gave their dry applause as he finished, and Lessie made fleeting eye-contact with him as he flashed her an encouraging smile. She was grateful to share the class with him — he always managed to boost her confidence.

She stood, notecards clutched in her trembling palms, stomach in knots, and prepared to make her way toward the front of the classroom.

The room suddenly faded with the rush of blood pounding in her ears, and she fought off a wave of panic as her fear was realized. She arrived with the familiar electric siphoning sound that closed with a *pop*, and suddenly realized she was falling, as though in slow motion, the air rushing past her face and whipping her hair. She faintly realized that they were in some sort of canyon before her awareness was brought to the screaming boy next to her. She lurched through the air to embrace him before they made impact with the advancing ground.

They were immediately engulfed in the white haze, and they stood, unscathed. "What's happening?" he asked in a shaky voice.

The light began to grow, radiating its warmth and brilliance, ready to take him Home. The sooner he left, the sooner she could get back to class. "You died, you're crossing over," she explained, trying to sound comforting.

He turned to her with pleading brown eyes, his chestnut hair encircling his head in thick waves. Her heart sank. She'd seen that expression before.

"I can't die," he spoke in a desperate voice. She felt her senses coming to a screeching halt. *Not again...*

She shook her head, angry defiance rising up in her chest. "You fell... It's your time..."

He grasped her forearm, his eyes growing more desperate as the spirits began to emerge from the light. "No, I'm not done yet! You *have* to take me back!"

She glanced from the spirits to the boy, torn with conflict. Could she bear the pain again that she had endured after saving Mitch? Was this boy truly meant to live? Was it her place to question him if he wanted to? What kind of gruesome sight would she be met with when she returned? She met his eyes once more, and was gripped by his fear and desperation. He wanted to live. She watched in anguish as he began to fade, just like Mitch had, and cried out, "Please! Take me back!"

No, not again...

"Please!"

She squeezed her eyes shut, her mind fighting to hold back, to let him cross over, but finally, her heart won. It was not her place to make the decision of life or death for this boy. Without further question, she relaxed and projected herself into the light.

The joy she felt was quite possibly even more powerful than the first time she experienced it. The light consumed her, filled her with immense indescribable love and purpose, and her elation overwhelmed her. She wanted to stay here — she *belonged* here. Never could she return, never again did she want to endure the pain and challenges of her restricting human form. Not after knowing this joy and fulfillment. How could this boy not want to be here? *Oh yeah, the boy.* The thought of him jolted her back to her mission. She could sense his desperation as her spirit faded at the veil. Reaching for his energy, and connecting with it, she pulled him back. With great effort, she forced herself to reconnect with her spirit. Her world went black.

"Lesley!" came a distant, familiar voice through the fog.

Lessie opened her eyes and groaned. It took her a moment to realize the greeting was directed at her. "It's Lessie." She was sitting in the gravel next to the boy's broken body with Stephanie — the same girl who had been there to save Mitch. She was already at work, the green glow illuminating the boy's chest. Lessie's throat tightened as her stomach turned. It was somewhat easier this time, perhaps because she didn't know him personally; but seeing the pool of blood under him, his lifeless eyes, his broken form and the unnatural angle of his legs was certainly *not* easier. She averted her eyes and glanced around, recognizing the landscape. She was somewhere in the Southwest, the red rocks and arid temperature becoming familiar to her since she had visited in her astral state several times already. She was at the bottom of a canyon, the orange and tan walls towering high above her, and the shade providing a welcome relief from the heat above.

"Right, I should have known that," Stephanie replied, bringing Lessie's attention back to the boy. Stephanie shook her head. "I just saw you, what, Thanksgiving? Usually I won't see the same Transcendent for another couple years. You have a quick turnaround!"

Lessie, not taken off-guard like the time before, began to mentally prepare her questions. "How many more of us are there?"

Stephanie smiled. "Quite a few. I wouldn't know how to put you in touch with any of them, if that's what you're asking. I haven't met any other Healers, either." She glanced up at Lessie. "That's what I'm called, by the way. A Healer." She scanned the boy's body after the green glow dissipated, and his eyes drifted shut. "This is an easy one. He died instantly, mostly from the shock of impact. But I cleared up the internal bleeding, and his heart is up and running again."

Lessie studied the boy, her thoughts traveling immediately to Mitch. "He's going to have a long road of recovery ahead of him..."

"Meh," Stephanie responded, shrugging. "He landed on his feet, his legs are broken pretty badly and his hips will be jacked up, but no spinal fractures or anything. Which is amazing. He's actually pretty lucky. Unlike that last guy!" She chuckled. "How's he doing, anyway?"

Lessie dropped her gaze, sighing. "He's recovering quickly, but emotionally... Not so good." She shook her head as she frowned. "I feel like I shouldn't have saved him." She shrugged her hands out to the side, looking questioningly at the boy on the ground. "Should I have even saved this guy?"

"Hey, now." Stephanie eyed her from under an arched brow. "If you weren't supposed to save them, then what good am I?"

Lessie considered her for a moment, letting her words soak in and ease her troubled mind as Stephanie smiled, her arms folded over her chest. And Nana *did* speak through Mitch that she did the right thing. She just wished she had more answers.

The boy took a labored breath. Stephanie eyed him, then nodded with approval. "Our work here is done." She lifted her focus back to Lessie. "Weigh your decision carefully before you go saving someone again, though."

The world vanished before Lessie could press her for more information.

"*Noooo! Aauugh!*" Pain ripped through her like a hot steel blade as her senses returned, and she dropped to her knees on the tiled floor as her world turned black.

Light filtered in through Lessie's closed eyelids, and she squeezed them tighter before attempting to open them against her pounding headache. *Where am I?* She allowed a groan to escape her throat, as though that could make her feel any better. Her whole body ached.

"Lessie?"

She felt a warm hand on her arm.

"Mmm..." she groaned again. "Adam?" She managed to slowly blink her eyes open, but her vision was too blurred to make anything out. "Where am I?" she croaked.

"The hospital," he said hesitantly.

"What?" She grimaced, blinking again, wishing her vision would clear. She wracked her brain for her last memory. Why would she be in a hospital? *Ugh, my head...* She brought her hand to her forehead, realizing her arm ached terribly as she did so, not to mention the IV connected to the inside of her elbow. Everything ached. She almost felt the same way she did after she returned from saving Mitch, only worse...

Her eyes popped open as her memory flooded back. The desert rocks, the boy in the canyon, his pleading desperation to live. *Ugh...* she moaned internally against another throb of her headache. She had no idea she'd react *this* badly to it; was not expecting it to be worse than when she'd saved Mitch. More memories coursed through her as she scrambled to sort through them, her body and head aching miserably all the while. Stephanie again, reversing his body's fatal wounds.

And then, the searing pain that ripped through her when she returned... She remembered screaming, wailing, and then, blackness.

"Does this have something to do with your epilepsy?" Adam questioned timidly.

Lessie blinked as the room slowly came into focus. She couldn't help but chuckle darkly inside. *Yeah,* she thought. *Something like that.*

"I'm not sure, Adam," she lied, her voice finally beginning to clear. "I don't know what happened."

He fidgeted with his thumbs in his lap. "The doctors can't find anything wrong, either."

"How long have I been here?" She tried to sit up, but abandoned her efforts as her pain increased.

"A day. You fell in English class yesterday. It's five p.m."

"I've been out for a whole day?" she gasped, staring at him incredulously.

He gave her a wary smile that didn't reach his eyes. "Y-ye-ah..." His face fell as he continued. "Your thing happened, right when you stood up in class to give your speech. Then when you came to, you started screaming and then... You collapsed. Unconscious."

Her eyes grew wide. That's right, she was in class, nervous about her speech. Nervous for this very reason, only this was so much worse.

He looked down at his knees. "It freaked me out. Freaked the whole class out. Mrs. Andrews called 911." He brought his palms to his forehead, and Lessie suddenly realized how beaten and worn he looked. The dark circles under his bloodshot eyes, his disheveled hair, his dry lips. "I've been losin' sleep. I've been here since school let out, I could hardly pay attention all day today. Your parents have been here all day, they finally went to get something to eat when I got here, but they seemed to be doing mostly okay with this. Emily was worried, too, but seemed sure you'd pull out of it." He lifted his head to meet her eyes again. "It's like she knows something about you that nobody else knows."

"Heh," Lessie chuckled nervously. "We *have* been best friends for a really long time."

He nodded. "Well. I've been praying for you. It's hard to

really trust God's plan when you don't know the outcome, ya know? But, I had faith."

"Mm," Lessie murmured halfheartedly, closing her eyes once more, sinking into the pillow.

"I mean, I knew you'd be okay, but I couldn't help but worry. Of course," he continued rambling. "Just have to lean on my faith. God has a plan for all of us."

"Adam?"

"Yeah?" His eyes lifted to meet hers, which she had opened slightly once she spoke.

"My head hurts. Can we just be quiet for a bit?"

"Oh," he replied, his face falling. "Sure. Sorry."

"Thanks," she sighed, closing her eyes once more. She tried to appreciate his concern, but their religious differences were not something she wanted to think about at the moment. She sensed more tension building every time his beliefs were brought up, and lying in a hospital bed in a great amount of pain was not the most ideal time to deal with it.

CHAPTER 24

AFTER BEING released from the hospital, the doctors unable to detect anything wrong with her, Lessie spent the next day at home, still feeling weak and unable to focus beyond her splitting headache. She escaped in her astral form, spending as little time in her physical body as she could. She finally began to feel normal again the following morning, and pushed herself through a full day of school with the residual tendrils of a headache grasping at the backs of her eyes and neck. She was eager to get home as she dumped her history book, sketchpad, and charcoal pencils into her backpack at her locker, dreaming of nothing but the comfort of her pillows and mattress in her darkened bedroom. She was planning on ignoring everyone, too. She checked her missed text messages and groaned.

>>*Hey Les, gonna be late today, want to wait for me at school? It could be another 30 min yet.*

She pursed her lips as she sent a text back to her father. >>*I'll walk to the park and get started on some homework. You can pick me up there.*

Well, eventually she would get home. It was a mild day for winter, so at least she could enjoy some fresh air and some distance from school while she waited for her dad. She slung her backpack onto her shoulder, swung her locker door shut and gave the lock a spin, and turned, only to stop dead in her tracks as she found herself face-to-face with Mitch Griffin.

She drew in her breath as her heart skipped a beat. She stared at him, braced for the unknown, lips drawn tight and jaw set. He shifted uncomfortably against his crutch, staring back at her with an expression she couldn't quite place. Was he upset? Mad? Scared? Torn? What was he even doing here? He had made it very clear he didn't want anything to do with her after their last encounter, and she was more than happy to oblige.

"They won't leave me alone," he finally muttered through clenched teeth. She still couldn't place his mood.

"Um..." Lessie glanced around nervously before returning her focus to him. "Who?"

"The fucking voices," he replied in a low rumble. "Dead people. Wanting me to tell people shit, like I'm some messenger boy."

She swallowed. "I don't know what to do for you..." she answered, readjusting her backpack strap on her shoulder.

"Tell her to shut up and leave me alone," he growled, his eyes narrowing.

Lessie shifted as her heart skipped. "Tell who?"

"Nana," he replied angrily, his voice rising, eyes boring into hers.

Her breath hitched. "She's back?" She grew hopeful at the prospect of more connection with her grandmother, unlike the fleeting moment she had the last time she spoke to Mitch.

Several students brushed by, each casting a curious glance at the unlikely pair consorting in the hallway. Mitch immediately grew self-conscious, anger rising in his face as his skin reddened. He squeezed his eyes shut, as though fighting the internal battle again, only harder. Grimacing, he finally said, "She's making me talk to you."

Lessie arched a brow. "What do you mean, making you?"

He groaned in aggravation. "I don't have a choice!" he exclaimed, throwing his right arm into the air and attracting the attention of several nearby students. "It's like these people are in my head!" He thumped his skull with his fingertips, glaring at Lessie, who took a cautious step away from him, biting her lip. "This *sucks*." He threw his finger at her. "And I'm still pissed at you for doing this to me!" His nostrils flared. "But your damn grandma insists that we talk, and I'm sick of her, so, let's go." He turned and began walking toward the exit, muttering under his breath, "Whatever, woman, I can talk about you however I want." Then, "Yeah, well, get out of my head then."

It took Lessie a moment to regain composure as she watched him limping away. She finally snapped out of her stunned trance and ran to catch up with him, her new burst of adrenaline chasing away the last of the fatigue and headache that had been clinging to her.

"Where are we going?" she asked as she reached his side.

He stared straight ahead, pushed through the doors, and left the school building with Lessie on his heels. He smoothly made his way down the steps. "The park," he finally snapped back at her.

Her brows furrowed. "Why...?"

"Because that's where you were going anyway."

Her skin prickled, feeling slightly invaded. "How did you know that?"

"I didn't." He flashed her an annoyed glare, thumped his

head with his free hand again, then continued to look ahead. "Nana told me."

"Jesus, Mitch, this is crazy... I—"

"I don't want to hear it!" he barked, stopping for effect and glaring at her before resuming his pace, making his way down the sidewalk.

She kept up with him, impressed at how quickly she needed to walk to do so. "Mitch, you're a *medium*!"

He scowled as he continued walking, his crutch landing on the sidewalk in a rhythmic clatter with every step of his left foot. "I'm a freak," he muttered. "I hope you know how much you fucked my life up."

His words lanced through her heart, just as painfully as the first time he had verbally attacked her in the hall. She opened her mouth to say she was sorry, wanting to say more but unsure of how to elaborate on her apology, but was interrupted.

"Yes, it *is* her fault!" He ground his teeth.

"Is she talking to you again?" Lessie asked carefully.

"She won't shut up!" Mitch spat back, and Lessie immediately snapped her mouth shut. Perhaps silence was the best option for the remainder of their walk. She hoped Nana would agree, for Mitch's sake.

By the time they reached the nearest pavilion at the city park, Mitch spun to face Lessie, causing her to stumble slightly as she backed away from him. They were alone now, and he was almost to the point where he didn't even *need* the crutch, which ignited a nervous unease inside of her regarding his uncertain emotional state. She swallowed hard and tried to keep her cool, folding her arms protectively over her chest.

"For the record, I don't want to talk to you."

Lessie nodded. "Understood."

Mitch's eyes narrowed. "But I don't have a choice."

"You said that."

He pursed his lips. Lessie remained stationary, her arms still folded, appearing calm and collected, unlike how she felt on the inside. He took a breath, and something shifted over his eyes as he began to speak. "She said you did the right thing. Saving me, and then saving that boy." His brows lowered as his eyes came back into focus. He fell silent, his expression questioning what Nana meant.

"I saved someone else," she offered. "That's why I was sick."

His brows furrowed deeper, but the shift went over his eyes again. "She said she was afraid to tell you about the side effects of saving people. She wanted you to believe you weren't allowed to, because she was afraid of what it could do to you if you tried it."

Lessie shook her head as she processed, her eyes squinted as she searched Mitch's expression. "Have you ever done it, Nana?"

Mitch's eyes went farther away. "No. I refused, not after what happened to my grandfather."

Oh my God, I'm talking to Nana... through Mitch... Her mind reeled, the flood of emotions combined with the new information was almost overwhelming. "What happened to him?"

"It killed him."

Lessie's breath caught so fast it nearly choked her. Mitch's focus came back as he locked eyes on Lessie's, and they stared at each other with mixed emotions, realization slowly setting in both of them that Lessie unknowingly risked her life for him. Finally he spoke again, softer this time. "She said the same thing could happen to you. Saving a soul puts too much of a strain on your own, the separation is too much, and the more you do it, the greater risk you take getting stuck on the Other Side." He looked confused now, almost torn. "She didn't want to take that risk. She hated that her grandfather did, and hated losing her mentor. She didn't want to see the same thing happen to you." He blinked, still wrestling with his mixed feelings, as he held Lessie's wide-eyed gaze, her mouth hanging open in disbelief. She shook her head. "How do you know that's how he died?"

Mitch's eyes remained unfocused. "She said as crazy as it sounds, he appeared to her in a vivid dream, wanting to tell her what happened, and to warn her, too." He cleared his throat. "She said she's sorry she never told you sooner."

Static prickled the air as the energy shifted, and Lessie rendered a guess that Nana had left them. It was just she and Mitch, and the air had changed drastically between them. She didn't know what to say. So, she said the only thing that came to her mind. "Thank you."

He stood motionless, his expression unchanging, as though he hadn't heard her.

She held his gaze silently for a moment. He seemed so torn, so lost, and her heart ached for him. "Are you gonna be okay?"

His expression shifted slightly. "I don't know."

She drew her lips together as her heart stung. She wanted desperately to reach out to him, but it felt as though there were a vast wall separating them, closing him off from the rest of the world.

A black SUV crunched through the gravel at the curb, and Lessie glanced over her shoulder as she caught sight of her dad waving to her from the driver's seat. "I gotta go." Mitch didn't respond. Her gaze fell to her feet before lifting to meet his eyes once more. "Thank you, really. I needed to hear that." She offered him a sad smile. "I was beginning to believe you were right. That I made a huge mistake, and should have just let you die. That was some pretty shitty guilt I've been carrying around." Her voice was almost a whisper.

His brows creased together as he drew in his lips. She let the moment soak as she made her way toward her dad's vehicle, then stopped and turned to find that Mitch hadn't moved from where she left him in his confused silence. She sighed, then pulled open the passenger door, climbed in, and closed it behind her, forcing herself not to look at him one last time as her father drove away.

"Sorry about being late. Who was that?" Sam inquired curiously, stealing a glance at her as he pulled out of the park.

Lessie sighed heavily, sinking into the passenger's seat. "Where do I even begin..."

MITCH LEANED AGAINST his crutch as he stood near a forgotten shelf in the corner of the living room, staring at a photograph in a dusty frame. A balding man with glasses and a dark goatee and mustache smiled back at him, with Mitch's much younger, thinner, and happier mother wrapped in his arms. He sighed as he traced his finger across the top of the frame, pushing dust to the edge. "Why won't you talk to me, Dad?" he whispered. He had been afraid to hear the man's voice, to know his thoughts of where life had taken his son, and how he handled his death. But after relaying the message to Lessie from her grandmother, and the comfort it brought her, he couldn't help but wish for his own source of comfort. He needed to know everything was going to be okay. Because, at that moment and ever since the accident, everything was certainly *not* okay. He was still angry at Lessie. He still wished he could have died — it would have been easier than living in the mess he was currently in. It seemed as though he should have, after all, but then... at the same time, it seemed as though he were meant to live. And he heard Lessie's grandmother's words, felt their truth inside of him as though they were his own thoughts. Lessie had done the right thing.

Not only that, but she risked her life. He squeezed his eyes shut, once again facing the memory of desperation, and the bright light.

"Everything okay?" Genevieve asked carefully as she entered the room.

He sighed, hanging his head. "I don't know," he answered honestly.

She nodded. "Well. I think everything *will* be okay."

He turned to face his sister, leaving his dad's image on the shelf behind him. "I hope you're right," he said quietly.

LESSIE CAREFULLY TURNED the pages of Nana's journals as she sat on the floor by her cedar chest, desperate to find any clues pointing to the death of Nana's grandfather. She had searched through them countless times already, focusing most specifically on the dates surrounding Aunt Jodi's death, but it was almost as though Nana didn't want to capture those moments. Delving back further into her earlier writings proved to be fruitless, as well. She suddenly paused, eyebrows furrowed, as she turned a page, then turned it back again. She hadn't noticed it before, but upon closer inspection, it seemed as though several pages had been torn from the binding.

She reached for her phone and selected Will's name from her favorites list.

"Hey, Les," he answered.

"Will..." she began, then closed her eyes as she reflected on all that had happened to her.

After a moment's pause, he asked, "You okay?"

She took a breath. "Barely," she replied quietly. "I did it again. I saved someone."

"*Again?*" he exclaimed. "How often is this going to happen?"

"Hopefully not much anymore. Apparently I risked my life." She drew her finger along the uneven crease in Nana's journal, tracing across the remaining scraps of torn paper.

Will was silent, before finally finding words. "Risked your life?"

"Mitch had another message for me from Nana." She recalled what Mitch had relayed to her, her voice fading as she told him how their great-great-grandfather died. "That's why Nana always got so weird when I tried to ask her about saving people. And she'd never give me a straight answer. That's why she was always so adamant about *not* saving people."

Will exhaled slowly. "Geez, Les, this... this is a *lot*. And it explains so much..."

"I know," she whispered. "But I'm still not sure what it means for your dad. How did he know saving people was possible? I mean, he had to have, right?"

"It seems like it."

She riffled through the pages of the journal, fanning the edges with her thumb. "I've been searching Nana's journals. I can't find anything, but it looks like if she *did* write anything, she tore the pages out. It's all I can find. It's almost like she didn't want any trace of information left behind about it."

"Her grandpa's death must have hit her pretty hard."

"Especially if it happened suddenly."

"How do you think she knew that's how he died?"

"I asked Mitch that. She said he appeared to her in a dream and explained what happened. I've been thinking about it so much. I wonder if he got sick the first few times he saved anyone, like how I did. What if he spaced out, off on a call, and she was there? And his soul never returned to his body?" She shuddered. She'd seen Nana, vacant and motionless, on calls several times. She couldn't imagine seeing her collapse, all life gone from her, without warning, never returning from her call.

"That would be pretty awful."

Lessie nodded as she shifted the phone to her other ear. "Awful enough to make her not want to talk about it. To make sure I never do it myself." She sighed. "We don't know if that all happened, but she did get the warning from her grandfather in her dream, either way."

"I just wish we knew how this matches up to everything that happened with Mom."

Lessie shrugged. "Well, Nana already said your mom was at peace with her death. She never got to tell that to your dad, though. He wouldn't let her. He just got mad that she didn't try to save your mom."

"He definitely must have known it was possible."

Lessie's heart ached for her uncle and grandmother. "We just need to find a way to explain it to him. Get him to understand that it was a misunderstanding."

Will sighed. "It's been eighteen years, Les. That's easier said than done."

Lessie frowned as she closed the journal and placed it back in the chest with the others. "We at least have to try. For Nana."

CHAPTER 25

LESSIE EXHALED deeply as she sank into her mattress, as though she'd been holding her breath the entire day. A weekend had passed since her experience with Mitch in the park — a weekend filled with distracted stewing over the message he'd relayed from Nana, along with the shock and disbelief that she'd actually gotten to *speak* to her deceased grandmother and former mentor. Not to mention the message itself — she could actually *die* from saving people?

She was tense all day, coming back to school after a mentally exhausting weekend, wondering if she'd have any run-ins with Mitch, wondering what he was thinking or feeling since they'd last spoken. Was he still mad? He seemed confused when she left him. Or was she just imagining things?

It plagued her mind through lunch, causing Emily to call her out on her distance, but Lessie tried to blow it off. As if right on cue, Lessie looked away only to meet the eyes of Mitch at the football table, as though he had been watching her from across the cafeteria the whole time. He quickly averted his eyes and refocused his attention on the conversation at his table, pretending he'd been absorbed in it all along.

She attempted to shut out her accumulation of distracting

thoughts that night by pulling up her social media app on her phone as she relaxed on her bed. She began thumbing through a series of pointless posts, and accidentally bumped the sidebar, displaying a list of members who were presently online. She huffed in annoyance, about to close and return to her mindless scrolling, until a little green dot next to Mitch's name caught her attention.

"The Universe has mysterious ways of speaking to us. There are signs everywhere, all the time." Nana's voice rang loud and clear in her memory as she stared at that green dot. A thought occurred to her, and she felt a driving force take over. Suddenly growing nervous, she tapped Mitch's name, and selected Private Message.

"Here goes nothing," she muttered out loud, and began working out a message with her thumbs.

>>*Hey. How've you been?*

Her heart picked up speed as she watched the indicator display that he'd read it. It nearly hammered out of her chest as the small ellipse showed up as he typed a response.

>>*Fine.*

Her shoulders slumped. *Fine? That's it?* She took a breath. *At least he responded.*

>>*Yeah right,* she typed back.

Again, the ellipse, and again, her heart sped up.

>>*What's it to you?*

She got to work on her response. >>*I guess since I feel partly responsible for you not dying I feel like I should check in on you.*

>>*What, are you God now?*

Lessie grinned, deciding to lighten the mood. >>*Eh. Still working on turning water into wine.*

A pause, and then, >>*lol*

Her heart nearly choked her. *Holy shit, did I just make him laugh?*

The ellipse popped up again, and she held her breath. >>*So. You don't just space out then...*

Did he really want to know about this? Was he getting past his anger? Her thumbs immediately got to work again. >>*Nope. Lots more to it than that.*

>>*Apparently. Still trying to make sense of all this.*

>>*I imagine that'll probably take awhile. Your life kinda turned upside down.*

Another pause. >>*Why are you being nice to me?*

A soft smile tugged at the corners of her mouth. >>*Well, I guess because you gave me a message from my grandma, which means more to me than you'll ever know. And I guess because I accidentally initiated you into the freak club.*

>>*Do I get a jacket?*

Her smile grew. >>*They're on backorder. Why are YOU being nice to ME?*

>>*I dunno. Kinda feel obligated, I guess.*

Her face fell. >>*Gee, thanks.*

>>*Whatever. So who's Nana? Besides your grandma, obviously.*

She bit her lip as she realized they were about to delve deeper into personal details. With a sense of surrender, she replied, >>*She could do it too. We're called Transcendents. It skips a generation. I have a cousin who does it as well.*

>>*Weird.*

She snorted a small laugh, and began explaining her "gift", smiling to herself as he responded with more questions, and she gladly answered. She pondered the absurdity of having a "normal" conversation with Mitch, and how drastically life had changed to get them there. >>*So, my turn. Has that been happening a lot?*

>>*Hearing dead people? More than I'd like.*

>>*Are you relaying the messages?*

>>*I try to ignore them. If I get away from people, the voices go away. Except in the case of your grandma. There wasn't any shutting her up.*

>>*Maybe you should just relay the message instead of running away.*

>>*What, are you an expert on hearing dead people?*

>>*I have my experience with dead people, in case you've forgotten. And in weird abilities. No use fighting it.*

>>*I'll take my chances. I'm the one-leg-wonder, I don't need to add anything else to my freak status.*

>>*I bet people would appreciate hearing from their loved ones.*

>>*Yeah. Just like Katie.*

>>*She was a dumb bitch. She doesn't count.*

>>*Damn.*

>>*Sorry. She was.*

>>*Eh. I agree. But yeah, not liking the idea of enforcing my freak status.*

>>*Just try it. You only have a couple months left of school anyway, then you never have to see these people again.*

>>*Whatever. I'm going to bed. Bye.*

She pursed her lips. >>*Goodnight* she reluctantly typed back. She relaxed back against her pillow. Finished or not, it was more of a conversation than she'd ever imagined having with Mitch. And it was *friendly,* too. She'd have to pay attention to signs from the Universe more often.

❖

MITCH BEGAN HIS day feeling uncertain, yet inexplicably re-freshed and renewed. The conversation with Lessie the night before was unexpected, and rather strange. He kept finding himself wanting to apologize to her for how he'd always treated her, and thank her for being nice to him, but couldn't muster the courage to do it. But even stranger yet was that he enjoyed the conversation. He was used to camaraderie, and suddenly being thrown into a life that not even *he* understood was un-settling. If this was his new life, and there was no escaping it, having someone to talk to who *understood* the challenges of being different was unexpectedly comforting.

But it was *Lester.* He'd picked on her relentlessly throughout high school; now suddenly they were supposed to be *friends?* He chewed the end of his pen, paying no attention to Mr. Edwards in his first period History class. *Were* they friends? No. That was taking it too far.

The bell toned, and the students gathered their books and shuffled toward the door as Mitch took his time, not wanting to trip anyone up as he resituated with his crutch. He eagerly awaited the day he could ditch that thing for good. He knew he was getting close.

Terry...

Mitch's spine tingled. He stood straighter, dropping his head back as he groaned. *Come on...* Could he not even make it past first period without a dead person trying to talk to him?

Tell Terry it's okay.

Mitch sighed, recalling his conversation with Lessie. *Relay the message instead of running away.* He glanced around the empty room as the last two students exited into the bustling hallway and Mr. Edwards took a seat at his desk, pushing his dark hand through his white hair.

Please, tell him it's okay, the female voice urged.

"Okay, fine," Mitch grumbled out loud, catching Mr. Edwards's attention.

"I'm sorry?" he asked.

Mitch sighed, meeting the man's dark, curious eyes.

"I'm. Um. Supposed to tell you it's okay." He felt a strange sense of relief flood into him, and the voice returned.

His loyalty to our marriage is kind, and beautiful, but is no longer serving him.

Mitch cleared his throat and relayed the message, and Mr. Edwards's eyes widened as he listened. "You deserve to be happy," Mitch continued. "She... She says y-you've been speaking with ... Um... Jane?" Mitch squinted; the name felt fuzzy.

Mr. Edwards nodded slowly, eyes still wide and disbelieving. "Jean. She's been volunteering in the library this school year," he explained softly.

"Okay, um... She — your wife — is saying that you two... um... Have something, and she wants you to be happy, and to... Uh..." He felt a sense of urgency, combined with laughter, pushing into him. "She says, 'Just ask her on a real date already.'" Mitch waited nervously, his palm sweating as it gripped his crutch. Mr. Edwards simply stared at him.

The old man's voice was a near whisper as he dropped his gaze to his desk, smiling softly in wonder. "That is exactly how she sounded when she was feeling bossy." He returned his focus to Mitch. "How do you know this?"

Mitch shook his head, averting his eyes. His voice was low.

"I just... hear people." A few students entered the room for the next class, and Mitch cleared his throat, quickly gathering his things, and hoping desperately that Mrs. Edwards was finished.

Mr. Edwards had already stood and was approaching Mitch slowly, with a mystified, distant look on his face. He shook his head sadly. "I never felt right moving on. I felt it would betray our marriage."

Mitch glanced at the students, who seemed absorbed in their own conversation. A few more had entered the room. Squinting up at Mr. Edwards, he asked quietly, "You don't think I'm crazy?"

Mr. Edwards let out a laugh that reached his eyes. "No! I've been a widower for quite some time now, and had my share of strange experiences. I swear my wife would change the channel on the television while I was trying to watch my detective shows. She hated that stuff. I knew it was her because it would flip to some sappy romance movie. She used to watch those all the time." His eyes shifted in reflection, a soft smile coming to his lips. "I've watched more of those damn movies after she died than I ever did while she was alive."

Mitch glanced at the floor, feeling a sense of warmth and contentment. "She wants you to be happy," he said, feeling her presence still.

Mr. Edwards met his eyes and smiled. He placed a hand on Mitch's shoulder, and said, "Thank you, son. I needed to hear this more than you know." He gave his shoulder a squeeze as his eyes softened. "You've really been through something... You have a special gift, and a great service to offer with it. Don't let being different get you down, or stop you."

Mitch dropped his gaze. "Thanks, sir," he said quietly.

❖

NATURALLY, A BROKEN version of Mitch's exchange with Mr. Edwards made its way around school, and by lunchtime Emily was eager to share the gossip with Lessie.

"Apparently Mitch is sharing messages from the dead to teachers now!" she said in an excited hiss at Lessie's locker.

Lessie brightened at her words. He took her advice...

"What's that look about?"

Lessie snapped her head up to meet Emily's curious eyes. "What look?"

"Whatever. But how crazy is that? I just can't help but laugh. Karma is great, right? He spends all his time giving you a hard time for being different, and now he's *way* worse off!" She grinned in satisfaction.

Lessie slammed her locker door harder than she intended, causing Emily's face to fall. "That's not fair, Em," she retorted. "I don't think I'd exactly call this *karma*."

Emily eyed her under an arched brow. "Okay, *why* are you sticking up for him?"

"I told you, I feel responsible for his mess." Lessie pushed past Emily and headed toward the cafeteria, and Emily quickly moved to catch up with her.

"Okay, whatever." She decided to change the subject. "Is everything okay with you and Adam? You've been kinda distant from him."

Lessie let out an exaggerated sigh. "Look, I've got a lot on my mind right now. I don't mean to be distant."

"Why don't you tell him that? He's worried."

Lessie tried to keep her focus on the lunch line as she grabbed a tray. Her eyes wanted to wander, to search, but not for Adam. To the football table.

She groaned inwardly. She had to quit thinking about Mitch. "Les?"

Her attention snapped back to reality. "Do you guys always discuss our relationship issues?"

"I just care about both of you, that's all."

Lessie studied Emily for a moment. "Well, I told you I have a lot on my mind."

"Like what?"

"Don't worry about it."

Emily dropped her gaze in defeat, and in turn dropped the conversation. They silently continued through the lunch line.

LESSIE'S HEART FLIPPED upon seeing the green dot next to Mitch's name as she checked her phone for what seemed like the hundredth time throughout dinner. "Looking for something?" Lynne had questioned with an arched brow after the fifth time, and Lessie quickly shook her head in denial. But as she helped clear the dishes, there was no denying she found what she was waiting for after checking her phone for the last time.

Lynne tried to press for questions as Lessie quickly dumped the dishes into the sink and eagerly took off for her bedroom, shouting over her shoulder, "It's nothing, Mom, just needing to talk to someone about a school project!" And she disappeared up the stairs, taking them two at a time.

>>*Hello,* she typed on her laptop after nearly leaping into her chair.

>>*Hey,* he replied, and she grinned. He didn't even hesitate.

>>*So, of course I heard the rumors, but good job today.* She hit *send* and grimaced. That sounded so corny...

>>*Ha. Yeah. I did my little magic trick on Mr. Edwards.*

She exhaled. So far so good.

>>*I know, I'm impressed. That you took my advice, that is.*

>>*Get over yourself.*

She pursed her lips, then let his words roll off her. >>*So... How did it go?*

>>*I thought you said you heard about it already.*

>>*I heard rumors. Those don't mean anything.*

>>*It went fine.*

She paused, unsure. >>*Really?*

>>*Yeah, he didn't think I was crazy, and felt better afterward, so. Whatever.*

>>*How do you feel?*

>>*Are you writing a book about me or something?*

She bit her lip. >>*Sorry, just curious.*

She held her breath as the ellipse showed up.

>>*I guess I'm fine.*

She pursed her lips, realizing he didn't seem to want to elaborate. A question occurred to Lessie. >>*Sorry if this is overstepping some boundaries... But has your dad ever talked to you?*

>>*No. And that's none of your business.*

She drew in her bottom lip again. >>*Sorry, I wasn't trying to pry. I just... can imagine how alone you probably feel.*

>>*Well, as far as I know I'm the only medium in my family. Or whatever the hell I'm called. You at least have a cousin like you.*

She raised her eyebrows. *Wow,* she marveled, *He listened to me.* She typed. >>*Actually, their family was estranged before I was born.* She decided to chance sharing the story about her family. She explained Uncle Ron's anger toward Nana, how he and his children left the family and never spoke to them again. How she learned that Aunt Jodi accepted her death, but Uncle Ron never let Nana explain that.

>>*Damn, your family drama is way more interesting than most people's...*

She grinned at his humor. >>*Well, when you're a superhero, you can expect your drama to be a bit different than the norm.*

>>*I thought you said we're freaks.*

>>*Aren't all superheroes freaks in their alter ego? ;).* She had a mini panic attack after realizing she just virtually winked at him.

>>*lol,* he replied, and she sighed with relief. >>*Sure.*

Her grin spread wider as a content peacefulness flowed through her. She felt safe to admit that a friendship was, indeed, growing.

CHAPTER 26

SPRING KNOCKED on the doors of mid March with warm breezes chasing away the chilly winter air. Rains drove through their tiny Southern Illinois town, refreshing the world and making way for new life and changes.

It built up a sense of need for connection in Lessie — namely with Emily, who had been growing agitated by Lessie's distance and unusual reserve. She had tried calling her out on it on several occasions, only to be met with denial from Lessie. Adam grew paranoid as Lessie seemed to disappear further into her own world.

"You ever gonna tell me what's up?" Emily pressed, sitting at Lessie's desk in her bedroom one evening, both of them quickly losing interest in the history assignment they were supposed to be working on.

Lessie chewed the end of her pen as she lay prone on her bed. She met her friend's eyes as the need for connection surfaced once again, and took a steadying breath. "Mitch... talked to me."

Emily squinted uncertainly at her friend. "What? When?" Lessie definitely detected an air of displeasure in her friend's voice.

Lessie quickly shifted her focus back to the glossy textbook pages. "Not too long ago." If several weeks counted as 'not too long.' "He had a message for me from Nana." She took a breath and retold the story. It felt like it had happened ages ago. She and Mitch had chatted online several more times over the past few weeks, developing a unique friendship that fulfilled Lessie in ways she couldn't quite define, and leaving her with a level of gratitude she'd never before experienced. She filled Emily in on Nana's apology, and her revelation that her grandfather had died saving someone.

Emily stared at her with wide eyes and a fallen jaw. "Oh my God, Les... So... First of all, why didn't you tell me all this sooner? And second, you put your life at risk? *Twice?*" She shook her head as she brought her gaze to the floor, and her brows suddenly creased. "You risked your life for that *asshole?*"

Lessie grew defensive as she pushed herself up into a seated position on her bed. "First of all, I didn't know I was putting my life at risk when it happened. And besides, asshole or not, he wanted to *live.* Who am I to make the call not to save him? If I'd let him *die,* can you imagine the guilt I'd have to live with?"

Emily snapped up to meet Lessie's eyes. "I thought you were questioning if you should have saved him at all? Why are you suddenly throwing this guilt story at me?"

Lessie squared her shoulders, her brows furrowed. "I know I did the right thing now! I got a freaking message from my dead grandmother, through a *guy* whose *life* I saved! Don't act like you know what this feels like! I'm dealing with shit here that you can't even begin to imagine, so... So quit trying to act like you know how I should feel!"

Emily recoiled slightly, her face falling. "Sorry," she finally said.

A silence fell as Lessie's own gaze dropped. "It's fine."

Before any further conversation could be made, Lessie's

phone chimed an alert of a text message. She retrieved it, grimacing as she read Adam's words. *>>Hey, just found out my Uncle Paul died...* Lessie's heart sank.

"What?" Emily asked in concern.

She shook her head. "Adam's uncle died..."

Emily sat up straighter. "Which uncle?"

Realizing Emily was afraid it could mean her own uncle as well, Lessie quickly said, "His mom's brother, Paul."

Emily relaxed slightly. "Oh, that's right." She nodded sadly in reflection. "He'd been battling cancer for awhile."

Lessie had already begun typing a response. *>>I'm so sorry. How's your mom?*

Her phone chimed. *>>Good as can be expected, I guess. Shook up. But we kinda saw it coming... so...*

Emily met Lessie's eyes sadly. "Guess we have a funeral to attend."

Lessie sighed. Though she felt guilty for her selfish thoughts, she couldn't help but feel a sense of frustration that she'd once again be faced with their obvious religious differences.

LESSIE SAT NEXT to Adam at the funeral three days later, as he focused somberly on the minister, who spoke of Paul's life with grandeur and affection.

"Paul was a sinner," he spoke, palms flat on the pulpit. "But! It was because of his faith, his acceptance of Jesus Christ, that released him of his sins and allowed him entrance through the gates of Heaven!" He outstretched his arms as he made this announcement, his voice booming. Lessie observed the riveted congregation as they nodded in agreement.

Gates of Heaven? she wondered with furrowed brows. *Allowed him entrance?*

"We are all sinners!" the minister continued. "But it is thanks to Jesus Christ, our Lord and Savior, for dying on the cross and *thereby!*" He paused, gazing out across the congregation. "*Freeing* us from our sins so that we may *all* return to the Father when our time comes."

More nods and soft murmurs from the crowd. *So... Do they think people like me won't go to Heaven?* she wondered with squinted eyes. She pursed her lips. *So, where exactly* would *I go?*

"Paul's time has come, Brothers and Sisters. God has a will, a plan, for each and every one of us. We do not know when it will be our time. Therefore, each and every day, we must live with *deliberate faith* in our Lord Jesus Christ, and serve him with honor and love."

Lessie squinted again, feeling herself growing tense. *Serve him? Isn't God in all of us? Shouldn't we answer to our inner wisdom? That voice of God within us all?*

She struggled with her thoughts and questions, and by the end of the service, Lessie had become rigid with frustration, and even more so from the effort she put into keeping her feelings to herself as Adam and his family grieved their loss.

SHE SHIVERED AS she pulled her jacket closer to her body, standing next to Adam as the minister said his last words before the casket descended into its grave. Adam's mother dabbed at a tear, and his father put a comforting arm around her. Adam swallowed as he lowered his head, his hands clasped in front of him. Lessie simply observed. The sadness was palpable, and the earth seemed to reflect the mood with its gray skies and impending rain, a mournful chill in the mid-March air. She felt her heart ache for the family. For Paul's suffering as he battled cancer his last few years on Earth; for Adam's mother, who lost a brother too young; but most of all, for their lack of knowledge as to where Paul's soul had departed. She dropped her own gaze as she was met with the stark reality of how different she was, what a blessing she possessed to *know* that death was not something to grieve, nor was Heaven a place they needed to gain special access to.

Yet, at the same time, it was a very lonely feeling. There would never be a way for her to share this knowledge with anyone, unless they themselves could cross through that veil and glimpse what awaited on the Other Side. How she wished they could know that God was not something separate from them, but *part* of them, *one* with them.

She tried to release her sadness. It did her no good to hang onto it.

She reached to clasp Adam's hand, and he met her eyes as he cast her a small, grateful smile. She returned it, with sympathy in her eyes that ran deeper than her sadness for his loss.

"WHAT'S EATIN' YA, kiddo?" Sam asked as he eyed his somber daughter, who was absently sweeping her paintbrush across a small canvas, no clear indication that she was trying to actually create something. She sat quietly at the kitchen table as Sam pressed his homemade dough onto a large round pizza stone. Lynne had gone out to meet a friend from her college days who was in town to visit, leaving the two alone for the evening, which was just as well for Lessie, as she didn't feel like interacting with anyone after the mentally burdensome day she'd had attending Adam's uncle's funeral and burial.

She felt her father's expectant eyes on her, and she sighed in resignation. "Our culture."

Sam drew his lips to the side of his face as he arched a brow. "That's pretty deep."

Lessie chuckled dryly as she stood and collected her brushes. "Yeah," she replied as she walked to the sink and flipped on the water. "I wish people could see what I see. Know what lies beyond, ya know?" She held the brushes under the running water, watching as the greens and blues and whites blended together, cascading toward the drain.

Sam nodded thoughtfully. "I wish I could see that, too."

She glanced over to meet him as he smiled softly at her. She returned her focus to the thinning paint, running her thumb through the bristles. "What made you different, Dad?"

"How do you mean?"

Lessie shrugged as she set one of her brushes aside and proceeded to the next. "You know, you were raised no different than Adam, believing all the same things, part of a devout family." She looked up to meet his eyes once more. "What changed for you?"

Sam pondered as he spread sauce across the flattened dough. "Well, I believed what I was taught for awhile. But, I just started thinking about things on my own, wondered why we believed in something we couldn't see, or couldn't actually prove." He gave his spoon a quick shake to rid it of excess sauce before setting it aside and retrieving the pepperoni. "My parents were pretty horrified when I tried to ask them about it. So," he shrugged as he finished assembling the last of the pepperoni. "I kept my questions to myself, went to church like a good boy, resenting the fact that I had no one to ask my questions, for fear that questioning would get me in trouble. And I thought, what kind of life is this? One in which we were discouraged from asking questions? Wasn't that how we were supposed to learn?" He paused as he retrieved the diced peppers and onions. "I felt controlled, and I didn't like that. Then, I met your mom." He smiled as he finished sprinkling the vegetables across the pizza. "The timing was so uncanny, her wisdom and understanding so powerful to me, that it almost seemed as though it were *planned* that she should be brought into my life. And that's when I started believing God was real, after all." He turned his head to face Lessie, who smiled at him with shining eyes. "When you were born, I promised I'd let you ask questions, *encourage* you to ask questions." He laughed to himself as he slid his hand into an oven mitt and grasped the preheated stone. "Turns out you don't really need to. You have all the answers at your fingertips."

Lessie snorted, rolling her eyes as she returned to the table to put away her brushes. "I don't know about *that*. I feel like I just have *more* questions. Adam seems so *certain*, ya know? They all do. Like Jesus was the best thing that ever happened to humanity, and they *have* to believe in him."

Sam closed the oven and set the timer, then turned to face Lessie, meeting her eyes. "Jesus had great messages, and deep wisdom. I just believe some of his messages got lost in translation, and misconstrued." He turned to the sink to wash his hands, and continued. "Jesus said we are all children of God, much like himself, the Son of God. I think he was trying to tell us we can be just as great as him."

Lessie smiled, dropping her gaze. "I believe we are."

CHAPTER 27

DISTRACTION CONSUMED Lessie through the days following the funeral. She pressed through each day with an eagerness to reach the evening, where she buried herself in her secret friendship with Mitch, finding refuge from their abnormal lives in each other's company.

Lessie's parents chose to ignore it for the most part, which she was grateful for, though she had overheard comments from the kitchen several times as she took off for her bedroom.

"Think it's a boy?" Sam muttered to Lynne.

"I don't know, she's been kind of weird about Adam, but I haven't heard anything about a breakup yet..."

"Who's she so eager to talk to then?"

IT WAS ONLY a matter of time before Adam couldn't take her distance anymore.

"What's going on, Les?" Adam urged as he met her at her locker before lunch.

She chewed her lower lip as she stuffed her art supplies and sketch pad into her backpack in preparation for class after lunch. "Nothing," she lied.

"Something's up. You've been quiet ever since the funeral. Is my uncle's death getting to you?"

She sighed as she shut her locker door, wondering if admitting her concerns would be the right thing to do.

"I mean," he continued, "I know the funerals you've been to have been a bit... different... so I can understand if it might be bothering you."

His words struck a chord inside of her, and she met his eyes under her furrowed brows. "Do you believe your uncle really was a sinner? Like that minister said?"

Students bustled by on their way to the cafeteria. Adam glanced around at the crowded hallway, then back at Lessie with uncertainty in his eyes. "That's what's bothering you?"

She hugged her arms to her chest and shifted on her feet, silently holding his gaze.

He shrugged. "We're all sinners. That's why we have to have faith..."

"Sinners, like we're bad people?" she asked, her voice soft and hesitant.

He glanced around the busy hallway. "Well, I mean we make mistakes..."

"Of *course* we make mistakes, don't you think God expects us to? What would life be if we were *perfect* all the time?"

"I..."

She didn't let him finish as she felt her confidence building. "So you mean to tell me, that since I don't believe in Jesus the way you do, you think I'm going to hell?" The thought angered her, and she took a steadying breath. A few students glanced curiously in their direction on their way to lunch.

"Lessie, calm down. You were just raised differently! But yes, I would love to see you accept Jesus so you can get to—"

"*Seriously?* You think God won't let anyone into Heaven if

they haven't accepted Jesus? What happened to everyone before Jesus came along? What happens to the people in other parts of the world who believe something entirely different? Who've never even *heard* of Jesus?"

"Look, my uncle just freaking died, I don't exactly appreciate being attacked for my religious beliefs." He glared at her, reclaiming his power.

Lessie sighed as she backed down. "Right. Sorry. I just don't really get it, okay?"

He nodded, softening. "You will."

She frowned. "No, I mean I don't get why people believe in Heaven being an exclusive club. It's just the Other Side, it's the only place there is to go from here. Getting all caught up in believing that we have to think a certain way to gain access kind of distracts us from the whole point of why we're here."

He squinted with uncertainty. "Excuse me, but do you have all the answers as to why we're here?"

She opened her mouth, ready to lash out her response, but quickly reigned herself back. "I know more than you realize," she whispered. She shook her head. "Sorry, I know you're still mourning. It wasn't fair that I threw all this at you. I'll keep my feelings to myself." She then turned and headed for the cafeteria, leaving Adam alone behind her.

For the first time since they'd started dating almost five months ago, Adam sat with his math team friends, and Lessie sat alone with Emily and Evan. "Les? Why isn't Adam joining us?" Emily questioned.

Lessie shook her head, her face falling. "Just... Kinda had an argument. No big deal, don't worry about it."

Emily and Evan exchanged a glance. "Hey, it happens," Evan

offered. "We all argue. Right, Babe?"

Emily, eyes still on her friend, nodded halfheartedly. "Right..."

DISTANCE ONLY GREW between Lessie and her friends as the next week wore on. She continued to chat with Mitch in the evenings, and their conversation progressed from simple talk of growing up and family life, to deeper subjects of Mitch's father's passing and Lessie discovering her ability. He'd fill her in on his secret meetings between classes with teachers, and the messages he'd relay from their deceased loved ones, and she'd share her experiences of crossing souls to the Other Side. He hadn't brought himself to share messages with fellow students, however, fearing the ridicule and rumors that would certainly come with it. Instead, he'd excuse himself for a bathroom break, separating himself from the student needing the message, and try to breathe until finally the spirit would leave him alone. Lessie was constantly fascinated by his experiences, and he slowly grew more fascinated by hers, as she shared her encounters with the dying and what happened when she crossed them over. His mind had opened immensely since their meeting in the park weeks ago, but it only enhanced Lessie's awareness of her and Adam's differences.

Adam noticed her reclusiveness had only grown since their last argument the week before. They'd talked lightly since then, said and accepted each other's apologies, but her continued distance seemed to develop a paranoia in him that he could no longer keep to himself.

He confronted her at her locker at the end of the school day, his dark blue eyes laced with concern as he hugged his books to his chest and leaned against the locker next to hers.

"What's going on?" he pressed as Lessie collected her books in her backpack.

She sighed as she closed her locker and offered him a sympathetic smile. "Nothing, Adam. Just have a lot on my mind, I guess."

"Can I drive you home?" he offered, his eyes still displaying the same morose uncertainty. He fidgeted with the corner of one of his textbooks.

She sighed, slumping her shoulders and casting him a pitying gaze. "I have an art club meeting. Dad's going to get me after work. But thanks, though."

They held each other's gaze for a moment before finally Lessie opened her mouth to tell him goodbye.

"Are we okay?" Adam broke in before she could speak.

Her eyes flashed with surprise as she quickly closed her mouth.

"I mean," he continued, "I thought we sorted everything out since the whole... funeral... argument. But you're still not talking, like you're in your own little world. What's going on?"

She shook her head. "It's nothing, really."

His brows fell in concern. "You know you can talk to me about anything, right?"

She gave him a sad smile, then stepped forward and rose up to her toes to press a kiss to his lips. He sighed into her, trying to allow the gesture to relax him.

She broke the kiss and stepped back, bringing her hand up to give his arm a squeeze. "I'll be fine. I'll talk to you later, okay?"

He nodded, forcing a smile. "'K."

LESSIE TRIED TO involve herself more in her friends' lives the next week, but the more she chatted with Mitch in the evenings, the more she lost interest in what was going on during the day.

"I talked to Will last night," Lynne said as Lessie came down for breakfast.

She brightened at her mother's words. "Oh yeah?" She suddenly realized she hadn't talked to Will in ages.

"I invited them to your graduation. Sounds like he and Camryn will be joining us." She smiled cheerfully and Lessie grinned in return, her heart taking flight.

"That's awesome!"

Lynne nodded. "I know Mom is smiling at us, seeing we've mended a few bonds."

"Uncle Ron may come around someday," Lessie offered hopefully. She thought back to her conversation with Will the night after she found out the dangers of saving people; that somehow Ron must have known saving people was even possible. But, was it possible to get Ron to understand that just because Nana *could* save people, didn't mean that was Jodi's fate?

Lynne simply sighed. "Maybe. But for now, I'm just going to appreciate having my niece and nephew back in our lives."

Lessie smiled in agreement. As Lynne drove her to school, Lessie punched a quick text to her cousin. >>*Mom just told me you guys talked last night. I'm so excited you'll be coming for my graduation!* Knowing he was probably still sleeping over in the Pacific time zone, she conjured the patience to wait for his response later.

She retrieved her phone from her locker before lunch, and her heart soared as she read Will's reply. >>*Yeah! We're excited! Don't tell Aunt Lynne, but we're going to try to talk Dad into coming with us.*

She grinned as she held her phone to her pounding heart, wondering if he and Cam would succeed. It would be the best graduation gift she could ever ask for. She was immediately jolted from her thoughts by a sudden voice next to her.

"Well, this is the happiest I've seen you in weeks."

"Adam," she breathed, then gave him an encouraging smile. "I just found out my cousins are coming for graduation."

He brightened with hope. "That's great!" he replied sincerely. They paused, silently smiling at each other, until Adam cleared his throat. "Look, I want things to go back to the way they were."

Lessie sighed, her optimism growing. "Me too."

"Can we put our differences aside and, I dunno, have fun again?"

Riding on her new high of emotions, she replied, "Yeah. I'd like that."

Adam grinned, relief visibly washing over him. "Want to see a movie with me this weekend?"

I could use a real date, actually, she thought to herself. "Definitely."

He exhaled and drew her into a tight embrace. "Thank you, Lessie," he said into her hair.

She smiled and wrapped her arms around his waist in return, soaking in the moment.

IF SHE THOUGHT her day couldn't improve more, Will's message to her that evening proved her wrong.

Les — video message me, I think me and Cam are making headway with Dad!

She wasted no time calling him, grinning as his excited face filled her screen. "Tell me *everything*," she urged.

"Cam and I had dinner with Dad. We decided we'd force him into conversation. It was hard, but we didn't back down. I didn't try to get into any of the stuff you and I talked about, but instead we talked about family values, about holding grudges, how all this anger all these years isn't healthy. We let him know that Nana told you why he left the family and that you told us. How Nana is gone now, there's no changing the past, and none of this is Aunt Lynne's fault, and it's not fair for his anger to keep us all separated from the family." Will sighed. "A lot of it was in one ear and out the other. It was ridiculous. Finally, Cam asked him if any of this is what Mom would have wanted. And that finally got a reaction out of him."

Lessie shifted, her heart beating faster. "What did he say?"

Will's face faltered. "Nothing. He just hung his head." He brightened slightly, and added, "But it was a reaction!"

Lessie shook her head, smiling softly. "So...?"

"So, Cam brought out the big guns, and got teary and told him she loved him, and didn't want to see him angry anymore, and wants to see him make amends with his sister."

Lessie nodded. "Did it work?"

"I think it got us somewhere. Only because Cam looks so much like Mom." His voice was lower as he dropped his gaze. He cleared his throat. "He said he'd think about it."

Lessie's grin lit up her face. "That's awesome! That's *huge*, Will!"

He chuckled. "I know. I never thought I'd see this day. We'll keep trying."

Lessie shrugged. "Just buy him a plane ticket and tell him he doesn't have a choice."

Will smiled. "Cam said that, too. I don't want to get him pissed off at us though."

Lessie sighed happily as she thought about her mother's reaction to seeing her brother for the first time in nearly two decades. She could only imagine she'd be elated.

"Thanks again for finding me, Les," Will said quietly, and Lessie lifted her head to meet his eyes through the screen.

"You've said that already," she answered with a smile.

"Well, you changed my life." His voice grew softer as he dropped his gaze. "I was in a pretty dark place before you came along."

Lessie sighed, wishing she could pull him into an embrace. "Not anymore, Will. And you've helped me more than you know, too."

He smiled as he met her eyes again. "Glad we have each other."

CHAPTER 28

LESSIE SIGHED happily on the way home with Adam, their movie date having been a success and rekindling emotions that had fallen dormant until then. She had nestled into him in the dark theater as he wrapped his arm around her, sharing popcorn and laughing at the comedy they had chosen to see. It was exactly what she needed, feeling revitalized and realizing that she'd been a bit too distant from her friends and overly absorbed in her secret friendship with Mitch.

"I'm glad we did this," Lessie said into the darkness as Adam drove, the night broken by oncoming headlights and the car serene with the radio playing quietly. He smiled in return.

"Me, too. We needed this." He glanced her way, sincerity in his eyes. "I really missed you."

"I'm sorry I've been so distracted." She reached for his hand and interlaced her fingers with his, resting their arms on the console.

"What's been going on?"

"Oh, family stuff, I guess. My uncle hasn't talked to my mom in over eighteen years. I've never even met him. My cousins are planning on coming to my graduation, and they're working on trying to get him to come, too."

"You can talk to me about this stuff, you know."

She sighed and nodded. "I know." She focused on appreciating his concern, though she knew she could never fully open up.

They kissed goodbye, embracing each other tightly, wishing they could prolong the moment. Adam leaned his forehead against hers, as her eyes fell closed. Their religious differences were a distant memory.

She carried a feeling of warmth and contentment with her as she made her way quietly up to her bedroom. After changing into pajamas, she checked her phone and found a message waiting for her from Will. Yawning, she tapped the message on her phone to open it.

Les, we got Dad a ticket. Her heart skipped a beat as she read faster. *He didn't exactly agree to come yet, but we're so close! Can't wait to talk more!*

She grinned, feeling a fullness in her heart. An alert appeared from her social media messenger, and she opened it as she sat down on her bed.

>>*Hey, haven't talked to you in awhile, you still alive?*

Mitch... Mixed emotions began coursing through her as she chewed her lower lip. After her wonderful evening with Adam, whom she'd been neglecting for too long, her secret friendship with Mitch suddenly didn't seem fair, or right.

But at the same time, she didn't want it to stop. *Couldn't* let it stop.

She replied. >>*Hey! Sorry! A lot has been going on.*

>>*You and Adam look like you made up.*

She squinted at the screen, her stomach turning. >>*Yeah, things are good. I've been kinda blowing him off. I feel bad.*

>>*Do you still like him?*

"What?" she whispered, shaking her head as her eyebrows creased. >>*What kind of question is that?*

>>*Just don't think you should string someone along if you're not really that into them.*

She narrowed her eyes as her heart beat harder. >>*Well, obviously I like him.*

>>*What was your problem before?*

>>*Religious views. Why do you care?*

>>*Religious views are a big deal.*

>>*Well we can work past them. What's your problem anyway?*

There was a pause, then finally, >>*Nothing.*

>>*Then lay off, my love life is none of your business.* She felt tense, her teeth clenched and her jaw set. Her stomach turned again.

>>*Look I just don't think it's fair to your little boyfriend for you to be talking to some other guy in secret.*

Her brows creased deeper. *Little boyfriend?* She remembered Adam sticking up for her to Mitch, how fierce and in control he had been, and borderline *mean.*

Of course Mitch would have a problem with him. His poor male ego was hurt. >>*Look I thought we were friends, now you're just being an ass. Like you always used to be. What's going on here? What exactly do you think we are?*

Her heart hammered, unsure of what to expect for a response as she watched the ellipse on the screen.

>>*We're freaks, Les.*

She sighed, then clenched her jaw again. >>*Maybe so. But I prefer to surround myself with people who accept me for it.* She took a breath, suddenly feeling pained, then typed, >>*Goodnight, Mitch.* And she closed the app.

She curled into the covers, staring at the dark wall as she

processed everything that happened. How could she go from feeling so complete and full of joy, to heartbroken and lost?

It took great effort for Lessie to keep from looking in Mitch's direction throughout the day Monday, especially at lunch. She couldn't help but catch sight of him a time or two, and each time she noticed he looked downcast and sullen, which tore at her aching heart. She tried to redirect her focus to her relationship with Adam, but somehow it wasn't as comforting as it was on their date the night before. The one thing that did genuinely cheer her up was the idea of seeing her cousins and, possibly, her uncle in just a few short weeks. She took refuge in those thoughts and strived to not think about Mitch the rest of the day.

Until she saw him at his locker after last period. She sighed as she watched him angrily packing his backpack. His crutch was finally gone, and he stood evenly and confidently on both feet.

Lessie adjusted her backpack over her shoulder, took a breath, and walked toward Mitch.

"What's going on?" she demanded, and his shoulders visibly tensed.

"Nothing," he finally said, stuffing the last book into his backpack and zipping it shut.

"Doesn't seem like nothing," she said. Several students shot them curious glances as they made their way through the halls. Lessie suddenly realized this was the first time they'd spoken in person since he relayed Nana's message to her in the park.

He slammed his locker door and turned to leave without so much as glancing at her. "Carter!" he called.

"Hey, man!" his friend replied from down the hall, smiling.

Mitch continued walking away from Lessie, as though she

didn't exist. Her heart shattered as she watched him leave, her throat tightening as he joined Carter at his side and the two disappeared down the hall.

She stood, breathing, unable to move.

"What the hell, Les?"

She jumped, then turned to face Emily, whose face was strewn with anger, her arms folded over her chest. "What was that?"

"Nothing," Lessie muttered.

"Didn't look like nothing," Emily replied.

"Well, it was!" she barked back, then turned to leave as quickly as she could, not wanting to speak to anyone anymore.

THE NEXT DAY Emily actively avoided Lessie, and Lessie's anger only grew stronger. She needed to redirect her focus on Adam, now more than ever. Though, somewhere deep inside of her, she realized she no longer wanted to.

He met her at her locker as he always did before lunch. "Everything okay with you and Emily?" he questioned.

Lessie sighed. "She's got her own issues," she replied. "But I'm fine."

"Okay, well, I was actually wanting to ask you about your Easter plans. Of course you're welcome to come to our family gatherings. But... My family and I would love for you to join us at church. Would you like to come?"

She tried to suppress her groan. An invitation to church was the last thing she needed while trying to stay focused and positive on their relationship. *Here we go again.* "Um, when is it?"

He chuckled, as though she should know this. "Uh, Sunday?"

She sighed, forcing a smile. "Sorry, we've never really made a big deal out of Easter. Kinda forgot it was coming up." She gave him a surrendering shrug. "Why not. I'll go." Maybe this would at least get Emily off her back, if she saw that Lessie was making an effort with their relationship.

He grinned. "Awesome." And he leaned forward to kiss her.

She sighed as she attempted to return his affection. But, she realized, the electricity was gone.

"HAPPY EASTER, DAD," Lessie greeted absently as she entered the kitchen Sunday morning.

"You too, Hon. You're doing the church thing again?" Sam eyed Lessie from behind his newspaper, bringing a mug of coffee to his lips.

She rolled her eyes. "Yeah. Giving it another shot."

The newspaper crinkled against the table as he smoothed his hands over the surface. "Are you liking his church?"

Lessie eyed him thoughtfully, then said, "Not... really."

"Why are you going?" He held her gaze as her brows creased, and he added, "I'm not saying there's anything wrong with it, you can do what you want. Some people need that sense of family that organized religion provides, and if you need that, you should go. But something tells me that's not what's going on." Lessie remained silent, uncertain of where to begin explaining her feelings. "You can talk to me," Sam spoke, interrupting her thoughts. "I was a teenager once, too, you know."

She rolled her eyes, but smiled warmly at him. "One with the ability to cross souls over to the other side, but all your friends just think you're spacing out?"

Sam laughed as he folded his newspaper on the table. "No. But I was a teenager." He smiled at her encouragingly, and she finally relented with a sigh.

"You know that boy I was talking to in the park that one afternoon you picked me up?" Sam nodded, and Lessie continued. "We've been talking secretly. He's the boy I saved when I got sick the first time." Sam's eyebrows rose as Lessie leaned against the table. "Apparently near-death experiences can result in enhanced psychic abilities. And he can now hear dead people."

Sam simply blinked at his daughter. Finally, he whistled an exhale, shaking his head. "Damn, sweetheart. I take it back. I wasn't a teenager like this."

Lessie chuckled, leaning back in her chair. "Told ya."

"So what's going on with this boy?"

She shrugged, running her finger along the edge of the table. "He used to pick on me because of my... thing. But, we started talking 'cause, ya know, he's weird now, too. And I've found that it's really nice to have someone to talk to who *gets* it."

Sam nodded. "I could see that." He held her gaze for a moment. "That was pretty big of you to be his friend after he used to be mean to you."

She shrugged. "I almost felt like I didn't have a choice. It just... happened. We talked for *weeks*. About *everything*. But, then he got all mad at me after Adam and I went on a date. For no reason."

Sam squinted. "No reason, huh? After you and Adam went on a date?"

"Yeah. Now he won't talk to me."

Her father nodded slowly. "Uh huh. You like this guy?"

Lessie's head snapped up from the table. "What? No! I mean...

I don't know, I used to sort of have a crush on him, which was stupid because he was so mean, but he's so cute... But that doesn't matter, we're just friends now!" She dropped her head once more. "Or, at least, we were. And I really don't know how I feel about him anymore."

Sam chuckled. "And how do you feel about Adam?"

Lessie shrugged, looking back down at her fingers. "Comfortable, I guess."

"But...?"

She sighed. "But not really... happy." She paused as she reflected on all the times she felt so at odds with him, and her memory drifted to the Valentine's dance, when Mitch relayed a message from the Other Side. Adam didn't believe in any of it. Everything that was her life, that was her reality, was nothing but fairy tales to Adam. She lifted her head to meet her dad's eyes. "And this religious difference thing really sucks."

Sam smiled softly. "So why are you doing it?"

"Because it makes him happy and we've been doing pretty good lately, so I guess I feel like I want to help things along."

"But does it make *you* happy?"

Lessie frowned, casting her gaze to the side. "No."

"So why are you doing it?" he repeated.

A million answers swirled through her head. She cared about Adam. She appreciated his friendship, and his ability to look past her abnormalities. She admired his confidence, and she felt she had become a better, more confident person since being with him. But she didn't feel accepted for her beliefs. She felt he wanted her to change, to accept his belief system as her own. And that would never happen.

It would be one thing to just stick it out until the end of

the school year. But then there was Mitch, and she wanted her friendship back with him. He was right, it wasn't fair to Adam if she was having a secret friendship with another boy behind his back. And, she had to admit, whatever she had with Mitch was more fulfilling than what she ever had with Adam. But should she waste her time with him if he was going to continue being the asshole he always had been? Did he really even deserve her friendship?

"I don't know, Dad," she replied quietly.

ADAM ARRIVED DRESSED in his Sunday best, looking handsome as always, but the chemical reaction his appearance used to ignite inside of her was gone. She forced a smile and climbed into the passenger seat of his car, her mind filled with questions and uncertainty after her conversation with her dad.

"I'm glad you're coming," he spoke as they pulled out of her driveway.

"Sure," she replied, forcing an encouraging smile in his direction.

She passively observed as the service took place, listening to the minister, watching the reactions of the people in the congregation, constantly hearing about eternal life, Jesus as king, Son of God, and many strange concepts she was becoming used to hearing since her relationship with Adam began. Those concepts still didn't resonate with her when she thought of the Heaven she was familiar with. There were no gates, there wasn't an entry fee, no man in the sky. She sighed as she sank into the church pew.

The people around her were happy to believe in these things. Adam was happy. And she realized, upon further reflection, that she was happy for all of them. To have something that brought them comfort, knowing where their souls went in the afterlife; if that's what they needed, then who was she to judge or tell them they were wrong?

But she didn't belong there. Of that, she was certain.

Lessie was quiet on the ride home, staring out the window as her mind turned over the possibility that things may be drawing to a close with Adam. It was a painful thought, as their relationship had been momentarily looking up for them. But, after her conversation with her father, and certainly after the church service and their differences being brought to her attention once again, she realized she didn't want to go on pretending. She just hoped she wouldn't completely break his heart.

"Lessie?"

She was jarred from her thoughts. She sat up and turned her head to face him. "What?"

"That was the third time I called your name, I was starting to think your thing happened again."

"Sorry, just thinking." She went back to staring out the window.

"About what?"

She sighed. *Let's see where this goes,* she thought, surrendering. "About your beliefs." She glanced over at him in time to see his face fall.

"Oh." He hesitated before asking, "What about them?"

"Just... Jesus being the King, Son of God, et cetera. The whole needing him for eternal life thing."

"I don't understand what you're not getting."

"What if he was just a regular guy who was just really enlightened? What if he was just trying to get us to see things from his perspective? To know that God is in *all* of us, not something separate from us."

His brows creased as he signaled a left turn and turned the wheel. "You kinda said that before, but I still don't follow."

She sat straighter in her seat, facing him. "We're all going to the same place, Adam. We don't need a ticket or a secret password. We just need to know how to live while we're *here*, before we get back *there*."

"Oh yeah? And how's that?"

She drew from her grandmother's wisdom. "Maybe our souls have to evolve. Maybe we're supposed to learn some kind of lesson, so that we can be more connected to the Source."

"Source?"

"Another way of saying God. What if God isn't a man in the clouds? What if we're all, like, *pieces* of the great God energy? And that energy, that power of God, is already in us? And we're just here to figure out how to tap into it? Or find our way back to it? What if that's what Jesus was trying to tell us?"

Adam shook his head as he turned on the road to her house. "That's not what the Bible says..."

"How do you *know*? What if it's just been misinterpreted all these years? Didn't Jesus say we are *all* children of God?" She felt alive just talking about it, playing the concepts over through her mind. Pondering the possibilities of what awaited in the great Beyond was like nourishment to her soul.

Adam did not reciprocate those emotions. Instead, she was met with fear and resistance. "How do *you* know?" He pulled into her driveway and parked in front of her house. He met her eyes, his own heavy with questions and uncertainty. "What if you *do* need to believe in Jesus, and all this time you don't, and what happens to you when you die?"

"What do you think will happen to me?" she asked, turning the question back to him. She already knew the answer. It was the advantage she would forever hold.

He blinked. "I guess you go to Hell."

"Aren't I a good person, though?"

"Well, yes, of course, but—"

"So the fact that I'm a good person doesn't matter, ultimately? What matters is that I believe in Jesus? What if I murdered people? Stole and lied and cheated? But so long as I believe in Jesus I can go to heaven?"

"I, well..." He looked genuinely puzzled.

She decided to shift to a different concept. "Do you ever question things? Is it wrong to question? To explore other possibilities? To find meaning and purpose in life outside of what our elders tried to instill in us?"

"I don't *know!*" he yelled, and she recoiled slightly, eyes wide. "I don't want to fight about this anymore," he said softly, staring at the steering wheel.

She sighed, looking down at her knees. "I'm sorry. I just... I believe what I believe, and I have... my own reasons to believe it's real. I'm not trying to take church away from you; I just don't want you to try to force it on me."

"I just didn't want you to miss out," he said quietly, slowly turning his head to her.

She smiled gently. "I'm not. Trust me."

He stared at her, as though trying desperately to figure her out, while at the same time trying to resist all the new questions she stirred within him. "What do you mean you have your own reasons to believe your ideas are real?"

Lessie shook her head. "I just do." Her heart told her to keep her secret to herself. But if she couldn't confide the reality of her life in her own boyfriend, then what kind of relationship was that? "I should go," she finally said.

He nodded, picking at his steering wheel with his thumbnail, his expression distant.

She took a breath, her heart tightening in her chest. "Maybe we need some time off..." Her voice was nearly a whisper. She could already feel the tears brimming.

He jerked his head over to meet her eyes. "Like, what? A... a breakup?"

She took in a shaky breath. "I..." Her shoulders slumped. "I just think we're too different, in some senses. I don't want to try to change you, and I don't want you to try to change me."

"I'm not trying to change you." His eyes were wide and pained as he gazed at her intently, desperately.

"Then you'd be fine with me never going to church with you again? You're fine that I don't believe in Jesus the same way you do?"

He returned his gaze to his thumbnail on the chipped vinyl on his steering wheel. He struggled to contain the pain on his face.

"It's fine. It's what brings you and your family and your community comfort. But I have different beliefs and, for reasons I can't really explain to you, that's not going to change."

"But we can believe our different things, and go on like we were before, can't we?" He finally looked up to meet her eyes again, and she could see his own tears welling.

She drew in her bottom lip, lowering her head. Could they? She thought about Mitch, and how much she missed their friendship already. She thought about her secret life, and how she'd have to continue keeping it a secret from Adam. And how that truly wasn't fair. Perhaps Mitch had a right to be angry with her, after all. A tear spilled as she looked up at him. "It's not the same. Too much life has happened, and is continuing to happen, and I think... I think our differences are going to make it too hard to stay together." Her chin quivered as another tear spilled. It pained her to not be able to tell him everything, to leave him in such confusion as to where her heart truly was.

"Is this what you really want?" He met her eyes, and the pain in his expression almost made her want to take it all back.

But she knew she couldn't. "I..." she whispered. "Yeah." She dropped her gaze to her knees.

A tear fell down his own cheek, and she swallowed against the shattering in her heart. Finally, he nodded, staring at the steering wheel.

She drew in a breath as the air in the car shifted. "So, I guess... I guess I'll see ya around."

"Yep."

She continued staring at her knees. "Thanks for everything," she said lamely.

"I'll see ya later." There was finality in his voice, but he wouldn't look at her. The pain in her heart was consuming.

"Okay." Another tear fell as she opened the door and pulled herself out of the car. "Take care, Adam..."

"Bye," he answered.

She choked on a sob as she shut the door and stood numbly in the driveway as he drove away. How could doing what she felt was *right* feel so painful? She felt broken and torn and a bit lost, lacking a sense of closure, like they were supposed to share one last kiss or embrace, give some sort of formal goodbye, before parting ways. She sighed. How could her grandmother's death be easier and come with better closure than a breakup with a guy she just wasn't clicking with anymore?

Wiping her tears with the back of her hand, she turned and headed back into the house.

CHAPTER 29

THE FIRST day back at school was harder than Lessie anticipated. She glanced around nervously as she shut her locker before first period, hoping Adam wasn't nearby.

"What's wrong with you?" Emily spoke, making Lessie jump.

"Geez, I didn't even know you were there."

"Yeah, it's like *you're* not even there." She gave Lessie a pressing gaze as she folded her arms over her English books.

Lessie sighed sadly. "I broke up with Adam Sunday after church."

Emily was silent, motionless, and unreadable. Lessie swallowed, then added, "The religious difference thing... It's just getting to be too much for me."

"I get that," Emily finally muttered. "But you couldn't stick it out til the end of the school year?"

Lessie blinked, hugging her Spanish books to her chest. "Are you mad?"

Emily exhaled in exacerbation. "I'm kinda not happy about our group being messed up, now, yeah."

Lessie opened and closed her mouth a few times, unable to form words.

Emily continued before Lessie could speak. "Just don't go

to church with him anymore! He could get over it! It's not like you're in church at school!"

Lessie glowered at her friend. "I've got a lot of other stuff on my mind, too, ya know! Church isn't the only thing driving us apart!"

"Like *what? Mitch?*" Lessie's breath hitched. "Does this have something to do with you two talking the other day?" Emily pressed.

Lessie desperately wanted to tell Emily of her communication with Mitch and the friendship they'd formed. How he'd been somehow changing, how she'd been drawing comfort from their conversations. How hurt she was that their communication had stopped.

But this Emily was not the Emily she knew and loved. "I can't... I can't really get into that right now," she said quietly. "I have to get to class." She was finished, no longer wanting to endure the hurt of her best friend's lack of support. Lessie turned and headed to the Spanish classroom, leaving Emily to stew in her own emotions.

Lessie's heart began to hammer furiously as she entered the classroom for third period English, which she shared with Adam.

He completely avoided eye contact with her, and she did the same, focusing intently on the lesson and glancing repeatedly at the clock, willing it to move faster so she could get out of Adam's presence. She escaped the classroom unscathed and sighed with relief.

Lunch was even worse. The tension was palpable. Lessie picked absently at her spaghetti, and Emily silently shoveled hers into her mouth with an angry determination.

"Um..." Evan spoke awkwardly. "You guys okay?"

Emily ignored his comment. "I met with the guidance counselor today."

"O-Okay...?" Evan replied, still glancing back and forth between the two girls.

"I've been looking at a school in Arizona. I think I'm going to apply."

Evan's mouth fell open slightly as Lessie's head snapped up.

"What?" Evan gasped.

"Since when?" Lessie balked simultaneously. "I thought you had decided on the Art Institute in Chicago?"

"For awhile," Emily replied with a shrug. "I kinda changed my mind. I just never said anything because I didn't want to hurt anyone. But, since it's okay to do things without concern for others' feelings, I figured, what the hell?" She glared directly at Lessie.

"Hang on, I—" Evan tried to break in, but was cut off.

Lessie glared back, feeling defensive. She gripped her fork. "Oh, then I guess you don't expect me to say, 'Good for you, Emily, I'm glad you're doing something to better yourself, even though I'll miss you terribly.' Or, 'I support you doing what's right for *you*.'" She seethed as she slammed her fork on her tray and stood from the table. "But I guess best friends aren't supposed to support each other's decisions, huh?" She grasped her tray and stormed from the table. Appetite lost, she angrily tossed her tray through the return window and made her way to the art room, where she attempted to find solace until the fifth period bell toned.

She'd never been so aggravated to have to share a class with Emily. She tried to ignore the piercing stare Emily shot at her as she blew into the classroom, slamming her art supplies on the table. "Great, now Evan is mad at me, thanks to you," Emily barked.

Lessie glared at her. "How is that *my* fault? You sure it has nothing to do with the fact that his girlfriend *blindsided* him? Maybe if you'd actually bother to *care* about other people's feelings instead of focusing only on *yourself*—"

"Oh, like *you're* so good at that? Gotta go breaking hearts instead of sucking it up til the end of the school year?"

"There's more to it than that!" Lessie screamed.

"Girls!"

They both fell silent as they turned to face Mrs. Finn, and realized the entire class was staring at them.

"Sorry," they both muttered. They didn't speak for the rest of the day.

"Everything okay?" Sam questioned hesitantly as he drove Lessie home from school. She had thrown herself into the car and slammed the door behind her, then proceeded to stare angrily out the window as he pulled out of the parking lot. He allowed her some silence as they drove, until curiosity finally got the better of him. "What's going on?"

"What do you think?" she muttered, pressing her face into her arm as she leaned against the window and continued to glare across the passing landscape.

Sam took a breath. "Is it that boy?"

Lessie huffed into her arm. "Part of it."

"You wanna tell me the rest?"

She fought against the sting of tears at the backs of her eyes, her throat tightening as she tried to focus on the fields and trees as they made their way home. It was everything she could do to hold back. If she opened her mouth, the tears would surely fall.

"Did something happen with Adam?" he asked carefully, glancing in her direction.

She broke. The tears spilled over and silently fell as her chin quivered.

Sam's face fell with concern as he reached to give her knee a squeeze. "Hey, what happened?"

"I broke up with him Sunday," she choked, and squeezed her eyes shut as her anguish flowed.

"Hey, it's alright..."

"No!" She sat upright and wiped at her freely falling tears. "It's not! Because now Emily is mad at me for breaking up our group. So *she's* not talking to me. So I lost my boyfriend, and my best friend, and Mitch is still ignoring me, too. I have no friends!" She choked on another sob as she brought her hands to her face.

Sam remained silent. Finally, he spoke. "Why don't you try talking to Mitch again?"

Lessie looked up from her hands, her brows lowered over squinting eyes. "What? He's the one who quit talking to me. Why would I try to talk to him?"

Sam shrugged. "Maybe you're just misunderstanding one another."

"He's a jerk, Dad. Why are you sticking up for him?"

Sam pulled onto their lane, slowing as he drove down the rock road. "I'm not necessarily sticking up for him. But you were happy while you two were talking, and, well, I just think there might be some unspoken... words." He fell short, as though there were more to say. Instead, he quietly glanced at Lessie, frowning.

"Unspoken words?"

"Just give the kid a chance, that's all I'm saying." He pulled into the garage, parked the car, and offered Lessie a sympathetic smile, which she only returned with frustration.

She went straight to her room, fuming with her anger toward Emily and Mitch. Of course she should have expected it from Mitch; he was always an ass before, so why should he be any different now? But... she could have sworn he changed.

She furrowed her brows, pursing her lips as she glanced at her laptop. She shouldn't allow him to treat her like that. Not after they'd come so far. Her dad was right; she should say something to him.

She opened her laptop, clicked on the messenger icon, and began typing.

Look, Mitch, I don't know why you felt the need to act the way you did the other night. Or why you quit talking to me. But I just want to let you know that I don't think it's fair. And I'm disappointed in you. I was proud of you for overcoming everything you'd been through. It seemed like you learned to make the best of your situation, maybe even grow from it.

But no. Apparently I was wrong. You're still the same asshole you always were before. Thanks for letting me down.

Hitting "send" only brought her temporary satisfaction. She tried not to think about any of it through supper. Lynne attempted to get Lessie to talk, but Lessie remained silent, saying she'd rather not, and to let Dad fill her in. Lessie excused herself after dinner and headed to her room, where she pulled open her laptop to send a message to Will, hoping that concentrating on their family affairs would cheer her up, or at least distract her from her sudden complete lack of friends. She was immediately sidetracked by a response from Mitch.

>>*I'm sorry.*

She stared at the screen for a moment, then began typing a reply.

>>*Well. Isn't that nice.*

Not long after, he wrote back.

>>*I'm serious.*

She blinked, feeling hopeful, but not quick to forgive. >>*What the hell was your problem anyway?*

>>*I dunno. I lost my leg and my football career all in one night. And most of my friends cuz now the dead talk to me. To name a few.*

>>*I get it. But you didn't have to take it out on me. All I've done was try to help you. And you sure as hell didn't deserve that.*

>>*I know.*

She cocked her head slightly. >>*You do?*

>>*Yes. And I'm sorry for that too.*

>>*You are...?*

>>*Yes. I'm sorry. Sorry for always being a dick to you, making your life hell, blaming you for ruining my life, all of it. You're right, I don't deserve your help.*

She reread his words several times. Was she still talking to the same person?

Before she could type a response, he added, >>*So I get it if you don't want to talk to me anymore.*

She sighed, drawing in her lower lip. >>*No, I do. I kind of don't have any friends right now. So I'll settle for you.*

>>*Gee, thanks. Why don't you have any friends?*

>>*I broke up with Adam and Emily got all pissed with me about it.*

>>*You did? When?*

>>*Sunday after church.*

>>*Ah. Religious differences.*

She smiled softly, surprised that he remembered their conversation about her and Adam's relationship. >>*Yeah.* She sighed, then added, >>*You should be happy now, since you gave me such a hard time about things going good for us last time.*

>>*Sorry.*

>>*Yeah, am I not allowed to be happy if you're not happy?*

>>*That's not it. Look I said I was sorry. For all of it. Everything. And I mean it.*

She leaned her face into her palm as she stared at the screen, drumming her fingers against the table. Hope glimmered in her, but it didn't quite replace the void in her heart from her broken friendships.

CHAPTER 30

LESSIE CAUGHT her breath in the foyer of the school building, having run in quickly to avoid the pouring rain. She removed her coat and gave it a shake, took a breath to gather her courage, and headed to her locker. She made up her mind to have lunch in the art room and completely avoid the cafeteria, and thus any possible run-ins with Emily, Adam, or Mitch. She sighed as her thoughts traveled to Mitch, realizing she still was unsure where their friendship stood.

She focused on her classes, forcing her mind not to wander to her former friends. Fourth period P.E. was harder than she anticipated, however, and her distraction led her to taking a basketball to the head. She was thrown sideways and landed hard on her arm. "Gah!" she screamed as she hit the polished hardwood.

A strained wrist had her sitting out the rest of the class. She climbed into the bleachers after receiving an inspection and an ice pack from Coach Benedict, and glanced hesitantly at Mitch before deciding to sit near him.

"That was graceful," he mocked, smirking, and nodding toward her iced wrist.

She rolled her eyes, while inside her heart leapt at his

acknowledgement. "What are you sitting out for?" she asked, braving conversation.

"All the running jacks with my knee," he replied simply. "It's getting better though. Just don't want to overdo it."

She nodded, feeling herself relax. "That's smart."

"I'm going to get back to it one day." He gazed out over the gymnasium as their classmates scrimmaged on the floor.

She gave him a small smile. "I'm sure you will."

He cracked a smile in return, leaning into the heels of his hands on the bleacher. He looked down, stretching out his left leg, and eyeing the fiberglass where it emerged from beneath the wrappings at his knee. She reveled in the sudden realization that they were talking amicably outside of the internet, and that she loved the sound of his voice...

"Hey boy, Lester tryin' to make some moves on you?" Blake jeered from the floor at the bottom bleacher, breaking Lessie from her thoughts. Mitch simply lifted his middle finger to him. Lessie's heart stopped as her breath hitched. "Whoa, dude! Chill!" Blake exclaimed. "She your girlfriend now or something?"

Mitch leaned his elbows on his knees and proceeded to lift his other hand, presenting the other middle finger.

Lessie's wide eyes darted back and forth between the two as Blake shook his head, rolling his eyes. "Whatever, man." He joined Dean and they both snarled, whispering amongst each other while looking in the direction of Lessie and Mitch. They laughed and bumped fists.

Lessie glanced at Mitch, who was now scowling at his knees, his shoulders raised to his ears as his hands pressed into the seat on either side of him. She dropped her own gaze and said in a quiet voice, "Look, if it's easier for you if I just avoid you, I can sit somewhere else."

He brought his head up to face her, his eyes narrowed. "What?"

"I mean, you have a reputation. I get it if hanging out with me might mess that up for you. I don't want to make your life harder than—"

"Shut up," he interrupted, and her eyebrows raised slightly as she closed her mouth. They locked eyes for a moment, until finally he said, "You think I'm the same person I was before? Those guys," he gestured in the direction of Blake, and continued, "they don't get it. I'm a freak to them, and not one of them has tried to get an idea of what I'm going through. It sucks. You're about the only person who's taken the time to show me any kind of support in this, and you're the *last* person I deserve it from." He shook his head. "So. Fuck what they think. You can keep your ass right here on this bleacher."

She blinked over wide eyes, then slowly turned her head to absently watch the basketball scrimmage, a smile creeping onto her lips. "Okay, then," she replied softly. His words stirred something deep inside of her. She swallowed and continued to watch the game, though her mind wandered to their conversation the night before. She cleared her throat. "So, uh. Is everything okay between us?"

He glanced her way, meeting her eyes, causing her to catch her breath again. "Yeah." He brought his attention back to the gym floor.

"So I don't have to worry about you being an ass to me again?"

"I said I'm sorry." He met her eyes again. "Can I make it up to you?"

Her heart stopped so abruptly she thought she'd pass out. "I was just giving you shit, Mitch, I don't expect you to—"

"Look, don't make things weird," he cut in. "You said last night you have no friends. I'll sit with you at lunch, how about that?"

She blinked, her mind reeling. "And that *isn't* gonna make things weird?"

He eyed her, squinting. "Do you not want to be seen in public with me?"

She surrendered with a sigh, her heart lifting as she felt certain she was in a dream. A smile tugged at the corners of her mouth as she stared out at the gym. "Fuck what they think."

Mitch met Lessie at her locker after P.E., ignoring the glances and stares from passing students. It took everything she had in her to keep from grinning like a lunatic as her heart hammered furiously in her chest. Oh, what she would give to turn the clock back to August to let herself know where she'd be at the end of the school year. She admitted it to herself: her crush on Mitch Griffin was suddenly, and undeniably, back full-force.

They found an empty end at a table full of mostly freshmen who didn't know them and didn't care, and sat down across from each other with their trays.

Lessie stole a quick glance in Emily's direction, making eye contact long enough to meet her angry scowl. Lessie quickly looked away, and almost involuntarily her eyes found their way to Adam, who was also staring at her, his face twisted in pain and confusion.

Lessie sighed as she dug into her ham sandwich, keeping her eyes focused on her lunch.

"What?" Mitch pressed.

"Adam," she admitted. "Pretty sure I crushed his soul. And I'm sure seeing me with you is not helping the matter."

"You don't have to sit with me."

Lessie shook her head. "I need to learn to not worry about what other people think."

"You seem okay with the breakup..." He eyed her carefully as he busied himself with his own lunch.

She shrugged. "It was a good relationship, but we're just too different. He did help me find a new sense of confidence, though."

Mitch gave a small nod. "Confidence looks good on you."

She cocked a brow, bringing her sandwich to her lips. "Mitch Griffin, did you just compliment me?" She suppressed a smile, feeling proud of herself for displaying her new confidence.

He kept his eyes on her, expression unchanging, bringing his own sandwich up. "Don't make things weird."

She smirked as she took a bite. After a moment, she asked, "What about your friends? Are they pretty much all a bunch of dicks, or are there any good ones? I mean, I can't really tell them apart. Their football jerseys all kind of blend together, and everyone calling me Lester kind of does, too..."

"Yeah, yeah, I get it," Mitch interrupted. "They're shallow. Most of them." He shrugged. "I've always been alpha dog, and they follow me around. I feel like harassing somebody, they harass them, too. I feel like having a party, they come."

"Living the dream," Lessie muttered sarcastically.

"It was how I got by after Dad died," he replied lowly, and her face fell. He sighed, bringing his voice back up. "Anyway. Carter's not bad. But he doesn't get it. He keeps telling me I should be glad I'm alive. That I'm lucky I'm alive." He scoffed, then grew quiet. "Everyone says that."

"Even though life as you knew it, and your hopes for your future, all died in that accident..." she replied softly as she stared at her tray. She recalled her mother's words, that the death of a dream was a lonely grief. She felt his eyes boring into her. Finally, as if drawn by a magnetic force, she lifted her own eyes to meet his. She detected a glimmer of appreciation, perhaps even relief, in their green depths.

"Yeah," he replied in the same quiet tone. A tingle crept up her spine as they held each other's gaze.

"What you doin' with Lester *again?*" came a jeering voice, breaking their reverie.

Lessie rolled her eyes as Mitch scowled, looking up at Blake, who was standing at the end of the table with his arms folded and brows arched, his face otherwise contorted into a sneer.

"Eating lunch."

"No shit, Sherman."

Lessie snorted into her sandwich.

Mitch stared at him in annoyance. "I'm pretty sure you mean 'Sherlock,' and, yes shit, now go back to your own table."

"Seriously Mitch? You leave me for *her?*"

Lessie scowled as Katie and all her perfect blonde curls joined Blake at his side, snarling just the same. Mitch sat back in his seat. "I recall *you* dumping *me.* By the way, thank you for that." There was genuine sincerity in his voice.

"Come on, guys, leave him alone," Carter broke in as he approached them, shooing the two away. They both left, rolling their eyes, and Carter's eyes fell on Mitch. "You can still sit with us, you know," he said gently. He glanced briefly at Lessie before returning his gaze to Mitch.

"I know," Mitch replied. "But I'm not."

"Did we do something?" Carter asked, his face falling with concern.

Mitch shook his head. "No. I just needed a change." He took a bite of his sandwich.

"Oh." Carter glanced at Lessie again, making momentary eye contact as she studied him, then returned his focus to Mitch once more. "Look, I don't have a problem with... whatever it is you're dealing with," he said, waving his hands around as he spoke. "And... I ain't judgin' ya, man. Just... I'm still your buddy."

Mitch sighed as his eyes fell back to his tray. "Thanks, Carter," he said quietly. Carter nodded once more, glanced a last time at Lessie, then left.

Lessie squinted at Mitch. "He doesn't seem too bad."

"Yeah. He's cool."

THE REMAINDER OF the week, and the following week, Mitch and Lessie continued to sit together. Every day, Lessie caught the same hurt look from Adam, and the same burning anger from Emily, as Mitch continued to catch flack from members of his former posse. And every time, they ignored the stares, the comments, and remained focused on each other, sharing stories about their previous lives, their friends and families, their adventures.

"Blake and Dean have always been annoying," Mitch explained Tuesday afternoon as they reached their table. "But, Blake's older brother always got the alcohol for our parties."

"I always wondered how that worked."

"Can I sit with you guys?"

Mitch and Lessie both drew their attention to Carter, who stood by the edge of the table with his tray in his hands, and hope in his eyes. They both raised their eyebrows, exchanged a glance and a shrug, and Mitch replied, "Sure," and pulled out the chair next to him.

The broad-shouldered boy took a seat and smiled hesitantly at Lessie. "Hey, I'm Carter."

She released a small laugh. "I know."

He nodded. "Right." Glancing back and forth between the two, he said, "I'm not interrupting anything, am I?"

"Nah," Mitch replied, smiling at his friend. "Glad you joined us."

"That table is lame without you there, man," he said, meeting Mitch's eyes. "Have Blake and Dean *always* been that annoying?"

"Yes," Mitch replied simply.

"Why do we put up with them?"

Mitch shrugged. "Beer."

Carter nodded in resignation, agreeing. Suddenly, a tall Hispanic girl with a pink stripe through her long, dark espresso hair appeared at the table, also holding her tray. Lessie recognized her as one of the Junior class cheerleaders. "Can I sit, too?"

The three looked up at her as she smiled cheerfully, and Mitch shrugged. "Sure."

"I'm Tess," she greeted, grinning at Lessie. She pulled up a chair next to Carter, and Lessie noticed the slightly darker shade of red on Carter's cheeks. Before they knew it, two other Junior girls joined them, sitting on Lessie's side of the table. Wren, who Lessie already knew from Art Club and also alto saxophone in the school band, was just slightly shorter than Tess; her highlighted, sandy brown hair was cut short and spiked in the back, and her smile lit up her large caramel eyes. Sami, another cheerleader, was significantly shorter, her wavy blonde hair drawn back in a loose ponytail, and her blue eyes smiling from her round, youthful face. Lessie couldn't help but notice the complete one-eighty her social life suddenly turned.

"So, I'll just point out the elephant in the room," Tess began, her dark brown eyes meeting Lessie's as she nodded between her and Mitch. "You two are a weird pair."

Lessie laughed nervously, already feeling out of place and now suddenly suffocated.

"Yeah," Mitch agreed with a shrug.

Tess raised her eyebrows, tilting her head as if to encourage him to go on. "So... What's the story? Weren't you always, like, a total dick to her?"

"Yeah," he replied again, his voice lower than before. Everyone stared at him, and Lessie showed no signs of adding commentary. Mitch sighed. "But, she gets what I'm going through, I guess."

Wren stared at Lessie with wide eyes. "He was an ass to you and you still decided to be nice to him?"

Lessie shrugged. "Sure, I guess," she replied hesitantly.

Tess shook her head, staring at Lessie. "Wow," she breathed. "That's, like, *so* nice."

"Like, *really* nice," Sami interjected. "I don't think I could ever be that nice."

"Me neither," Wren agreed.

Carter met Lessie's eyes. "Just so you know, I never called you Lester."

"You just watched while everyone else did," Tess cut in, pursing her lips.

Carter scowled at his tray. "Like you have room to talk."

"What's *that* supposed to mean? I'm nice to everyone!"

"You weren't nice to *me* just now."

"I call it like it is! You got a problem with that?"

His face reddened as he glared at her. "You don't have to throw me under the bus!"

Lessie watched as their bickering escalated, until finally, Tess snatched her tray and bolted to her feet, spewing off Spanish obscenities under her breath. Carter suddenly grasped her slender, brown arm in his massive palm, and she immediately halted with a look of indignation. She narrowed her eyes and opened her mouth to curse at him further, but before she could speak, he cut in with a pleading voice, "Will you go to prom with me?"

The silence was palpable. She stared with wide eyes before slowly placing her tray back on the table. Her entire disposition melted like snow in the springtime. "Oh my God, yes," she breathed, her eyes shining. She sank into her seat and grasped his hands in hers as his own eyes widened in disbelief. "I've been hoping you'd ask me for, like, *weeks.*"

"Oh my God, really?" Carter replied through a relieved exhale, a grin forming at the edges of his mouth.

Tess nodded enthusiastically, beaming, as she grasped his face in her palms and pulled him to her. She planted a heated kiss to his lips, and if his elation were something tangible, he would have floated straight to the ceiling.

Lessie watched the entire scene with a partially open mouth. As Carter brought his own hands to Tess's face and deepened their public display of affection, Lessie closed her mouth and brought her wide-eyed gaze to Mitch, who was simply smirking and shaking his head. "Does this sort of thing happen often?" Lessie asked, arching a brow.

"Tess has always been a wild card," Wren answered with a shrug and an eye roll as she turned her attention to her lunch.

LESSIE ENTERED ART class with a new sense of peace and fulfillment, reflecting on the sudden friendship that surrounded her at lunch, and still carrying an element of shock that that friendship mostly consisted of the social class she used to try to avoid like the plague. She found her table and absently opened her sketchbook.

"You disgust me," Emily hissed, breaking Lessie's thoughts. She snapped her head up to meet Emily's burning eyes. They hadn't spoken in over a week.

Lessie's brows creased. "I know that feeling," she replied lowly. She held Emily's gaze, challenging her, until finally Emily huffed and went back to her own table, fuming.

"You two gonna be okay?" Lessie's classmate, Meagan, asked as she sat down on the other side of her table.

Lessie shook her head in frustration. "I don't even know what to think."

"She'll come around. There's something cute about you and Mitch together."

Lessie blinked, her eyebrows raising. "Wait, what?"

Meagan shrugged as she flipped through her own sketchbook. "I mean, everyone's talking about you two. You're kind of a weird couple, but I like it." She smiled innocently at Lessie, who continued to stare in disbelief. "It's like West Side Story, ya know?"

Lessie glanced sadly at Emily, who was ignoring her at this point. "Or Romeo and Juliet," she muttered, hoping Emily would hear. Lessie shook her head, looking back at Meagan. "We're not exactly a 'thing,'" she stated.

"Oh," Meagan said, furrowing her brows. "It sure looks like you are."

❖

EACH DAY, LESSIE enjoyed her new friendships and the sense of open acceptance that came with it, looking forward to lunch with the appreciation that, for once in her life, she actually felt like a normal teenager.

She grinned as Wren and Tess met her at her locker after school that Friday.

"Mitch doesn't have a date to prom. You should go with him," Tess said as she folded her arms over her chest and smiled.

Lessie's face immediately fell. "I wasn't planning on going," she muttered as she stuffed her books into her backpack.

"Well, plan on it now," Tess responded.

Lessie narrowed her eyes. "Prom is next weekend. I don't have a dress, and I doubt I can get a hair appointment this late."

"We'll take you shopping, and my mom does hair as a side gig," Wren fired back and folded her own arms across her chest. "Next excuse?"

Lessie huffed out an exhale. "He's nominated for prom court, he wouldn't want someone like me as a date..."

"*Dios mio,*" Tess retorted, rolling her eyes. She then asked pointedly, "You like him, don't you?"

Lessie grew rigid. "We're friends," she answered firmly. "That's it."

"Well, then I'll go with him," Wren said, cocking her head slightly, arms still folded. Lessie's skin prickled as she opened her mouth to protest, but quickly stopped herself. She pressed her lips together and clenched her jaw. Wren giggled, bringing her finger up. "See? Don't like that idea, do ya? You *do* want to go with him!" Tess grinned at her friend's smooth play.

"Okay *fine, yes* I would go with him. If he asked me. Which he hasn't." Lessie shrugged her backpack over her shoulder.

"I can fix that," Tess replied, and as if right on cue, Mitch entered the hallway. "Mitch!" Tess called, waving her hand, and Lessie's stomach flipped as she drew in a breath. Tess grasped him by the arm and pulled him into their circle. He eyed them curiously with a small smile. "Do you have a date for prom?"

His smile faltered. "I'm not sure I'm going..."

"Yes you are, you're up for king," Wren said, rolling her eyes.

"That doesn't mean I want to go..." he muttered.

"Why don't you ask Lessie to go with you?" Tess pressed, arching a brow as she folded her arms again.

He blinked, meeting Lessie's eyes, and she went rigid as her heart began hammering. She opened her mouth to tell him he really didn't have to, but he cut her off. "I was thinking about it for awhile, actually..." He admitted in a quiet voice. Her insides nearly imploded. "Just wasn't sure if you'd actually want to go. Much less, go with me."

She stared at him with wide eyes and a slightly fallen jaw, until finally, she shook her head, and replied, "Of *course* I'll go with you!" Heat immediately rose to her cheeks. "I didn't think *you'd* want to go with *me...*"

He chuckled nervously as half a smile tugged at the side of his face. "Well, then, I guess it's a... a date. Or whatever you want to call it."

Lessie felt heat creeping up her neck as she shifted on her feet. "Don't make things weird..."

Tess and Wren grinned as Mitch recomposed himself and said, "Well, luckily I've got a tux on back-up. Just couldn't decide until now." Lessie's knees grew weak at the visual. He glanced at Tess and Wren. "You guys mind if we tag along for dinner?"

Tess brightened, and smirked. "You better be joining us!"

He flashed Lessie a warm smile, and her stomach nearly dropped out. Her sweaty palm gripped her backpack strap tighter. "Sounds like a plan, then."

"Great," Lessie squeaked, forcing a smile.

CHAPTER 31

"YOU DON'T look too thrilled," Genevieve commented at breakfast. It was the morning of prom. While Genevieve wished she could attend, it was an invitation-only event for anyone outside of the junior and senior classes.

Only a year ago Mitch was picking Katie up in his jeep, eager to dance the night away with their friends, and finish the night getting drunk at Blake's house afterward, living life as though they owned the world. He tapped his prosthetic foot against the table leg. Things were certainly different then.

"I'm struggling with it, I guess," he responded, stirring his spoon through his cereal. He felt guilty saying it out loud. He felt a strange sense of excitement about having Lessie as his date, after all the progression their friendship had made. He wanted his emotions of spending the evening with her, and a group of *real* friends, to override his feeling sorry for himself and the unexpected turn his life took, but he couldn't bring himself there. Those emotions weighed heavier on him that morning.

Genevieve's face fell. "You're up for prom king, you should be excited."

He swallowed, shrugging as his chest tightened. "The old me got nominated. I'm not who I used to be. And this is just another reminder that I'm not who I was. That my old life is dead. And so is my future."

She squinted and leaned against the island counter, watching him thoughtfully. "You're right, you're not who you used to be. You're better. And your life changed, yeah. But your future can only be dead if you are. And you're not. You're alive." She paused, then added, "You *lived*." She studied him as he stared into his cereal bowl. "What happened, Mitch? You've been, like, *happy* lately. Now, all of a sudden, you're not."

He shrugged, his gaze unmoving. "I have been, yeah. But I still lost a lot, and I'm only going to be reminded of that tonight. Can't expect me to be happy *all* the time." He abandoned his breakfast and stood from the table, silently making his way back to his room.

She frowned in sympathy. "But you gained so much more..." she whispered as he shut the door behind him.

LESSIE MARVELED AT the crystal chandeliers, the black drapes, gold decorations, and glittering lights. A local reception hall had been rented for prom, and its sweeping foyer and vast ballroom made Lessie feel as though she'd stepped into a life of royalty. But with Mitch at her side; broad shoulders clad in his tuxedo, piercing green eyes that would be on *her* that night; she felt as though she'd stepped into a dream. Her stomach had been turning all week at the prospect of the night. The thought of dancing with him made her so nervous she almost felt sick.

She glanced at Mitch as they gathered with their group at their reserved table, and frowned as his adam's apple bobbed in his throat. "What's up?" she asked, leaning closer to him. Her own nerves began to dissipate upon realizing that he just may be more troubled than herself. He shook his head, pressing his lips together. She couldn't help but chuckle. "Hey, *I'm* supposed to be the one who gets nervous at social events. *You're* the cool, popular one who does this all the time!"

He gazed out over the dancefloor as colored strobes flashed through the dark ballroom to the beat of the music. "That's the problem."

Once they finally made it to the floor, dancing seemed forced, and Lessie's heart sank. What she had been so nervous about was becoming more and more of a disappointment as the night wore on, and she was beginning to feel as though even his smiles were forced. She questioned herself — perhaps he truly *didn't* want her as his date. They gathered at their table once more, Tess and Carter giggling amongst themselves, Wren and Sami enthralled in each other. It was nearly a half hour until coronation.

A loud thud suddenly caught everyone's attention.

"Damnit!" Mitch exclaimed as his face twisted in pain. He lifted his left knee and clutched it to him as he grimaced. The pain was suddenly replaced with anger. He cursed several times before finally, Carter interrupted.

"Dude, you just stubbed your toe, chill..."

"Shut up!" Mitch barked as he whirled on his friend, still clutching his leg and glaring. "What do you know about how I feel?" He growled in anger, pressed his hands to his head, then abruptly turned and left.

Everyone stared in silence with wide eyes. "I'll go talk to him," Carter stated quietly as he stepped forward, but was stopped by a hand on his chest.

"No," Lessie interrupted, meeting his eyes. She took a steadying breath as she dropped her hand to her side. "I'll talk to him." She ran to follow Mitch into the foyer.

"Mitch, *stop*," Lessie demanded, catching up with him just as he was pushing through the large glass door. She grasped his arm and pulled him back, and the door slid shut with a *click*. "What was that all about?"

He clenched his teeth and shrugged her hand away from his arm. "Forget it," he grumbled, averting his angry eyes to the far wall.

"No, that was obviously something," Lessie replied persistently. "You stubbed your toe and then freaked out about it."

"I don't *have a toe!*" Mitch suddenly burst, eyes flashing, causing Lessie to jump back with a gasp. She swallowed against a lump in her throat as he threw his arms in the air. "I don't have a fucking *foot!*" His chest heaved with his breath, and he stared into her nervous eyes as she waited silently for him to calm down. He exhaled, standing straighter as he closed his eyes. He slowly lifted his eyelids, and he spoke in a frighteningly even voice. "I've finally accepted that I lived. I'm starting to feel like I can accept my new... life... But shit like this," he gestured toward his left foot, "when I feel pain on a part of me that doesn't even exist? It's a constant slap in the face that everything I hoped for is *dead.*"

His words ignited a fire within Lessie's heart, and she burned with a desire to reach out to him, console him, but most importantly, awaken him. She narrowed her eyes and set her jaw. Stepping forward, she lifted her hands and took his face between her palms as she locked onto his green irises. She silently noted the spark of electricity she felt at the contact. "You were obviously not meant to make a career out of football, Mitch," she stated firmly, her voice nearly a whisper. "You begged me to keep you alive because you *knew* you were meant for far greater things."

He stared into her eyes as her words sunk in, unable to move or speak. Finally, he lifted his hands and placed them over hers, his touch cold against her skin, and slowly removed them from his face. Her heart hammered. He showed no emotion, and she suddenly realized she was terrified. "Mitch..." she whispered, her voice pained, but he released her hands at her sides and left, making his way back into the ballroom. Tears stung at her eyes as her heart constricted. She swallowed against the growing lump in her throat and shakily turned to follow him, having nowhere else to go.

The band slowed their upbeat tempo to a smooth and steady rhythm as the lights dimmed. Lessie watched Tess and Carter wrap themselves in each other's arms, as Wren and Sami did the same. Her eyes found Mitch, who was leaning against their table with his arms folded over his chest, watching the couples as well. His gaze was distant, his expression lost. She approached him with trepidation. "I'm sorry..."

He lowered his head, sighed, and stood to face her. Finally, he met her eyes, and held out his hand.

She stared at his open palm for a moment before finally lifting her own, hoping he couldn't see her hand shaking as she took his, and her heart hammered harder as the heat of his grasp encompassed hers and drew her in. The same humming electricity returned. He led her onto the dance floor and slid his arm around her waist as he held her hand against his chest, and she nervously brought her own arm around his firm shoulders.

They were so close. She could feel the heat from his body,

smell the spice of his cologne on his neck. Her heart fired rapidly as her stomach flipped. How she had longed for this moment, yet now, she no longer knew how to feel, and wished desperately to know how *he* felt.

"I'm not upset," he said quietly, as though reading her mind, and she felt her tension release. "You know how to throw your punches, though," he added, his voice softer yet.

She didn't respond. She didn't know how to. She simply stared out across the dance floor as they moved in slow circles, wishing this moment with him were under different circumstances.

"So, thanks for that," he added, and she finally took a small step back so that she could meet his eyes.

"For what?" she asked.

He shrugged as he let go of her hand and slid his around her waist with the other, causing her stomach to flip again. She hesitantly brought her free hand up around his shoulders, marveling at the reality that his arms were actually around her, and hers around him. Their eyes remained locked on each other's. "Telling it like it is and making me pull my head out of my ass."

Her heart lightened as a small smile began to tug at her lips. "I meant it," she finally managed to say. "That you're meant for greater things."

He returned her smile with a sigh and tightened his hold on her waist, drawing her closer to him. She strained against her weak knees as she felt her body melt into his, almost as though she belonged there, and she braved wrapping her own arms tighter around his neck. She breathed him in as she allowed her fears and uncertainties to release, enjoying the moment for whatever it was, as they swayed in unison to the music.

CHAPTER 32

THE RIDE home was silent as Lessie pondered their individual lives, and where their tragedies, and choices, had brought them. She stole glances at Mitch as he drove, but his eyes and features were unreadable as he stared into the night, gripping the steering wheel. His crown lay forgotten in the backseat. He seemed cheerful enough as he received his title of king, smiling from the stage and meeting Lessie's eyes as she clapped enthusiastically. She silently enjoyed watching Katie Sommers lose the title of queen to the girls basketball MVP, Avery Michaels, as well.

"See? Nobody cares that you can't play football right now," Lessie had said later that evening. "Or that you hear dead people." He regarded her with a smile that didn't reach his eyes.

As he slowed to a stop on her driveway, she drew in a nervous breath, and turned to face him. "Come with me."

He met her eyes with hesitation. "Where...?"

"Just walk with me. Come on." She pushed the door open and climbed out of his mom's SUV, and met him at the driver's side door as he stood to join her, eyeing her curiously. He followed her to her favorite tree, where they stood at its roots in the thin grass and watched the stars for a moment. Lessie took a breath, drawing from Will's wisdom and guidance through the months he helped her emotionally recover after Mitch's accident. "Things are going to constantly... trigger you."

His brows creased. "Okay..."

She turned to meet his eyes. "I know. Because the same thing happens to me. Sometimes, without warning, I'll see your empty eyes staring from that steering wheel." Her voice cracked as she clung to her strength. "You have no idea how that haunted me..."

He swallowed, but remained silent. She took another steadying breath, then continued. "But I have to force myself to remember where life has taken me since then. And I realize... I wouldn't trade it for anything." She turned her head to face the stars again as the weight of her words filled her chest. "I'd do it all over again."

He pressed his lips together, for the first time realizing that he was not alone to bear the pain of his accident. He stared at her as the moonlight illuminated the smooth curve of her face, her dark eyelashes accentuating the crystal blue of her eyes as they shined with her emotion. As though driven by an unseen force, he reached to lace his fingers into hers, and she turned her head, her surprised eyes piercing into his as her breath hitched.

"You saved my life more than just from that accident, you know," he said in an almost whisper.

A tear slipped down her cheek, and she reached to draw him into an embrace, pressing her face into his shoulder as she drew in a ragged breath. After he recovered from momentary shock, he let out a breath as he wrapped his own arms around her, pulling her closer. He brought his hand to the back of her head, pushing his fingers into her hair, as the other hand pressed firmly against her back and held her against his beating heart. She was overcome with a profound desire to tell him how much she cared about him, to speak from her soul how he'd saved her life, too, and taken her on a journey far greater than anything she ever could have imagined. How eternally grateful she was for his mere existence in her life and all that he'd taught her. But her words remained unspoken, as she breathed in his energy and let her tears stain his shirt, clinging to him with the fierceness of her surging emotion.

MITCH SMILED FROM the end of the hall as he watched Lessie collect her books. She stood upright, her shoulders back and head high as she tucked a loose strand of hair behind her ear. It was as though she were a completely different person from who she was mere months ago. But then, so was he.

It was the Monday after prom weekend, and constantly his mind traveled back to their embrace under the tree, as she cried against him. He wished he had kissed her. Scolded himself for missing an opportunity.

He felt an elbow bump against his arm. "Hey, man," Carter said as Mitch turned his head to face him. The burly blonde nodded in the direction of Lessie. "You better not let her get away. Don't want to slip into the friend zone." He pursed his lips with an arched brow as he briefly met Mitch's eyes, then left without another word.

Mitch took a breath, and approached Lessie at her locker. "Want me to drive you home?" he offered, and she grinned as she reached to close the metal door. Before she could answer, her eyes went vacant as her face fell, and her jaw went slack. Mitch's expression shifted to concern. "Les?" He searched her eyes, but he only found emptiness. "Oh," he said to himself, realization setting in.

He stood waiting, wondering where she was, who was dying and getting to cross over at that moment. The broken memory of the bright light came to mind, and his missing foot tingled as a crawling sensation made its way up his non-existent calf. He gave his prosthetic leg a shake, then returned his focus to Lessie, who was still gone. His eyes wandered the halls as several students stared at them, stared at Lessie, then moved on. God, he used to make so much fun of her for this. He sighed, a sick sense of guilt turning his stomach. He then caught Emily's eyes.

She glared at him from across the hall, standing motionless as the sea of students ebbed around her. He held her gaze, un-moving, unfazed.

She stormed up to him. "That's *my* job," she seethed.

He cocked a brow. "You haven't exactly been there for her lately."

"And what gives *you* the right to be there for her?" She brought her face within inches of his, her eyes shooting daggers, but he remained unaffected. "If that's what you're actually *doing...*"

He sighed, rolling his eyes as he crossed his arms and leaned against the locker behind him. "I fail to see why you care."

"Because I'm her best friend."

He laughed. "Fine way of showing it."

She threw her hands up. "You're unbelievable! What does she possibly see in you?"

He blanched at her comment, but quickly recovered. "Look, if you're her best friend, you should care about her happiness, and what *she* wants. She didn't want your cousin, and you should probably support her even if it means breaking up your little group."

Emily's face fell under creased brows. "She told you all that?" She then shook her head, closing her eyes, then opened them again, meeting him with a piercing gaze. "Wait, you *listened?*"

He rolled his eyes. "Don't act so surprised."

She stared at him, bringing her hands to her hips, her expression distrusting. "What do you want with her?"

"I don't *want* anything."

She squinted. "Well, I don't trust you. You've always been an asshole, why should things suddenly be any different?"

He pressed his lips together, still leaning against the lockers with his arms folded, then kicked out his prosthetic leg, drawing attention to it from under his cargo shorts, and crossed it over his right ankle. "Things change."

Emily drew in a breath, still scowling. "I guess so," she finally muttered, then turned and left.

Mitch brought his attention back to Lessie, just as her eyes came back into focus. She blinked several times, shaking her head, then met Mitch's eyes. "What did I miss?" she asked.

A smile tugged at the corners of his mouth. "Oh, man, it was *crazy*. Mr. Meyers's snake escaped from the biology lab, everyone in the hallway was screaming, running around, and you're just standing there, and I tried to get you to move, but—" He stopped and grinned at Lessie's bewildered expression.

Finally, her own smile began to creep in, her eyes squinting as her head tilted. Then finally she laughed.

And he realized he loved that sound. He'd have to try to get it out of her more often. "Come on, I'll take you home," he said, and she grinned, agreeing.

His thoughts traveled to prom night as he pulled into her driveway once again, but his emotions were in an entirely different place. His heart hammered as she turned her head, smiled sweetly, and said, "Thanks for the ride. See you tomorrow." Her smile shifted to a grin, her white teeth shining in friendly admiration, and his heart hammered harder. He forced a smile in return as she grabbed her backpack, slung it over one shoulder, and left the car.

Don't let her get away, a voice pressed, and suddenly he found himself jumping from the driver's seat and shouting, "Wait!"

She raised her eyebrows and approached him slowly, her head tilted and thumb looped in her backpack strap. He swallowed, licked his lips, and gathered his courage. "I just wanted to... I mean, I should have... Or..."

She smirked, arching a brow, but remained silent.

He huffed an exhale, set his jaw, and stepped forward. He squeezed his eyes shut, and her eyes flew open wide as he captured her lips with his. The wind picked up as if choreographed for this moment, blowing her hair to the side as electricity arced through her body, and she instantly melted into him. Her backpack fell to the ground as she wrapped her arms around his neck and he brought his palms to her face. The current that pulsed between them was breathtaking, almost blinding, as fireworks erupted around them, the rest of the world completely forgotten. It was as though he were reaching into her soul.

"Whoa..." Mitch breathed as they separated, staring dazed into each other's eyes. Lessie chuckled as heat crept into her neck, her arms still enveloping his shoulders, and his hands still on her face. He stroked her smooth cheek with his thumb, and laughed. "I should've done that a long time ago..."

Her cheeks flared as she grinned. "Better late than never," she replied with a laugh, and claimed his lips with hers, smiling against him as their hearts took flight in unison, and he wrapped his own arms around her waist, drawing her in tighter.

"Ahem," a gruff voice interrupted them, and they jumped nearly five feet apart, the color drained from their faces.

"Oh my God, Dad, we were just—"

"Sir, I am *so sorry*—"

The two fell silent as Mitch saw his life flash before his eyes. Lessie's father stepped off the porch and approached them slowly, his expression stern and unamused, the muscles in his jaws flexing. Mitch swallowed against his hammering heart, and Lessie stared with wide eyes and burning cheeks.

"You must be Mitch," Sam said in a low rumble, meeting Mitch's terrified eyes.

"Y-yes, sir," he stammered.

Sam's eyes slowly moved from Mitch, to Lessie, then back to Mitch again, and his expression slowly softened as humor glinted in his eyes. "'Bout time you two figured your shit out."

A stunned exhale burst from Lessie's chest, as Mitch's jaw dropped. Sam grinned with a chuckle as he clapped Mitch on the shoulder, and Lessie threw her head back with relieved laughter, as Mitch attempted to learn to breathe again.

LESSIE COULDN'T STOP smiling as she finished her homework in her room that afternoon. Her heart nearly soared out of her chest as a message from Will flashed across her phone as she sat in front of her laptop at her desk. She could almost see him smiling through the text. >>*We did it. We talked Dad into coming!*

She let out a squeal as she leapt up from her chair, nearly

unable to contain herself. Her heart exploded with emotion as she typed her response, and read Will's story of how they finally convinced Uncle Ron to at least let go of some of his grudge.

>>*Have you mentioned anything to your mom yet?* Will texted after his story was complete.

>>*No, I wasn't planning on mentioning anything until you had a definite answer from your dad.*

>>*Good idea. You should probably give her a heads up, though. I'm sure she's got a lot of mixed feelings about him and we don't want to catch her off-guard.*

>>*Yeah but I think her priority is reconnecting and moving on. She misses him.*

>>*I'm sure it'll all be fine then. You did tell her about Nana crossing Mom over, right?*

Lessie froze, eyes wide, breath caught in her chest as her mind scrambled through memories of her roller coaster of life since last November. >>*Oh shit... Will, I got so caught up in Mitch dying and saving his life and my relationship junk and high school... I wanted to tell Mom and Dad when I found out but with everything going on with Nana's death I didn't think it was the right time, then my life kinda took over... I never told them...*

She felt like a complete flake, her head falling forward into the palm of her hand.

There was a pause before Will responded. >>*Um... you might want to tell them that too... maybe make sure they're sitting down for all of this...*

Before she could process all of this any further, her thoughts were broken by her mother's voice, causing her to jump.

"Lessie!" Lynne called from the bottom of the stairs. "Emily's here to see you!"

Lessie's heart stopped. She bit her lip as she set her phone down and returned to her seat at her desk. "Come on up!" she shouted back.

Emily appeared in Lessie's doorway, and the two stared at each other in awkward silence. "Hey," Lessie finally spoke.

"Hi," Emily replied, her gaze falling to her feet.

Lessie watched her for a moment, but Emily remained motionless. "What?" Lessie finally spoke, stating it more than asking.

Emily sighed heavily and entered the room, closing the door behind her and sinking into Lessie's mattress. "I miss you."

"Oh, I see everything still revolves around you and *your* feelings," Lessie grumbled, turning back to her computer screen.

"I'm serious. And I know I've been unfair. I'm sorry."

Lessie glanced over her shoulder as Emily hung her head, picking at her thumbnails with her hands in her lap. "Unfair is an understatement," Lessie mumbled, then sighed, turning in her chair to face her. "I miss you, too."

Emily looked up cautiously, her face sullen. "I know you weren't happy with Adam," she began. "But I just really liked what we had going. Plus, he's my family, and I felt protective of him, too."

"I broke up with him because didn't want to finish off the last month of school *pretending*. It would have been nice to have some support."

"I know," Emily sighed. "I should have supported you. And now a lot has happened. I missed getting to go to prom with you. And you and Mitch have something way deeper going on than I thought, and I realized... I really hate not being part of your life."

Lessie frowned, lowering her head. "I hate it too. My life is a lot different now..."

Emily nodded as tears welled in her eyes. "I... see that he changed. That he's different. And I guess I need to accept that."

Lessie nodded, meeting Emily's eyes.

"Evan broke up with me, too," Emily added in a choked whisper.

Lessie's heart sank as her face fell. "Oh, Em... I'm so sorry."

Emily released a sob as she dropped her face into her hands. "It's my fault, too. I've been selfish this whole time."

"Well, coming out and saying you're ditching us all for a school in Arizona was a bit of a shock..."

"I'm sorry!" she cried. "I just wanted to get far away from here!" She sucked back a sob and continued, "We've been strained ever since that day. It's really sucked."

Lessie nodded slowly. "Well, I think it's good that you did something for yourself. If you feel like you belong in Arizona, more than Chicago like you first talked about, then you should go. You shouldn't let anything hold you back."

Emily nodded slowly, turning Lessie's words over in her mind.

Lessie sighed, her gaze returning to her knees. "That's the same kind of support I would have liked to have."

Drawing in a shaky breath, Emily replied, "I support you. I'm glad you did what you needed to do for your happiness. Even if you're hanging out with someone who used to be a total *ass* to you, I realize maybe you had some kind of weird premonition that you two were just... meant to be."

Lessie smiled, reflecting on the electricity she felt with Mitch earlier, and her heart flipped again as she recalled their kiss. He *kissed* her... "Maybe so," she replied, and her smile softened as she met Emily's eyes. "I wish you'd take the time to get to know him. He's a different person. Or, maybe he's who he's always been, and he's just suppressed it all these years and it's finally getting to come out. Either way, he's a pretty amazing guy."

Emily nodded again. "I believe you." Her chin began to quiver. "You two seem really close..." Her voice cracked as another tear fell. "I feel like you replaced me..."

Lessie exhaled heavily, pitying her friend as she pressed her face into her hands. Lessie stood from her chair and came to the bed, sitting next to Emily and pulling her into a hug. "I didn't replace you," Lessie said as Emily fell into her shoulder. "He *is* kind of my boyfriend now..." Lessie grinned at the thought, then continued, "But you'll always be my best friend."

Emily slowly sat back, nodding as she wiped her cheeks. "I'm happy for you," she said, smiling over her quivering lip.

Lessie chuckled, grabbing a tissue box from her nightstand and passing it to Emily. They sat on the bed in silence, staring at their knees, until finally Lessie sighed and fell back on the mattress. "I think I'm falling in love, Em..."

Emily smiled. "I think you already did that, all these years you've been crushing on him."

Lessie shook her head. "That was just a stupid crush. This is different. It's... deeper. Just getting to know him over these last couple months... We have this *connection*. I thought for sure we were doomed to be just friends for the rest of our lives... But..." Her mind traveled to their kiss again.

Emily smiled, meeting Lessie's eyes. "You're a hot mess..." she said with a laugh.

Lessie smirked, blushing, then said, "Thanks for coming over. I really did miss you."

"Thanks for still being my friend."

Lessie grinned. "Always."

LESSIE ABSENTLY TWIRLED spaghetti noodles on her fork, her mind pulled in too many directions to keep track of. She was still elated from her moment in the driveway with Mitch, relieved that she and Emily's friendship was restored, and thrilled that Will and Cam successfully convinced their father to come out to visit and possibly mend the family rift. She slumped into her chair. But how could she have forgotten to ever fill her parents in on that *important* detail Nana had shared with her? Why Uncle Ron left the family in the first place?

"Is this a teenage girl thing?" Sam asked, breaking Lessie's thoughts.

"Huh?" She lifted her gaze to meet his eyes.

"You seem pretty down for finally getting somewhere with that boy you have a crush on," he said.

Lynne arched an eyebrow, fork halfway to her mouth. "Got somewhere? Got where?"

"That Mitch kid was kissing on her in the driveway," Same replied with a smirk.

"Oh *really...*"

Lessie groaned. "Guys, there's something I need to tell you."

Sam's face paled, and Lynne returned her fork to her plate. "He got you pregnant already," Sam said in a glowering voice.

Lessie threw her head back. "Oh my *God, Dad!*" She sighed heavily. "It's about Nana and Uncle Ron and Aunt Jodi."

Sam exhaled, his shoulders relaxing. Lynne tilted her head. "What about?" she asked.

"Nana told me what happened. Right before she died. But...

you guys were so preoccupied with her death and the funeral and everything that I didn't want to burden you with that extra information. Then I started dating Adam and everything happened with Mitch and I just forgot, I guess."

"*What*, Lessie?" Lynne urged.

Lessie took a steadying breath. "Nana said she was the one to cross Aunt Jodi over."

A heavy silence fell over the dinner table. Finally, Lynne and Sam both broke it.

"*What?*"

"How is that even possible?"

Lessie shrugged. "She's not sure either, it was the first and only time she got called to someone she knows, and someone who isn't the same age as her." She swallowed her nerves, then continued. "She tried to tell Uncle Ron at the funeral, hoping it would comfort him, but instead he got mad at her for not trying to save Aunt Jodi. He cut her off and left before she could explain that Aunt Jodi was at peace with her death."

Lynne's eyes narrowed. "How was she supposed to save her? She didn't know that was possible... Did she?" Lynne squinted at her daughter.

Lessie hung her head and groaned. "Ugh I can't believe I didn't tell you any of this... I'm *so sorry...*"

"Better now than never," Sam said. "Go on with the story."

Lessie took another breath. "Nana came to me through Mitch, now that he's a medium because of his near-death-experience thanks to me, and told me that her grandfather died because he tried to save someone, and that the same thing could happen to me, but instead of telling me that when she was alive, she made me believe saving people was forbidden."

Lynne's face reddened. "Why wouldn't she tell you the *truth?* You mean to tell me you could have *died* those two times you saved people?"

"Promise us you will never try to save anyone again," Sam cut in.

"I don't plan on it," Lessie grumbled. "Listen, I don't know why Nana handled it the way she did, but she's gone now, and it is what it is. I've filled Will in on all this, and he and Cam have been working on trying to get Uncle Ron to come with them to my graduation."

"Wait, *what?*" Lynne burst. Sam rubbed his forehead with the heel of his hands.

"And he succeeded..."

Sam and Lynne exchanged a disbelieving glance. "Do you think any other families are having these kinds of conversations at the dinner table?" Sam said, hoping for comic relief.

Lynne rolled her eyes. "Lessie, this is a lot to process."

"I know, I'm sorry. I was so sidetracked by Mitch's issues, and the breakup with Adam, and the fallout with Emily..." Tears welled in her eyes.

Lynne sighed. "It's fine. You've had a lot on your plate. Let's go back to the part where you said my brother is coming to visit."

Lessie looked nervously up at her mother. "Is that okay?"

Lynne chewed her lower lip, then nodded. "Of course it is. I'm not sure what to expect, but I just want our family back together."

CHAPTER 33

LESSIE SLID across the vinyl-upholstered booth as Mitch slid in next to her, and she smiled at the contact of his hip against hers. They met at The Depot for lunch after gathering at school to retrieve their report cards and the last of their things, saying their final goodbyes to that chapter of their lives. They grinned with the relief of a stressful week of finals being behind them, and an exciting, open future ahead of them. Mitch pressed a kiss to her lips before popping a french fry into his mouth, and she laughed. They couldn't get enough of each other.

"So, I wanted to ask you," Lessie began, still grinning as she met his eyes. "Would you want to come to dinner at my house tomorrow night?"

He shifted in his seat, eying her hesitantly. "Dinner at your house? Like meet your family?"

Her expression didn't change as she shrugged. "You already met my dad, and that went surprisingly well. But, yeah, I guess you'll kind of meet my Uncle Ron and my cousins Will and Cam." She paused as reality began to set in. She had already filled Will in on her conversation at dinner with her parents about updating them on the family details as well as informing them of Ron's visit. "Are you sure your mom will be okay with this?" Will had asked her. Lynne had shown some hesitation, but Lessie had assured Will she'd be fine, it's her *brother,* she wants nothing more than to mend the family bond. Lessie swallowed. Her estranged brother, who left his sister to handle all the family affairs with the passing of their mother on her own... Lessie's eyes became distant. She pulled herself out of her memory with Will and back to the table with Mitch. "And... I'm kind of meeting my Uncle Ron for the first time too... And my mom hasn't seen Ron in over eighteen years..." She swallowed as she stared at her food, internalizing what could await her the next day.

Mitch's eyebrows raised as he slowly chewed the end of another french fry. "That's a big deal... Not sure if I should walk in on all that." He studied her as she continued staring at her food. After he finished chewing, he added, "Uncle Ron... That's the one whose wife died, right? That your grandma crossed over?" His expression was hesitant, almost nervous.

Lessie's eyes grew wide as her jaw fell slightly, and she finally lifted her head to look at him. "Oh, no... Mitch... I wasn't even thinking about your..." Her voice trailed off as she shook her head. "Never mind, that was stupuid of me to ask, I don't want to put you on the spot, if, you know, Nana or Aunt Jodi try to say something. I hadn't even thought of that. You probably shouldn't come..."

He gave her a small smile as he shook his head. "I like that you forget I'm a freak," he said with a hint of laughter in his eyes. They held each other's gaze for a moment, until finally, Mitch spoke, his voice soft. "It's fine. But, yeah, I think I'll pass. Not because I don't want to, but because this kind of sounds like a personal family thing, that maybe your new boyfriend shouldn't be thrown into just yet." She nodded, and he relaxed with the relief that she seemed to understand. He squinted slightly as he added, "You said your mom hasn't seen her brother in over eighteen years?

She chewed her lip, shaking her head slowly. "I have no idea how this is going to go over. Mom has had to deal with a *lot*, including her mother getting sick and dying, and her brother wasn't there for any of it. Not even her funeral. I think I take for granted that my mom is so compassionate, so understanding. Both my parents are."

Mitch gave a small understanding nod. "Yeah, I mean, my sister is one of the most understanding people I know, but if this were us and she had to take care of Mom dying and I were MIA, she'd be pretty damn pissed."

Lessie swallowed hard, realizing how royally this could backfire. "Shit."

Mitch gave her knee a squeeze. "I'm sure everything will be fine. But I'm here for you if you need anything, like rescuing you from a huge family feud or something."

Lessie tried to smile, but couldn't. She appreciated his offer, but her stomach twisted at the realization that she may end up needing to take him up on it.

WILL GLANCED HESITANTLY at his father to his left. The old man stared out the small window, his gaze following the runway to the horizon, bathed in the orange glow of sunset. Cam nudged her brother, drawing his attention to his right, and she gave him a half-smile and a shrug. He sighed.

"You okay, Dad?" he asked carefully. He didn't have a relationship with the man, so showing any kind of care or concern was somewhat foreign to him. But after the weeks they'd spent trying to coax him into this very trip, he felt a strange bond begin to form.

Ron shrugged, his sallow, wrinkled face remaining expressionless as he continued staring out the window. "I can't imagine being welcomed into her home," he finally replied in a gruff voice.

"Of course she will," Will responded, hoping the nerves in his voice went undetected.

He and Lessie had spoken not long ago, after she called him and frantically poured out her fears of her mom *not* being okay with this. It had crossed Will's mind as well, but ultimately Lynne said herself that she wanted to forgive and move on. They had to take her word for it.

"She was thrilled when me and Cam showed up," he reminded Lessie during their phone call. "Your mom is obviously a wise, compassionate, forgiving woman. I remember her saying when we were there that grudges and resentment were only toxic emotions that would eventually poison the soul. So I would think she'd put the past behind her when she sees Dad again? Right?" He wondered if he was trying to convince himself just as much as he was convincing Lessie.

"She *wants* to forgive you, Dad," Cam said, leaning forward to join the conversation. "She already has."

"Just remember none of this is her fault," Will added, followed by a nervous swallow. "Aunt Lynne and her family have nothing to do with Nana or Mom."

Ron continued staring out the window, his mind wandering to buried memories, his thoughts unspoken.

"Mama, can you save people?" He had been so curious about

his mother's ability, fascinated by the mystery from a young age. He couldn't stop asking questions, his thirst for knowledge never seeming to be quenched.

He remembered his mother looking uncomfortable at the question. She was always so happy to tell him about her ability, always so open, though she urged both her children never to speak of it in public. She had exchanged a quick glance with her husband, whose gray-green eyes seemed to hold a dark secret he was keeping for her. Ron was too little to understand what transpired, though he sensed the unease.

She had cast him a soft smile. "If it were possible, sweetie, it would be far too dangerous." She patted his knee. "Let's not speak of that anymore." She gave him a gentle, yet stern look. "My job is to bring people to Heaven. Nothing more."

Heaven. The Other Side. Where Jodi was... Where his mother had taken her... He thought for sure she could have brought her back, could have reversed what had happened, could have saved their family from the pain and heartbreak that eventually tore them apart.

"Nadine," young Ron overheard his father say to his mother. He knew eavesdropping was rude, but he couldn't help himself. He had an insatiable hunger for knowing more about his mother's mysterious life. "Should you have even told him that much? You basically said it is possible..."

"It will be fine! I didn't say that entirely, and I said it's dangerous. If he asks again, I'll make sure the subject is closed."

Ron squeezed his eyes shut as the memory dissipated. His mother had never spoken of it again, and he hadn't either, even after his sister was born and she became full of her own questions. As he grew, and adulthood chased away the innocence of childhood, he learned to suppress his hunger for knowledge, though his curiosity and secret knowledge still lay beneath the surface.

The plane began to taxi down the runway.

He never anticipated having to apply his secret knowledge to his life on a personal level.

A silent tear slipped down his ashen cheek as he held the black urn in his hands. How could she be gone? How could everything be gone? He had two small children, and he couldn't imagine having to raise them without his partner at his side. Couldn't imagine having to grow old without her. They had so many unfinished dreams, so many unanswered prayers, so many hopes and visions that never came to fruition. And now she was gone.

A hand touched his shoulder, jolting him from his thoughts.

"Ron, honey..." came his mother's gentle voice.

He quickly brushed the tear from his cheek, blinking. He cleared his throat, signaling he was listening, but unable to form concrete words.

"I just want you to know, I was there..."

His heart stopped, and he slowly turned his head to meet her eyes.

"I just thought you should know. I took her Home... and she was—"

"You what?" he interrupted, his voice rough and strained.

"It was—"

He whirled on her, interrupting again. His eyes burned. "You let her go?"

Nadine's face fell at the strike of his words. "Ron," she said, "It doesn't—"

"Why didn't you bring her back?" he shouted, scarlet anger flushing his cheeks as fire blazed in his eyes. His mother took a step back, her expression shocked and hurt.

"I couldn't!" she insisted, eyes wide with pain.

"Don't give me that bullshit, Mom. I've heard you tell Dad it's possible before! You broke our family!"

She was too stunned to speak, staring, crushed, as her son flashed her one last glare, turned on his heel, and left.

He never spoke to them again.

>>ON OUR WAY, *should be there in 20 min,* Will texted, and Lessie nearly dropped her phone as her heart hammered and her hands shook. Will, his sister, and father spent the night at a local hotel after arriving at the airport late the night before. Will and Lessie had made arrangements for them to come over after breakfast, and planned to spend the day at home as Ron and Lynne adjusted to having each other back in their lives. Lessie grew nervous at the prospect of all the unknowns, including their family dinner that night.

>>*Okay, I'll let Mom and Dad know.*

>>*Is your mom okay?*

Lessie glanced at her parents; her mother checking the food inventory in the fridge, and her father cleaning the kitchen. She recalled her conversation with her father the night before while her mother was in the shower, her nerves about the unknown outcome of the next day's events beginning to get the better of her.

"Your mother has always been more understanding and forgiving than anyone I know," her father had reassured her.

"Yeah, but she's still human," Lessie argued, her accumulating fears bringing more uncertainty to the surface. "What if she's been resentful of Uncle Ron and just suppressed it all these years? What if all that comes out tomorrow night?"

Sam shook his head. "There's no way of knowing. But I feel it's better to risk an emotional explosion than to miss the opportunity to reunite them at all. We all know she misses him. That's the most important thing here."

"But what if there *is* an explosion?"

Sam gave her shoulder a reassuring squeeze. "I'll help keep her calm. You just relax and be proud of yourself for pulling this off in the first place."

Lessie frowned. "That was all Will and Cam."

Sam smiled. "They would have never even been in the position to try if you hadn't come along and pushed things forward."

Lessie tried to let his words take hold, but her fears still remained in the forefront.

Lynne met Lessie's eyes as she looked her way while closing the fridge. "They'll be here in twenty minutes," Lessie said, clutching her phone. Lynne and Sam exchanged a nervous glance.

>>*We're as ready as we can be,* she wrote back to Will.

By the time the rental car was on their driveway, Lessie was nearly coming out of her skin. "They're here!" she screeched, her nerves completely consuming her. Sam, shifting on his feet against his own nerves, joined Lessie at the door, and Lynne slowly approached behind them.

Lessie pushed the door open, and a heavy tension stretched through the air. Lynne drew in a breath, eyes wide, as her hands flew up to cover her mouth. Lessie felt like she could puke.

A breeze blew across the silent landscape as the gaunt, balding man stood with his two grown children on the front porch, staring at the woman he'd grown up with, and left behind years ago. Finally Lynne gasped, "Ron, I... I can't believe you're really here..."

His chest rose with a nervous inhale. "I can't, either. But my kids drove a hard bargain." Tears welled in Lynne's eyes, and Ron added quietly, "I don't expect you to welcome me with open arms." Will and Cam exchanged a hesitant glance from the front step, and Sam and Lessie stood frozen in the foyer.

Lynne quickly shook her head, swallowing back tears. "Of course I'm going to welcome you," she said, her voice strained. She cleared her throat. "You're my brother. I... I've got a lot of emotions right now..." Her raw honesty caused a tear to finally slip to her cheek. She blinked hard against it. "But you're here. I didn't think this would ever happen. Come in!" Her demeanor shifted as she shook herself from the cascade of emotions and tried to allow herself to accept what was happening. Lessie felt her shoulders drop, not having realized how much they had tightened against her neck.

Lynne ushered her family inside the house. She hugged Will and Cam, expressing heartfelt thanks for the work they had done on their father. She then took Ron's shoulder in her hands. He went rigid at the contact. "Listen, the past is behind us," she said, meeting his eyes. "A lot has happened, a lot of which I'm upset you missed, and that I had to experience without you. But Mom would want it all to just be forgiven, and that's what I want, too. Can it be water under the bridge?"

He nodded slowly, shocked and silent. The mention of their mother sent a flicker of pain across his features.

Will and Cam made themselves at home as Lynne introduced Ron to Lessie, and the family immediately dove into conversation, doing their best to make Ron feel comfortable.

"DINNER IS SERVED!" Sam announced later that evening as he carried a large roast pan laden with a thick, sizzling ham, perfectly caramelized and covered in pineapple rings. Everyone settled into the dining room around the large spread of steaming dishes.

"That looks amazing!" Will complimented, sitting at one end of the table, his sister to his left, and Lessie next to her. Cam agreed, admiring the spread with bright eyes. Ron sat to Will's right, still appearing somewhat stiff, but at least more at ease than when they had arrived that morning. His sister sat next to him.

Sam grinned proudly as he placed the ham in the center of the table. "Hopefully it tastes as amazing as it looks," he replied, then seated himself at the head of the table between his wife and daughter. Soon, everyone began digging in.

"I wish Mom could be here for this..." Lynne suddenly mentioned, breaking the silence that was only previously filled with the clinking of forks against plates and the shuffling of food.

Ron stiffened. "I like how it's going, like this." His voice was low and gruff, and Lessie exchanged a nervous glance with Will.

Lynne's face fell. "She would have loved you being reunited with us."

Her brother's eyes narrowed. "If she were still here, I wouldn't be."

Fuck, Lessie thought.

"And she's not here, so let's just move forward from where we are," Will cut in, a slight crack in his otherwise strong voice.

Lynne knit her brows as she took in her brother. "I thought you being here meant you forgave her..."

Ron held her gaze evenly. "I accepted that you didn't have anything to do with it. That has nothing to do with me forgiving her."

"But that doesn't matter, because she's gone," Will attempted to rescue again. Lessie held her breath.

Lynne placed her fork alongside her plate, clearly growing defensive. "She's gone, and I had to take care of that whole process alone."

"Yeah, well, she's not the only one who died," Ron said, his voice louder.

Tears welled in Lynne's eyes. "We all were affected by Jodi's death, Ron."

It was his turn to place his fork on the table, though with a bit more aggression than Lynne had. "You seem to be missing the detail that our mother could have changed things," he said through gritted teeth.

Shit, shit, shit. Lessie locked eyes with Will, hoping he could hear her brain's distress signal.

Will audibly placed his hands on the table. "Let's all take a breath here—"

But Lynne was already standing up, tossing her napkin from her lap to her plate. "I'm thrilled that our kids came around, Ron. I thought maybe you had, too. But clearly you won't ever change."

"There's nothing to change," he spat back, "And frankly I wish *she*—" he threw a finger at Lessie, "left my family out of all this!"

Lessie's jaw dropped as her heart broke.

"Don't you *dare* talk about my daughter that way! She did your children a favor! Unlike anything *you* ever did for them."

Lessie shook herself from her stunned silence and stood from the table, grabbing her phone as she recalled Mitch's offer to let him know if she needed him to rescue her. She began punching out a text message to him as she slowly made her way to the living room, tears blurring her vision. >>*Remember you said you'd help if I needed anything?*

>>*Uh oh, what?*

>>*I kind of want to leave...*

>>*I'll come get you*

Lessie tried to tune out the rest of the explosion as she sank into the couch, tears staining her cheeks and shoulders fallen in defeat, but she couldn't help but hear the rest of it.

"We can't change the fact that my wife is dead, can we?" Ron shouted.

"You act like Mom killed her!" Lynne fired back.

"She might as well have!"

"What the *fuck!*" Lynne was screaming now, and had grabbed a fork and chucked it at the floor.

"Honey—" Sam interjected, reaching for Lynne's arm. She shrugged him away as she started in on Ron again.

Cam leaned in to Will's ear. "Let's get him out of here." Will nodded.

>>*On my way,* Mitch texted.

>>*Thank God.*

Lynne continued to unleash her pent-up emotions on Ron, angry at his years of absence and hurt by his inability to forgive, while Ron fired back with arguments, solidifying his stubborn emotions. Will and Cam executed several failed attempts at getting Ron to come with them, to get outside and cool down, while Sam was facing the same situation with Lynne. Lessie simply sat on the couch and cried.

Finally, after several more pieces of silverware were thrown and a glass was knocked over, soaking the table cloth, Will grabbed his father by the shoulders and forcibly moved him in the direction of the front door. Tears were in Cam's eyes as she met Lessie's hurt expression on their way through. "We'll fix this," she said, her voice unconvincing.

Lessie stood and returned to the dining room to join her father. "I texted Mitch to come get me, sorry I fucked all this up."

Sam's face fell. "You didn't, I got this," and reached for his wife's shoulders to pull her toward the kitchen.

She shoved his hands off her once again and followed her brother, nephew, and niece toward the foyer in an uncharacteristic fit of rage. The doorbell rang.

"I'll be back," Lessie said to no one in particular as she pushed past the mess of angry family members and quickly darted for the front door.

MITCH STOOD WITH his fists in his pockets, shoulders tensed at his ears, backlit by the front porch light. *What am I getting myself into?* he thought. Even his inner voice sounded nervous. "Thank you," Lessie breathed, and he inhaled with a sudden sense of purpose brought on by the relief he saw in her eyes. She took his elbow and spun him away from the mess inside the house and off the front porch into the cool night air.

Go back.

He stumbled, missing the step. "Dammit," he grunted, correcting his balance. Lessie gripped his elbow tighter, her concerned expression telling him she assumed it was just his bad leg that tripped him. If only. He tried to calm himself down. He knew this could happen, but hoped he'd be in and out of there before it had a chance.

Go back to the house.

"Jesus Christ," Mitch groaned, stopping as though an unseen force were causing him not to move.

Lessie tried to keep moving, but stopped when she realized Mitch wasn't moving. Fear was etched in his face as he glanced over his shoulder to the front door. Will was pushing his father onto the front porch as Lynne continued yelling from inside the house, light from the foyer spilling out into the night.

Go to him, the voice urged.

"What's wrong?" Lessie asked, but a terrified awareness crept in as Mitch turned to face her family.

Time can heal some wounds, but forgiveness heals all. He must understand this.

Instinct coursed through Mitch's veins like an electric current. The voice belonged to Jodi, which he inexplicably knew without question. For a moment anger shot through his mind — he came to rescue his girlfriend, not relay messages to her uncle from his dead wife. He instantly tried to stifle the anger, and his gaze traveled helplessly to Ron as his stomach twisted. *Here we go*, he thought to himself, realizing he wasn't ready for this at all, much less okay with it, bracing himself as though he were in a roller coaster car, climbing the tracks of a steep hill. Mitch brought himself to stand in front of Ron, who met Mitch's eyes with anger and frustration. Will, whose hands were still clutching his father's shoulders, shot Lessie a questioning glance as to why her boyfriend was suddenly impeding their progress.

Mitch took a breath and squared his shoulders. "Y-your wife," Mitch began.

Ron's brows creased. "What the hell is this?"

Ronnie...

Mitch squeezed his eyes shut. The voice was adamant, driving him to speak for her as though he had no choice. "Ronnie," he repeated. He met Ron's widening eyes, and was suddenly hit with a sense of knowing that Jodi was the only one who ever called him that.

"Who the hell are you and what is this," Ron said in a low rumble, more as a statement than a question, the crease in his brows growing deeper as anger burned in his eyes.

"Mitch can... hear people who've... passed..." Lessie explained nervously, jumping to his side, glancing at Mitch with concern as he swallowed back his growing nerves.

Ron grew even angrier as his face reddened and eyes narrowed. "Did you all plan this? Put him up to this?" His nostrils flared.

"No!" Lessie exclaimed. "He's my boyfriend, I was just trying to leave!"

"Dad, listen—" Will cut in, but this time Ron threw his hands off his shoulders, his eyes locked on Mitch's.

"I'm not so sure I appreciate this little set-up you all had—"

"Dammit, Ronnie, pull your head out of your ass and listen to me!" Mitch suddenly exclaimed, feeling taken over by Jodi's spirit, and he brought his palms up to his face as distress momentarily lanced his eyes. The family fell silent as everyone's wide eyes fell on him, the only sound coming from the crickets chirping in the night. Mitch swallowed hard again as he glanced at everyone — Lynne on the front porch, Sam's wary hand on her shoulder, Will and Cam on either side of their father, who was breathing heavier. Mitch regained composure. "Sorry, those were her words..." he said, his voice softer, gesturing to the open air behind him. "I hear these voices whether I like it or not," he tried to explain, not sure if it would help. "And trust me, I don't like it."

"I swear we didn't set this up," Lessie cut in.

Bewilderment cracked Ron's expression, their only saving grace being that Ron was no stranger to people with unusual abilities. He stared at Mitch, and Mitch knew in his heart he had Ron's attention. He cleared his throat. "She said..." He closed his eyes again, listening, tuning in. "She said to find forgiveness. This is the way things were meant to be."

"Meant to be?" Ron shouted, brows lowering over flashing eyes. "Her leaving me alone to raise those two little kids without her? Mom could have *saved* her! I can't forgive that!"

Lessie and Will grew even more tense as they exchanged a glance. Sam and Lynne both took a hesitant step closer.

Mitch squeezed his eyes shut as waves of emotions that weren't his own coursed through him. "She couldn't have saved me," he said, Jodi's voice speaking so strongly that he now felt as though she were *in* him, *part* of him. Everyone listened with bated breath as Ron went rigid, staring wide-eyed at Mitch, who made nervous fleeting eye-contact before vacancy came into his gaze, and his voice fell into a disconnected whisper. "I didn't want to be saved."

"W-what?" Ron asked, his own voice dropping, disbelieving.

"I was at peace, Ronnie," Mitch spoke for Jodi, staring blankly into the air. "It was simply my time. I know it seemed too soon, and unfair, but it was how my life was meant to go, and I accepted that. I told your mother that, too." Mitch paused, then added, "She would have saved me if I'd wanted it."

Ron fell silent. He had been too angry to hear his mother's words, all those years ago when she admitted that she was *there*, that *she* was the one who brought Jodi, his partner, his best friend, the love of his life, to the light. He felt as though his mother were telling him that she was the one who took Jodi away from him. Shame flooded him with the force of a tidal wave as he hung his head.

Mitch's voice broke Ron from his agonizing trance as his empty stare remained on the air in front of him. "She would have brought me back if I'd asked her to. But it was my choice. This was meant to be our journey — where mine ended, and yours began anew."

"Anew?" Ron repeated in a questioning growl. "It destroyed me."

"It was your choice to let it destroy you, Ronnie. Every challenge in life offers us a choice: to grow, or fall."

Ron squeezed his eyes shut, fighting back the tears that threatened to emerge. He fought against his impending surrender. He fought against his anger at his mother, who was now dead, and at his sister, whose eyes he could feel on him from the porch behind him. "I fell..." he finally choked. His eyes misted as he drew in a ragged breath, and said, more loudly this time, "I fell."

Cam reached for her brother's arm behind their father's back and squeezed it tight as her own tears escaped. Will's throat constricted, his heart heavy, as he lifted his opposite arm to grasp his sister's hand in return. He'd never had a relationship with his father. Ever since his first calling at thirteen years old, he'd felt shut out, unaccepted, rejected. But watching his father break, tears falling freely down the grown man's cheeks, struck a note deep within his heart.

Sam reached for Lynne as her hands went to her mouth, eyes wide, as she watched her brother's walls crumble.

Lessie fell silent as she stood next to Mitch, watching as not only Ron's life changed before her, but Mitch's, too. The bravery he displayed was unlike anything she'd ever seen before, and her feelings for him grew even stronger.

Mitch finally lifted his eyes, a new light shining in them that hadn't been there before. He seemed to glow with a sense of purpose. His gaze fell on Ron, whose body was now shaking as he leaned against the table, face concealed in his hand. "It's not too late to build back up from this," he said quietly. "She knows you can, and will."

Finally, Ron lifted his head, his eyes wet and bloodshot. He brought himself to meet the watery gaze of his children. They looked so much like their mother, and so grown up. So much life had progressed, and suddenly the realization of how much of it he'd missed crushed him as fresh tears fell from his eyes. "I'm so sorry," he finally broke in a raspy whisper.

Lynne sucked back a sob as Sam squeezed her tighter, and Camryn suddenly grasped him into a tight embrace. "Oh, Daddy," she cried, and she buried her head into his shoulder. He returned the embrace forcefully, holding her tightly against him, clinging to her with fierce desperation. Will watched, tears streaming from his own eyes, and joined in the embrace. Ron lifted a shaking arm around his son's neck as he drew him in with Cam.

Lynne sobbed audibly again, and slowly made her way to

the three. She met Ron's wet eyes. "Are we gonna be okay?" she whispered, her voice cracking. Without words, he pulled his sister into the embrace.

Lessie continued to observe, deeply moved by the scene in front of her as tears caught in her throat. She wanted to join her family, yet at the same time she was acutely aware of Mitch, who seemed to be back in himself again, looking shaken and forlorn. He shifted uncomfortably as he watched the small group clinging to one another, letting their tears flow freely. He cleared his throat and quietly said, almost to himself, "Excuse me," and turned to head back to the driveway toward his car.

Lessie met her father's eyes. Sam smiled softly, and gave her a nod, which Lessie returned before turning on her heel to follow Mitch. Sam placed his hand on Lynne's back and softly guided everyone back into the house.

LESSIE CAUGHT UP to Mitch as he reached for his car door, and she took his hand before he could open it. He exhaled slowly, surrendering to her touch, then lifted his gaze to the vast expanse of stars in the inky sky. A cool breeze blew past him while crickets and frogs carried on their symphony.

"You okay?" Her voice was soft, her eyes filled with concern.

Mitch slowly nodded, and blew out a breath. "Yeah. I am." He turned his head, bringing his gaze from the stars to meet her crystal eyes, and offered her a small, genuine smile. Lessie smiled in return. He turned his head to bring his eyes back to the stars once more, becoming lost in his own thoughts.

Lessie's eyes remained on Mitch with deep admiration. "That was amazing. What you just did," she finally spoke.

Mitch gave another slow nod, and leaned his body against

the car. "Thanks," he responded, shifting his weight between his legs. He took a breath, then added, "I couldn't have done that if it weren't for you."

Lessie smiled as she sidled in closer to him, leaning against the car, sliding her palm along the inside of his arm and lacing her fingers into his. He squeezed her hand. "Do you have any idea what you did for our family tonight?" she said in a near whisper.

He exhaled slowly. "I feel like..." He stopped, falling short as he let out a low chuckle.

Lessie smiled. "What?" she pressed, eyeing him curiously as he continued to stare at the night sky.

A shooting star slid through the black night, and he watched with reverence, finding a sense of comfort in it, almost as though it were a sign from the Universe.

"I feel like I'm part of something way bigger than myself..." he finally spoke as he dropped his head closer to hers, his voice hushed yet unrestrained.

Lessie's heart lifted at his words, and she pressed herself to him, squeezing his hand. "You are," she whispered back. She rested her head on his shoulder as they took in the magnitude of where their journeys in life had brought them, and they returned their gaze to the expanse of stars glittering in the heavens.

CHAPTER 34

MITCH STUDIED his reflection in his full-length mirror, adjusting his black tie over his dark green shirt. He balanced on his right leg, his crutch tucked carefully under his left arm. He glanced at his prosthesis leaning against the bed, before returning his attention to his tie. He tried to smile, stretching his lips over his teeth, closing them, then allowed his face to fall. His thoughts traveled to the night before, the fiasco outside Lessie's front porch, and Jodi's message to Ron. His eyes left his reflection, following the memory, the power of what he'd experienced that night. He'd never experienced anything so profound; except, of course, the connection he felt with Lessie. He had drawn her into a fierce embrace under the stars as they leaned against his car, kissing her deeply, feeling as though he could cling to her forever. He didn't want to think where he'd be in life without her friendship and support.

A laugh startled him, and he glanced toward his doorway to see Genevieve smiling. "You look good, bro," she said, folding her arms under her chest.

He sighed. "Thanks."

She appeared behind him in the mirror as he fidgeted with his tie once more. "You excited to graduate?" she asked.

"Yeah," he replied simply.

"What's wrong?"

He merely shrugged.

She tried to make eye contact with him in the mirror, but his gaze dropped as he smoothed his shirt where it was tucked into his black slacks. "This isn't another Prom problem, is it? Mourning the old life?"

He shook his head, cracking a small smile. "No. I think I'm getting past all that."

She released a smile to match his, then grew serious again as she said in a soft voice, "You wish Dad was here." He glanced up to meet her eyes.

"Yeah," he replied, just as softly.

"Does he ever talk to you?"

He shook his head. "I guess I've been a little afraid to hear from him. But... today I kind of hoped I would."

"What do you think he'd say?" She watched him curiously while he placed his graduation cap on his head and adjusted the tassel. He then removed it and turned to face her.

"He'd be really proud of you."

Her expression shifted as they held each other's gaze.

He continued. "You grew a lot after he died. Into a better person. You were the only one of us who showed any kind of strength. I think he'd be really proud of who you are now."

She dropped her eyes to the floor, a soft smile tugging at the corner of her mouth. "Thanks," she said in a near whisper. She then brought her focus back to his eyes. "He'd be proud of you, too."

He sighed, nodding slowly. "Maybe. I don't think he would have been before. I was an asshole. To everyone. Especially people who didn't deserve it." He frowned as he hobbled over to take a seat on the bed and began rolling up his left pants leg. His stomach lurched like it always did as his eyes traveled over the purple flesh that ended just below his knee. He wondered if he'd ever get used to the sight. It was disturbingly alien to him. "And look what I've done," he rasped. He began working the silicone sleeve over the stump of flesh, then reached for his prosthetic leg. "I had a scholarship to the same school he went to. To follow in his footsteps." He slid the peg at the end of the sleeve into his leg, and stood to click it into place. He silently sank back into the mattress, his shoulders slumped as he smoothed his pants over his left leg.

Genevieve joined him on the edge of the bed, sinking into the mattress next to him, placing her hands in her lap. She glanced up at him. "Yeah. But look where it's taken you. You get to follow your own footsteps now."

His pensive expression remained on his bare fiberglass foot as he nodded slowly.

She continued. "Considering what you've been through, I don't think any normal person would have recovered as well as you have. So," she shrugged, "you're pretty strong, too."

"I almost didn't."

She grinned and nudged him with her elbow. "Until Lessie came along."

He smiled warmly at the thought of her.

"She really saved your life, Mitch."

Mitch chuckled at the irony of her words. "Yeah. She did."

She smiled. "And you've become stronger and happier."

He nodded, shuffling his left foot on the floor.

"And Dad would be proud."

He paused, then squeezed his eyes shut against the tears that suddenly stung at the backs of his eyes, and he fought to hold himself together. She placed her hand on his back and he took a breath, letting a tear slip, which didn't go unnoticed by Genevieve. "Holy shit, what's this?" she said quietly, moving her arm to embrace his shoulders. "Emotion?"

He finally let go, pulling her into a hug and allowing himself to cry, to release everything, all his anger and sadness and frustration, his loneliness and need for approval, everything he'd battled all the years since his father's death, and then everything he had bottled up since his accident. He let it all out on her shoulder. She gripped him tightly in return as her own tears fell. "I love you," she whispered.

"Love you, too, Gen," he choked in return. He sat back, wiping his eyes and composing himself.

She smiled, wiping her own. "Feels good, don't it?"

He let out a watery laugh. "Sure."

She then gave his knee a squeeze and said, "Ya know, Dad probably doesn't need to say anything. I think we said everything for him."

LESSIE MET UP with Emily at school as their families left to find seats in the gymnasium. Their caps were pinned neatly in place, and their dark green robes hung loosely from their shoulders. Emily grinned at her friend. "This is it," Emily said with bittersweetness in her voice.

Lessie returned the smile and nodded. "Yeah. I still can't believe you're leaving..."

Emily rolled her eyes. "Whatever, I'll be here all summer yet."

Lessie grinned. "Guess it's off to community college for me."

"You decide what you want to go into?"

Lessie shrugged. "I feel drawn to business management, for some reason. Nothing that deals with interacting with people, though." She grimaced at the thought of spacing out during an important meeting.

Emily laughed. "The perfect job will land itself in your lap, don't worry."

Lessie smiled at her friend with warmth and appreciation.

The students were organized in the hallway outside of the gymnasium, and as the band played "Pomp and Circumstance," they began their walk toward their seats near the stage. The ceremony went by quickly. Adam, naturally, was Valedictorian and was the first to walk across the stage, and Lessie sighed sadly as she noticed the struggle in his features. He hadn't been the same since their breakup. She clapped loudly as Emily walked, and just as loudly for Mitch.

She glanced toward the bleachers, smiling at her parents, as well as her uncle, and cousins; three people who had only just entered her life months ago, and days ago, but she couldn't imagine life without. She reflected on all that had changed in those few short months. How she'd started the school year timid and embarrassed by her ability, and not only found confidence, but strength in herself as an individual. She'd lost her grandmother, yet gained insurmountable knowledge, and even greater friendships. She met Mitch's eyes and smiled. It was his friendship she was most grateful for; and the change, growth, and strength he'd shown in such a short time inspired her. *It's our challenges that shape us into better, stronger people,* she recalled her grandmother saying. She learned first-hand that Nana couldn't have spoken truer words.

Lessie grinned proudly as she walked across the stage, and into life's next chapter.

MITCH'S EYES TRAVELED over the crowd of families and friends packed into the bleachers. A sense of peace settled into him now that the school year, and graduation, were over. His moment with Genevieve earlier that day awakened something inside of him, and he smiled at her words. That their dad would be proud.

He reflected on the challenges and hardships the year brought with it. *Every challenge in life offers us a choice: to grow, or fall,* Jodi's words echoed in his mind. His missing foot tingled. He certainly had grown... His mind wandered to Lessie. He never imagined she, of all people, would make such an impact on his life, or would become such a valuable friend. It almost made everything worth it.

He smiled to himself. Strange how one could end up finding gratitude in trauma.

He glanced up toward his mom and sister as they waited for the crowds to disperse as everyone left the bleachers, and did a quick double-take. A balding man with glasses, a dark goatee, and mustache was smiling warmly back at him. The man winked. Mitch squeezed his eyes shut and opened them again, but he was gone.

He blinked, then whispered, "Thanks, Dad." He was knocked forward and broken from his thoughts by a body crashing into his back and arms wrapping around his shoulders and chest.

"We did it!" Lessie exclaimed.

He beamed as he turned to face her, her arms remaining

around his shoulders. "We did," he replied, pulling her closer. His eyes shifted as sentiment coursed over his features. "I really don't know where I'd be without you..."

She smiled warmly. "Same here," she whispered.

He chuckled. "You'd be just fine, as strong as you are."

She grinned and brushed her cheek against his as she pulled him into an embrace, inhaling deeply against his neck. She felt a deep sense of belonging as the electric current of their connection fueled her with new life. He wrapped his arms around her waist and drew her into him, breathing her in.

"Get a room!" Will jeered with a playful smile as he, and the rest of Lessie's family, approached them. Lessie and Mitch reluctantly separated, rolling their eyes while reflecting Will's smile. Their hands remained tightly clasped.

"Congratulations, you two," Sam said with a grin.

"It's been quite a year," Lynne added. The warmth in her eyes spread to her brother as she glanced over her shoulder, meeting his gaze. "For all of us." They exchanged a smile.

Lessie's own heart warmed, and she grinned as Will met her eyes. "You're gonna come out to visit us this summer, right?" he asked. He shifted his focus to Mitch, and smiled. "Both of you."

"Definitely," Mitch responded without hesitation, wrapping his arm around Lessie's shoulders and squeezing her into him. "I'm ready for the next adventure, how about you?"

He met her eyes, and her grin brightened as she slid her arm around his waist, ready to face any new adventures life brought their way. "Absolutely," she replied.

AUTHOR BIO

A BIG DREAMER in a small town, Jami Christine expresses her dreams through art, literature, and music. Embarking on her soul-searching journey at 13 years old, Jami navigated the waters of human emotions; both turbulent and serene, murky and clear, toxic and thriving; and has been passionate about assisting others on their own soul journeys through many healing arts modalities, and now, through the adventure of fiction.